Forbidden
Post-Apocalyptic Sci-Fi Action Romance
Marteeka Karland

Forbidden
Post-Apocalyptic Sci-Fi Action Romance
Marteeka Karland

All rights reserved.
Copyright ©2025 Marteeka Karland

ISBN: 978-1-60521-935-6

Publisher:
Changeling Press LLC
315 N. Centre St.
Martinsburg, WV 25404
ChangelingPress.com

Printed in the U.S.A.

Editor: Katriena Knights
Cover Artist: Marteeka Karland

The individual stories in this anthology have been previously released in E-Book format.

Table of Contents

Forbidden (Forbidden 1) 4
    Chapter One..5
    Chapter Two 15
    Chapter Three...32
    Chapter Four...49
    Chapter Five..68
    Chapter Six..80
    Chapter Seven...92
    Epilogue...99
Neighborhood Watch (Forbidden 2) 101
    Chapter One...102
    Chapter Two 110
    Chapter Three...120
    Chapter Four...132
    Chapter Five..146
    Chapter Six..158
Sleeping With the Enemy (Forbidden 3)...172
    Chapter One...173
    Chapter Two 183
    Chapter Three...196
    Chapter Four...209
    Chapter Five..219
    Chapter Six..234
New Beginnings (Forbidden 4) 250
    Chapter One...251
    Chapter Two 263
    Chapter Three...273
    Chapter Four...283
    Chapter Five..293
    Chapter Six..309
    Chapter Seven...315
Chocolate Kisses (Forbidden 5)..322
    Chocolate Kisses 323
Marteeka Karland 337
Changeling Press LLC..338

Forbidden (Forbidden 1)
Post-Apocalyptic Sci-Fi Action Romance
Marteeka Karland

Anna Garrett has lost everything to the Gothe'maran invaders. Like an avenging angel, Khan sweeps into punishes those who have wronged her. Then she learns his identity. He is General Khan Mak'un -- known as Khan the Merciless. The man Earth thinks is responsible for its genocide.

Khan has been sent to stop the bloodshed any way he can. He doesn't expect to find the fearless Anna doing everything in her power to find him. Khan's duty to his people proves to be just as much a part of him as this woman who has captured his soul. He knows he will never let her go, even though her love will probably cost him everything.

Chapter One

Holding the blood-soaked body of her baby, Anna screamed. Her living room was a bloodbath. The bastards who had so viciously murdered her family had already disintegrated her husband's corpse. Now they were advancing on her. They'd dispose of her son's little body without wasting any effort.

They were the Gothe'maran. Other worlders with the features of humans but a vicious killing streak no dictator on Earth, past or present, could ever hope to match.

Part of her mind was conscious of the three men deciding her fate. She didn't think she could stomach being part of the deplorable process that would bring more such monsters into the universe. Her mind and body couldn't survive being brutally raped day after day. When they found out that she was incapable of having more children, that they couldn't use her as breeding stock, and they would kill her.

Perhaps that would be for the best.

She'd never even had time to draw her weapon, and her first instinct had been to help the two most important people in her life, not to kill their attackers. Now her main focus was her infant son. Perhaps she should have felt more for her husband, and she was sure she would later, but now she was lost in a mother's grief.

Then, just beyond the three hulking monsters, in her front yard, another man approached through the haze of the smoke-filled air. He wore the uniform of the Gothe'maran, and she thought he was even taller than the giant soldiers before her, but his features, save the midnight hair escaping his helmet, were obscured in the distance. Her gaze froze on his approaching form.

He stopped.

She stared.

Silently, she pleaded for his aid.

The first warrior reached her and yanked her to her feet by her hair, breaking her rapt gaze. Her son slid from her arms to the floor. Suddenly everything in her screamed at her to fight. Where before there had been a willingness, if not an eagerness, to just get it over with, to surrender to their sadistic handling until she finally succumbed to the arms of death, now she was taken over by an all encompassing need to fight. If she was meant to die, she'd take a few of the bastards with her.

Anna didn't just feel the need to defend herself, she wanted to kill. She wanted to do to these bastards what they had done to her family. Never thinking herself capable of killing, no matter how essential, she drew her weapon and fired into the belly of the assailant holding her up on tiptoe by her hair. Blood splattered from his back, bathing his companions in the black, almost gelatinous substance. She quickly turned to the next-closest attacker and tried to fire, only to find her gun wouldn't discharge a second time. The Gothies had now drawn weapons, and she knew she only had seconds to live.

Glancing behind the warriors, she saw the newcomer within arm's length of them. Without a word, he reached around one man's neck and gave a sharp twist. The *crack* of snapping vertebrae seemed deafening, and the last Gothie turned to face the newcomer.

"General?"

The look of surprise and indecision on the monstrous face of her attacker was unexpected. The

Gothe'maran were infamous not only for their brutality, but for their extreme control over their emotions during battle. Nothing caused a Gothie to show weakness.

Before the last soldier could decide whether or not to shoot his comrade, a smoldering hole appeared in the exact center of his chest. He gave a howl of rage that turned to extreme agony. The hole grew wider and acrid smoke rose from the wound as it crept toward his throat and lower abdomen. Ash fell from his body as it was consumed by the strange weapon. The stench of burning flesh was almost overwhelming.

The man who had just saved her life stood looking at her with harsh black eyes. As usual for one of his race, those black eyes gave away nothing of what he was feeling.

Had he not been what he was she might have found him handsome in a darkly masculine way. His face held harsh angles from his straight nose to his chiseled cheekbones and almost square chin. A pale scar ran vertically from just above his left eye, slightly off center down the length of his face. But instead of detracting from his handsomeness, it only enhanced his special brand of dangerous, manly beauty.

He took a step toward her, reaching out with one hand. She retreated two steps, raising her presumably useless gun with unsteady hands. She knew she needed to pull the trigger, knowing that doing so -- if the damned thing fired -- could mean the difference between life and a miserable death. But that same instinct to fire on her would-be killer insisted she not shoot the man before her.

She felt drawn to him. Something inside her wanted take his hand. The man whose people had just slaughtered tens of thousands of her own in a single afternoon, including the two most precious in the world to her. Self-loathing permeated her mind. And shame.

She gripped the gun more firmly and tried to take aim at him, only to warn him off. This man was important to her. She needed him. He needed her. She knew he needed her as surely as she knew she needed to breathe. Confused, she looked away, and her gaze fell to the body of her son. *Alex. Oh, my precious Alex!*

Grief overtook her once again, and she staggered to his tiny, lifeless body. As she took him in her arms and cried into his little neck, she felt a stillness come over her. Her crying slowed somewhat. This was a terrible tragedy, something that never should have happened, and there would be hell to pay for it, but she would survive. She would survive because the man before her would have it no other way. She couldn't help her husband or her son now, but she could help him.

She looked back at him in astonishment. Those feelings were his, not hers. What the hell was going on?

He took a tentative step toward her again just as the medallion on his collar beeped. He pressed it to his throat as he spoke in his own language.

The conversation lasted less than a minute. When he finished he looked at her once more. "I'll find you again," he said slowly, his harsh accent very thick. Then he was gone. But so was the body of her son. Taken right from her arms.

"No," Anna whispered. Then in a gut-wrenching wail, "NO!" She fell to her knees and wept bitterly until she embraced an exhausted sleep.

Sleep was no comfort though. Her dreams were filled with her husband and baby's screams. Several times she woke from her resting place on the floor where her family had perished. Several times she cried herself back to sleep, unable to move from the only place she could feel close to them. She didn't even have bodies to bury. No way to find closure.

It was only later, when she had managed to move deeper into relatively safe UWA territory, she learned the man who had saved her life was the general in command of the forces trying to conquer what was left of the United States of America and the United World Army. He was General Kahn Mak'un. Also known as Kahn the Merciless.

* * *

Anna gasped as her body became a heated, sensitized version of itself. She could feel his hands moving over her flesh in the most tender of caresses. As he feathered light touches over her breasts and followed them with a wet lick, she arched into him, offering him whatever he wanted to take. She felt her nipples tighten, harden with the exquisite torture, and she barely held in the whimper that threatened to escape. She didn't want the pleasure to end. Maybe this time would be different.

He trailed his lips down her body, his hands never forsaking her breasts, until he found the little indention of her navel. There he laved that sensitive spot before starting his downward descent. Her hands speared through his mass of dark hair, trying to hold to the illusion.

Just before he would have delved into the nest of curls at the apex of her thighs, he stopped and looked at her over her outstretched body. "You are mine, as I am yours. Never think I'll allow you to be lost in this madness my people have started on your world. When I find you I will give you pleasure of the flesh, but I'll also give back to you some of what you've lost."

He buried his face in her cunt then, finding her clit

with the uncanny accuracy she always expected of him. The cry she tried so valiantly to suppress emerged and Anna screamed her pleasure…

And woke herself from yet another dream that left her heavy with an unfulfilled, aching desire that no amount of masturbation could ever possibly ease. She knew. She had tried many times over the last several months.

Every night was the same since she'd first seen Kahn the Merciless. He came to her in dreams and left her more aroused and sexually frustrated than she thought she could bear. In a way, she felt guilty that she should welcome Kahn in her dreams even though many months had passed since she'd lost her family in the Pilot incident. In her heart though, she knew she had to move on. She still grieved, but she had to dwell in the land of the living.

Was she insane to want to give her body to the man who was most likely responsible for everything that had happened on Earth? Was she finally losing her mind? Maybe. All she knew for sure was that she had to find him. Only then would she find the relief she so desperately needed and the answers he so cryptically hinted at.

* * *

Anna's dreams intensified each month. Every night, Kahn the Merciless took her to new heights of ecstasy only to leave her hanging there, unfulfilled.

It had been two years since her family was murdered. Two years Anna had spent preparing herself to find the nemesis of her dreams and find answers for all that had happened on Earth. Answers for what had happened to her. She had searched every form of media she'd had access to for anything about Kahn the Merciless. The funny thing was, there were no pictures of him prior to the Pilot incident. After that, he appeared several times but he was never photographed with a weapon in hand. Apparently he did his killing through his army.

As she entered the recruiting office of the Somerset, Kentucky, branch of the United World Army, Anna prepared for the questions to come. Questions there was no way she could answer truthfully.

The sergeant, an African American named Mahoney according to the nameplate in front of him, sat behind a desk that looked too small for his massive frame. He wore camouflage fatigues with the sleeves rolled up to expose burly forearms covered with a myriad of scars and tattoos. His shaven head, also sporting scars, gleamed in the harsh fluorescent lighting of the underground recruiting office. A tattoo of some odd Celtic-looking design covered the majority of his head. Anna wasn't sure exactly how tall the man was, but she was sure he topped her own five feet six by several inches. She didn't think she had ever seen a more intimidating human.

"I want to enlist," Anna said.

"And you are?" he asked, barely looking up from the stack of folders before him.

"Anna Garrett. I'm a registered nurse and I'd like to do all I can as close to the Front as possible."

She knew that would get his attention. The life expectancy of soldiers fighting on the front lines was less than two tours of duty. That of Mobile Army Surgical Hospital unit personnel wasn't much better.

As she expected, the sergeant's head snapped up and his dark-eyed glare pierced her. It was a few moments before he actually spoke.

"You're aware the Gothe'maran do not

distinguish between medical and combat personnel?"

"Of course," she said.

"Then why?"

"I believe I can do the most good there. It is where the most people are needed." The response was, of course, total bullshit, and the sergeant would have to be moronic not to know that, but it was the expected answer to that question. There were only two reasons anyone would ask to be assigned to the Front. One was condoned, the other was not.

He regarded her a moment. "I'll have to pull up your civilian file. The UWA needs people at the Front too badly for me to dismiss anyone willing to go, but we will not help someone commit suicide."

"I understand. Would you like me to save you the trouble and tell you my experiences with the Gothe'maran?"

Again, she saw the surprise at her straightforwardness and had to smile inwardly. Humans were nothing if not predictable. It was a wonder they had managed to last this long in the war. All good humor faded with that thought.

Sergeant Mahoney sat back in his chair and regarded her thoughtfully. "Where are you from?"

"It's called Pueblo, Kentucky, but you will know it as the Pilot."

At the mention of the Pilot, the obviously battle-hardened man blanched. "Dear God! And you expect me to believe you aren't suicidal?"

"Sergeant, I want to kill as many Gothies as I can. Now, as a surgical nurse, I probably won't have the opportunity to actually kill any at all, but maybe I can patch together a few of our men and women who can."

"Well," he said, his focus once again on the files and papers scattered on his desk, "if there are no other more recent incidents, you've cleared the waiting period by exactly one day, but I suspect you did that on purpose." He referred to the mandatory two-year enlistment waiting period set up by the UWA just after the Pilot incident. Too many men and women had thrown their lives away needlessly after that massacre, and Earth didn't have the people to spare.

"I watched them butcher my husband and my son, Sergeant. The only reason I'm still here is because I can still have children." A lie, but then again so was the rest of her story. "I should have been on a transport back to their home world, but I managed to get away after I killed a couple of them." God help her if anyone found out differently.

Mahoney sighed. "You realize that just being a nurse isn't going to cut it at the Front. There will be other training you'll need before we can send you in."

"What other training, Sergeant?"

"For one thing, the doctors and nurses at the M.A.S.H. units there do more than surgeries. They actually have to go into the field and get the wounded more than half the time, so you're going to need some training in emergency evacuation and medical intervention. That can take at least six months to complete at best."

"Would it help speed things up if I told you I am a nationally registered emergency medical technician paramedic as well as a nurse?" she asked with a smirk. She knew very well it would make a difference. She had been planning this since the day her family died... and *he* left. "I'm perfectly qualified in the areas you just mentioned."

"I see," Mahoney said. He paused to stare at her as if sizing her up. "Well," he finally continued, "I'll run this by the regional commanding officer and see if we can get you out there in a couple of days." He stood and offered her his hand. "I'll be in touch, Ms. Garrett."

When she would have pulled her hand from his, his grip tightened. "I want you to really think about what you're doing, Anna. That place is as close to hell as anyone can ever see. Some of the weapons they use are designed to make the torment last as long as possible. They make what they used at the Pilot look like squirt guns."

Anna smiled. "Thank you, Sergeant. I'm making this request with my eyes wide open. I know what I'm getting myself into." That statement was only partially true.

She knew about the Front, but she didn't know about Kahn the Merciless, and he was the reason she was going there in the first place. She knew that, if she could survive, she would eventually find the man because his forces would push back the battle lines and the chances of her getting captured were great. She was taking a huge gamble that he'd see her before she was killed, but it was one she had to take. She had dreamt of the man every night since he had saved her and two things were very clear to her -- he needed her more than ever, and if the dreams didn't stop soon, she'd probably die from unfulfilled lust.

* * *

A week later, she sat on a bus filled with determined, if frightened, men and women headed to a little place near what used to be Lexington, Kentucky -- the state's own little piece of hell nicknamed the Front. She was going there intending to be taken as a prisoner of war by a race of people who didn't take prisoners. She was walking into the lion's den and, God help her, she had never been more excited in her life.

Chapter Two

"I don't care if you have his leg," Anna snapped to the enlisted nurse. "The Gothies will be here long before we could possibly get it packed for transport." They made their way through the M.A.S.H. unit, preparing for the latest attack. Anna had been in Lexington three months, and was now the most senior medical staff member.

She felt for the young soldier, she really did, but they didn't have time for niceties. "Give him a choice, Lieutenant. He can either stay here and hope the Gothe'maran will be so kind as to reattach his leg before they kill him, or he can be moved out with everyone else and lose it. And I don't plan to leave anyone behind."

Other than herself, of course. She'd make sure she was captured and damn the consequences. But she got the feeling that *he* knew what she had planned and would be waiting for her.

Suddenly, there was a flash near Anna's surgical suite. A deafening silence followed it, as if all sound had been simply sucked into a vacuum. The air around her seemed thick and unbreathable. Dizziness swamped her and she fell to her knees with a jarring thud. Her hands instinctively flew out to grasp whatever was in reach to steady herself. As the room spun around her, she looked up… and her eyes locked with those of Kahn Mak'un.

He stood in the doorway of the tent, his soldiers fanning out to check the other collapsed bodies round the room. She thought that odd because the Gothies usually just killed everyone they came across. He moved toward her. Her last thought before the blackness claimed her was *He's found me at last.*

* * *

What had happened to the humans was tragic. And those deplorable acts had been done in his name. Kahn could see the fear on the faces of those people of Earth he met as he walked through the tiny camp. They knew who he was and thought they knew what he stood for. He had never been a part of the zealous faction of his government that had invaded Earth, and he certainly never condoned the slaughter of these people, of *any* people. All of this had been done behind the king's back. All in the name of "saving the race."

His people were warriors. Unfortunately, in their blood frenzy, most of those who had come to Earth in the beginning had forgotten that honor had to be met in battle. No matter what a superior officer ordered. There was no honor in killing women and children. The madmen that had started this had brought tens of thousands of his homeland's warriors, and Kahn doubted that there was a single one left who had not forsaken his honor for the kill.

Now, he had to clean up the mess. And that was proving as difficult as he expected. These people had lived in terror for almost three years. His job now was to round up every last warrior and get the hell off this planet. Some of them had heeded the return call, but more than half of them had not. They had chosen to continue their "search" for Earth women to bear children who could be raised to fight in the stead of homeland warriors. Gothe'mar then could fight wars without risking the lives of their people, thus expanding their empire. The notion was not honorable. It was disturbing that so many warriors had gone along with it.

In truth, Kahn suspected most of them simply enjoyed the violence. Such was the nature of his people. It was why they were taught to control their baser instincts from the time they were able to learn higher skills, even before they were of schooling age. Extreme emotion had no place in Gothe'maran society.

Now, it was taking all his control to keep from savagely killing every rebel warrior he came across. They had shamed him. They had shamed his people. And they would pay for every drop of blood they had shed.

Especially that of his woman's family.

True, he would not have been able to claim her had her husband been alive, but he would gladly have let her go if it would have meant she would not have been tormented by the loss. He doubted he would ever forget her cries of anguish as she knelt over her baby. Still, now he felt only overwhelming joy. His soul had found its mate. This time he would not let her go.

He stood there watching her as she was overcome by the *tol'sun* -- the silent light. Her hair and skin were as pale as the rays of sunshine on this light-filled world. Slight of form, she still had lush curves that he could discern through her clothes. He itched to remove the offending garments to see the body of his mate.

She found him just as she gave in to the vertigo caused by the passive weapon. As he watched her slump to the ground and felt her acceptance of him, he thought that maybe, just maybe, he could claim her without causing her more grief. Because he knew there was no way he could let her go now that he had found her again. She was his, and honor, as well as his every instinct, demanded he claim and protect his mate at all costs.

"Round up the warriors for transport. Give medical assistance to the humans," Kahn said to his second, Kiril.

"Commander," came Kiril's low, rumbling voice. "Shall I have the ship prepare for your woman?"

As always, Kiril knew where Kahn's primary focus was. "Yes. I will take her aboard before the effects of the *tol'sun* wear off. She needs to adjust to her new life as quickly as possible."

"And if there is too much damage to be undone?"

Kahn thought a moment before he spoke. What he was about to tell Kiril would shake the foundation of the Gothe'maran. "I don't think that will be a problem, my friend." He looked Kiril in the eyes. "She can hear my thoughts when my emotions are high, as I can hear hers. Not to mention our mutual need of each other. It is almost unbearable for both of us."

Kiril's normally impassive features registered surprise for an instant before he snorted. "Unlikely, Commander. Telepathic abilities exist only in true mates and then only after they have been bound for many years. You jest with me."

Kahn's gaze didn't waver. "I never jest, Kiril. This you know."

Kiril's face paled. "Great Mother," he whispered. "You have been mates in past lives, then. Many lives if you connected with her so fast. And with someone not of our race? It is forbidden."

"Not of our race? I wonder." The implications hung heavily. Gothe'maran warriors may have slaughtered tens of thousands of their own people.

"You suspect these people of Earth are related to us?"

Kahn sighed. "Preliminary testing from scans and the microscopic tissue sample of the baby suggest the humans may be more closely related than previously thought. We will know more when we have her permission to take a blood sample."

Kiril grunted. "Is the child still in stasis?"

"Yes. His injuries were fully healed, but Medical Command thought it wisest to have his mother near when they brought him out of stasis."

"Another difficulty in getting your woman to adjust. She will not be pleased her son was not returned to her."

"She doesn't know he's still alive."

Kiril actually laughed -- something Kahn had never seen. He hadn't even known Kiril was capable of laughter. "Good luck, my friend. If she is a Gothe'maran by nature, her anger at being kept from her child will be unparalleled. I'm glad I'm not the one to have to tell her."

Kahn shared his second's amusement. He was actually more fearful that, once she became comfortable with their mind sharing, she would manage to glean the information directly from his brain than he was of telling her himself. He would have to keep her occupied with other things until he could broach the subject. Kahn smiled a bit before sobering. "There is much still to be done here, Kiril. Many warriors are still killing, and it's up to us to stop them."

"What would you have me do, General?"

"No mercy, Kiril. No mercy."

"As you command."

* * *

Anna awoke still a bit lightheaded. She also found she was quite comfortable for the first time in several months and did not want to spoil the pleasant feeling by opening her eyes and finding it all a dream. She lay there, dozing, not caring what had happened, not wanting to think beyond the wonderful feeling of a soft bed beneath her and warm covers over her.

"Are you aware you snore when you sleep, *tarae*?"

Anna jackknifed to a sitting position, the covers falling to her waist. Kahn the Merciless sat beside the huge bed… *smiling*. In her search for this man, she had seen hundreds of photographs of him, and none of them could have prepared her for the devastation of his smile. All those angles, all the fierceness in his eyes, simply melted away. Even the scar seemed to diminish. He looked at her with a gentleness, a tenderness that took her breath away. She was speechless.

He was dressed in dark gray. His leather-like pants hugged muscular thighs and his shirt and vest were open, revealing a tanned expanse of very powerfully built torso. His hair hung in waves to his shoulders, giving him a wild look that sent a liquid gush of heat through her body. She was drawn to this man. Everything in her screamed for him.

"What? Nothing to say? From the woman who would give herself willingly to a people she knows to be deadly simply to find me? I expected a tirade of some sort at the very least."

Teasing. He was *teasing* her! When the chuckle emerged from deep within his chest it was all she could take. Her hand shot out, grabbed the nearest pillow and hurled it at him. It hit him square in the face.

She gasped. Had she really just hit Kahn the Merciless in the face with a pillow? Of all the hare-brained, idiotic things to do! She flung herself across the expanse of the bed and made a mad dash for the door, only to be snagged in mid flight by a steely arm around her middle. The laughter at her ear was the last thing she expected.

"You're probably the only person on several worlds who would dare throw anything at me, *tarae*. You should know you have nothing to fear from me. Can you not feel it?"

The only things she felt were his breath feathering her cheek and the clenching in her belly. She almost melted on the spot. But she realized she *could* sense what he felt. His amusement -- and his lust for her.

She looked back at him. He had all her answers. Would he give them to her?

Gently, he took her shoulders and turned her to face him. "In time, *tarae*, I'll tell you everything."

"How…"

"Later. I need you. Now."

It was only then that Anna realized she didn't have on a stitch of clothing. Not that she cared. She could actually feel his intense need for her. Amazing! But she wasn't sure what part of those feelings was hers and what was simply her experiencing his feelings through their strange bond. She only knew she needed him more than she had ever needed anything in her life. It was unsettling to say the least.

Anna knew what she was feeling was unnatural. This instant attraction was too much, too fast to be completely her own. When she considered her obsession with him, she knew there was something more going on than she was able to understand. But there was simply no way she could fight it. She needed his body and needed to give him hers. And this attraction, this desire, was getting stronger by the second until they threatened to spontaneously combust with the heat of their mutual lust.

With a fierceness she hadn't known she possessed, Anna flung her arms around his neck and plastered her mouth against his. Her tongue thrust between the seam of his lips, plundering, ravishing, using her kiss as the outlet for the pent-up lust she had not been able to express for the last two years, three months and fifteen days.

Anna ate at his mouth, licking and biting, the aggressor. A first for her. Somehow, she managed to rid him of his shirt and vest and began working on the fastening of his pants. She felt the lust in him. He was as wild as she, but holding himself back for her benefit. The effort he exerted was tremendous, and she felt him tremble with it both inside and out.

Once she managed to unfasten his pants, her hand found him, hot and oh, so hard. She probably would have been impressed with his length and girth had she been able to form a coherent thought, but her only consideration at that moment was getting him inside her. As soon as possible. Now.

She gave him a mighty shove, and he stumbled back onto the bed. With him on his back, his legs hanging off the edge, she advanced on him. She caught first his surprise, then the passion growing impossibly more intense. She was going up in flames and taking him with her.

Kahn pushed himself onto the bed a bit more, and she followed him, climbing up his body to rest her sex against his. Anna felt his cock pulse and twitch, burying itself between the moist folds of her pussy to rub against her throbbing clit. She heard the animalistic growl and thought it was Kahn at first, only to realize it actually came from her own throat. One part of her was shocked into total oblivion while the instinctual part was actually in heat. She couldn't control this side of herself.

Don't try, love. Not now. Not this time, Kahn's voice spoke in her head.

It was too much. Anna impaled herself on the cock of Kahn the Merciless.

She screamed.

* * *

Kahn was lost. He had never experienced anything like this. Anna buried her face in his neck and bit hard, forcing a startled grunt from him even as she eased the sting with a wet lick. She rode him with an abandon that bordered on insanity. He was in her mind. He knew what she was feeling -- he felt it himself -- but his Anna was not used to such powerful emotions. She needed fulfillment and guidance. It was up to him to be her anchor.

She rode him faster and harder, her grunts and squeals of pleasure testing his resolve as his hands caressed her. He knew she needed release above all else. Only the satiation of her body would bring back her sanity. His thumb found their joined bodies and circled her clit. She immediately started to convulse around him as her first climax hit her. She grabbed hold of his thighs, throwing her head back and shrieking her pleasure.

Still she rode him. The friction was almost unbearable, and Kahn knew his tightly held control was about to snap. Her hips gave a little twist as she sank down on his cock, and it was all he could take. He grabbed her hips so tightly he likely bruised her, rising to meet each of her thrusts with a savage one of his own.

He gave a mighty plunge when he felt her muscles start to spasm once more. His hips ground into hers, seeking to get as deep as possible before he emptied himself into her. On a roar, his climax hit him. His eyes clenched shut, his muscles bunching as he bucked underneath her, driving himself ever harder until the last drop he had to give spilled into her tight, grasping cunt.

She collapsed on top of him, her breathing as ragged as his own. His arms slid easily around her and gently stroked her back. He was about to roll them to their sides and cover their spent bodies when he heard the *hiss* of the electronic door opening.

Mikkril De'Kar stood just inside Kahn's bed chamber. He was not as tall as Kahn and his musculature wasn't as impressive, but it didn't make him seem any less menacing. He was leader of the rogue warriors and also Kahn's father's youngest brother.

"Disgusting!" he spat in English. "She is human! Our people will never tolerate you succeeding your father while you bed the human whore."

Kahn had no doubt his uncle used the local Earth language hoping Anna understood his words. The lieutenant accompanying him stared straight ahead. Kahn immediately flipped Anna onto her back, kissing her briefly to muffle her small squeak of shock.

"Rest, *tarae*. I must deal with this. I will return as swiftly as I can." Anna's cheeks were crimson and he could feel the shame radiating from her in waves. He smiled once more at her, hoping to reassure her as he stood to greet the intruders. Grabbing a robe, he ushered the men outside his bed chamber.

"I assume you have a good reason for disturbing me by bringing this *bakkara* to my quarters?" Kahn's voice was quiet, deadly.

"Mikkril is condemned, General. Coming here was his last request." The lieutenant did not apologize, though Kahn could see the apprehension in his eyes.

"Why did you not think to warn me?" Kahn barked more harshly than he'd ever spoken to a junior officer. Volume wasn't needed when menace worked better, but anger had overridden his usually steely control.

The lieutenant did not hesitate. "His request was an unannounced audience with you, General."

Kahn crossed his arms over his chest, looking down at his uncle, head held high. "You have it. Speak."

Mikkril sneered. "I only wanted to confirm my suspicions that you bedded a human, and I have a witness." He gestured to the now startled lieutenant. "You will release me or I will see to it you will never be king."

"My fate and that of the mate chosen for me by the Universe is no concern of yours. We will accept whatever is to come." Kahn couldn't believe his uncle actually thought he would escape death. True, Mikkril hadn't been judged by the king as of yet, but there was little doubt the man was guilty of genocide and attempted slavery. Just looking at Earth was all the proof anyone needed. The only reason he was even given this much of a reprieve was because he was the king's half brother.

"Ah, but did you know she cannot have another child?" The smirk on Mikkril's face indicated he thought Kahn unaware of that fact. "I should think that will affect your… affection… for her. Think about what you are doing, Kahn. You cannot rise to power with a barren wife. You'd be spitting in the face of a thousand years of tradition." Mikkril turned to the lieutenant. "Take me back to my cell. I'm finished here."

Mikkril. Always the royal bastard. Literally.

Gothe'maran society held dear the idea of family. Men and women mated for life, but their ultimate goal was to mate with the one the Universe had created for them. Their soul's mate. Mikkril's father had dishonored his wife by taking a mistress and fathering another child. The people had demanded he relinquish the throne. As a result, Kahn's father had assumed the throne while still in his boyhood years. A boy leading the mighty Gothe'maran was not readily embraced. Fortunately, Kerrek had not only gained the respect and trust of his people, he had made the Gothe'maran thrive. By taking a human mate, Kahn risked having his people question him as their rightful king when the time came to take his father's place, but he was confident that could be worked out.

But right now, none of that mattered. Mikkril had dishonored himself and his entire family. He would pay with his life at the hands of the king. The only thing that mattered to Kahn was the woman on the other side of that door who was currently coming to terms with their torrid lovemaking.

* * *

After Kahn left, Anna lay quietly, gathering her emotions. She had never experienced anything quite like the sex they had shared. Okay, so "sex" was a fairly bland term to describe what they had done. Fuck like rabbits? Now there was a term! She was stunned by her own behavior, and by the feelings running around in her head. Unable to contain her nervous energy, she jumped up from the bed and paced restlessly.

When they'd had sex, she could feel what Kahn had felt, from the overpowering lust to how silky her skin felt to him when she'd glided over his body. But once the experience was over, she could no longer feel those emotions. It was as though he had simply turned himself off. Now, she only felt an occasional flicker of something. Annoyance, anger, pity. Then it was gone like it never happened. What the hell was happening to her?

It wasn't long before Kahn quietly opened the door and slipped in once again. As he entered, his gaze snared hers and he began to disrobe. Anna had thought him handsome before, but now that she had time to appreciate all of him, her breath caught in her throat, her chest constricted and her body went up in flames... again.

He looked like a bronzed god. He towered over her own sturdy frame by almost a foot, and was very heavily muscled. Vein-roped arms as thick as her thighs, a chiseled torso so steely only the skin made it soft to touch and molded, thick, defined legs all bespoke the power this man wielded.

Perusing Kahn's legs had probably been a bad idea because her gaze was inevitably drawn to the male flesh now hardening between them. If his body was a work of art, his cock was the Rembrandt. She knew he was large -- she felt the evidence in the tenderness between her own legs -- but she hadn't realized how perfectly made his sex really was. She could distinguish each vein running the length of it, and the large, mushroom-shaped head darkened from red to a deep purple with his desire. Like everything else, his cock was in proportion with his body, which made him long and mouth-wateringly thick.

* * *

For his part, Kahn was definitely not immune to his mate's inspection. Just watching her lovely azure eyes run over his body got him hard. She had wrapped herself in the sheet, but he remembered her form perfectly. She was slight by the standards of his people. He was surprised he hadn't broken her with their wild mating earlier. Slender arms and legs joined a body boasting generous breasts and hips. Her work at the Front had reshaped her body and he found this one just as appealing as the fuller version of two years earlier. The mass of flaxen curls covering her head and sex was his undoing. His people were dark, bronzed. Anna was like the precious pearls of her world -- creamy white from head to toe.

Lust surged through him, answering both her feelings and his own.

"Anna." His voice was husky to his own ears. "I have need of you again but there are things we must discuss." She blinked and he registered her surprise that he knew her name. "It should not surprise you. You know my name. I seem to remember you calling out to me several times a few minutes ago." He smirked and irritation radiated from Anna.

"That's a bit different, *Kahn the Merciless*," she mocked. "Everyone on Earth knows who you are."

There was a silence between them as Kahn tried to figure out how to tell her about her son.

The moment he let that thought slip, he knew it had been a mistake.

She froze. "What about my son?"

Kahn gave her a wry smile. "You're becoming more comfortable with the mind merge. That's good, but I must confess, your timing could be better."

She cautiously stepped toward him. "What about my son," she repeated. It was a demand, not a question.

Kahn told her without preamble, "He lives."

His sense of Anna's emotions went suddenly blank. In the next second, she drove the heel of her hand upwards into his chin, snapping his head back and making him stagger backwards. "Bastard!" She clawed his face, slapped him, punched him, kicked him with all her strength. "What have you done to him? If you've harmed him, I'll kill you myself!" Her anguished screams tormented his heart.

Kahn let her beat on him a while before enfolding her securely in his arms. Great sobs racked her body as she cried brokenly. He knew she was not even aware that she clung to him instead of seeking his death. "Please don't hurt my son. I'll do anything you ask. Anything." This last was a ragged plea. Her heart was breaking all over again and Kahn suffered with her.

"*Tarae*, never, never would I harm you or anyone you love. For any reason. Least of all a child." He gently urged her to look at him, tilting her chin upwards and framing her face gently in his large, battle hardened hands. "I know you've believed all these years my people were bloodthirsty monsters, but we are not. When our emotions are out of control, our passions rule our minds but that is precisely why our race seeks emotional control above all else. I know you can feel it in me, when you feel my emotions pull away from you. The only thing we place above control is the protection of our family. For that, we would do whatever necessary." Kahn gently guided her to the bed, as he straightened the sheet covering her, and they both sat down. "Even such honorable things as that can be twisted, and that is what happened with your planet."

"Where is my son?" Her question was put to him in a whisper, her tortured eyes brimming with tears.

"You remember the day we met?" When she nodded, he continued. "My second, Kiril, scanned the dead. Just as a man's heart can stop and his lungs quit working and there still be a chance he can be saved, so it was with your son."

"Impossible! He was literally torn apart. I remember there being so much blood…" Her voice trailed off as she slipped backwards into the memory.

"It is very possible, Anna. On Earth a hundred years ago, a man with no heartbeat was dead. There was no bringing him back. For us, it's not so much a matter of heart and blood activity as brain activity."

"So? Without oxygen, the brain dies. Without blood, there is no oxygen. You get the point? Once the brain starts dying, it's only seconds before the damage is irreversible. Alex had been dead too long."

"For your people, yes. Not for mine."

"I don't understand."

"We can repair cells in the central nervous system up to a point. Your son was placed in stasis to prevent further decay of his cells, and the damage to his body was repaired. All the damage. It is as though he was never injured."

Kahn watched Anna's eyes grow bigger with each word. "Impossible," she breathed again. "What you're suggesting is totally impossible."

"We've been perfecting the technique for a thousand years. I assure you, it is very possible."

"Have you seen him?"

"Only in his stasis chamber. Once we get to Gothe'mar, and you are present, Medical Command will bring him out of stasis and you will have your son back."

"But, if he's okay, why keep him in stasis?"

"It will be less traumatic for Alex. Sometimes there is a brief pain when the cells of the body are, for lack of a better term, jump-started. He will want his mother."

Anna smiled. Then she burst into tears once again. "Oh, Kahn. I can't believe I could be getting my son back! Even if I don't, just getting to see him again will bring me peace." She sniffed, wiped her nose, then pinned him with blazing blue eyes. "If you're lying to me, Kahn, I'll kill you."

Kahn did his best to block his amusement. She was truly Gothe'maran in nature. Holding her gently, he kissed the top of her head. "All will be well, *tarae*. Trust me."

She looked up at him, her gaze calculating. "I will. For now."

Chapter Three

Still wrapped in the bed sheet, Anna walked around the stark room where she and Kahn had been staying since he had taken her from Earth. The only furniture seemed to be the large bed and a small table with one chair. There were two doors, one of which was open, the room beyond it dark. The color scheme was a colorful gray, dark gray and more gray. Even the bedclothes were gray. There appeared to be bare steel for floor, walls and ceiling with only a thin rug for carpeting. The only sound was a quiet but ever-present roar.

"How long before we get to my son?"

"The *Kol'cha*, my flagship, is the fastest ever built. We should arrive at Gothe'mar in about ten hours."

"Once we get there, when will I get my son back?"

Kahn smiled gently at her. "We will go straight to Medical Command. It will take several hours for them to complete the restabilization process, but we will be there for all of it if you wish."

"I wish. Definitely."

Trust him. Those words were so easy to say, yet so hard to do. What could she do? Never in her wildest dreams did she ever imagine she'd get her son back. Now the only way that was going to happen was if this man decided to take her to him.

She continued to quietly pace the room. Finally deciding she needed a bath, she turned to Kahn. "I need to clean up. Is there a shower I can use?"

Kahn looked at her for a long moment, as though sizing her up. "There is a bath. Let me show you."

He led her to the open door, and the lights came on when she stepped over the threshold. There was no toilet, but a huge, oval shaped pool surrounded by exotic, very colorful plants -- the only color in the whole place.

"Thank you," she said, and turned her back on him, expecting him to leave. She wasn't surprised, though, when she felt his large hand on her bare shoulder.

"Anna," he whispered, hoarsely. She knew he was hurting. He tried to hide it with smiles and kindnesses but she knew he desperately wanted her to trust him. To love him. Part of her did. But another part of her knew that he could have found her at any time and brought her son to her.

Shrugging him off, she climbed into the water, and slid beneath until only her head remained above it. He turned to leave, and she had intended to let him go, but the thought of being alone was unbearable. "Wait."

He half turned to her, his expressionless face grating on her nerves. Why couldn't the man just fucking say what was on his mind!

"Because it's not in my nature. But I will try to be more open with you."

She forced a breath of air out of her lungs in frustration. "Then why don't you just tell me what you want from me? I can't feel you, and I can't read your expression... you're going to have to give me a little help here."

He took a step toward her. Okay, so it was more like he was stalking her than simply moving in her direction, but she tried to ignore that.

"I want you, *tarae*. I want your body and your mind. Your soul already belongs to me, but I want you to acknowledge it freely."

Maybe too much wasn't good either. "Kahn, I don't even know if I *like* you or not. I'm certainly not in love with you. I know that's what you're getting at. I can feel it now."

"But you want me. I feel that in you."

Much as she wanted to deny it, she couldn't. She couldn't be around him without wanting to feel his body against hers again. As his hungry gaze raked her naked form beneath the water, a fresh rush of heat exploded through her body. She didn't need to be able to hear his thoughts to know what was on his mind.

She was supposed to be mad at him, but she was finding it difficult to concentrate when he stalked her in all his naked glory, his cock jutting out proudly from the dark curls between his legs.

"I need you. I've never needed a woman more."

Anna desperately wanted nothing more than to welcome him into her arms, her body, but she couldn't. Not now. Not until she knew for sure he was the man she hoped he was.

"Kahn, you've got to give me some space. I can't do this until I know for sure I can live with the consequences."

He paused as he slid into the water behind her. "All right, *tarae*. We'll take it slow." He kneaded her shoulders, lessening the tension she hadn't realized was there. She sighed at the exquisite pleasure.

"Tell me something. What does that name mean you keep calling me?"

"Well." Kahn took a deep breath. "*Tarae* are domesticated pets, but still one of the most vicious creatures on Gothe'mar." Kahn moved closer, his breath tickling the back of her neck. "But the thing about *tarae* is, they breed so fast, if they didn't have a natural enemy they would probably take over the planet."

"Uh huh." Anna got a funny feeling in the pit of

her stomach. "The point?"

"The predator that hunts the *tarae* is a very large, winged creature like a falcon or hawk on Earth but much, much bigger. He must hunt, and *eat*, many *tarae* a day if he is to survive."

"Uh huh." She was repeating herself, but when his mouth slid over her neck, when she could feel his immense need of her, her vocabulary dried up and her IQ dropped fifty points. "Does this bird have a name?" she asked, looking back at him.

His grin became positively wicked. "They are called a *kahn*."

Heat suffused her body at the implication. He would have her. It was inevitable, and she knew it with every fiber of her being. Her only dilemma was trust. She couldn't take the chance now. If he was right and she was about to have her son back, she couldn't be with a man she didn't trust.

But her body had other plans. He resumed his gentle massage and his hands on her bare shoulders and back sent tingling shivers straight to her pussy. She groaned and leaned into him. His lips were back at her neck and jaw as he kissed a path from ear to collarbone. If he didn't stop, she'd throw herself at him again. She had to stop this somehow before she did something she'd regret.

Pushing away from him, she slid beneath the water's surface. Eyes closed, face upturned, she came out of the water, smoothing her hair back from her head. She turned away from him, moving to the other side of the small pool before turning around. When she did, she couldn't miss the ravenous look in his eyes.

They sat there in the water staring at each other a long moment before Kahn finally broke the silence. "You make going slowly difficult."

His sultry voice made her wish things were different. She wanted simply to go to him, fuck him senseless, until neither of them could move. Her breasts felt heavy and full. She knew without looking that her nipples were hard. All she had to do was brush her fingers against them, squeeze them, and she'd be so hot for him, she might be able to forget why she shouldn't fuck him.

"Touch yourself, *tarae*," Kahn whispered. "If you won't let me give you pleasure, please yourself. Let me watch."

Anna was helpless to do anything but what he asked. She desperately needed release. Her own need was bad enough, but she could feel what he wanted from her as well, and it was driving her mad with unfulfilled desire. It was like her dreams all over again.

Her hands found her breasts and she massaged the full globes. Filling her hands, she pushed her breasts together and licked each tip impulsively. She shuddered at the sensation her own tongue created. Taking one peak into her mouth, she sucked and nipped gently, sending a flood of warmth straight to her cunt.

She didn't know if the moan was hers or Kahn's, but the sound was definitely encouraging. Sliding one hand to her pussy, she ran a finger along her folds until she reached the small opening and dipped the finger inside. Savoring the sensations, she then circled her clit several times until her hips rocked in time with the movement of her fingers.

Making eye contact with Kahn was not the smartest thing she'd ever done, but once she did, she couldn't look away. Nor could she simply sit there with him so close and not want him to touch her. She needed to come and she didn't think she'd be satisfied with anything less than his cock pounding deep inside her.

He rose and moved toward her slowly. When he reached her, his hand shot out to her hair and he pulled her head back roughly so that she looked up at him. The fear that coursed through her at his forceful gesture, and the evidence of his straining control blazing in his eyes, made her even more aroused.

Not bothering to ask permission, he grabbed her by the waist and lifted her to sit on the edge, spreading her legs and diving between them with his face. Anna thought she'd die, the waves of pleasure were so intense. Her clit burned where his tongue touched it, and her breasts tingled with each touch of her fingers and mouth. Kahn's heady growls were a powerful aphrodisiac and she almost came.

Almost.

Before she could stop it, a vision of her son's bloodied body filled her mind and all thoughts of sexual release vanished, leaving her empty and a little ashamed.

* * *

Raising his head, Kahn sighed. He kissed her belly and hugged her middle a moment while he got his breathing under control again. He had pushed her too hard. Once again, he'd let her down. When would he ever stop making mistakes with the only woman in the entire universe that mattered to him?

"I'm sorry," he said, muffled by her abdomen. "Forgive me."

Anna clutched his head to her middle. He could feel her shame, but also her need for him to anchor her in such a difficult time for her. She was trying to put aside her own wishes for the welfare of her son and for that he thought he might die from loving her. Anna was everything a Gothe'maran man could want in a wife.

Desperately needing to get her talking to him, to help her be comfortable with him again, he turned to the subject most on her mind. "Tell me about your life on Earth, *tarae*."

"You never ask the easy questions, do you?" Anna took a deep breath. "I'd never given the future much thought beyond looking for you. I wasn't even sure I *would* find you."

Kahn smiled. "I know, sweet. But *now*. What do you want from the future?"

Anna thought a moment. "I'm really not sure. Beyond getting my son back and him being whole and healthy, I don't know what more I could ask of the future." She thought for a moment. "I suppose I never really cared what happened to me before you found me at the Front. My thought was to get to you by any means necessary, but I never truly expected to ever see Kahn the Merciless a second time. I think I just wanted the nightmare my life had become to be over. Either you'd find me and explain the madness happening on Earth or the Gothe'maran would kill me. Either way, that phase of my life would be over."

"And what of your life before?"

Anna swallowed. "I loved my husband deeply." Her voice was husky, rough. "My little boy? It goes without saying that I loved him more than my own life. I would have given my own to save his, but they came out of nowhere. I didn't have time to act, to prevent anything. When it was over, what could I have done that would have made any difference? Your scientists may be able to bring Alexander back to life, but I knew ours couldn't. I worked in the medical field ten years before the Pilot incident. I knew nothing would save either Alex or Mark."

Anna retreated, gliding to the opposite edge of the bath without turning to face him. "My life was happy, Kahn. Every married couple has problems and we were no exception, but I would have gladly spent the rest of my life with him, raising our son." Kahn felt the emotion compress her chest. She hurt talking about this.

The gentle lapping of the water was loud in the ensuing silence as he moved to gently touch her shoulder. "If I gave you the opportunity, would you give your account of what happened at the Pilot?"

Anna wiped tears from her cheeks with the heels of her hands and sniffed. "Why? What good could possibly come of it?"

He hesitated, unsure how to phrase his next statement. "When we get to Gothe'mar, there will be a trial going on. The man responsible for leading the rebel warriors to Earth is being tried for what your people would call crimes against humanity. There are statements that he alone was responsible for recruiting the warriors he unleashed on your planet, and that he gave them explicit instructions to wipe out every living thing on your planet save fertile females, but there have been no witnesses from Earth to describe firsthand what actually happened from Earth's perspective." Kahn gently turned her to face him, his eyes locked to hers, waiting for a reaction. "Mikkril says Earth was in the middle of a civil war when they got there. They were only trying to end the killing."

Anna gasped. "But you *saw* them kill my family!"

"No, Anna. I saw them vaporize your husband's body and come after you. I didn't see them actually kill anyone. After that incident, the only killing I saw was my warriors killing Mikkril's."

Rage almost consumed her. She wanted to lash out, to hit something. To kill something... someone. Kahn couldn't blame her. "So you're telling me there is a possibility your people will be convinced we did this to ourselves? We killed each other on such a massive scale? What about the death camps? How will he explain them?"

"Your history is replete with similar incidents, as is our own. As is just about every race in the universe. It's not uncommon. You can prove that's not what happened."

"What about Alex's injuries? He was hit with a Gothe'maran weapon. Won't that make a difference?"

"Certainly. Medical Command will testify to such, but they need your account to back them up and fill in the rest of the story." He lowered himself into the water so that he was face to face with her, looking at her from eye level instead of towering over her. "Can you do this?"

The determination to avenge her son and husband in the only way given to her was very strong. She would get her point across to the king. She would make him see Mikkril for what he really was. A murderer.

"I'll do whatever you need me to, Kahn."

He enfolded her in his strong embrace then. Nuzzling her hair with his chin, kissing her temple. Simply holding her. And she let him. He drew some comfort in that. "I'm sorry, *tarae*. All this has been more difficult on you than it had to be and I am the cause. I should have told you about Alex from the start."

"I guess I'm as much to blame as you are. I'm the one who practically attacked you when I first woke up." She smiled, a little, sad smile. "Just let me work it out. I will, in time."

"I know you will. Unfortunately, there is something else."

"There's more?" Her disbelief and dismay were clear.

"Yes. And I honestly don't know how to explain the rest to you. It will be difficult for you when we reach Gothe'mar, and there will be little I can do to help until the trial is over."

"What do you mean, 'difficult'?" Her wariness sharpened her features, and she looked at him through narrowed eyes.

Before he could answer, the intercom chimed softly.

Kahn swore under his breath. "Speak," he barked.

"General, Military Command requests you speak with them immediately." The voice was clipped, but neutral. He tried to bury his apprehension, but wasn't sure how well he succeeded. *Here it comes.*

"Alex?" she whispered. Kahn shushed her with a quick touch of his finger to her lips and a kiss to her forehead.

"Inform them I will contact them at once. Establish the link to my office in ten minutes. Kahn out."

He focused on her once more. "No. If something were wrong with Alex, Medical Command would be the one to contact me." He paused, warring with his sense of duty and his sense of responsibility to her. He could see by the look on her face that she knew something wasn't right.

"Kahn?" She searched his eyes, his face, his mind.

"You said you trusted me for now. Can you trust

me a little farther?"

"What's that got to do with this? What's happening?" she asked without answering his question. She wasn't going to deal well with this. Not that he blamed her.

"I don't have time to explain now and I may not see you again until we dock." His grip on her shoulders tightened. "Whatever happens, believe in me. I promise, I'll take care of you and Alex. Whatever the cost."

"You're scaring me, Kahn." Her face had gone pale and he could feel the adrenaline rush through her body as if she were preparing for battle.

"Don't be scared, *tarae*. I'll take care of everything. You just have to trust me."

Anna replied softly, "That's a lot to ask."

Kahn sighed as he got out of the bath and dressed. It wasn't much, but at least she hadn't completely rejected him. Before he left her, he looked at her one last time. "I love you, *tarae*. If you never believe anything else I tell you, believe that. Cling to that no matter what happens."

Kissing her lightly on the mouth, he left.

* * *

Kahn's presence hadn't actually been required for the curt statement from Military Command that he cease all contact with Anna. His father could simply have issued the order and been done with it. As head of Military Command, Kahn knew Kerrek had a job to do. As his father, Kerrek knew that if he extracted a promise from his son face to face, Kahn would not break that promise. Not that Kahn had been given a chance to explain the situation. The order was given, Kahn had acknowledged the order, and the "conversation" had been terminated.

Damn them all!

He could only guess what Mikkril had said to shift the blame from himself. Well, Kahn supposed he'd find out soon enough.

They were docking on the main spaceport orbiting Gothe'mar. They were here and Anna still didn't know the prejudices that awaited her when she actually met Mikkril. If his people felt the same as Mikkril, if they were not willing to accept an off-worlder mate to their future king, Kahn wasn't sure what he'd do. As current ruler, Kerrek could smooth things over a bit if he chose to, but would he? Kahn could only guess what was in his father's mind.

Still, Kahn had promised to take Anna to Alex first thing, and that was what he intended to do. He just hoped he didn't have to disobey too many commands to get it done. Duty had never seemed so heavy. And it struck him that nothing had ever been more important to him than his duty to his planet and his people.

Until now.

* * *

When the two warriors came to escort her to the planet's surface, Anna was a little disappointed. She had expected Kahn would be there to take her to her son. Instead, the two silent giants flanking her took her to a small spacecraft that was to carry them to the surface of Gothe'mar. No matter how many times she tried to get the sentinels to tell her where Kahn was, she got no answer. In fact neither of them spoke to her, or even looked at her, except to give her orders.

Time seemed to crawl as the three of them sat in silence during the two-hour trip to the surface. Why they had to take a spacecraft at all was a mystery to Anna. She remembered vividly having her son vanish from her arms, and watching Kahn disappear. It seemed like a wasted effort, but she'd endure it. In silence. She'd be damned if she'd complain even once.

When she finally exited the tiny craft, she was met by Kahn and three other imposing looking men. The relieved smile she flashed him faded as she caught the look in Kahn's eyes. Merciless didn't even begin to describe it. She could feel the desperate hope within him that she'd trust him, but beyond that nothing else. And his features certainly gave away nothing.

"Medical Command has recommended you be present when they awaken your son," one of them said. Funny, he looked remarkably like Kahn. His expression gave away nothing, but something in his voice disturbed her. He sounded almost... disgusted. Like he was looking at a particularly revolting insect. "I am Kerrek. You will come with us."

Anna gave Kahn a brief, questioning look before nodding her agreement. She didn't think she could have spoken if she wanted to, she was so nervous. She was going to get her son back!

The foursome led her down a series of crowded hallways, each becoming less and less congested. When they reached a hall leading to a large, gray door, Anna found her entourage was alone. No one spoke until they finally stopped before the entrance and Kerrek turned to her.

"You will do as instructed by the doctor without question," he said.

"Of course. Thank you for letting me be with my son for this."

The man just looked at her. When he spoke, disdain and contempt oozed from every word. "You are here because Medical believes it will be less stressful for the boy. Your feelings in this matter are of no concern to me or anyone else. If it were not for Medical's strong insistence you be present, you wouldn't be."

Anna was stunned. Something was very wrong. She looked to Kahn, but he was not facing her, nor was anyone else. He desperately wanted her trust, though. She could feel the need beating at her stronger than any of his emotions ever had before. The necessity for trust was so powerful, it created a stabbing pain in her temple and she almost fell to her knees.

Somehow, she managed to walk steadily through the door when it *whooshed* open. In the center of the room was an incubator-like contraption. Knowing in her heart that machine was where her son lay, she headed for it, unbidden. A vise-like grip on her shoulder stopped her, causing her to wince. One of her escorts effectively, and painfully, halted her approach. He never once looked at her.

A very tall, very slender man was working at the various terminals surrounding the place where her son rested. He looked up as soon as the doors closed again.

"Is this the mother?"

"It is," Kerrek acknowledged.

"She has no weapons of any kind?"

"None. My son brought her here and has assured me she carries no weapon. She can do no harm you will not be able to prevent."

Anna's head whipped around to the man she now realized was Kahn's father. Did this man think she would harm the people who had saved her son's life? "I would never try to hurt anyone who has tried to help Alex."

"Silence!" he roared at her, his face a mask of unbelievable anger. "To even presume you would be capable of doing harm to someone in Medical

Command is ludicrous. We are concerned that you would undo all the good this man has done for the baby."

"What?" Anna whispered. She simply couldn't believe what he was implying.

"It may be acceptable to terminate your own children on Earth, but on Gothe'mar, you would forfeit your own life for even attempting it. We protect our children." The superior, condescending look combined with the rage flashing in the man's eyes was completely wasted on Anna.

She was lost in her own rage.

Before she could even form the thought, she backhanded him with all her strength using her closed fist. Everyone in the room moved to subdue her. One of the big men slapped her hard enough to split her lip. Still another hit her full in the stomach, then her side as she bent double. But even though the force of the blows made her want to vomit, they could not stop the fight in her, or stem her words. "How *dare* you! Your people slaughtered my people by the millions, including my husband and my child!" She struggled against the impossibly tight male hands holding her back from further attacking Kahn's father. "I don't know who you are or what your function is on this Godforsaken planet, but if you want to blame someone for killing that baby over there, look in the mirror. You! Your people! Your warriors!" Anna continued to lash out at her captors, even Kahn when she recognized his presence to her left. She kicked and scratched, even bit when she could. "Alex was killed by a Gothie weapon!" Her voice dripped disdain. "Even if I was able to take the damn thing from one of your warriors, how could I possibly know how to use it?"

Kahn's father looked to the doctor who was

shielding the incubator with his own body. The doctor nodded. "The child was killed by a standard issue destabilizer. I do not know if Earth possesses anything similar but in order to fire one of ours, she would have to have been fitted with a controller chip specific to the weapon in question. I found no such chip in the data files when she was scanned upon boarding General Kahn's ship. She would not have been able to fire any weapon of our world without it, and would not have been able to remove it without leaving trace particles."

"Do they have anything similar, Kahn?"

"They do not, Father." Kahn's voice was soft.

"You're sure?"

"Absolutely. Besides, when I got to this woman and the boy, she had not even drawn her weapon and there were no Gothe'maran weapons near her." Kahn's voice was carefully controlled. Even through her anger and grief, she sensed his wariness, his unwillingness to give away too much. God! She hated not knowing what was going on! And at this moment, she hated Kahn most of all.

"Did you see a warrior kill her husband or her son?" Kahn's father looked openly inquisitive. It was obvious this information was new to him. Information he wasn't sure he liked but, since it came from his son, he had no choice but to believe.

"No, but I did witness a warrior disintegrate the body of her husband. That warrior's attitude was not... reverent. At the time, I assumed from what I *did* witness that the three warriors present had something to do with the death of the man and the child."

"Interesting." An emotionless mask was once again in place. Anna decided she hated Kerrek almost as much as the men who had killed her husband. Kahn had come to her aid, but she wasn't sure she'd ever be able to forgive him for not actively helping her when she had been hit or, most especially, when she had been accused of murdering her own son. She was sure Kahn had known his father believed she'd killed Alex before they ever reached Gothe'mar.

Now that she was beginning to come down from the adrenaline rush, her face burned with pain and her stomach felt like something inside of her had torn. Breathing hurt and she was losing the ability to even stand up on her own. She would have slumped to the floor if not for Kahn keeping her upright.

The doctor came to her side, running a small scanner around her body. "She is bleeding internally from a ruptured spleen and a punctured lung. And a head injury. I must repair her first, then I will bring the child out of stasis." His examination stopped suddenly. He looked at her, surprise evident. "You cannot have children."

"No," she gasped. "Having Alex... almost... killed me." Breathing *really* hurt. "My husband... d-didn't..." Another gasping breath. "... want to p-put... me through that... again." Kahn and the doctor were now helping her into a machine that looked vaguely like a tanning bed. "Had a... tubal... ligation." God, she *hurt*! Why was *any* of this important?

"Relax, madam," the doctor said. "This will take a few minutes. You'll not feel any pain, only a warmth. It should be relaxing once the process gets underway."

Anna closed her eyes and simply gave herself into their hands. She hurt too badly to fight them anyway. If they honestly believed she had killed her own son, she was up shit creek without a paddle. For the second time in her life, she succumbed to the black blissfulness of unconsciousness.

Chapter Four

"Father." Turning away from his woman -- *his* woman -- in the healing tube was the hardest thing Kahn had ever done. "I know Mikkril is your brother, but I do not believe he is telling the truth about what happened on Earth." He had to be careful here. Kerrek loved Mikkril as if they were full-blooded brothers instead of half brothers. Kerrek would acknowledge Mikkril's deception if it could be proven, but he would not accept half-baked theories and assumptions. "Look at all the evidence and listen to what this Earth woman has to say. It can only serve to give you more information. You can decide later how much weight to give her statement."

"Listen to her?" Kerrek sounded incredulous. "After she assaulted me?" He paused, looking suddenly weary. "I fear I already know the truth of it." He looked at Kahn fully. "You think she is telling the truth?"

"I do," Kahn said without hesitation.

Kerrek spoke to the doctor, "Can you repair her internal damage?"

"Yes, sir. I can even repair the damage to her reproductive system if you wish it."

Kerrek gave Kahn a sidelong glance and spoke softly, knowingly. "Do you wish it, my son?"

Kahn actually blushed, horrified. *He knows!* "I -- Father --"

"Do it," Kerrek said, grinning at Kahn. "This woman is your future queen and she will need to have more babies."

Now, *this* was unexpected. "Wait," Kahn said, raising a hand in the doctor's direction. Turning to his father he said, "You have no problem with a union?"

How could he not have known his father would have seen things this way?

Kerrek shrugged. "The Universe directs us in ways no one can predict. Given the fact that so many of our warriors were eager to sacrifice an entire world to 'preserve our people,' perhaps it is time Gothe'mar learn that all life is precious. Not just the lives of our own people. If this woman has captured your heart, who am I to forbid a union?"

"My relationship with her is... complicated," Kahn said somewhat uncomfortably. There was no way Kerrek was going to believe any of this.

His father only smiled. "I can imagine. Mine with your mother was, also." The king chuckled as if remembering. Then his merriment faded and his eyes misted over.

"You miss her a great deal." Kahn's voice was soft, quiet with respect.

"She was my soul's mate. I will find her in the Chamber of Souls when my spirit departs this body." He smiled. "But, yes. I miss her a great deal." Kerrek paused and looked at Kahn. The force of that stare was enough to make even Kahn the Merciless squirm. "Kahn," Kerrek said, carefully, "is this Earth woman your soul's mate?"

Kahn's mouth went dry. "Yes," he managed. How would his father react?

Kerrek merely smiled. "So your time has come. It's not something I expected -- no one has ever found a soul's mate outside the Gothe'maran people. This will be the bridge they need to accept Anna as their queen. It is the very heart of our beliefs."

He clapped Kahn on the shoulder. "I will go now. Don't leave her side. If this had happened between your mother and I, she would have skinned me alive when she got out of that healing tube. I'm sorry I treated her so harshly, Kahn. You should have said something." He paused. "That's something else you're going to pay for." Still chuckling, his father turned away to consult the doctor and dismiss the guards who had accompanied them.

Anna's anger at Kahn had been bitter. He knew she had trusted him to protect her and he had failed. Had he better prepared her for what was going to happen when she reached Gothe'mar, told her she was being accused of her son's attempted murder, she might have been better equipped to deal with everything. As it was, he had led her into a situation that could very well have gotten her killed. Instead, he had bedded her. Eagerly. He chose to try to get her to accept him, to trust him, instead of telling her the king of Gothe'mar suspected she had murdered her own son. Anna trust him? Probably not in this lifetime.

That had cost her, too. One simply did not assault the king. She was lucky she had survived. She wouldn't have if Kahn hadn't stayed the guards when he did. Not that she would see it that way. Not that she should. His father's last words haunted him. He had denied her in front of his king and his people, not to mention his father, something she would never forgive.

Right now, Kahn could only wait. He had to be the first person she saw when she came out of that tube. He had to gauge her feelings through the link so he would know what he needed to do to regain her trust.

"Sir." The doctor was speaking to him now. "Shall I proceed? I need to see to her injuries."

Kahn hesitated only a moment. "Yes. Proceed, but do not repair her reproductive organs. It must be her choice." He started to turn away, but faced the doctor again. "Can you identify the problem she had with her pregnancy that caused it to be difficult?"

"Yes, sir. It is easily correctable. A minor problem with the shape of her uterus. Fixing that should solve any problems for birth in the future."

"Then hold your findings and keep them ready. If she decides she wants this, we'll do it later."

"As you wish, sir." The doctor turned back to Anna's healing tube. "This will take a while, sir. Go rest. I'll call when she's close to regaining consciousness."

Waiting had never been harder.

* * *

When Anna opened her eyes, Kahn's face was the first thing she saw. At first she smiled. It must have all been a very unpleasant dream.

Then the tall, thin doctor came into view. "How do you feel, madam?"

Not a dream after all. Well, shit.

She sat up, swinging her legs over the side and remaining that way for a moment before answering. "Fine. Will I still be able to see my son?" Her voice was bitter and she forced herself not to look at Kahn. If she did that, he'd see her hurt. If he didn't already feel it. She'd give almost anything to be able to block her feelings from him at that moment.

"Of course. All is ready. We are simply waiting for you," the doctor said, not unkindly. "Please follow me and do not touch your son until I tell you. This process is delicate and cannot be disturbed or he could be in danger."

Anna followed him without a word. Let him stew. If he even cared. She couldn't feel him and didn't want to try.

Gazing into the encasement, she got her first look at her son. The tiny boy was resting comfortably on his back, one hand tangled in the tuft of dark hair on his head. It was like he was sleeping peacefully in his crib.

Grief over losing him, joy at finding him again, all the emotions were so overwhelming, she staggered and would have fallen into the contraption had it not been for Kahn's steadying hands. She immediately shrugged away from him and focused her undivided attention on what was happening to her son.

When the doctor flipped a few switches and pushed a few buttons, the incubator started to hum with life. Soft lights surrounding the baby on the inside began to glow softly.

"Beginning cellular restabilization. This will hurt him for a couple of seconds, but will pass and the process will be completed. Do not touch him or the healing tube until I tell you it is safe." The doctor waited for her to acknowledge his words before he turned away again and flipped another switch.

As she watched, Alex sucked in a breath and then screamed so that Anna's first instinct was to snatch him up, but Kahn held her back, whispering, "Wait, *tarae*. Only a second or two more."

Anna looked to the doctor, beginning to feel frantic. Tears slid down her face unchecked. She could not bear another second of this. Her son needed her... again. And unlike the last time, she would be there for him.

"Please! He needs me," she sobbed.

"You may go to him now, madam. Cellular restabilization completed, patient's vital signs normal. Congratulations, madam."

Anna didn't wait to hear the doctor's last statement. She rushed to Alex the moment he'd let her and was now cradling her son against her chest, comforting him and crying with him.

After a few minutes, Alex's cries stopped and he looked at his mother. "Hello, booger." That name had always made him giggle. This time was no exception. The child giggled through the tears and started cooing and gurgling as any five-month-old should do.

"I need a bottle for him and some baby food." She looked to the doctor for help, but Kahn had a bottle already in hand.

"Give him this and I'll see what we have on Gothe'mar that is similar to what you would give him on Earth."

She took the bottle without acknowledgement and began feeding her son. She only hoped they would let her finish this one thing before they took him away from her. There was no doubt in her mind that they would take him. Worse, she knew there was nothing she could do. Fighting would only cause her more injury and distress her son. Frustrated, lost in despair, she knew she was beaten.

"He needs a diaper and clothes. And he is used to sleeping with his Buggly Bear." She started to cry again despite her resolve not to. "Some... someone will have to... rock him to sleep because... I-I've never put him to bed by himself," she said between sniffles. "And he n-needs... a n-nightlight." She was rambling and she knew it, but couldn't seem to stop herself. Giving him up this time would kill her. Without Kahn to sustain her, she knew she would grieve herself to death.

Then she felt strong, warm arms surround both herself and Alex. Even as angry as she was at Kahn, she couldn't stop herself from turning to him for help.

"I can't let them take him away from me, Kahn,"

she sobbed. "Please help me. I'll do anything, anything! Just please don't take him from me." She was crying uncontrollably now, to which Alex pulled back and looked at her, then at Kahn, then back at her and started giggling.

Normally, that would have been enough to stem the flow of tears, but it only made Anna cry all the harder and hug her squirming son closer. She knew that the next moment could possibly be her last with him and she wasn't letting go for anything.

"*Tarae*, relax. No one is going to take Alex from you." Kahn released her and led her to the door. "Come. Let's get Alex to our room. He needs rest."

Not trusting the reprieve, Anna clung to Alex. The relief was almost as overwhelming as the earlier grief, but she held on to her control. She wasn't sure why things seemed to have changed, but she wasn't questioning her good luck. Lord knows she deserved a little for a change. Kahn guided her to a suite and into the bedroom where a gigantic, very comfortable looking bed awaited her. There was an assortment of infant clothing and supplies in one corner, and Kahn brought her a fresh diaper and a sleeper.

"Here. Dress him for bed. He will need sleep."

He was right. Alex was rubbing his eyes even as he tried valiantly to avoid that awful creature called sleep. Anna changed and dressed him. Crawling into the big bed with him, she sang softly as she rocked gently back and forth, Alex wrapped snugly in her arms. It wasn't long before he doddled off, looking as peaceful as an angel.

"We need to talk, *tarae*." Kahn's voice was husky with emotion she couldn't feel. But when she turned to him, the feelings suddenly swamped her. *Sorrow. Overwhelming sorrow.*

Her grip tightened on Alex and the child whimpered but continued to sleep.

"Please, let's talk, then you can rest with him. You both need sleep, but we need to clear the air so we both know exactly where we stand." The Kahn standing beside the bed pleading with her was not a Kahn she had ever met before or even suspected might exist. He looked like a lost little boy. Vulnerable. *This is because of me.*

She let his feelings flow over her and deciphered them as best she could. His sorrow stemmed from the possibility that she would not be able to forgive him. He believed there might be no hope for him. And he just might be right.

"Will my decision have any bearing on whether or not I get to keep my son?"

Kahn's startled expression told her all she needed to know about that. He had no intention of trying to use Alex to keep her in his life. Hearing him say it, however, was a step in the right direction for him. "Of course not! Alex belongs with you. No one will deny that anymore."

"Then, if it's all the same to you, I'd rather spend this time with Alex. I don't much feel like talking to you right now, Kahn. I'm really not sure I ever will again."

She turned her back on him, cuddling herself against the body of her son, and tried to ignore his devastation. It wasn't easy. He didn't say a word. He respected her wishes, but the depth of his despair almost caused her to change her mind.

No. He had to truly understand how much he'd hurt her, betrayed her. He was apparently so ashamed of her that he had let her be beaten, and almost let her lose her son because he wouldn't defend her. Because he seemed to be afraid of letting his people know he was involved with her.

Which brought up another question: just how involved did he see them? He'd said he loved her, but were their definitions of love the same? She tried to tell herself that she owed it to him to give him the benefit of the doubt. After all, he had given her Alex back and that was worth more than she could ever possibly repay, but she just couldn't bring herself to forgive and forget that easily.

She'd sleep on it. If she still hated him in the morning, she'd ask him to take her home. If not, she'd talk to him. It seemed the only reasonable thing to do at this point. He'd just have to understand.

* * *

Kahn was smiling, his hand outstretched while he held Alex with his other arm. Anna tried to take his hand, but found the gap just too big to bridge. But he had Alex. She had to try. She could almost grasp Kahn's hand…

Alex laughed. The sound was haunting somehow instead of joyous. Kahn looked at the little boy and grinned a "proud poppa" grin, then turned his gaze back to her. He was no longer smiling. Instead, there were tears in his eyes and his hand slowly dropped to his side. He seemed to be falling away from her.

But he wasn't. She was falling away from him.

She tried to find a hold, but all she found was air. She was reaching into nothingness and the two people she loved most were slowly but surely falling away from her. She screamed…

And sat up in bed, drenched in sweat and gasping for breath.

One quick look to her right assured her Alex was still sleeping.

She needed to splash a little water on her face

and get a drink. Anna carefully and quietly gathered all the pillows she could find on the bed and arranged them around Alex. Sliding out of the bed, she made her way to the dimly lit bathroom.

As she pressed the button that would give her cool water, she looked in the mirror over the sink to confirm her suspicion. She looked as bad as she felt. She ached in her chest and upper abdomen and even though there were no marks, her face felt like it should have been black and blue. Her eyes had dark shadows underneath them and her skin was damp. Her lips were so pale, they almost disappeared into her face.

Dropping her head and bracing herself on the countertop with her hands, she bit back a sob. She'd been hard on Kahn. Damn hard. True, she had reason to be, but his misery wasn't wasted on her. She knew he was only trying to do the right thing for himself and his people. Knowing he was so off balance, she was miserable because she wasn't big enough to put aside her anger and try to see things from his point of view. She just couldn't understand why he hadn't told his father about her. Why had he treated her as if he didn't know her? Like they didn't have intimate knowledge of each other.

She began to cry. Losing Kahn was going to be harder than she thought given the short time they had known each other. Then again, she had wanted him on some primitive, emotional level since the first time she saw him. She could forgive him for anything except not wanting her. He might want her in private, but if he could not acknowledge their relationship in public, before his people or even his family, she could not be with him. She would not be his mistress. She had more self-respect than that.

Lost in self-pity, she turned around when she

heard water sloshing gently behind her just as Kahn raised his big body out of the bath.

"Anna." His voice was husky, rough. His eyes were bloodshot and he looked almost as bad as she did. But he was still beautiful to her. So beautiful it hurt.

Water clung in a mesmerizing array of droplets to the fine hair on his chest and arms. The dim light accented the hollows and sinew making him look more powerful and sexier than ever before. Instantly, her pussy began to weep with wanting him. But it was the ache in his voice that drew her undivided attention.

She looked at him. Really looked at him. The sorrow in his face mirrored her own, and a little sob escaped before she could stop it. She almost ran into his arms. Almost. Pride held her legs rooted in place and stubbornness raised her chin.

"*Tarae*. Please. I was looking out for both of us." His face was shadowed and it was hard to read the emotions there, but what was inside was another story. "I was trying to be a leader instead of a mate." He rubbed his eyes wearily with a hand. "My family has held the throne of Gothe'mar for over a thousand years because the people believe my family held their best interests at heart. I feared they would not accept a queen not of Gothe'mar on the throne."

"I don't understand." Her eyes narrowed.

"My father is king of all Gothe'mar. My family has reigned for longer than any ruling family in recorded history. It is my duty to lead and look after our people, to put their lives above my own. I have been burdened with this since I was first old enough to understand what it all meant. I have always been taught that my people's needs come before my own." He moved a little closer to the pool's edge, closer to

Anna. "As my father has recently pointed out, in thinking of my duty to my people, I neglected the most important duty of all -- that to you. Our relationship is not about me solely. Without you, there would be nothing. I would be nothing." She could feel him will her to look at him, and she couldn't help but meet his gaze. "I should have treated you with more respect."

"Yes. You should have." Anna wanted him with all her being. She wanted to reach for him, to move into his arms and feel his body around her. She could feel part of her soul being torn apart knowing that she could never be what this man needed. Her heart was breaking.

Kahn moved toward her a little more, his arm reaching out to her before he dropped it. "My father approves of our union. He seemed a bit amused by the situation I've managed to create for myself where you're concerned. He will help me figure out how to see you accepted by our people."

"Kahn," Anna stated warily, not sure how to express herself without further hurting him. "I can't be anyone other than who I am. If you think your people can't accept me as I am, then I'm sorry. I won't live a lie even to please you."

"I would never ask that of you."

"What were you thinking when you treated me like you did? You were obviously concerned about it then. Why should I believe things have changed now?" Anna was trying very hard to express her anger, her hurt, reasonably. All she really wanted to do was rush into his embrace and fuck him until neither of them could move. Either that or slap his handsome face.

"It was a mistake. A huge mistake. One I'll regret for the rest of my life. I asked for your trust, then showed how little I deserved it."

This side of Kahn was *so* unexpected. This was a man who commanded armies, who was to be king of his world. He inspired fear and dread in the hearts of all who saw him. Yet he was willing to show Anna just how vulnerable he really was when it came to her. She was torn. If she walked away from him, he probably wouldn't drop his pride a second time. On the other hand, if she gave in, he'd know he just had to act contrite and she'd forgive him anything.

In the end, she searched her own heart. She couldn't make herself believe that Kahn was anything other than an honorable man. He had been unsure of how to handle things, probably for the first time in his life. Second-guessing himself had proven to be a mistake and he was admitting it. How bad could he really be?

Before she could change her mind, Anna pulled her sleep shirt over her head and slid her panties off her hips, stepping out of them as she walked to the tub. "We'll sort things out." She slipped into the water and into Kahn's embrace, feeling the squeezing sensation around her heart ease a little. When he would have claimed her mouth, her hand came up against his lips to stop him. "This is to get the physical relief we both need and can't fight, Kahn. Things are far from settled between us. Do you understand?"

"Yes, *tarae*. But it is a beginning." He smiled at her, a tender smile full of love and relief and hope.

He did kiss her then. Slowly, languorously, savoring the very essence of her. Anna knew he needed her as much as she needed him and it was a heady sensation. She thought she would climax from his kiss. His feelings were hers and she knew how much he appreciated the dance her tongue was doing with his.

It was impossible to tell which feelings were her own, but she didn't care. The only things in the world that mattered to her were this man in her arms, and the baby sleeping on the impossibly large bed in the next room.

"We have to be quiet, Kahn. I don't want to wake Alex," she breathed. How she managed to form that thought was beyond her. She could hardly think of anything other than the talented mouth currently moving over her own.

He chuckled and it warmed Anna's heart to know she had driven the desolation from him by just accepting him once more. "I don't think I'm the one you need to silence, *tarae*. I seem to remember you making quite a bit of noise the last time."

"Did I? I thought it was you bellowing when you filled my cunt with your cream." She knew what the crudeness of her words did to him. She could feel the lust rise within him, within herself.

"Perhaps we should try it again." His voice was a growl. "See who screams as she gets pounded with my cock."

That did it. Anna knew she needed him inside her, riding her, taking her body any way he saw fit. The recent emotional upheaval needed release, and the man she loved was going to provide it in spades.

He palmed her ass and lifted her until she instinctively wrapped her legs around him. She rubbed her cunt against his heavy erection and felt his muscles tense as he suckled her neck. As he lifted her just a little higher, probed her slick opening with the head of his cock, she found his mouth with hers.

Instead of the quick entrance she expected, Kahn slipped just inside, halting her movements with his strong grip on her buttocks. He moved his kisses to her breasts and sucked one nipple into his mouth. The water supporting her as much as possible, Anna let her head fall back.

Kahn began to increase the pressure of his mouth on her nipple. Still he wouldn't let her ride him as she wanted to. He held her against his body so that she was unable to get more of him inside her no matter what she tried. Her breast ached and throbbed where his mouth was attached, making her pussy spasm around his cock. Her juices mingled with the water lapping around them. Her clit pulsed in time with her heart, and she could feel her impending orgasm just out of reach.

"Please, Kahn. I need you inside me," she pleaded. "Give me more of you. All of you."

Kahn growled as he thrust into her. The emotions swirling inside him were chaotic. She felt his need to be a gentle lover this time warring with his need to claim her as his, to dominate his mate into accepting him. He didn't just need her body, but her. All of her. Everything that was her.

"What do you want?" It was more demand than question. "What will it take to get you to come?"

"You," she gasped. "Your cock. Ramming into me. I need your cock, Kahn." She could only whimper now. She was coming apart inside. Still he didn't move more than a fraction of the pace she needed. The teasing only served to drive Anna higher and higher without ever reaching the pinnacle.

"Look at me, Anna," Kahn said, halting all movement now.

She didn't want to meet his gaze. Though she knew he needed her, wanted her, she also knew there was a reason he thought his people wouldn't accept her. She knew she shouldn't want him, knew his people probably wanted him to marry someone befitting their future king -- one of them. But she couldn't get enough of this man. God help her, she loved him with all that she was.

"Anna." His voice was gentle yet gruff with emotion and lust. When she finally did look at him, it was through a haze of shame and desire mingled with love and so many emotions she couldn't name them all. His piercing eyes bored into her soul and he paused a moment before he spoke.

"You do not fully understand the bond between us, *tarae*. It cannot be denied by you because you think I believe you unsuitable for me, and I cannot deny it simply because my people might not want their future king mated to an off-worlder. I swear to you by everything that I am, I am your mate and Alex's surrogate father first. I'll be a king second. I'll do my duty to my people, but my family will always come first from this moment forward."

"And if your people don't accept me? If you have to choose between your people and me and Alex?" Anna had never been so unsure of herself in her life.

"Then we will leave. We will build a life together with love, and Alex will know that we love him and each other."

Anna knew in her heart that Kahn was telling her the truth as he saw it. So she simply clung to that and hoped it would be enough. "Make love to me, Kahn," she whispered.

And he did.

The slow, even thrust of his hips began again. The slick, gliding sensation of their bodies melding beneath the water was heady indeed. It didn't take long before Anna was as frenzied as she had been earlier, and she wrapped her legs around his waist, locking her ankles.

She ground her pussy onto his cock as she twisted her hips, threw her head back and cried out. Kahn's grip on her ass tightened and his nostrils flared with his effort. He released one cheek of her buttocks to run a finger down the seam and gently delve into her rear entrance. When he pushed past the tiny ring of muscle, Anna only suppressed her scream by biting his shoulder. The sensation was almost overwhelming in its pleasure. When he added the second, then the third finger, she had had all she could take.

"Oh my God. Kahn!" She exploded onto his cock, his fingers up her ass. Never had she felt so full. His grunts came with every stroke as he fucked her with a fever she'd never known existed, the corded muscles, tendons and veins of his face, neck and arms straining his skin. Just as her own climax was ebbing, he gave one mighty thrust and her name on his lips made a guttural, primitive sound in his own passion.

They clung to each other, the water rocking their bodies gently as if to soothe and relax them. Kahn spoke first.

"You are my life, my sweet Anna. Give me your trust and I promise I will not disappoint you again. Give me your heart and I'll treasure it always."

Anna stiffened. "You've got to give me time, Kahn. I promise to try to trust you, but it's not just me now. I can't afford to stumble into another situation like before. Do you understand?"

"You wouldn't be a good mother if you didn't take that into consideration. Of course I'll give you time." He kissed her forehead. "You will be asked to testify at the trial tomorrow. Will you at least trust me to see you safely there? It wouldn't surprise me if Mikkril tried to hurt you before you can speak out against him. His life is on the line, after all."

Anna looked at him, startled. "I never thought of that. Alex will be the most vulnerable. Since I'm obviously no match for a Gothe'maran warrior." She thought for a minute. "I'm not thrilled about this. We have a long way to go, Kahn, and since I don't have much of a choice, I know we'll be safer with you than anyone else." When he looked a bit crestfallen, she sighed. "I'm sorry if I sound harsh, but taking chances with my son's life is not the way I'd choose to test how much I can trust you. From my viewpoint, I simply have no alternative. I may have issues with you, but you're the only Gothe'maran I believe actually cares if we get there alive or not."

Anna searched deep down for a gut feeling to tell her what she should do. "I think I do trust you. Even though things got a little out of hand when you brought me to Alex, I know you didn't expect me to pick a fight." Needing to lighten the mood a little, she said, "I caught you off guard when I slugged your father, didn't I?"

Kahn groaned. "Don't remind me. You would have been killed if I hadn't intervened. I don't think anyone in our whole history has ever hit the king before."

"King. God, Kahn. I can't believe your father is the king of Gothe'mar! That you're next in line to be king. This whole situation is ludicrous." She would have laughed if she hadn't already started to become aroused again. His cock was still inside her, causing the most delicious sensations to thrill her cunt once more.

He chuckled. "Being heir to the throne has its advantages."

"Oh yeah?" Anna wiggled her hips to draw his

attention to their joined bodies. "Like what?"

"If I were anyone other than the king's firstborn son, I would be on duty, not in this bath making love to my woman."

"Hm. And if you were king?"

He flashed her that wicked grin. "My woman would be making love to me instead."

Anna laughed, feeling lighthearted for the first time in a long while. "I guess it really is good to be the king."

Chapter Five

No matter what Kahn said, Anna wouldn't leave Alex with someone while she sat before the tribunal. Both he and his father had offered assurances that the boy would be safe and that she would most definitely get him back immediately afterward but she wouldn't budge. Kahn supposed he couldn't blame her. She had said it would take time to trust him again. Trusting him with her son's life was most definitely last on her list and that was as it should be.

Fortunately, the child was asleep when the time came for his mother to face the man she would speak out against, and Anna carefully made her way to the witness box. She shifted Alex so that he lay on her shoulder, and the child grunted at the movement but remained contentedly asleep.

"We understand that on Earth there are hearings such as this and that the witness against the accused swears to tell the truth before the court. Is this accurate and something you recognize as binding to you?" The king presided over all tribunals and he was the one to whom it fell to determine the accuracy of each witness's testimony. One thing he had always told Kahn was to find out what held the word of each species that entered the witness box and make them swear to it.

"Yes, sir."

"Then, by your rules of court, do you solemnly swear to tell the truth, the whole truth and nothing but the truth, so help you God?"

Anna blinked. Kahn could see the surprise on her face at hearing the familiar words. Then she smiled. "I do. Of course."

When asked to relay her experiences during the

war, Anna painted a gruesome picture. She described the tortures her people endured individually, and what she had seen at the death camps abandoned near the Front. She gave an account of the equipment found at one of these camps, and there was no way it could have been anything other than Gothe'maran in nature.

Mikkril looked at her impassively as she relayed her account. Try as he might, Kahn could not read the man's intent in his expression. He could have been merely a spectator for all the emotion he gave away.

Kahn noticed her embrace tighten on Alex as she told how he and her husband had been slain. There were tears in her eyes and on her cheeks, but her voice was steady and sure. She never took her eyes off Mikkril.

When the representative of Gothe'mar was finished questioning her, Mikkril's representative stepped forward. Kahn held his breath. This would not be pleasant. He just hoped Anna could control that temper of hers. He smiled. Then again…

* * *

Anna didn't know how in the world Alex had managed to sleep through the proceedings so far. Thank God he had though because she absolutely refused to let anyone else have him. Even for a second. She was so nervous, she just knew she'd wake him with her trembling.

Courage, tarae. *I'm with you.* Anna warmed at the encouragement from her lover. *Lover!* Man, she was in way over her head. His eyes were focused on her and she took courage from his words and his intimidating physical presence.

Gothe'maran courts were held in what looked like a very large cathedral. The "judge," in this case the king, sat behind a very large desk to the left, and the accused sat in the middle of the stage. Each witness stood in a box facing both king and the accused. The "lawyers" moved around the space in between but were very careful not to obscure the view of the accused. From what Anna gathered, it was the right of the accused to not only face his accusers but to make them face him as well.

Now, it was Mikkril's representative's turn to question Anna. She had a feeling this wasn't going to be pleasant.

"Ms. Garrett, you say your world was not in a civil war. Is that correct?"

"Yes, it is." Apparently, Mikkril was sticking to the story that he had been trying to save Earth from itself.

"Then can you explain the events just prior to the arrival of the Gothe'maran warriors?"

Anna frowned. "I'm not sure what you're referring to."

The representative was a very tall man, almost as tall as Kahn, and he had obviously practiced using his height to intimidate. Anna was sure as hell intimidated.

He looked down his nose at her. "Do you expect the king to believe you can remember to the last detail the battle you just described but you cannot remember the effects of a nuclear blast on your own homeland?" He sneered.

A light dawned and Anna sat up a bit straighter. "I always assumed the Gothe'maran had set off that explosion. I think everyone on Earth did, too."

For the first time since the trial had begun, he faltered. Unfortunately, he picked up smoothly. "Would it surprise you to know that bomb was set by a faction within your own country?"

Without hesitation, Anna shook her head and said, "No. It has happened before. Groups of radicals, or even one individual acting alone but in the name of a group, have performed such acts of terror before. It doesn't constitute a civil war."

"Yet your country was at war."

"But not with ourselves."

"No!" He pointed at Anna to emphasize his statement. "With a country vastly inferior in technology to your own. A war they had no hope of winning."

Anna remained as calm as she could. "On paper, maybe. But if you'll look into Earth history a bit, you'll find that the group of countries in the region you're referring to has a long, bloody history of war, dating back thousands of years. You'll also find that such people usually find a way to beat technology and 'civilization.' They were doing plenty of damage, just in bits and pieces. They knew the one thing America would never stand for was her soldiers coming home in body bags. The factions who were left to do the fighting after the governments fell took out one soldier at a time. It adds up after a while."

"But Earth is still fighting amongst itself. Do you deny that?"

Anna was getting confused. She reached for Kahn with her mind hoping he could feel her confusion and help her out. She couldn't reach him this time. *Damn.*

"I suppose you could say that, yes."

"You see, Your Highness! She admits it!" Mikkril's representative was triumphant. "If it had not been for the Gothe'maran forces taking control of Earth, they would have annihilated each other."

The smile Mikkril gave her was pure evil. He

obviously thought he had won a victory. And from the way the king was nodding his head, he just might be right.

"Your Highness." Anna looked to Kerrek. "I'm confused."

Mikkril's counsel barked a laugh. "You're human. It does not surprise me."

Kerrek speared him with a look. "Darkin, you will keep quiet when I am addressed or I will have you removed. Further, you will not insult any witness in this tribunal for any reason. Such shows disrespect by you and the one you represent." Kerrek's voice was quiet but even more menacing than Kahn's could be. "I will take any such action in the future as a personal insult."

The tribunal went dead quiet. Anna wasn't sure of the significance, but Mikkril paled and so did his representative. After one last menacing glare at Darkin, Kerrek returned his attention to Anna. "You wish to pose a question, Ms. Garrett?"

Anna looked warily at Mikkril before answering. "Yes, sir. Are our definitions of civil war the same?"

The king's eyebrows rose a fraction. "I'm not sure I see where you're going, Ms. Garrett. A civil war would be when a planet or empire is divided and separate sects fight amongst themselves for control of the government or to form a government of their own."

"But you see this as being separate sects within the same government?"

"Of course. What's your point?" The king looked annoyed, and in a race that gave away very little through facial expressions, that meant he was most likely *very* annoyed.

"Well, sir, Earth isn't ruled by *one* government.

Each country has its own form of government and there are literally hundreds of countries in the separate continents."

The whole room came alive with murmurs. Anna looked behind her to find Kahn, wanting his reassurance. As she did so, she heard excited whispers being exchanged, and Kahn didn't look happy at all. Unfortunately, when she turned back around she could see that Mikkril looked very pleased indeed.

"Silence!" the king roared. "I'll have order in this tribunal or I will excuse everyone in the viewing gallery."

"Your Highness." Mikkril's delegate again. "I ask you to dismiss the charges. It is obvious that Mikkril De'Kar understandably misunderstood the goings on of Earth. He was only trying to protect Earth from itself."

"Absolutely not. There is still the matter of the genocide he ordered."

"A misunderstanding as well, my king. He was not committing genocide but trying to get the populace under control when they refused to stop the bloodshed."

"That's a bit of an overkill, don't you think?" Anna said dryly.

"Ms. Garrett, I'll give you the same warning about speaking when I'm spoken to. I am in control of this tribunal." Kerrek's emotions were really showing now, and he looked livid. Which likely meant he was ready to commit murder. "I've had about enough of your double talk, Darkin. It is clear to me that Mikkril is responsible for the bloodshed on Earth."

"But, Your Highness! He was only trying to save lives. Theirs as well as those of the Gothe'maran people. His methods might have been a bit harsh, but they were working. Earth ceased fighting itself. Given time, he would have added Earth to the Gothe'maran empire, thereby adding females to breed fighters. Our warriors would not have to battle to expand the empire and the Gothe'maran people would be the envy of the entire universe!"

"To my knowledge, this empire has never encountered a planet as divided as Earth." Kerrek's tone said he had heard enough. Anna held her breath. This was it. "And yes, I can see how one might mistake Earth's squabbles as a sign of government upheaval, but the killing of women and children has never and will never, *ever* be condoned. For any reason. General Kahn spoke here about how he liberated a so-called 'death camp.' His report was chilling even for a race that has thrived on war and bloodshed in the past." He now looked at Mikkril, his eyes chillingly angry. "Mikkril, if there is ever a need for war, Gothe'mar will defend itself with its own warriors, without breeding a race of slaves for that purpose. That you both are using this as a defense for your actions shows you are not honorable."

Kerrek took a deep breath, obviously not liking what he was about to do. "Mikkril, you are found guilty of all the accusations against you. For your crimes, you will forfeit your life. For forsaking your honor and tarnishing the honor of my son and therefore myself, the king, your death will be prolonged and most painful. My son and I will decide your fate within the day." Picking up a previously unused gavel, he said, "So be it." And slammed the instrument against the desk with a resounding *whack*.

* * *

Kahn looked into the eyes of his half uncle as his father pronounced his judgment. Absolutely nothing.

Mikkril gave away nothing of what he thought or felt. It wouldn't be like Mikkril not to try something violent. No man who had so brutally murdered children would go quietly to his death.

Anna clutched her child and seemed to turn her concentration to the sleeping boy, kissing the back of his neck as his head lay on her shoulder. Mikkril lunged for her, but she didn't turn to face him until it was too late.

* * *

Anna! Kahn's voice inside her head snapped her to attention. Mikkril was almost upon her. With one mighty lunge, the evil man grabbed for her. Anna tried to swing away from him, putting herself between Mikkril and Alex, but her movement was too late. Mikkril had already gained a solid hold on Alex and her momentum only served to rip her child from her arms.

Her anguished shriek filled the hall and she threw herself at Mikkril but he was ready for her attack. He backhanded her as she approached, once again using her momentum against her. With a battle cry he darted up the steps toward the back of the hall, Alex, now awake and screaming in fright, tucked under one arm.

Heedless of the pain that exploded through her skull, Anna scrambled up the steps after him, her only thought to get to Alex. An arm around her waist restrained her, and she fought it like a wildcat.

"Let me go! Alex!" she screamed over and over, a mad, hysterical scream. It was just like the nightmare she'd lived for over two years. In her dreams, she was never able to get to her son.

"Please, madam. Let the general take care of this." She didn't know this man, but he was wearing the uniform of the Gothe'maran. Anna looked around her and saw that Kahn and Kerrek were both racing after Mikkril along with a host of soldiers.

Kahn, please save Alex. She willed him to hear her. She wasn't yet as sure of the bond as Kahn was but put all her faith in it and in Kahn.

She stilled. Trust Kahn to save Alex? Did she? Only a couple of hours ago she thought she would likely never trust Kahn with Alex's life. She had to get to Alex, no matter what. No matter who was trying to get him back for her. She would not lose him again!

* * *

Kahn raced down the back steps into the bowels of the great hall, his father just behind him. Mikkril might not live long enough for that long, painful death he had coming. How Mikkril thought stealing Alex would help him he had no idea. Maybe a quick death was what he wanted. Kahn growled as he tried to devise ways to take out Mikkril without harming Alex. The trick was to get Mikkril close. Kahn had to make sure he either had a clear view of him or that Mikkril put the child down. Anything else would put Alex's life in jeopardy and that was something Kahn would not even consider.

Destabilizer in hand, Kahn rushed through the dimly lit passageway, listening for any sound that might indicate which way Mikkril was headed. When he stopped at an intersection, his father stopped at his side. "Do you hear the child, Kahn?"

"No… wait!" Kahn tilted his head. "There. A muffled cry. Left."

Without another word, both men sprinted down the hall as quiet as the warriors they were. It didn't take long before they could hear more.

"Are you sure taking the Earth whelp was a good

idea?" Darkin. For him to be there so fast, this had to have been planned.

"It was the only way I could be sure I'd make it out of the hall alive. Kahn would never risk hitting a child, no matter what race it is." Mikkril's voice oozed contempt.

"Its cries will lead them right to us. You're a fool, old man!"

"So... silence... it!" Mikkril hissed through his teeth.

Kahn rounded the corner just as Darkin raised his own destabilizer and aimed it at the now screaming infant.

"NO!" With a battle cry he fired at Darkin, hitting him square in the chest. The man howled in agony, his clothing burning away, then his flesh. In moments, Darkin was nothing more than a pile of ash.

Behind Kahn, Kerrek fired at Mikkril but his shot went wide and was absorbed by the wall. Mikkril shot at Kahn, just missing his head, as he snatched up the child and sprinted down the corridor. He had to get to Mikkril before he made it to the spaceport just outside the Judgment Hall. If that happened, he would lose Mikkril in the crowd.

Fortunately, someone had thought of that. Mikkril had just reached for the door adjoining the spaceport when it burst open to reveal about twenty warriors. Caught, Mikkril turned around and looked at Kahn.

"You have me, Kahn," he said, menace dripping from his every word. "But I have the Earth bastard. Guarantee me safe passage out of the empire and I'll spare its life."

"I cannot do that. You have been fairly tried and sentenced." Kahn's voice was hard, but reasonable.

"Have the honor in death that you forsook in life."

"Will the little Earth bitch forgive you when she finds out you could have saved her son?" He sneered. "I bet she won't be so accommodating between the sheets. I'm doing a service to the empire by getting rid of both of them. You could have never taken her to mate anyway. The people would not stand for it."

"Your words are for nothing, Mikkril. I will kill you, the child will live, and Anna will be my mate and the future queen of Gothe'mar. There is no other option."

"There are always other options!" Mikkril was obviously losing his control. Kahn knew he had to do something fast or Alex was as good as dead.

"Not this time." Kahn fired.

* * *

"Alex!" Anna pushed her way through the crowd of warriors that surrounded her as she chased after Kahn. She was just in time to see him drop Mikkril with a single shot to the head. She moved as quickly as she could, but Kahn reached Alex first, catching the child as Mikkril's grip slackened. The large man toppled to the floor minus his head, shoulders and most of his torso.

Kahn's mind was blocked to her, but she could see his rapid breathing and the pulse beating frantically at his throat. When he handed Alex to her, his hands shook.

Anna hugged her child, soothing him as best she could, and watched Kahn. He had fallen to his knees when he made the dive to catch Alex. Now he sat flat on the ground, arms braced on his bent knees. He was still breathing hard as Anna cautiously approached him.

"Are you all right?"

Kahn looked up at her, anguish on his face. "Alex?" he croaked.

Anna blinked. "He seems to be fine, but I'll feel better about it once I get him to the doctor. I need to make sure."

"Thank the Universe." A smile played at his lips. "Let's see to Alex."

"Yes. Then we need to talk."

"Of course, *tarae*."

Chapter Six

The doctor gave Alex a mild sedative and placed him into the same tanning bed look-alike that had healed Anna's injuries before. She was reluctant to leave him, but the doctor assured her Alex would be well watched after and any injuries he had sustained would be completely repaired. Still, she refused to go far. Kahn did manage to get her into a lounge of sorts equipped with a food dispenser and a couch.

After getting her a cold drink, Kahn sat down with an arm around Anna and said, "Don't worry. He'll be all right."

"I can't help it, Kahn. I just got him back and I'm so afraid I'm going to lose him again." Staring at her untouched cup, she sounded bleak even to her own ears.

"Anna, look at me." When she complied he said, "No matter what, no matter who tries to say differently, I swear to you on my life and the life of my family and my people, I will never let anyone take Alex from you or harm him in any way. You're my mate, Anna. Your family is mine as mine is yours."

"I've not consented to be your mate. I'm still upset over my arrival here." Anna pouted but she wasn't really mad. Her heart rejoiced that he still spoke in the permanent sense.

Kahn chuckled. "You're my mate whether you want to be or not. The Universe has already decided for us. Your only choice is whether or not you choose to stay with me."

"Oh, Kahn." She loved him, she really did. But there were still some considerations. Unfortunately, Kahn was intent on distracting her from dealing with those issues. He placed a gentle kiss just below her ear, then sucked the lobe into his mouth and nibbled just a bit.

"Now," he said between kisses as he made his way down her neck and moved a hand to the buttons of her blouse. "What did you want to talk about?"

"Um, Kahn…" She breathed his name gently, her mind and body turning eagerly to the pleasures he was offering. "I can't stay here. On Gothe'mar. Oh heavens don't stop that!" The only thing separating his hand from her taut nipple was the lace of her bra.

"And why is that, *tarae*?" His voice sent chills down her back and heat coiling in her belly. She was sorely tempted to simply let him take her however he wanted.

"Because you're going to be a king." She was rapidly beginning to lose her ability to carry on any sort of intelligent conversation.

Kahn pulled back to look at her. "Now why would that make you want to leave? I would have thought any Earth girl would want to be a queen." He smiled teasingly.

"Kahn, I can't change what I am. I'm not Gothe'maran. Even though your people aren't the bloodthirsty savages I once believed, I don't think that they would accept me as the wife of their king. I might be happy for a while, but seeing you and Alex both miserable wouldn't be worth it."

"You've heard several of my people agree with Mikkril, haven't you?"

"It's pretty hard to miss."

Kahn traced circles on the expanse of soft flesh left bare by the modest length skirt he had slid up her thigh. "Did you happen to notice all the ones who were determined to make sure you were unharmed when you rushed after your son?"

"What?" Anna was genuinely perplexed.

"All the soldiers you had to push your way through to get to me and Alex after I killed Mikkril." He waved his free hand in the air for emphasis.

"Well, yes. But I thought they were going after you."

"Did it *look* like I needed their help?" He sounded and *felt* almost offended.

Anna couldn't help but giggle. "You were doing pretty well on your own, but they were your warriors. It only stands to reason they would follow you."

"And did you happen to notice that the majority of them were forming a defensive ring around you, not trying to find an opening to help me?"

"Well, now that you mention it..."

"Anna, the people of Gothe'mar are more adaptable than even I realized. We guard our loved ones zealously and my family has ruled for over a thousand years. Not because the line was unbroken, but because the people loved us enough to *allow* it. We've always held our honor above all else and did the right thing, no matter the personal cost.

"My father and I had a long talk while you slept." He took a breath. "I'm not sure how to explain all this to you, but I'll do my best.

"It is a Gothe'maran belief that each soul has one true mate. Each life, the souls seek out one another in hopes of mating yet again. The problem is, there is no predicting where in all the Universe one soul will find the other, therefore the odds of finding one's soul's mate are extremely low. But --" he lifted a finger to punctuate his point, "-- if the souls do manage to find each other, they create a bond like you and I share. The more lives they spend together, the stronger the bond becomes.

"Usually, it takes several years of being with a mate before the bond starts to manifest itself. The more lives spent together, the quicker the bond is established. We shared a bond from the moment we first saw each other. According to my father, there has only been one other couple in living memory to have accomplished such a thing: he and my mother.

"It is one of the reasons my family has ruled as long as they have. The very foundation of this belief demands that the ruling family be true to each other. The very fact that we are soul's mates guarantees Gothe'mar will accept our union."

"Just how do we go about proving such a thing? Surely everyone won't just take our word for it." Anna was enchanted, yet still a bit skeptical.

Kahn chuckled and brushed her nipple through the lace again, lazily. "In part, yes. But should there be a challenge, we will have to prove our link. A simple matter really.

"Anyone wishing to challenge our mating may do so. Once a challenge is made, the couple and the challenger must go to the Chamber of Souls. The Chamber houses souls awaiting rebirth and they alone can attest the validity of the claim of mates." Kahn tucked his fingers under her bra to gently pinch her nipple, eliciting a groan from her. "What you are forgetting is that Gothe'mar is home to a race of people who value honor above all else. If the people questioned my honor, I would not be accepted as king in the first place. With Mikkril's disgrace and conviction, there is no one who would question my honor."

Anna's senses were beginning to overload again. She loved what he was doing to her body and was not ashamed to let him know. She purred and stretched against him, inviting him to do more. He was only too happy to oblige.

Kahn sank to his knees before her, wrapping his arms around her middle, and took her taut nipple into his mouth through the lace of her bra. Anna's fingers twined in his hair, hugging him to her as she whimpered in need.

"Feel good, *tarae*?"

"Oh yes. Sweet God, yes!"

He grunted his approval as his clever fingers found the clasp and unhooked the lacy scrap, pulling it away to reveal the creamy treasures before him. He buried his face between her breasts and kneaded them softly as he occasionally lapped and nipped each ripe peak.

Anna knew the pleasure he could give her and surrendered to it. He would take care of her. He would take care of her and Alex. Everything was going to be fine. She smiled as she hugged him to her. Everything was going to be fine. Except...

"Kahn?" Her voice was a squeak as he started moving down her belly, gently pushing her into a more reclined position as he did so.

"Hum?" His slide southward didn't hesitate in the least, even when he reached her skirt. He simply pushed it past her hips and slid her panties to the side. Slowly, he swiped his tongue from her opening to her clit.

"You said your family... dear God, what are you doing?"

Kahn circled her anus with his tongue before sliding one finger gently inside. "Making love to you, sweet. Now what were you going to say?"

His voice was annoyingly calm and Anna puffed a breath of air upwards, causing a tendril of hair that had fallen over her forehead to stir. How could he be so calm when he had her tied in knots?

Kahn looked up at her and smiled. "A warrior's control is almost limitless."

Anna snorted. "We'll have to see about that," she said as she squeezed his finger with her inner muscles. "Just how in control would you be if your cock was buried there instead of your finger?" Their link flashed with heated lust and so did his eyes. Anna smiled wickedly.

"Say what you will so that I can take what you so generously offered." If talking dirty to him was the key to his lust, then Anna figured she was going to have loads of fun in the future. The not-too-distant future from the looks of things.

"You said your family has ruled for a thousand years. Do you mean passed down from father to son?"

"In most cases, yes." Kahn slid another finger into her ass and idly circled her clit with his thumb. "If a son is too young or unable to assume rule, an elder sister or uncle is sometimes appointed."

Anna stilled even though the sensations he was creating were about to drive her crazy with needing him. "What if a king can't have a son?"

Kahn shrugged. "Such has never happened. I don't think a man has ever sat on the throne who wasn't capable of producing an heir."

"What if it wasn't the king, but his wife? What if she couldn't have children?" Her desire was waning. She wasn't going to cry. No way. If this was the end, then she'd take what he wanted to give her and pleasure him in return, but she would leave. She would not tie him into a marriage that could not produce an heir to a thousand-year heritage.

Kahn stopped the slow play of his fingers.

"Anna, love. What are you trying to say?"

"You know what I'm getting at." She shoved him away, but he only leaned into her.

"Why is this bothering you? It does not even apply."

"Of course it does! Kahn, let me up."

"No. Not until you say what is in your heart, Anna."

"Can't you tell?" she asked, almost bitterly. "You seem to have a pretty good grasp on this thing between us. Tell me what I'm thinking."

"All right." Kahn didn't move an inch. His face became blank as he looked intently at her. "You think to leave me because you can't have children. You think that tradition will ultimately be more important to my people than the happiness of their future king. You think --" He paused, capturing her chin and turning it back to him when she looked away. "You think that I will become bitter or dissatisfied because I will not father a child to ascend the throne when I give it up."

"Okay. So you summed that up nicely."

"Have you learned nothing about me?" he said softly, and Anna caught the hurt in him.

"I know you love me, Kahn. But this is serious stuff."

"First of all, if it had been that important to me, I could have fixed your reproductive system when you were injured upon your arrival here. I could also have had the doctor repair the problem that made you have a difficult delivery of Alex in the first place."

Anna sucked in a breath. "Really?"

"Oh yes. In fact, the doctor at Medical suggested it but I told him not to. If you want that procedure done, it is up to you. But it will be because you *want* more children, not because you think I *need* them."

Kahn raised a hand to her mouth when she would have spoken. "Secondly --" His fingers, meant to silence, turned caressing as his gaze lingered on her lips. "I already have a son to take the throne so there is really no need of any of this discussion."

Anna stilled, truly puzzled. "You never mentioned you had children."

"I do. He's a little over two years old, though he has the mind and body of a five-month-old."

The breath rushed into Anna's lungs as she stared, not daring to believe what she was hearing. "What?" she whispered.

"Perhaps you've met him. His name is Alex and his mother is a hellcat when it comes to his safety so I know nothing will happen to him. If you choose not to become fertile again, I see no reason you should have to."

Tears overflowed her eyes as she flung her arms around Kahn. He was accepting Alex as his. But what of the Gothe'maran people?

"They will gladly accept him. You'll see. Everything unfolds as the Universe intends. They will accept him and love him."

The fingers Kahn had in her anus slid almost free only to be reinserted with a third. His thumb on her clit resumed its lazy circles. "Now. Where were we?"

* * *

For the first time since he met her, Kahn felt Anna give herself fully into his care and he was determined he wouldn't let her down again. Starting right now. He would love her good and proper this time.

His head dipped to her cunt once again and he tasted her, pulling gently at her engorged clit. The fingers he had embedded within her slid free and he crawled up her body to press his full weight on her. His hand fisted in her hair and he searched her face. "Tell me you want this union, Anna."

"Yes. I want you."

"Now and forever?"

"Always," she breathed.

It only took a swift tug of his breeches and his cock slid free. He rolled off her to his side, maneuvering her so that she rested her back against his chest. Positioning himself at the slick entrance to her pussy, he paused once again.

"Tell me you love me." It was not a request or a question. He demanded her love.

She smiled. "With all my heart, forbidden or not, I love you with everything that I am."

He surged forward, groaning as he thrust into her body. Her soft cries were music to his ears as he slowly, but deeply took her. She met his forward push with a backwards one of her own and soon the writhing of her lithe little body made him hunger for more. Harder. Faster. Deeper. He wanted all she had to give him. He wanted to give her all he had to give.

Lifting her leg, he slid down to give himself better leverage and began to thrust in earnest. The sharp, staccato rhythm of flesh slapping flesh was punctuated by her cries of pleasure with each smack. He knew he wouldn't last long, but he wanted all of her. His body and his link as her mate demanded it. He knew she was on the edge and would soon find her own release, but not yet. He stopped and pulled out.

"Wha -- Kahn, why did you stop? I need..." She was struggling to turn over. She wanted to mount him and bring release to them both, he knew.

"Hold still, *tarae*." He pulled his cock back just a little to the entrance of her ass and pushed slightly.

"Kahn. I'm not sure about this."

"Just relax. You know I'll make it pleasurable for you." He kissed her cheek and whispered, "Trust me."

She relaxed immediately and turned her head to smile at him.

"Push outward with your muscles. Push against me and it will be easier for me to get inside you."

Anna did as he asked and he slowly entered her. He knew he caused her some discomfort, but he also knew he made her hot. She was even more eager than before, if that was possible.

"That's it. Let me fuck your sweet ass, just like you wanted it."

"I did offer, didn't I?"

Kahn chuckled. Once he had worked himself all the way inside her, his balls resting against her upper thighs, he reached around her and pulled her back to him by her breasts.

"Now. I fuck you."

And he did. What started as something slow and gratifying turned almost savage in its intensity. Kahn surged into her again and again until sweat slickened his chest and back and ran down his temples.

Anna desperately sought leverage so she could meet him thrust for thrust. Finally, she blindly grabbed his hip and found what she needed.

Their lust was mutual. Each felt the need of the other and it only increased as they reached their climax.

Anna came first. She screamed and bucked, digging her nails into Kahn's firm ass as she pulled him to her. Kahn's cock pistoned rapidly until his own orgasm exploded from him in great spurts. He held her, his cock still buried, until the last of his seed was spent.

They lay like that for a time, catching their breath. Then a soft chime interrupted their peaceful afterglow.

"General. There is a problem. You and Ms. Garrett are to report to the Temple Beyond immediately."

Kahn froze. "Explain," he barked.

"Mikkril's son."

Fucking damnation! The little bastard was going to try to avenge his father. *Of all the idiotic things*!

"I would speak with Kazar before this."

"Not possible, General. He has already entered the Temple Beyond."

"What is it?" Anna asked tentatively.

"Mikkril's son, Kazar, is questioning our union. He shares his father's prejudice. He will not want you in a position to be queen so he seeks to discredit both of us."

"Maybe you'd better explain this a little better."

Kahn helped her to her feet, straightening their clothing, then ushered her out the door. He took her to a transportation unit that would take them across the continent to the Temple. Once they were seated and the unit was moving, he began to speak.

"Within the Temple Beyond lies the Chamber of Souls. When a challenge of mates is made, the couple and the challenger enter the chamber. If the couple are true mates, the souls rejoice and the Temple is filled with an amber light as witness to their happiness." Kahn looked at the rapidly moving scenery, obviously not liking what came next. "The energy needed to do this is drawn from any life within the chamber. The only way to survive is to be joined physically with a mate. Under normal circumstances, the challenger would appear to age a few years at most. But the stronger the connection between mates, the more energy the waiting souls will draw."

"Hm. Sounds a bit dangerous," Anna commented.

"It can be. Which is why it is seldom used. And then only when the throne is in question." He turned to her now. "A link like ours will destroy Kazar. But I'll just bet there'll be no talking him out of this."

Chapter Seven

The Temple Beyond was the largest structure Anna had ever seen. Its four spires rose elegantly into the clouds and the sun reflected off its walls and windows like gold and diamonds. It looked like a massive cathedral, only hundreds of times bigger and more ornate.

At the top of the steps leading to the temple doors, they were met by a thin, aging man dressed in gold from head to toe. The High Priest, she figured.

"The situation is grave, my son. Kazar will listen to no one, including myself and the king."

Kahn's expression was neutral, but his feelings were volatile to say the least. She was afraid he'd explode any second. She was definitely glad she was not Kazar. "And you expected anything different? If the souls do not kill him when this is over, I probably will."

The priest gave Kahn a stern look. "You will do no violence in this temple, Kahn. Future king or not."

Kahn growled and tugged Anna after him as he made his way through one great hall after another. Finally, he came to an intricately carved door plated in silver and surrounded by windows. Anna couldn't see anything inside. It was either pitch black, or the windows were tinted.

"Kazar!" Kahn bellowed. "Get your sorry carcass over here and let's be done with this."

A man almost as tall as Kahn and even more solidly built approached them. Anna stepped behind Kahn as she saw the menacing look on the man's face.

"Gothe'mar will never have a human, or anyone not of Gothe'maran heritage, on the throne. You lie about your claim that she is your soul's mate."

"You're a fool, Kazar. If we step into that chamber, you'll die. My link to Anna is at least as strong as Father's was to Mother."

"My father risked everything rather than see a human share the throne. I can do nothing less," Kazar stated. He seemed resigned. He was obviously doing what he thought honor demanded.

"You disgrace your family and dishonor me," Kahn growled. Anna took his arm, guiding him away from his cousin.

"Let's just do this. If he dies, then you'll have satisfaction without getting that priest all upset."

Kahn turned to her. "Do you know what I meant by 'physically joined'?"

Anna took in an exasperated breath. "So we'll hold hands going in. Let's just get this over with."

"No, Anna." He grabbed her shoulders and looked at her. "We have to have sex and this little worm will be there the whole time."

"So," Anna swallowed, self-consciously looking at Kazar, "if we aren't... *joined*, then we age too?"

"Exactly."

"Do we have to enter the chamber joined?" Anna was getting a bit apprehensive. No way did she want to have sex for an audience.

"No," the priest supplied. "You will have several minutes to complete the union. You will know when the time is right to join your bodies."

Anna looked to Kazar. "Where will he be?"

"On the far side of the chamber. But he will be able to see us the whole time."

"What if he tries to stop us from joining? You know. Tries to take us with him?" Anna was getting really concerned.

"The souls will not let that happen, assuming

you are true mates," the priest said. "This is usually done to embarrass the couple held in question. However, if your link is as strong as Kahn has suggested, it could very easily, and most probably will, kill Kazar."

Kahn walked to his cousin to stand toe to toe with him. "Do you understand that once you enter that chamber with us, you're as good as dead?"

"If the souls even recognize this human. I'm betting you're the one who will be sadly mistaken." Kazar turned to the priest. "Open the doors."

The priest shrugged. "So be it. Let it stand that Kazar, son of Mikkril, so challenges Kahn and Anna, son and near daughter to Kerrek, in their claim of soul's mate. Enter the Chamber of Souls."

Kahn tugged at his clothing angrily. Anna assumed she was to do the same and removed all but her underwear. "Can I leave this on until we get inside?" she whispered to Kahn.

"No. You must enter the chamber as you will be born again. Flesh only."

Anna couldn't help herself. She glanced Kazar's way and sure enough, he was stripping as well. *Well, shit.*

* * *

Kahn entered first, a few steps ahead of Anna, followed several seconds later by Kazar. Once he and Anna were both inside, Kahn immediately began to feel a sharp rise in energy. Then he understood.

Kazar knew they were mates. And if he didn't know the power drain would start immediately, he probably suspected. Looking to Kazar, the man had his eyes closed as if meditating.

"Anna! Get out of the chamber!"

She looked at him in alarm as the heavy door

shut with a deafening *clang* before she had even a chance to obey him. "What's happening? My skin is crawling."

"If we don't join immediately, we'll be killed along with Kazar."

"So, join with me! What's the problem?"

The power around them glowed a brilliant amber and was growing brighter every second. Kahn could feel his life being drained. All the while Kazar never made a sound. The energy began to hum all around them, focusing on Anna and himself.

Then everything stopped.

Kazar stood frozen, his face considerably older and his hair whitening at the temples. The priest's face was immobile at the window, his mouth open as if he were stopped in mid word.

Kahn looked at Anna and immediately went to her. She looked at him questioningly. He shrugged, not knowing what was happening as he took her in his arms.

Brother and sister. Welcome. Do you wish to join us? The voice was neither male nor female, one voice, yet many voices.

Kahn blinked and looked at Anna. "Join you?"

In life before life.

"You mean, our souls joining you here? In this chamber?" Anna asked.

Yes. If you release your bodies, you can live here until needed.

"But," Anna said, "we are needed. Right here. Right now. Kahn is the future king of Gothe'mar. He can't leave now."

Ahhh. I see. You have mated in many lives. Your essence sings to us. Join, so that we may rejoice in the union.

"You mean, right now?" Anna squeaked.

Kahn chuckled. "I think they're giving us the opportunity to join before they use up our life force."

"But they're watching!"

"So is Kazar. What's different now than when you stepped into this chamber?"

"I thought Kazar and maybe the priest would be the only ones. But now we're being watched by God only knows how many!"

Kahn lowered his voice. He knew the effect he had on her when he talked dirty. She might think he was the only one affected by it, but he knew better. "Let them watch. I'll fuck you senseless and every soul for a thousand generations will bear witness to your screams when you come. We'll fuel their lusts until they assume their next life."

Anna drew in a sharp breath. Kahn knew she would definitely give him all she had now. He'd have to make a note for future reference: Anna liked to be watched. She let her nails lightly score his rigid chest before dropping one to his rapidly hardening cock. "Hm. You know, there's one thing I've wanted to do since the first time I fucked you."

And she dropped to her knees.

Anna's hands slid up and down the powerful columns of Kahn's thighs. Looking up at him put her almost at eye level with his cock. As it was, his balls were right there, just begging for attention. Without touching his now very rigid shaft, she sucked one testicle into her mouth, licking it gently before repeating the motion with the other. Kahn's groan caused a trickle of moisture to escape her cunt and a single drop fell to the tile underneath her. Continuing her erotic exploration, Anna gave his cock a wet lick from base to deep purple tip. She caught the drop of pre-come on her pass before she took half of him into her mouth.

He hit the back of her throat and she almost gagged before she could relax enough to swallow. That done, she was able to get a bit more of him into her mouth with little trouble. Kahn's hands grasped her hair tightly as his hips gave a little thrust and he shouted out as her throat contracted around his cock head. Anna was afraid he might lose his load before he got inside her, but that was all right with her. She was enjoying this more than she ever thought possible. She could hear the moans and echoes of pleasure all around her and could have sworn she was in the middle of an orgy. But one swift glance around her showed only Kazar, still frozen. And the amber light getting brighter and brighter until it was almost crimson in its intensity.

Kahn dragged her away from him, pulling her hair hard. "On your back. Now!" he barked, but his hands shook as he followed her and attempted to guide himself within her. It took two tries before he hit what he wanted and without another wasted second, Kahn plunged into her.

The energy swirling around them built their own sexual energy to an impossible high, which, combined with their unique bond, created a maelstrom of erotic bliss unlike anything ever before experienced by either of them. Anna wasn't aware of Kazar's sudden and immediate decline as his life force was sucked out of him. Neither was she aware that the crimson light had now become a brilliant yellow and was rapidly increasing to a blinding white. All she was aware of was Kahn's savagely handsome face above her, his cock inside her and the orgasm to end all orgasms approaching with brutal speed.

She wrapped her ankles around Kahn's neck,

lifting herself to meet his every thrust. He stayed on his knees, locking his hands and forearms around her thighs to give him leverage in the pounding he was giving her. Her breasts bounced violently as he slammed into her again and again, over and over. Sweat slickened both their bodies and puddled where their skin touched the tiled floor.

"Fuck me, Kahn! The energy…" Anna cried.

"Come! Now! Come, Anna!" Kahn bellowed his climax as Anna convulsed and writhed so that he was barely able to stay joined to her. They rode wave after wave of white-hot pleasure, their bodies using every last ounce of energy they had to give. As the spasms faded, so did the light, until a soft amber glow was all that remained.

Too tired to do anything but pull his spent body from Anna's, Kahn tugged her close and gave in to the blackness.

Epilogue

He awoke with Anna still at his side, but they were in his bed chamber, in his bed… and across the room a stout woman sat in a rocking chair with Alex, giving him a bottle. Kahn wearily pushed the hair out of his face and carefully sat up so he wouldn't disturb Anna.

"Ah, the sleeping beauties awake," the woman said with some amusement. "We were beginning to think you would sleep the rest of the week away."

"Week?" Kahn said, confused.

"Oh, yes, sir. You and your lovely lady have been asleep for three days and nights. This little fellow has been missing his mother." Alex turned his gaze to Kahn and smiled, letting milk dribble out of the corner of his mouth before going back to his bottle.

"Alex?" came Anna's sleepy voice.

"He's fine, *tarae*, and in good hands from the looks of things. Do you need more rest?"

"No, but I could use a toothbrush really bad."

Kahn laughed. "In the bath chamber, love. I think I'll join you."

Once they had showered and taken the necessary grooming and personal hygiene steps, Kahn and Anna entered the bed chamber once again. Alex had finished his bottle and gone back to sleep. The nursemaid stood with the little boy in her arms and looked to Anna.

"Would you like to hold your son, madam?"

Anna looked at Kahn. "Perhaps his father should have that honor."

Kahn was startled -- moved to tears. One escaped before he could stop it as he looked at the sleeping boy who was now his son. Taking Alex in his arms, Kahn just stared at the perfect little human. "He's so beautiful." He looked at Anna. "Thank you for allowing me this. For trusting me."

"I love you, Kahn. Thank you for saving my son."

"Thank you for giving me a son to love, for giving Gothe'mar a future to look forward to. And thank you for loving me. I love you, too." He watched as Anna brushed a tear from her own cheek.

"Let's go introduce Alex to his people," Kahn said as he put an arm around his beloved mate.

"With pleasure."

Neighborhood Watch (Forbidden 2)
Post-Apocalyptic Sci-Fi Action Romance
Marteeka Karland

Impossible Choices...

Mikkarn and Kiril both want the same woman, but even though they have shared women in the past, have *needed* to share, this is one woman each of them wants to possess -- by himself.

Mara, an Earth doctor studying under Mikkarn, is drawn to both men, but her sense of propriety simply will not let her accept what her heritage tells her is wrong. How can she love two men at the same time? Desperately needing each man's touch, she gradually come to the realization that neither man alone will do. She wants them both!

Can a soul have more than one mate -- or is it *forbidden*?

Chapter One

"Mikkarn, over there," Kiril whispered, pointing to a small group of humans working frantically on a badly wounded man in the crowded refugee center.

"By the Universe! His whole belly's been blown away." Mikkarn winced as he glanced back at his boyhood friend, now bodyguard. "Our Earth contact will have to wait. Time is of the essence."

Kiril cleared the way through the chaos and filth so Mikkarn could scan the man's abdomen -- or what was left of it -- for a quick assessment of the injuries.

"Who the hell are you, and what the hell are you doing to my patient?" A tiny woman stepped between Mikkarn and the dying man.

"Doctor Mikkarn Tovel. I am in charge of the relief sent from Gothe'mar by Medical Command. This," he gestured to Kiril, "is Commander Kiril Cha'marn, my bodyguard."

"It's about damn time! I'm Doctor Mara Jenson. We've been expecting you for days." She turned back to her patient. Digging in her jacket pocket, which bulged with its contents, she came out with a pair of small scissors. "I'm your contact and Earth representative. I'll take care of the paperwork later. Right now, I need your help." Mara cut away bits of the man's shirt and Mikkarn saw there were actually two wounds, though one was much larger than the other.

Mikkarn moved his scanner over the man again. His wounds were fatal. The healing tube wouldn't be ready in time to save him. Still, Mikkarn had to try. He barked a sharp set of instructions into the communicator at his throat.

Not getting the results he wanted, he backed

away from the patient and spoke with a deadly calm. "We don't *have* a few minutes. Get the computers online *now*."

The man's vital signs were failing, fast. Mikkarn was losing this battle.

Without warning, the man screamed, a blood-curling howl that raised the hair on the back of Mikkarn's neck. A bright red fountain of blood erupted from the gaping wound, and Mara and her staff scrambled in an effort to stem the flow.

"I told you to hold pressure!" Mara snapped. Grabbing a nearby towel, she pressed it to the man's abdomen and looked over her shoulder at Mikkarn. "Are you going to stand there, or do something?" Her vivid green eyes pierced him straight to his soul.

"We are making the final preparations. I can transport him directly into the tube in five minutes."

"This guy doesn't have five minutes!"

Mikkarn moved closer to do an intensive scan of the man's brain. Kiril had not interfered until this point, but he placed a restraining hand on Mikkarn's shoulder. "Kiril, I need an exact reading of neurological decay." Not saying anything, Kiril backed off.

"There is a steady drop in brain function." Mikkarn made eye contact with Mara again and winced at the anger he saw there. "He's losing too much blood to maintain oxygen levels."

Her disgusted snort actually caused a physical ache in his chest. Why her opinion of him mattered at all was beyond reasoning.

"No shit. You think?" Mara drawled as she dug into another pocket and handed a roll of tape to the woman next to her.

"Sarcasm isn't helping." His reply was harsher

than he intended and his anger self-directed. He had absolutely no idea what to do before technology took over. His patient was dying right before his eyes.

"You're the one with god-like medical knowledge. Do something!" Mara's desperate accusation hung between them. Mikkarn hated to admit there was nothing he could do until the computers were linked and engaged.

"Not without the proper equipment," he replied tightly.

Mara looked at him in disbelief. "You're kidding, right?"

No matter how much she affected him, her mouth was getting on his nerves. "Do your job. I'll do mine. You keep blood and oxygen going where it's supposed to and I'll get the computers ready to operate the healing tube."

As she turned from him, his attention never left Mara or her team. Unfortunately, when she bent over the patient to grab something just out of reach, the fabric of her pants stretched tightly across her backside. He blinked as an unbidden image of that shapely rear clothed in nothing but his hands stabbed into his consciousness.

Damn!

It took his team just shy of five minutes to ensure all was ready for Mara's patient. Mikkarn looked down at the dying man just as Mara spoke to her nurses.

"No, squeeze them in. He needs blood too badly to let it drip on its own, and we don't have a pump."

"That's not advisable, Dr. Jenson. This is untyped blood." Mikkarn almost felt sorry for the nurse who spoke. Almost. Mara knew what she was doing, and any delay in carrying out her orders could very possibly cost this man his life.

"Just do it!" Mara snapped. "Or leave. I really don't care which."

Another nurse, who wisely kept her head down, squeezed a bag attached to a tube coming from the patient's mouth, while another nurse pressed the man's chest downward with a considerable amount of force in a steady rhythm. Mara had one hand inserted past her wrist inside the man's gut.

Blood was everywhere.

"If you're done fiddling with your fancy gizmos, we could really use a little help here." Mara's voice was strained, incensed. Almost accusing. She never even glanced at him.

Mikkarn ignored her biting comment. "You must remove your hand from his body." His irritation was of no consequence. The only thing that mattered was getting this patient to a healing tube safely.

"If I do that, he'll bleed to death in seconds. I'm plugging his aorta."

"Transfer will be instantaneous. You will move on my mark."

She looked at him then. "You better be right about this."

Mikkarn didn't flinch. "Ready? Now."

Mara removed her hand.

* * *

Mara's first encounter with her mentor, Dr. Mikkarn Tovel, and the brooding bodyguard, Kiril Cha'marn, was a mixture of intense emotions. The instant she'd pulled her hand from the dying man's belly, her patient simply vanished. For several seconds, Mara knelt where she was. Talk about anticlimactic.

Well, that was until she got a good look at Mikkarn, and his silent shadow. The adrenaline rush she had experienced during the life and death struggle was quickly replaced with a surge of lust so strong, she sat flat on her butt in dismay. These men were as different as daylight and dark, but she was hard-pressed to decide which man was the sexiest.

Mikkarn was exceedingly tall -- perhaps six feet seven inches -- towering over her own five foot three inch frame. Exceedingly tall and very lean, wearing a loose-fitting white shirt and pants. His muscled, vein-roped forearms were bare, and when he moved she caught glimpses of a nicely chiseled chest. His eyes, though ice blue, held a wealth of warmth in them, welcoming her within their depths. Lightly tanned skin and a lustrous head of long, blond hair completed a man she could have created in her fondest dreams.

The other one, the silent, looming one, probably sprang from her worst nightmares.

Kiril was heavily armored, but Mara doubted he was anything other than one solidly built warrior. He couldn't be anything else. His skin was a rich mocha color and black eyebrows revealed the hair color hidden by his helmet. His eyes were so brown, they were almost black, and she knew those eyes saw straight to her soul… and found her lacking.

Once she recovered herself, and the necessary introductions were made, Mikkarn took Mara straight to her patient. She could see for herself the machine working to repair damage no Earth surgeon would have had a prayer of fixing.

"I greatly admire what you were able to accomplish today. I doubt anyone among my own people could have saved that man under the same circumstances."

For a moment, she thought he might be making fun of her and Earth's "primitive" medicine, but something in his eyes said otherwise. She just stared at him a moment, not sure what to say.

"Well, we didn't save him, did we?" It was a statement more than a question. "You said the magic words and he vanished off to Neverland where he will emerge whole again. My thanks to you." Mara was certain her irritation radiated off her in waves.

Mikkarn sighed. "I am trying to compliment your skill."

"Coming from the *Masters of the Universe*, that's a very great compliment indeed," she drawled. "Why is it, by the way, that you can bring the dead back to life, but you have this aversion to a little blood?"

He blinked. "You think the blood bothered me?"

Mara shrugged. "It seemed the logical conclusion. Besides --" she did her best to pin him with a sharp look, difficult when looking so far up just to catch his gaze, "-- I'd rather think you didn't like *any* blood than that you just didn't want to dirty yourself with *human* blood."

He backed away a step, surprise in his azure eyes. "Mara, I came here to help your people. All life is precious to me."

"Then why didn't you help me? Why did you just stand there, jabbering about your computer?" She knew she was being belligerent, but couldn't seem to stop herself.

"Because I simply didn't know what to do. Everything is computerized on Gothe'mar. There are very few places left where actual physical contact with a patient is necessary. I can diagnose any problem and tell our computers what has to be done to save a patient, but I cannot actually perform the procedure myself. No doctor in Medical Command can. It simply isn't necessary."

Well, *that* was pretty straightforward. Mara

blinked several times, trying to absorb what he had just told her.

"You mean, you don't do even the most basic procedures? No sutures, no closed reductions? Nothing?"

"No. That is what the computers were designed for. It's guaranteed to be a sterile procedure, the antibiotics are automatically administered, and the chance of error is cut by eighty percent. Everything entered into the computer is checked by two other failsafe devices." He shrugged. "It seemed like a good idea at the time."

Mara almost laughed. Almost. Recent events being what they were, she didn't find it that amusing just now.

"Well, in case you hadn't noticed, this isn't Gothe'mar. If this is all the help your people have sent, you've all wasted your time." She turned her back to him. In the space of one breath, Mara felt the last hope of Earth's wounded slip away. The Gothies couldn't help.

"Wait!" Mikkarn grabbed her arm, forcing her to stop. "We have everything on the way. There will be enough equipment here to help everyone in a few days." If she didn't know better, she'd think he almost sounded desperate for her to agree with him.

But she couldn't.

"A few days," she said, disappointment creeping into her words. "What about the people who need help now? And how much longer will it take to set up your equipment once it arrives?" Mara waved her arm to encompass the whole camp. "Look around us. Do you think most of these people have that long?"

For a moment, his eyes held hers. Then he dropped his gaze. "No. They don't."

Mara could see the pain in his features. Maybe she was being too hard on the man. After all, he was only doing what he could. "Look," Mara sighed, "there's not much you can do here. There is a doctor in place running the equipment you have working and we need much more of those wonderful computers of yours. Do what you can. We'll make do until you can get things running from your end."

He turned from her without another word. It was strange, but Mara thought she could almost feel the sorrow in him. She watched the tall, brooding physician leave the camp, his head high. She was so preoccupied with the emotions welling up inside her that she almost missed Kiril's intense scrutiny.

He looked at her with disapproval. For a handful of heartbeats, neither broke the gaze. It was a contest of wills. Mara raised her chin several notches in an effort to keep from backing down. No man cowed her. For any reason. And she'd be damned if she'd start letting this one because his buddy got his feelings hurt.

But she couldn't keep it up. She actually felt bad about the dressing down she'd given Mikkarn. He was trying to help in the only way he could. She knew that. She had taken out her frustration and disappointment on a man who didn't deserve it. Lowering her gaze, she turned away.

She had more important things to worry about than a man's ego.

Chapter Two

Two years later, she was still trying to convince herself she didn't give a damn what either man felt... or thought. That was the most perplexing thing of all. There were times she swore she *knew* what one or the other of them was thinking. Since she first met Mikkarn and Kiril on Earth, she'd thrown herself into the work she'd started soon after arriving on Gothe'mar. She blamed her "insight" on nothing more than exhausted paranoia. Maybe if she kept telling herself that, she'd start to believe it.

She'd been given an opportunity to study medicine on Gothe'mar and had grabbed it with both hands. Anything she could learn that might help her people in the future, she would. The work had been hard and mentally taxing, but somehow she learned the complex system of computers and how they related to both Gothe'maran and human physiologies. She was, so far, the only human to complete a residency.

And that was only the beginning.

She was actually teaching the Gothe'maran a thing or two about hands-on medicine. At least, she was teaching Mikkarn. He had a thirst for medical knowledge to rival her own. Since that day on Earth when they first met, he had worked as tirelessly as she had.

They spent almost every working hour together and were so attuned to each other they could anticipate what the other needed, which only confused her more. It was both uncanny and disturbing. Was she really catching his thoughts, or was it all an illusion born from the incredible professional relationship they shared and her own heightened response to him physically? Mikkarn was one hot man and Mara wanted him, badly. Their close working relationship had opened her eyes to the highly intelligent, compassionate man he was. She also sensed a dark side to him. Death was something he simply could not accept, and Mara was certain that was what drove him so hard. Still, Mara wasn't sure she had ever been attracted to anyone as strongly as she was to Mikkarn.

And through it all, there was Kiril. The silent shadow.

He was always there. Watching.

When they were on Earth, he served as a bodyguard for Mikkarn. Here on Gothe'mar, Mara wasn't sure what their relationship was. Kiril was a constant presence, like a guardian angel... a very frightening guardian angel. Something about him scared the hell out of her. It wasn't anything he'd ever said or done so much as his body language. This man was dangerous.

In more ways than one.

Every time he looked at her, she felt the effect physically. He wanted her, that much was certain. His heated, visual caresses and possessive gestures said as much. He never let another man approach her other than Mikkarn and, even though he didn't speak much, he never missed an opportunity to touch her, to stake his claim without saying a word. He was always gentle with her, tender even, and a simple touch from him was enough to make her skin tingle every time.

Mara looked out her picture window. The beauty of this planet never ceased to amaze her. Because of the rotation of Gothe'mar and the orbit of the planet's ringed moons, the sun never fully rose or set on this part of the planet, leaving it bathed in perpetual twilight. The plant life adjusted accordingly and there were species of vegetation that could be found only in this region. Mara sighed. She really loved it here.

Unable to help herself, she focused on the residence where the objects of her obsessions lived and laughed. If those two men wanted anything to do with her, other than professionally, they had a funny way of showing it. Neither had offered to spend time with her outside work, and she knew they both had their share of women.

That didn't stop her from fantasizing about them.

Her fantasies had begun to take on a life of their own. Especially when the men and their women were around the pool. She could easily imagine being one of those women. She didn't really care which man she imagined touching her. Their images would overlap. She could never really keep them separated. Just thinking about what they did inside that house with those women made her jealous, and she had no idea why.

It also made her wet and horny as hell, and she knew exactly why.

She had it bad.

She'd have to get over it, because she simply didn't have time to strike up a physical relationship with either of them. God forbid it should lead to anything more, anything serious. Nothing could get in the way of her goals of taking this advanced technology back to Earth, and, hopefully, leaving a small piece of human medicine behind.

Dimming the window for privacy, Mara turned out the lights and headed for bed. Not that she expected a good night's sleep. She'd given up expecting that months ago. If her rest was to be disturbed, at least her dreams made the long hours worthwhile -- dreams where she experienced the pleasure both men could give her.

Mara sighed. Exhaustion. It had to be exhaustion causing her insomnia. She'd been pushing herself at a grueling pace ever since she'd arrived on Gothe'mar. What else should she expect?

But what a pleasant way to lose sleep.

Giving her pillow a solid punch, she drifted off to sleep, welcoming the sinfully erotic dreams she hoped would follow.

* * *

Mikkarn held Mara tightly as he thrust into her tight, grasping cunt with all his might. Mara knew she was wet and welcoming, as always.

She whimpered as she wrapped her legs around his waist, resting her heels on his ass and giving herself leverage to fuck him as vigorously as he fucked her. Her nails raked his back with cutting force as she writhed underneath him, a woman well in the arms of passion.

Mara clutched Mikkarn's steely arms as he rode her body. His blue eyes darkened in his ecstasy and he looked like some angelic demon. His beautiful face was almost fierce as he fought for... something Mara couldn't quite grasp. He needed something, something she could give him, if she only knew what it was.

He growled as he lowered his head to hers, kissing her deeply, plunging his tongue into her mouth over and over, mimicking their wild fucking. Closing her eyes, she moaned as she threaded her fingers through his hair.

Only, his hair was too short, cut almost to his scalp.

When he raised his head, she was looking into the gentle, passion-glazed eyes of Kiril. In one smooth motion, he rolled her over, letting her straddle his hips as she rode him at her leisure.

He palmed a breast in each hand, pulling the nipples, pinching them gently. Mara cried out, throwing her head back.

Grabbing her hips, Kiril surged upward, driving his cock as deep as he could. No way he would last long. Her sweet, tight cunt grasped him until he thought he'd die from the pleasure. He loosened the pins holding her hair in place and tangled his fingers in the unruly mass.

He needed more.

Pulling her down for a kiss, Kiril groaned as he rolled them once again. He plunged into her, one hand roaming down her body to her ass, urging her to move with him.

He growled, pulling her head back by the hair so he could see her face when she came. To his shock, it wasn't Mara's sea-green eyes that gazed back at him, but the icy-blue eyes of Mikkarn.

He wanted to stop. He wanted to pull himself out of Mikkarn's body, but he couldn't. All he could do was pound the man's ass mercilessly.

Mikkarn's own cock was straining upwards and a drop of pre-come oozed from the tip. Without thought, Kiril took Mikkarn's cock in his hand and pumped in time with his own thrusts.

Mikkarn's manhood throbbed.

Kiril's balls tightened...

* * *

Mara's scream that echoed in each man's head as they both woke, panting and sweating. Each in his own bed.

The dreams were about to drive Mikkarn crazy. He couldn't continue to work with Mara in his present state. He went up in flames every time she came near, but he had two damned good reasons why he couldn't pass her off to someone else in Medical Command.

First, she had knowledge he wanted almost as much as he wanted her. Secondly, and this was really the more important reason, he absolutely couldn't stand the thought of another man working so closely with her.

That was the least of his worries.

Kiril. They had been friends since boyhood. Kiril looked out for the weaker Mikkarn. Kiril had always been there to watch over him, had insisted on going to Earth with Mikkarn as a bodyguard. He'd made the request to a "high official in Medical Command." They'd spent a great deal of time together the last couple of years and were very attuned to one another. Perhaps that was the reason for Mikkarn's dreams. The gods knew the only thing on his mind since meeting Mara was very carnal, very sweaty sex.

Mikkarn wasn't sure if Kiril realized the intensity of sexual frustration he was experiencing, but for the last year or so, Kiril had gone out of his way to find willing women for some much needed relief. It had started out simply enough. Kiril would introduce Mikkarn to a woman who just happened to be with the woman he had for himself. The night would be spent rather pleasantly, in private.

Then the time came when Kiril only brought one woman. Things had gotten a little out of control and they had shared her, with very satisfactory results for everyone. Since then, they had shared women often.

But they had never had sex with each other. Never *wanted* to have sex with each other. What in the Universe was happening to him now? Mikkarn sighed. It was all becoming wearisome. His obsession with Mara, his growing attraction to Kiril -- nothing made sense anymore.

As he gazed out the partially dimmed window, he caught sight of Mara standing in front of her own window. Their respective dwellings were close together, something he loved to hate, and her shapely form, clad in a knee-length tunic, was clearly visible. It was the only time he had ever seen her hair fixed any way but in that severe bun.

Backlit softly, her hair surrounded her like a brilliant flame, the tresses tumbling about her face in an unruly mass of curls.

She paced restlessly, glancing toward the house often. Suddenly, she stopped and stared, transfixed by… something.

Confused, Mikkarn looked out the window to his left. Kiril had arrived.

With a guest.

* * *

Mara couldn't believe her eyes. Kiril stood by the pool, his arms wrapped around a painfully thin, fair-haired woman, kissing her with enough passion to curl any woman's toes.

Mara knew her. Tamche was a Gothe'maran nurse who worked with Mara and Mikkarn. Mara had seen Tamche with Kiril several times over the last couple of weeks. Not that Mara was paying attention, of course. She just happened to notice. She also just happened to overhear the woman talking to other nurses about her plans to seduce the handsome doctor and his equally sexy bodyguard. From the one conversation Mara had witnessed, she realized Tamche was determined to have one or the other of them as her lover, "… until she could find a suitable mate…"

Bringing her thoughts back to the present, Mara realized Tamche was beginning her quest. Mara watched as Kiril cupped his hands underneath

Tamche's ass and picked her up. Mara took a step back. She should leave. This was *private*.

But she didn't. *Couldn't*. It was almost as if her will was no longer her own. Her heart rate quickened, as did her breathing. A rush of heat curled inside her followed by a drop of moisture trickling from her sex.

Kiril carried Tamche up the two steps of the deck and set her on her feet. Mara watched in fascination as Kiril actually yanked Tamche's blouse open. Tamche pulled her arms against her body. Apparently she wasn't expecting him to start this outside. Kiril bent his head close to Tamche, saying something. Mara could see his lips move while he tugged the material from Tamche's shoulders. His hands caressed her back and Kiril unhooked her bra. Mara could hardly breathe.

Kiril moved Tamche closer to the pool's edge. He was so tall, when he dropped to his knees, his face was in perfect position for his lips to catch a nipple. He turned so that Mara had a good view. He kneaded Tamche's very small breasts, tugging the nipples and alternately sucking each of them into his mouth. Kiril wrapped his arms around Tamche's tiny waist.

Tamche's head fell back. Mara could almost hear her moan. She knew she should not intrude, but she could no more look away than she could cut off her own hand. Or stop the moisture from soaking through her panties.

She watched as Kiril unzipped Tamche's red flower print miniskirt and slid it down her hips. She wasn't wearing panties. Mara gasped with Tamche as he shouldered her legs apart and licked her cunt. One slow swipe. Tamche grasped his shoulders and pulled him closer, her head falling back once again as she squealed her pleasure. Mara heard her this time, even through her closed doors and windows.

Mara moved closer to the window, absently pressing a hand to it as the other found her breast. She watched Kiril lower his mouth to Tamche's cunt again. The woman's legs gave way and she stumbled to the deck with Kiril's mouth still tightly fused between her legs. With Tamche on her back, spread out before him, Kiril settled in to feast, the heavy muscles of his bronzed back rippling as he appeared to make himself more comfortable.

Mara kneaded her own breast, pulling at her nipple when Tamche cried out. Kiril dipped his head to Tamche's intimate folds once again and Mara let her hand trail from her breast down her belly to the waistband of her panties. She hesitated only a moment before dipping her fingers to comb gently through her curls.

As Kiril entered Tamche with a finger, Mara finally gave in to her desire and glided one finger between the drenched lips of her pussy. She was shocked at how wet she was. Moisture had literally drenched her panties. The musk of her own arousal filled the air around her as she found her clit and moved in slow but persistent circles.

She watched with envy as Tamche received obvious pleasure from Kiril. *Her Kiril.* That thought followed her to orgasm. She ducked her head as she silently reached her peak. Shock waves pulsed through her body, the ultimate satisfaction.

What am I doing? Her post orgasmic bliss vanished before she could appreciate it and she was suddenly ashamed of herself. She'd just been a peeping Tom as her co-worker was mouth- and finger-fucked by one of the two men who had starred in her fantasies for the past two years. Flushed with guilt, Mara glanced up to see Kiril ushering Tamche inside.

Kiril stopped at the doorway, turned to capture Mara with that sharp gaze she'd always tried to avoid. The blood left her face. She looked away but couldn't keep her gaze from his for long. When she looked back, there was amusement on his face as he touched a finger to his brow in salute and grinned. Then he followed Tamche inside.

Chapter Three

Kiril smiled. He had never been so turned on in his life! He knew from the moment he greeted Tamche that Mara could see them. Everything he'd done had been to see her reaction. *So, little Miss Proper likes to watch? Interesting.* He had this whole week's end to get her wound up. Come the next work cycle, he intended for her to do a hell of a lot more than watch. Oh yes. He wanted her to be a very active participant indeed.

There was only one problem. From what he had observed over the past several months, the little minx seemed to have a thing not only for himself, but for Mikkarn as well. Under normal circumstances, he'd have no problem with both of them simply fucking her until they'd had her every way imaginable. He just seemed to want to keep this interesting woman for himself.

By the Universe! What was he doing? He was about to spend a week's end with yet *another* woman he wasn't remotely attracted to while just across the way was this gorgeous woman he'd been dreaming about since he'd first laid eyes on her two years ago.

For now though, he'd whet her appetite. She liked to watch? He'd give her something to look at.

* * *

When the video-phone chimed, it startled Mara so badly she blew a mouthful of milk out her nose. Somehow she knew who it was. It was just a question of which one. And if she would actually answer.

After twenty chimes, she realized the caller wasn't going to give up. Slowly, carefully, she answered. Kiril's grinning image stared at her from the display screen.

"H-Hello?"

"Did you like what you saw?" His voice was deep, gruff, and oozed sexual depravity. The sinfully beautiful muscles of his bare chest made Mara's stomach clench and her pussy let loose a gush of moisture in welcome to the promise held within that voice and body.

"What do you want, Kiril?"

Kiril's laugh and the accompanying smile sent shivers down her spine. Both served to let her know she had no hope to escape the sexual web of this particular predator.

"Only to know how you enjoyed watching me mouth-fuck a woman while you masturbated."

The crudeness of his words should have insulted her. She had never let anyone talk to her like that before. In fact, she'd put many a man in his place for saying less to her, but she simply couldn't say anything to this man by way of reprimand.

She swallowed. "I'm sorry about that. It was rude of me."

Again, that sensual display of amusement. "Perhaps, if you... beg... nicely, I'll forgive you. Just this once."

"Now," Mara said, annoyed, "why would it matter to me whether or not you forgave me?" *Swine*!

"Simple, sweetheart." His voice was just a bit too smug for her liking. "I'll have to forgive you before I make you scream as you come with my cock buried deep inside your creamy cunt."

Mara flushed from her hair to her toes, her body suddenly awash with a fine sheen of sweat. Her voice caught in her throat and she trembled. Somehow she managed a weak, "You're delusional."

"Am I?" he asked. "Then I'm sure I won't see

that gorgeous little body at your window again, will I?"

Mara sucked in a breath. He definitely wasn't going to let this rest. Common sense finally made an appearance and she disconnected the call without another word.

But not fast enough to cut off that infuriating laugh of his. The one that said he would indeed hear her scream as he made her come, his cock buried deep inside her creamy cunt.

* * *

Once his screen went dark, still chuckling to himself, Kiril made his way through the house to the big "playroom" he and Mikkarn had created. Tamche's shrill squeals rang through the halls and headed straight to his spine, traveling upwards, making his head feel like his brain was going to erupt out his ears.

When he entered the room, his friend was drilling the woman's ass from behind. Both on their sides, her leg was draped over his and he kneaded her breast roughly. An erotic sight, one Kiril had seen many times before.

As soon as Kiril stripped off his shirt and started unfastening his pants, Mikkarn rolled over to his back, taking Tamche with him, still embedded in her ass. Tamche had her eyes tightly closed, keening at the top of her lungs. Kiril winced at the sound. She was destined to shatter his eardrums. He didn't think she was even aware he had entered the room, much less that he was about to cram his long, heavy dick into her already stuffed body.

He met Mikkarn's gaze as he climbed onto the bed. Mikkarn nodded and spread his legs slightly to make room for Kiril. Kiril positioned himself as he reached for his cock to masturbate so he'd be hard enough to enter Tamche's body, only to realize he was already impossibly hard. *Force of habit.* It had been so long since jerking off hadn't been necessary. He couldn't remember when he had gotten hard without it. *Mara.* It obviously wasn't Tamche he was hard for.

As he placed his cock at the opening of the obviously natural blonde spread out before him, Tamche's eyes flew open. She looked a little apprehensive. He guessed she hadn't taken into account their size. Kiril grinned at her.

"Are you ready, my dear?" Kiril asked.

"Yes. Do it," she panted. "Fuck me."

"Watch as he enters you," Mikkarn said next to her ear.

Tamche moaned as she watched. "That's so fucking hot!" she exclaimed as she pushed back against them.

"It is. Definitely." Only Kiril was no longer looking at Tamche enveloping him. He was looking to his left out the picture window where the dimmer had been left off.

In the fading light outside, Mara's motionless form was clearly visible as she looked out her own lighted window. Staring at them. There wasn't much light in his playroom, only a soft lavender glow from the little sun/moonlight entering the window, but it must have been enough for Mara to see exactly what the three of them were doing.

Kiril grinned as he looked back to Tamche and Mikkarn. Tamche was off in the land of bliss, obviously getting the fuck of her life. But Mikkarn…

Mikkarn was looking out the same window, into the same window. At the same woman. Wearing the same grin. *Well, shit.*

* * *

She was watching. Just like he knew she would be. Mikkarn had watched Mara himself when Kiril had welcomed Tamche. He had seen her fondle her breast, watched her hand drop below her waist. He'd known the exact moment her orgasm overtook her. He'd known she hadn't made a sound. It would be typical of her. She wasn't the screaming type.

Correction. She *could* be the screaming type if she'd just lose that damned control. She wouldn't be like Tamche, though. He'd seen Kiril wince when he first entered the room. He'd winced more than a couple of times himself. He'd never been one for bondage -- that was Kiril's thing. But now would be a really good time for a gag.

Mikkarn kept his eyes on Mara as he thrust repeatedly into Tamche. The woman was definitely getting her pleasure, but he honestly didn't give a damn. Right now, he only had eyes for Mara. Tamche was deliciously tight though. So tight he could feel Kiril's movement every time he thrust. When he felt him pause, he couldn't help but catch the other man's gaze.

Kiril's face was… hard. He had a look about him. Like he was saying "back the hell off!" When Kiril looked to the window then back at him, Mikkarn knew what was going on. *Well, shit.*

Mikkarn kept his rhythm steady. He didn't particularly like Tamche, but he didn't want to hurt her by having to explain why they had suddenly stopped. Judging by the sounds coming from the woman sandwiched between them, she couldn't really have cared less what they were doing, as long as they kept doing *her*. Her shrieks were increasing incrementally and she was thrashing about so much Mikkarn wasn't sure he could keep inside her.

Kiril grabbed her hips, holding her still enough to finish her orgasm. No way either of them was getting off this time. That sound alone prevented it. As Tamche's screams and squeals reached a pinnacle, Mikkarn glanced out the window once more. Mara hadn't moved. He wished he could read her expression, but he was too damned far away. When he glanced back, Kiril was staring out the window. This was going to be difficult.

Tamche finally collapsed and fell silent, breathing rather heavily. "That was amazing," she panted. "Is this what I'm in for all weekend?"

"Perhaps," Kiril said. "For now, I think you could use some rest." Kiril disengaged himself from Tamche's pussy.

"Mikkarn and I have some things to do, so you won't be disturbed. Shower, get a bite to eat, take a nap. We'll be back later."

Mikkarn didn't argue. He simply rolled Tamche over so he could slide out of her gripping ass and placed a soft kiss on her cheek. "Rest up." He playfully swatted her on the rump and left with Kiril, wondering what his friend was up to.

* * *

Kiril stalked down the hall, through the kitchen, and out the back door, jerking various articles of clothing on as he went. He was seething. But not for the reasons he should be. Universe be damned! He wasn't sure why he felt this intense need to share women with Mikkarn, and he damn sure didn't *want* to share Mara. But something inside him made doing anything else almost impossible. These feelings would be the death of him! Unfortunately, his anger and confusion caused him to lash out, and the only one around for that was Mikkarn.

"Just what the hell were you thinking?"

A slow smile spread across Mikkarn's face. "Apparently the same thing you were."

"You know what I mean," Kiril snapped. "What would you have said if Tamche had seen you staring at Mara?"

"Look," Mikkarn said, crossing his arms. "I'm not in love with Tamche. I'm not sure I even *like* Tamche. I wouldn't set out to intentionally hurt her, but facts are facts." Mikkarn punctuated himself with a finger pointed at Kiril's chest. "You said she approached *you* about this weekend. I have no problem giving her all the sex she can handle, but I won't pretend I care about her when I don't." Mikkarn sighed and ran his hand through his golden hair, mussing it slightly. "I'm not saying it's not fun, but damn it, Kiril, I'm tired of this. Tired of meaningless sex to ease my frustration. Are you even remotely interested in any of the women we've been with lately?"

"No," Kiril said without hesitation. "I've found the woman I want and she's right over there watching us."

"Then we have a problem, my friend. Because she's the one I want, too."

Both men stared at each other. "She's the one," Kiril hissed. "I felt her hurt along with her fascination. You will stay away from her."

Mikkarn took a staggering step backward, a look of utter confusion on his handsome face. Kiril was about to turn away when Mikkarn narrowed his eyes and said, "And if I don't?"

Kiril spoke through clenched teeth. "Then I will show you why I am one of the most feared warriors on Gothe'mar."

Mikkarn grunted. "May the best man win, Kiril."

He stuck out his hand.

Kiril snorted as he took it. "Yeah. As long as it's me."

* * *

Mara sobbed brokenly. Her lovers were with another. They had betrayed her and she hurt more deeply than she ever thought possible. She could feel the pleasure they took in Tamche's body, and the pain in her chest increased.

She floated over the trio, their images blurred through tears that ran unchecked down her face. She knew she was dreaming, but couldn't seem to break free, even when it was the only way to end this terrible pain.

The incredible sensations flowing through them assailed her. Their pleasure was hers, and she hated them for it.

"Mara…" Mikkarn's voice was a whisper in her mind.

She wrapped her arms around her body, trembling with the desire coursing through the two men, desire that was also her own.

"Come to us." Kiril's voice this time. "We will give you pleasure beyond your wildest dreams." He looked up, straight into her eyes, her soul, as he thrust deep into the body of Tamche.

Uncontrollable lust swamped her, combined with unbelievable anger. Anger at Tamche, anger at Mikkarn and Kiril, and anger at herself.

Tamche had no right to be with either man. The woman didn't care about them other than as her latest conquest. That fact was something she flaunted daily. Mikkarn and Kiril didn't care about Tamche other than as a means to release their own sexual frustration. She could feel the truth of that in her dream. Even knowing all that, even knowing they willingly took pleasure in the other woman's body even as they wanted to take Mara into their bed, she still would have given everything she had to be in Tamche's place at that moment.

She wasn't sure she could ever forgive herself for that. She should have had more self-respect. She deserved much better.

With anguish in her heart, Mara closed her eyes and screamed...

* * *

Mara woke, her body covered in sweat, her heartbeat pounded, and her chest constricted painfully because of the images she had witnessed, and because she just *knew* Mikkarn and Kiril were with Tamche at that very moment.

And they were most likely fucking the bitch into oblivion.

Desperation built within her. She was losing herself, and she had to regain control. Her whole life was about control. If she wasn't in control of her own body, how could she possibly hope to control the knowledge of life and death she had worked so hard to learn?

"What's the time?" Her voice shook.

A monotone, but slightly female, voice responded. "Twenty-three hundred hours, Earth Standard Time." Gothe'maran time being roughly the same, that meant the sex bars should be in full swing.

Gothe'marans mated for life, but until then they took their pleasures often. Sex bars here were as prevalent as sports bars on Earth.

Mara saw her problem as sexual frustration, and that was a problem she intended to solve.

Tonight.

* * *

Mara didn't have much in the way of sexy clothing, but she figured she could manage. Deciding to go simple, with her favorite pair of jeans and a white silk blouse, she put on a touch of makeup before heading to her personal shuttle. As she lifted out of the driveway, Kiril stood at the huge window in the same room where he and Mikkarn had fucked Tamche. He stared at her, a little, knowing smile on his face.

Ain't life a bitch.

Resolving not to think of either of them, she reached for her determined mindset and headed straight for the most depraved club she knew. Her first step inside was into almost total darkness, which served to heighten her other senses. The smell of smoke, slightly stale sweat, and strong Gothe'maran liquor assaulted her, and she wrinkled her nose. The only well-lit section of the whole bar was the stage in the center of the room. The sight going on there was one that brought back disturbing and, strangely enough, painful memories.

Two very large Gothe'maran males -- okay, so *all* Gothe'maran males seemed to be abnormally large to her -- were being sucked off by a dark-headed, dark-skinned woman on her knees in front of them. One man had his hand fisted in her hair, while the other one bent over to fondle a plump breast.

Mara looked away. She couldn't see a damn thing! The lighting was practically nonexistent and with her eyes wandering back to the stage every couple of seconds, she was sure they'd never adjust enough to find a table or even make her way to the bar.

She definitely shouldn't have come here. Especially not alone. She stood out like a sore thumb, which would have been good if she had really wanted to be noticed. As she started to make her way farther into the bar, she ran into a leather-wearing, whip-wielding, body-pierced thug she wasn't sure was actually going to take "no" for an answer.

Finally convincing her would-be Romeo she wasn't interested, she glanced back toward the stage and watched, transfixed, as the woman, her almost black skin lustrous from the sweat of her exertion under the heavy lighting, raised one leg to hook around the hip of one of the men. Once he had guided himself inside, he grabbed her ass and lifted, allowing her to wrap the other leg around him.

Feeling her own pussy clench in response, Mara sucked in a breath as she turned her attention to the bar and ordered a drink. A strong one. Downing it in one gulp, she let her eyes snap back to the stage.

The second man had maneuvered behind the woman. He greased himself liberally with a gleaming lubricant and slid easily into her ass. After a little adjustment, the trio began to move in harmony, the cries of the female almost as loud as the moans of the two men.

Is that what Mikkarn and Kiril are doing with Tamche right now?

The thought annoyed her more than anything else, and she decided she'd get no peace here. Mindless sex with a complete stranger was *not* what she needed. She didn't want to think about what she *did* need.

Mara knew she'd made a mistake. She wasn't sure exactly what she'd expected, but this was *way* more than she bargained for. Her head was spinning. It was time to get the hell out of Dodge.

As she turned to leave, her eyes having adjusted to the dim interior, she noticed various acts of sex being played out before the eyes of anyone who cared to watch. Women were fucked by multiple men, and these scenes made what had gone on at her neighbors' home seem domestic. Women were flogged by their Masters, men forced still other women to suck their cocks or the cocks of other men. One woman was flogged until she screamed, then fucked by another woman wearing an impossibly large dildo. All that, combined with the smells and sounds and the heat of so many bodies in one place, was nauseating.

She needed to leave. *Now*.

A woman lying spread-eagle on the bar with a man's face glued between her legs snagged her attention. How in the hell could she have missed all this before?

She had almost made it to the door when an arm snaked around her middle and pulled her up against an impossibly strong chest. *Oh, God. No*! She struggled wildly, afraid those around her would think it was all part of the show. The man grunted, tightening his grip.

"It's okay, Mara. It's me, Kiril." His voice, right next to her ear, sent cold fire racing down her spine. Gooseflesh rose on her arms and hot, liquid need wet her pussy. God, he smelled good. His clean, slightly spicy, masculine smell surrounded her, overriding the sickening scents of the bar.

Mara stopped fighting and relaxed somewhat against him. She felt his breath on her neck and couldn't suppress a sigh as she tilted her head to give him better access to her. She felt more than heard his chuckle as she savored this moment. Finally, she was in the arms of a god.

Chapter Four

It felt good to finally have her in his arms. This was where she should have been from the moment he first saw her. Her body was warm, soft, curvy. A woman's curves. He inhaled deeply, nuzzling her neck. Her sweet smell was intoxicating.

Kiril felt her hurt. She didn't know anything about soul's mates and the mental connection that developed, but she definitely knew something wasn't right. Well, that, and she was livid. Not that he could blame her.

When she pulled up outside the club, he never thought she'd actually try to enter. He was even more surprised she'd gotten in. In addition to the fact she wasn't Gothe'maran, she wasn't exactly their normal clientele. He'd followed her inside with every intention of dragging her back out again, but he had trouble getting to her through the crowd. He'd been stopped several times by women offering sexual favors, which was normal. That was why everyone was there, after all. Eventually, though, his patience ran out. He had to get Mara out of there.

When he found her, he rethought that notion. She was watching the woman getting eaten out at the bar. She'd been moving steadily toward the exit, but her attention was definitely not on where she was going. He grinned. Maybe he could use this to his advantage.

"You really do have a thing about watching, don't you," he whispered close to her ear. She shivered in his arms.

"No. It's just hard to miss." Her voice trembled slightly.

"Would you like to offer yourself to me while all

these people watch? Would that make you hot?"

She jerked away from him and turned around. "No! Absolutely not!" Her eyes were wide, and she looked panicked.

"Relax, sweetheart." He moved forward and reached for her face, stroking her cheek. "You don't have to do anything you don't want to do. You seem so interested in watching, I thought you might like being watched."

"I -- I could never --" she stammered. "What if someone from Medical Command saw me?"

He pulled her close. "It wouldn't matter. I'm sure there are officers here -- there usually are. Besides, no one said you had to." He kissed the top of her head, then gently turned her around, her back to his chest. "Now, look." He pointed back to the bar. The woman's head and shoulders were hanging off the edge and the bartender's face hidden between her thighs.

A man standing next to the woman, tweaking her nipples, unzipped his fly and pulled out his cock. She immediately turned her head and opened her mouth to take him. His thrusts were shallow and slow at first, but soon he was pounding away at the woman's mouth.

"Did you enjoy watching Mikkarn and me fuck Tamche?" he whispered, kneading her shoulders and giving her ear a nip. She shivered, but said nothing. "Did you come that time, too? I know you came when I ate her out."

"That's really none of your business," she said, so softly he barely heard her. "I want to leave. I don't like it here."

"Really? Your nipples are hard and your breathing is much too fast. I'd say you were enjoying yourself. Should I see if your cunt is wet?"

She whirled around and raised a hand, presumably to slap him. Hell, he'd have slapped himself for that remark. He caught it easily and pulled her to him, pinning her wrist behind her back. She stared up at him with angry eyes.

"I will not let you touch me in public," she bit out. The fact she didn't say she wouldn't let him touch her at all didn't escape his notice.

He grinned. "But you do like to watch."

"No! It's just…" She looked away, back to the bar. "It's hard not to watch when it's right in front of you," she said softly.

"And Mikkarn and I? You didn't have to look out the window. You were in your own house."

"I'm sorry." She didn't say the words so much as mouth them. He saw the tears glisten in her eyes and felt like a complete idiot. He didn't want to make her cry. But he knew what was bothering her.

"Mara, you don't have to feel bad about liking to watch. It's arousing. That's why most of these people are here. To be watched. To watch."

"But you didn't expect me to be watching. I violated your privacy."

"Actually, you didn't." When she looked back at him in confusion, he said, "Mikkarn left the window undimmed on purpose. At least I think he did."

"He what?" Her eyes were wide in surprised outrage.

Kiril chuckled as he took her hand and led her to a nearby corner. When her back was against the wall and he was sure she wasn't able to bolt on him, he said, "You obviously have no idea what you've been doing to us these past two years. I've wanted you since the first time I saw you. Apparently Mikkarn feels the same. I, however, intend to keep you for myself."

When she opened her mouth to protest, Kiril dipped his head and captured her lips with his. He plunged his tongue into the depths of her mouth and groaned. She tasted like heaven. In her shock, Mara didn't respond at first, but it didn't take long for her to slip her tongue around his and sigh.

When she accepted his kiss, he decided he'd seduce her. Right here. He wanted her to enjoy this walk on the wild side. Pressing his body fully against hers, he let her feel all of him. His cock hard against her belly, his muscles bulging with suppressed desire. Her body felt better than he could have ever hoped, and he wondered why he had waited so long for this in the first place.

Mara accepted him eagerly, tangling her fingers in his hair. The pain she caused to his scalp when she pulled him to her neck only fueled his desire for her. Kissing his way down her neck, he tugged her blouse open and nuzzled her breast. She let out a soft cry and jumped a little, trying to pull his head up, but he simply licked a long path across her exposed flesh and she changed directions. Now she pulled him against her chest, and he wasn't about to waste the opportunity.

Her breath came in pants, and her chest heaved. Gently tugging her blouse, he exposed one ripe nipple and gave it a wet lick. This time, she actually whimpered. *Finally, a sound. This is good.*

Kiril watched as the bud became increasingly hard. "Your nipples are beautiful. They crave my touch." Mara's eyelids drooped. She was feeling the moment rather than watching what he was doing. That was just how Kiril wanted her. He didn't want her to think about where they were, but he wanted her to enjoy watching the sex going on around them. Not that anyone could actually see the two of them. They were half hidden by a tall, gargoyle-like statue. Still, he wanted to prove to her how much she could enjoy this.

"Watch the woman at the bar," he murmured. "I want you to come when she does."

When she sucked in a breath, probably to protest, he bent his head and sucked her nipple, nipping gently when she groaned. Finding the other bud with his fingers, he pinched and twisted it lightly through her blouse and bra. A fine sheen of sweat formed on her body. Her breathing grew more labored and he knew she was on the brink. Roughly yanking her clothing away from the other breast, he pushed their generous mounds together and sucked both nipples hard.

The woman at the bar shrieked her climax and Kiril knew it was time. "Come for me, Mara," he said as he repositioned his mouth to receive more of her. "Come now."

Mara hooked one leg around his hip and ground her sex into his thigh. Her fingers tightened in his hair to the point of pain and she gave a soft cry as he carried her to orgasm. Kiril continued to suck and lick until she loosened her grip on his hair and her breathing returned to normal. He kissed her cheeks, her eyelids, her nose, then he straightened her top, cupped her face, and kissed her lips gently.

When she opened her eyes, he smiled at her. "Now, wasn't that fun?"

* * *

Kiril's words were like a bucket of ice water thrown in her face. Her cheeks warmed and a sharp pain stabbed her belly. She'd acted like a whore. Worse, he'd treated her like one. There was no way she could keep the tears at bay, but she'd be damned if she'd let him see. Shoving past him, she ran for the door and kept running until she reached her personal shuttle. She didn't know if he followed her -- most likely not -- but she wasn't taking any chances. Powering up, she sped away.

She desperately wanted to go anywhere other than home. Going home would be tantamount to running straight to Kiril and she didn't know if she would ever be able to face him again. All she had brought with her was enough money to get into the club and to buy her drinks. No way she had enough for a hotel. Besides, she couldn't avoid him forever unless she moved.

She cried so hard on the way home, it was a wonder she didn't wreck. Her tears had slowed somewhat but hadn't stopped altogether by the time she pulled into her driveway. And she had a whopper of a headache. Neither of them deserved her tears. She had seen Kiril and Mikkarn's sexual escapades and knew something like this would happen. They could have Tamche, as far as she was concerned.

Stomping into her living room, she stripped as she locked the door and made her way to the bathroom, leaving a trail of clothing behind her. A shower was a necessity. She smelled like smoke. Worse, she smelled like Kiril. His masculine scent, wild and spicy, still enveloped her.

The last two years of her life had been spent lusting after those womanizers! And she had no one but herself to blame. She had wanted to be different from all the other women. So much for daydreams.

When she finished her shower, her skin bright red from the too hot water and the vigorous scrubbing, she heard a pounding at the front door. *Well, shit.* Putting on her robe, she decided she'd tell him to get lost.

"Mara. Open up. It's Mikkarn."

Mikkarn? Curious, she pulled her robe tighter around her and opened the door.

Mikkarn didn't enter her home so much as explode into it, taking her with him. Before she could protest, he picked her up and marched down the hall until he found her bathroom.

The bathroom? "What are you doing?" She pushed against him. "Put me down."

He set her on the counter and took her face in his hands. Tilting it to the light, he examined her face for several seconds.

"Will you stop?" She captured his wrists. "What the hell are you doing?"

"You've been crying."

Mara's gaze shifted away from him. "So? It's nothing. Certainly not something I'm sharing with you."

"Kiril told me what happened," he said as he busied himself with wetting a washcloth and started to wash her face. The gesture was totally unexpected and not unwelcome, but she'd be damned if she'd show weakness again tonight.

"God! Why won't you two just leave me alone?" She hopped off the counter, rushing out of the small space. Despite her protests, his presence was comforting. That was definitely something she didn't want him to know. "What is it with you guys? I've spent two rotten years right across the street, and you've never even so much as struck up a conversation outside of work. Then all of a sudden, Kiril practically begs me to watch him have sex with Tamche by the pool and he said you're responsible for leaving the window undimmed while you guys fucked her.

"Then Kiril follows me to the bar and..." She

trailed off, knowing her cheeks were probably a very bright shade of red.

Mikkarn smiled a slow, wicked smile. "Well, you didn't have to watch, you know. I only left the window clear because I saw you get yourself off watching Kiril and Tamche."

"Damn it! I do *not* like to watch! It's just hard not to when you guys are fucking every woman within a ten-mile radius!"

"Hmm." Mikkarn rubbed his chin in contemplation. "If you don't want to watch, what do you want?"

"I don't know!" she snapped.

Silence.

Mara sighed. "I just know that my daydreams came to life only to turn into a nightmare. Now, I'll just stick to my daydreams. Only maybe they'll take a different form. Now --" she started down the hall to the door, "-- if you'll kindly leave, I need to get ready for bed. I'm tired and --"

Any further explanation was cut short when Mikkarn pulled her into his arms and silenced her with his lips.

She struggled a little at first, but his mouth molded itself to hers with insistent gentleness. He coaxed a response, angling his head until he covered her lips at just the right position. She sighed, and he slipped his tongue inside, gently licking. She couldn't help herself. Try as she might, she couldn't fight the feelings that had been building for the past two years. Something deep inside her yearned to mean something to this man, even though her better judgment warned her against it. She wanted to be more than just a one-time fling. She wanted the daydream.

Funny thing was, she wasn't so sure *he* didn't

want the exact same thing.

That thought brought her to her senses. She broke the kiss, but he used that opportunity to make his way down her neck. His hands caressed her back while his lips carefully sucked her face and chin. Chills ran down her spine, and her hands gripped his muscled shoulders. "Mikkarn. Please stop. I can't…"

"Why?" Mikkarn didn't break contact with her. "Because of what Kiril did?"

"Because of what you are. I've wanted you so long, I'm afraid what this will do to my heart." She knew she was going to cry. She couldn't help it.

"What do you think I am? Is it because of the women, or because I'm Gothe'maran and you're human?" Mikkarn never stopped his pleasurable torment of her neck and collarbone.

"Because you have so *many* women," she wailed. "I don't want to be another notch on your headboard come morning! My feelings have nothing to do with you being a Gothe'maran man. They have everything to do with the fact that you're just like every *human* man I've ever met. Once you get what you want, you leave. I don't think my heart could stand that, and I have no idea why!"

Mikkarn raised his head and looked her straight in the eye. "Mara." His voice was just a breath, less than a whisper. "When I get through with you tonight, you'll know just how special you are to me. And I promise, there will never be another woman in my heart other than you."

Dropping his hand to the belt holding up her robe, Mikkarn tugged it free. Mara immediately pulled the lapels of her robe together. This was more embarrassing than being caught masturbating. She stumbled backward, moving farther down the hall, still clutching her robe to her body. This didn't *feel* right. Something was missing. Something very important. She only stopped when her back met the wall.

"Please leave now," she said. "I want to be alone. I don't want this."

Mikkarn approached her carefully. "I don't think that statement is entirely true, but I'll respect your wishes." He cupped her face gently and urged her to meet his eyes. "Next time, I'll respect your *other* wishes." He smiled. "You want me, and not just because you're curious. Something about me touches something deep inside you…"

He stopped. Then he backed up, a strange expression on his face. Mara could have sworn she actually felt his discomfort. *Impossible*! "Unfortunately, I'm not the only one you crave." Mikkarn's smile was tight, as if the effort was solely for her benefit.

"What's going on? How can you *know* that?" Mara was beginning to panic. This was all too weird. If she didn't know better, she'd swear the two men could actually read her mind sometimes. The thought was not comforting.

Mikkarn shrugged and said simply, "Because you're my soul's mate. Kiril thinks you're his soul's mate as well. I guess this is something he and I will have to work out on our own." Stepping close to her once again, he brushed his lips against hers gently. "We'll talk later. In the meantime --" his grin was positively wicked, "-- keep your eyes open. You might see some interesting things." He winked.

As he retreated down the hall to the front door, she screeched after him, "I do *not* like to watch!"

* * *

The house was eerily quiet when Mikkarn returned. He knew Kiril was there, knew Tamche was still there as well, but he didn't hear a sound anywhere. Then the sharp staccato sound of flesh slapping flesh caught his attention. As he made his way up the stairs, the sound grew louder, accompanied by muffled cries and harsh groans. In the playroom, the sight he witnessed was... disturbing. Not because of the act itself, but because of the savage, angry expression on Kiril's face.

Tamche was face down -- the ball gag he'd wished for earlier firmly in place -- but lying on one hip with her knees together. Her wrists were tied to the bedpost and she seemed stretched almost uncomfortably. Hell, no way she wasn't actually in pain. It looked like her shoulders might dislocate if any more pressure was put on them.

On his knees behind her, Kiril had a bruising grip on her hip and thigh as he pounded ruthlessly into her ass. He was red-faced, the veins in his neck prominent as he strained for release. Over and over he thrust himself into her back opening, faster and faster as he growled and grunted loudly with each thrust. He slammed into her one last time with a fierce shout, and then pulled himself from her ass roughly, and shoved her away. Jumping up, he stalked across the room.

Mikkarn immediately moved to the bed and removed the restraints and the gag from Tamche. Gently rolling her over, he asked, "Are you all right?"

Tamche opened her eyes and gave him a weak smile. "All right? I've just had the best fuck of my entire life. What do you think?" She laughed softly as she stretched. "I think I'll keep him."

Mikkarn looked to Kiril, whose expression was just short of murderous. He glanced at Tamche before going to his friend. Tamche had spread her legs and she shuddered as she brushed her clit. She froze when her fingers ventured farther, to her ass.

"Kiril, you didn't come. What happened?" She sounded as puzzled as Mikkarn suddenly was. Why had Kiril held back?

"What happened?" Her voice was very angry indeed.

Face still red, his whole body actually shaking -- most likely from anger -- Kiril looked directly at Mikkarn and pointed an accusing finger at him. "You fucked her, didn't you?"

Before Mikkarn could respond, Tamche looked from one of them to the other and with eyebrows raised said, "Of course he's fucked me. You were there." Her tone was a bit condescending, but Mikkarn tried to focus on his friend. Something wasn't right.

Kiril turned his furious gaze to her and spat, "I don't mean you! Why would I be upset about him fucking *you*?" His eyes found Mikkarn's again when he shouted angrily, "I'm talking about Mara, you *bakkara*!"

Mikkarn silenced anything Tamche was about to say with a hand on her shoulder. "Let's discuss this later, Kiril. You're being disrespectful."

Tamche brushed aside Mikkarn's hand and turned to Kiril. "Why would you care if he's fucked Mara? She's nothing but a silly Earther who thinks she can pick up a few tidbits of knowledge. And *why* didn't you come in my ass? You sounded like you got off nicely." She grinned at him as she slithered from the bed and wrapped her arms around his neck. "You know I'm very wealthy. Promise to master me in the bedroom like that every night and I'll take you as my consort until I find a male worthy of me to take as a mate."

Mikkarn winced. He had begun to feel very sorry for Tamche, but remarks like that reminded him the woman could fend for herself. She was on her own now, and it was time she was on her way as well.

"I don't mean to offend you, Tamche, but something urgent has presented itself. We must cut our week's end short," Mikkarn said, still trying to be diplomatic. Women might be as ruthless as men, but he believed they should be treated with respect. After all, it was from them that their children were birthed and nurtured.

"No. I'm not leaving until this weekend is over. You promised me I'd be fucked until I couldn't walk straight." She lay back and spread her legs. "So fuck me again. Now, Mikkarn."

Mikkarn could see the woman expected to be obeyed. She had closed her eyes once again and grasped her knees, pulling them to her chest. Her cunt glistened with her juice, and her musky scent wafted in the air. It made Mikkarn slightly nauseated.

"No, Tamche. You may rest here if you wish, but our involvement sexually is over." He turned to Kiril. "Out. Go to the pool and wait for me there." When Kiril snarled at him, looking like a wild beast with his teeth clenched and his hair in such disarray, Mikkarn said softly, "She remains untouched by me. We need to *talk*." The tension seemed to lessen somewhat in his friend. It must have been pretty heavy because Mikkarn actually felt lighter. Not much, but better.

"You will not leave!" Tamche screeched. "*I* say when this is finished! *No one* leaves me without my permission!" The skinny woman looked furious. Mikkarn could feel a headache coming on.

He sighed. "And how do you propose to keep us here? I don't think you can *make* us perform."

"You will. Or perhaps I should concentrate on Mara." A contemplative look crossed her features.

"Yes, I think perhaps it's time for Mara to realize she's a guest on this world. A guest who is *tolerated*, not wanted."

Yep. No doubt about it, there was definitely a headache in Mikkarn's future. He watched Tamche dress, not sure exactly what to say. Warning her against doing anything to Mara was out. That would only increase its likelihood. She moved with all the grace of a queen and looked at him over her shoulder.

"I want Kiril, and I intend to have him. He won't make a suitable mate, but he will be one hell of a consort. Tell Mara she can have him when I'm finished." She turned to leave then but paused as the door slid open at her approach. "That is, unless I decide to keep him." She smiled, then walked out.

Mikkarn watched her walk to her personal shuttle and pause when she would have slid into the cockpit. Tamche looked to Mara's house, where the other woman stood gazing out her living room picture window. Tamche waved to Mara then turned to the pool area, where Kiril presumably waited, and blew a kiss. Then, thankfully, she left.

Mikkarn took his time going to Kiril. The other man needed to cool down, and Mikkarn needed to talk himself into telling Kiril what he thought was *really* going on. Grabbing a tube of lubricant as he headed to the pool, Mikkarn had a feeling he'd probably need it.

Chapter Five

Mara watched with a heavy heart as Tamche's shuttle lifted off. She hadn't missed the intimate gesture directed poolside as Tamche left, and she definitely hadn't missed seeing Kiril lower himself, naked, into the water. No doubt about it. Mara needed to find a way to distance herself from both of them.

She could leave. She had definitely thought about that, but she had come to love and respect the people of this beautiful world, so it wasn't just the two infuriating men in her life here she'd miss. Besides, she was never one to quit.

She'd given as much as she had taken. Hopefully, the Gothe'mar would remember doctors needed hands-on knowledge of their patients. All the technology and automation was great -- wonderful -- but there had to be a balance, and she had proven that on Earth. Her goal was to combine both approaches to medicine, and she felt pretty sure that would be accomplished.

She was about to ready herself for bed, again, when she saw Mikkarn step out the pool-side patio door, strip, and get into the pool with all the grace his sleek body implied. The light from Gothe'mar's moons created a silvery glow around the two men in the water, and her mouth went dry, her heart rate skyrocketing. What would it be like to be equally naked and in that pool right now?

She couldn't help herself. She was mesmerized. There was no way in the world she could have stepped away from that window if her life depended on it. She *had* to watch them, even if it was something as innocent as an evening swim. *Innocent. Yeah, right.*

* * *

Mikkarn knew Kiril was hurting. He also knew Kiril was confused. The other man was starting to put everything together and he wasn't sure he liked what he saw.

How could they have been so blind? Mikkarn had had a "connection" to Kiril almost from the moment they'd met. He had never considered it was anything more than a deep, abiding friendship. Now, he was convinced it was more. Was it possible both Kiril and Mara were his soul's mates? One thing was certain, Kiril would probably fight it. He was nothing if not traditional.

"She wants you, Kiril." Mikkarn removed his own clothes to join the naked man in the pool. "She's just fighting it because she wants me, too."

Kiril snorted. "She is my soul's mate. She cannot have you."

"And what if I were to tell you she was my soul's mate, too? How would you feel about that?"

Kiril slowly turned to face him. "Impossible. There is only one mate for each soul in the universe. It is common knowledge."

"Is it?" Mikkarn asked, quietly.

"If that is true, there could never be balance in our relationship!" Kiril was becoming angry, something that Mikkarn felt acutely. It was the last piece of evidence he needed to convince himself he was right.

"If that were truly the nature of the relationship, you'd be right. Mara cannot have two soul's mates while each of us has only one. Our very nature would destroy all chance any of us could have for a happy existence. Gothe'marans mate for life. How could either of us accept that we must share our mate with the other?"

"I *will not* share her!" Kiril made a valiant effort to calm himself. Mikkarn felt the conflict in his mind, saw it on his face. "She is… precious. She's not like the women we've shared in the past, and I will not cheapen her by asking that of her."

"And if she insists, if I insist?" Mikkarn's voice was quiet, almost a whisper.

Kiril narrowed his eyes. "Say what you mean, Mik. We've never minced words with each other before."

Mikkarn took a deep breath. This was it. "She is your soul's mate, as she is mine. But *you* are also *my* soul's mate. As I am yours."

"You're mad! How could that possibly be…" Kiril's comment was lost as he seemed to lose focus on Mikkarn and turned himself inward. "She is watching us," he whispered. "And the images she's having are… vivid."

Mikkarn couldn't control the surge of lust if he tried. He'd caught her spontaneous fantasy, too. Before Mikkarn could respond, Kiril sucked in a startled breath and his sharp gaze snagged Mikkarn's. Kiril had felt Mikkarn's desire. If Kiril didn't realize that Mikkarn had reasoned this correctly by now, he never would.

Kiril lunged for Mikkarn and grabbed him by the hair, tilting his head back, seeming to tower over Mikkarn even though he was the shorter man. "By the Universe, you *are* mine! I will take what I've been denying myself all these years."

* * *

As Mara watched, the two men appeared to talk for a few moments. Nothing more. But Mara's lust rose with every second. Sweat dampened her body and her own intimate moisture dampened her panties. Suddenly, there was nothing more she wanted than to see these two men please each other. Why? Who knew, but she wanted to see Kiril buried balls deep in Mikkarn's mouth. Or ass. She wasn't picky.

The conversation appeared to turn into an argument, with Kiril angry enough to hit Mikkarn. Finally, unbelievably, Kiril reached for Mikkarn and jerked his head back by the hair, saying… something. Mara thought he might actually harm the other man, but instead, he hefted himself onto the ledge of the pool. The erection he sported was a sight to behold, but Mara only caught a glimpse of it before it disappeared into Mikkarn's mouth.

Mara gasped at the same time she imagined Kiril did. She couldn't believe this! The pleasure on Kiril's face alone was enough to send her into orgasm had she been touching herself. He leaned back, giving Mikkarn the room he needed to move, resting his hands on the pool's edge.

With Mikkarn's hair flowing free and his lower body in the water, it should have seemed like just another woman giving Kiril head, and good head judging by his expression, but Mara actually *felt* the difference. It was almost like she had put her mind in Kiril's. She was shocked that Mikkarn was doing such a thing, even more shocked to discover she liked it, but the thing that made her cunt ache with maddening desire was that she knew Kiril was going to be buried in Mikkarn's ass very soon.

Sure enough, Mikkarn crawled out of the pool and leaned his elbows on a nearby table, presenting his ass. As he looked over his shoulder at Kiril, his face was savage, strained in his desire, and Mara could see his cock, proudly standing up from the blond hair at its base.

Kiril reached for the tube Mikkarn had dropped near his clothes. He greased himself, sliding his glistening cock inside the other man's ass in slow, persistent strokes. He continued tentatively for a while before grasping Mikkarn's hips and increasing the pace and strength of his thrusts. Soon, he was pounding almost viciously, and Mikkarn was meeting him thrust for thrust as he reached a hand to his cock and stroked himself.

It didn't take long before Kiril's hips began to convulse erratically as they met Mikkarn's buttocks. Mikkarn's fist pumped furiously, and as Kiril threw his head back and arched his spine, Mikkarn sprayed the ground with his seed, shuddering and grinding his ass back against Kiril's groin.

Mara's own release came at the same instant. Her head fell back and she had to grasp a nearby chair for support. She actually cried out her pleasure. Given the fact that she hadn't been touching herself, she was very surprised -- probably why she hadn't clamped down on the sound as she normally would have. Thank goodness the men couldn't hear.

But they could see.

And they were both staring straight at her.

Mara decided to simply ignore them. Leaving her window, she discarded her robe and curled up in her bed. Tears stung the backs of her eyes and she didn't know why. She had no expectation that either man would profess undying love to her. She wasn't even sure she *liked* them. But seeing them with Tamche, and especially with each other, had changed something inside her. She didn't want them to be with another woman ever again. She wanted them to be with her.

Both of them.

And that was impossible. Even if Earth allowed such an unconventional union, the very foundation of Gothe'maran religion and society would forbid it.

Tomorrow, she would start looking for a new sponsor at Medical Command. She was probably stuck in the house because it was provided for her, and she'd feel like a jerk asking to be moved. She would just have to figure out a way to live near to Kiril and Mikkarn, knowing they were with other women, without her heart breaking.

She let the tears flow freely. Best to get that over with so she didn't do it at work. How she was going to face Tamche the next day, she didn't know. With one last sigh, she drifted off to sleep, and into the dream world that had plagued her for the past two years.

* * *

"You should be with us. You belong with us, as we belong to you." The male voices were fused together, but she would know them anywhere. Mikkarn. Kiril. Together, they were even more beautiful than when heard separately. A perfect harmony she desperately wanted to be the melody for.

"Ah, but you are. You always have been." Kiril's voice at her ear sent shivers spreading through her already tingling body. His arms snaked around her middle from behind and she snuggled against his chiseled chest.

A callused hand found her breast and plucked the nipple gently. "Your body responds so beautifully to our touch," Mikkarn rumbled, his mouth tantalizingly close to her left breast. The erotic puff of air as he spoke raised the fine hair all over her body. Her nipples were impossibly hard, needing his touch -- their touch.

Desperately, she tried to pull away. "You're both trying to consume me!" Mara gasped as Mikkarn's clever tongue dipped into her navel with a wet lick. "I'm my own person! I say who I want. I will not be forced into any relationship, no matter how mutual the attraction."

Kiril's growl reverberated through her body a second before his mouth fastened onto her throat. He bit -- none too gently -- before soothing the hurt with a swipe of his tongue. Mara shrieked and bared her neck even more to him, unable to resist the lustful temptation as moisture rushed from her pulsing cunt.

"This is not just any relationship, Mara," Kiril growled. "Our souls search for each other in every lifetime. Only the luckiest find their mate. Only the strongest love, the truest hearts, find their mate in more than one life."

"How can you both be my mate? None of this makes any sense!" Mara was frantic to escape.

Her body had other plans.

Mikkarn's lips found the other side of her neck, kissing, nipping. The contrast to Kiril's more forceful touch was astounding.

"We will come to you." They again spoke in unison. "We will win your heart, and your soul will recognize us for what we are…"

* * *

Mara's neck throbbed and her hand covered the spot Kiril had bitten. Her sheets were tangled about her body and she struggled to kick free.

Taking a deep, calming breath, she climbed out of bed and headed for the shower. Maybe she could find some peace in helping others. Maybe she could forget how wonderful it was to be in the strong arms of both men.

Men she knew, without a doubt, she loved with all her heart.

* * *

The dreams were always welcome to Kiril. This one especially because he knew beyond any doubt that Mara was his -- theirs.

Which brought along a whole new set of circumstances. As he stretched his naked body, Mikkarn stirred next to him and Kiril smiled. They had enjoyed exploring each other after the explosive coupling by the pool. Kiril got out of bed and padded silently to the window.

"Mikkarn, did you ever think it possible to have more than one mate?"

"Not until tonight," he said as he joined Kiril. Mikkarn had been silent most of the time since that first mating. Now that the connection was realized, Kiril was surprised they hadn't seen it before.

"I understand now why I've always had the need to be near you all these years, even to the point of requesting to be your guard when I was second in command to General Kahn himself." Kiril placed his hand on his friend's shoulder. "You have always been very important to me."

Mikkarn smiled. "I know. If it hadn't been for Mara…"

"I know, Mik." Kiril took a calming breath as he looked out the window, through the night, to Mara's home. "Do you think she will understand?"

"I suppose that is up to us. I'm still not sure of all she feels, but she is confused. She knows something is not right when she is with only one of us, but I don't think she realizes why."

Kiril shrugged. "Or maybe she just doesn't think it's possible to love us both."

Mikkarn turned sharply to face Kiril. "Then tomorrow, we prove to her she can."

* * *

Mara's dreams were filled with images of Mikkarn and Kiril. Sometimes together, sometimes with her. Always, they expressed their love for each other, and for her. Now she knew these feelings weren't hers alone.

She was more confused than ever. *Why was she catching their thoughts?* She had looked into the whole soul's mate thing after Mikkarn's reference. She wasn't sure how much she believed, but she was hard-pressed to find another plausible explanation for her insight into the two men's thoughts and feelings. Telepathy only existed on Gothe'mar between soul's mates.

Scrubbing herself vigorously, she pulled herself together. She had work to do. Her personal life would have to wait.

As Mara left for the hospital, she couldn't help looking toward their house. Had their night been as eventful as her dreams had been?

Mara sped off. She was *so* in over her head!

As she made rounds, she tried to pull herself together. It was all she could do to concentrate on her patients. Thank goodness this was Gothe'mar. Everyone was simply waiting their turn with a healing tube. All of them would be completely well by this time tomorrow. Rounds were more a habit for her than a necessity.

Mara was charting on her last patient when the one person she didn't want to see sauntered into the lounge. Tamche leaned casually against the doorframe.

"Congratulations, Mara. Your... um, physical... approach to medicine has been well received."

Uncomfortable, Mara stood and straightened her

lab coat. "Thank you."

Tamche smiled sweetly. "I didn't mean it as a compliment."

"I'm sorry. I don't understand."

Moving casually around the room, running a finger over various pieces of furniture as if anything in the room was of more importance than Mara herself, Tamche laughed softly. "Our technology makes your methods obsolete. You can never hope to make enough of an impact with anything you can do to gain the respect of Medical Command." Finally, Tamche stopped and faced Mara from across the room. "You're a mascot. A cute but unnecessary addition to our team. It is my opinion that you're wasting everyone's time and resources with archaic and barbaric equipment we will never need."

Mara blinked, taking a small step back. "I'm sorry you feel that way. I'd hoped to make everyone understand that Earth methods could be used as a means to improve your own."

"How can such a primitive culture improve on a thousand years of technical and biomedical research?"

Mara shook her head. "I've been working with you for two years. Why are you doing this now?"

"Because you need to know your place!" Tamche transformed from a smiling, if condescending, colleague into the most alien, hate-filled person Mara had ever seen. "You don't belong here. I suggest you leave before you make the wrong people angry."

Mara shrugged. "I think you know I'm not going anywhere, Tamche."

"Oh, but I think you will." Tamche pulled a gun from behind her back and aimed it at Mara. An Earth gun. "Killing you with a weapon of your own people will prove none of you belong here. They'll send everyone home, but you won't care." Tamche smiled again, an unholy, evil smile. "You'll be long departed from the Universe."

* * *

Kiril's attention was uncharacteristically divided. Mikkarn had spent the day in the mainframe chamber adjusting the failsafe alarms on the recently implemented interventions for human patients. Kiril had nothing to do and he tried to blame that for his restlessness. The cause of his agitation, however, lay in the fact that they hadn't seen Mara all day.

Kiril tried to reach for her mind, to catch some emotion from her, but he felt nothing. Knowing how focused Mikkarn needed to be, Kiril refused to bother him. Kiril was simply having a tough time accepting that he had two soul's mates. Such was unheard of.

Pacing down an aisle between the massive machines, Kiril stopped in his tracks. He stilled and concentrated. Something wasn't right.

I'm going to die. Mara's voice was clear in his mind, her extreme fear calling out to him.

"Mik! Mara's in trouble!"

The other man was already sprinting from the other end of the cavernous chamber.

"Go, Kiril! I'll follow!"

Not pausing even a moment, Kiril hurried through the three security checkpoints, reaching for Mara as he went.

Where are you, Mara?

He didn't hear her voice, but he caught images of her surroundings… and her attacker. *Tamche!*

The room was familiar, thank the Universe, and he ran as quickly as he could, shoving people out of his way. When he reached the door he was sure led to Mara, he didn't stop to collect himself, or to wait for help. He simply disengaged the lock and burst in.

A mistake he only hoped he lived to regret.

Chapter Six

Mikkarn wasn't far behind Kiril. The simple fact that Kiril had to maneuver through the crowded halls ensured that. When Kiril reached the door to the lounge, Mikkarn expected to be able to catch up. Instead, Kiril opened it and roared inside.

His battle cry was cut short by a loud *BANG*, and Kiril halted abruptly.

Mara screamed and lunged for Tamche.

"Mara! Don't!" Mikkarn's cry was frantic.

It was too late. Mara already held Tamche's wrist above her head, struggling with the gun. Not waiting on the outcome, Mikkarn simply grabbed Tamche from behind with one hand and the gun with the other. Tamche struggled wildly and Mikkarn wasn't sure how long he could hold her.

Before Mikkarn could decide what to do, Mara landed a punch to Tamche's jaw, effectively knocking the kicking, screaming woman out cold.

"Kiril," Mara whispered, and she turned deathly pale.

Turning around, Mikkarn watched as Kiril fell to his knees, his eyes wide, his skin pale and glistening with sweat. Blood oozed steadily from a wound to the right side of his chest. Mikkarn could hear a sickening sucking sound with each breath Kiril took.

Mara was at Kiril's side in a flash. Pulling a small pair of bandage scissors from her pocket -- she had always insisted on carrying items she would normally have used if she were on Earth -- she cut away his shirt. Removing her lab coat, she wadded it into a ball and pressed it to Kiril's chest. "Hold this."

He activated the communication unit on the wall as he followed her instructions, cursing the need to remove his personal comm device when he'd entered the mainframe chamber that morning. They would have to wait precious seconds before help arrived.

Mara searched the room methodically until she found a sandwich wrapped in plastic. Carefully unwrapping it, she tossed the food aside and knelt beside Kiril. "Remove the dressing."

Mikkarn did. Blood still oozed, but not in great amounts. The gurgling sound persisted.

Mara carefully placed the plastic over the small wound in Kiril's chest. "Hold that by the edges."

Again, Mikkarn did her bidding as she dug through those ever bulging pockets until she came out with a roll of tape. Tearing three long strips, she taped the plastic down at three edges.

"We need to get him to a healing tube," Mikkarn stated as several Medical Command personnel entered the room.

"No, really?" Mara's voice dripped with sarcasm. "I never would have guessed."

"Are you always such a bitch in a crisis?"

"Only when people state the obvious."

Kiril moaned and both bickering doctors turned their attention back to him. "If I make it through this, I'm putting you both over my knee." Kiril's voice was weak, but Mikkarn couldn't help but smile.

Mara's soft bark of laughter sounded suspiciously like the beginnings of a sob. "If I *let* Mikkarn make it through this, I'll help you spank him."

Mikkarn grasped Mara's arm firmly, a gesture meant to comfort. "Let's get him on the stretcher."

* * *

"Faster! Move it!" Mara tried to hurry the three men who had responded to Mikkarn's call for help into pushing Kiril's stretcher *faster*, but they refused to listen to her.

"This hospital is full of people, Doctor." One of them, a big, burly man, spoke calmly. "Commander Kiril will be fine when we get him to the healing chamber."

"Where's Mikkarn?" She had lost him after they'd loaded Kiril and started off with him. How *dare* Mikkarn abandon her and Kiril!

"He's calling ahead to make sure the healing tube is readied," the same burly officer explained patiently. He pushed the stretcher at the impossibly slow pace, as though he had all the time in the world. He sounded like he was talking to a child, which only annoyed Mara more.

"Do you even understand the seriousness of his wounds? His lung has collapsed, possibly both lungs, if the bullet ricocheted inside him. He could very well die without immediate intervention." Mara knew she wasn't getting through to the man. She only hoped nothing delayed them from getting him to a damned healing tube.

Gritting her teeth, Mara decided her best course of action was to go ahead of the stretcher and clear the way. They were about halfway to their destination when a sudden surge of panic almost brought her to her knees. *The damn tubes are full!* Mikkarn's intense emotion caught her up in the maelstrom and she screamed her rage, never questioning the certainty of what she now knew, or how she knew it.

"No! Fucking hell! I *knew* something like this would happen!" Mara stopped the stretcher and shoved it in the opposite direction. Toward the ER.

"What in the Universe are you doing, Doctor?" Big and Burly asked. "I thought you were anxious to get Commander Kiril to the healing chamber?"

"It's full and he can't wait."

"What do you mean it's full? There's always a place for the very sick and injured." He redirected the stretcher, again heading them in the opposite direction.

"Would you listen to me? We've got to get him to the Emergency Room. It's the only place that has the equipment I need!" Mara was becoming desperate. Where the *fuck* was Mikkarn?

"This is not the time for you to play the hero, Doctor." Big and Burly sounded impatient. "I'm sure you've learned much, but I will not let you endanger Commander Kiril with your barbaric medicine."

Mara didn't even bat an eye. She picked up the first object she saw -- a chair -- and swung it with all her might at the hulking guard. The other two guards immediately moved to subdue her but Mikkarn's authoritative voice commanded them to stop. "You will bloody well do what she tells you to! More than half the tubes are down for upgrades and there is no place to put Kiril."

"It's about fucking time!" Mara snapped. "Help me!"

"You two --" Mikkarn indicated the remaining two guards, "-- see to him. Get him to the ER as quickly as you can."

Kiril was deathly pale, his lips taking on a faint bluish tinge. Mara led the way, as she and Mikkarn heaved the stretcher into motion. When they wheeled Kiril into the ER at breakneck speed, several nurses turned to Mikkarn for instructions.

"Get Dr. Jensen whatever she needs." Mikkarn hooked Kiril up to various monitors as Mara cut away the rest of his clothes to look for more injuries.

"I need the chest cart." Detaching herself from

everything but her patient, Mara didn't glance up. She needed to know exactly what she was dealing with, and she needed to do it effectively. No distractions of any kind.

"What's she going to do, Doctor?" The fresh-faced nurse watched in fascination as Mara gowned up.

"Just do what she says. Seconds count." Mikkarn was actually wondering the same thing. He couldn't fault the nurse for asking.

"Okay." Mara turned to Mikkarn. "Here's the deal. Kiril's most obvious injury is an open pneumothorax. The bullet caused an opening in the pleural space and his right lung has collapsed, making adequate air exchange impossible."

"I know what it is, Mara. How do we fix it?"

Mara felt her face heat up in her embarrassment. "Sorry." Moving to a cart in the corner of the room, she started looking for the supplies she needed. This *archaic* equipment was the only thing that could save Kiril now.

"We have to drain the air and blood, if there is any, so the lung can fully expand again."

Mikkarn rolled his eyes skyward. "Again, that's obvious. *How* do we do it?"

"Lighten up! If you had paid attention to me when I built this damned cart, you'd know," Mara snapped. Taking a deep breath, she rolled her shoulders to relieve the tension. "I'm sorry. You're right. I'm a bitch in a crisis."

Mikkarn smiled. "Just tell me how to help you."

"I want a thirty-eight French chest tube. I think there is only a pneumo, but if there's blood in the pleural space, the larger tube will be helpful." Turning to the nurse at Mikkarn's side, Mara said, "I need some

Betadine, size six sterile gloves, and a local anesthetic." She pressed a button to raise the stretcher to a comfortable level for her to work. Leaning close to Kiril, she brushed her lips to his. "Hang in there. This will hurt, but when I'm through, you'll be able to breathe easier."

Kiril managed a weak smile. "I trust you. Do what you must."

A rush of tears threatened to spill from her eyes. She absolutely could not lose this man. Looking to Mikkarn, she realized the same was true of him. She would be lost without either of them.

Taking a deep breath, Mara spoke to the nurse again. "Do you remember how to ready the Pleurevac? I'll need you to do that while Mikkarn and I put in the chest tube."

The nurse nodded her head and pulled out the sheet of instructions, fumbling with them as she tried to set up the equipment. Thank God the English to Gothe'maran translation had been included in the package. Checking for the correct amount, the nurse filled the atrium with sterile water and hooked it to the suction device.

Mara nodded her head in satisfaction. At least someone had paid attention to her.

"Raise your right arm over your head, Kiril. Mikkarn, glove up." Mara put on her gloves as well and carefully cleansed the proper area, explaining herself to Mikkarn as she went. "Imagine there is a line from the very center of his armpit running the length of his side to his waist. We'll call this the mid-axillary line. We want to make an incision horizontally slightly in front of this line. Count the spaces between his ribs. You want to go into the sixth space, which should be at about nipple level in a man."

"Would you two please stop talking about me like I'm a piece of meat?" Kiril looked annoyed, *felt* annoyed. "I'm not some cadaver for you to practice on, Mikkarn. Let Mara do it."

Mikkarn chuckled. "What? You don't trust me?"

Kiril snorted. "Sure I do. But I trust her more at this instant."

Mara tested the syringe of anesthetic. "You're going to feel a stick, then a stinging sensation. This will numb you locally. Once I make the incision, you'll feel some discomfort as the tube goes in, but it should be bearable."

Kiril nodded. His breathing was becoming more labored and his oxygen saturation was dropping slowly, but steadily.

Mara made her cut. Quick, clean. She carefully broke through the subcutaneous tissue over the rib and punctured the tissue inside with her clamp. She swept just inside the incision with her finger to check for organs or adhesions in her immediate path. Taking the plastic-like tube in her clamp, she inserted the blunt end until about half the tube was inside Kiril's chest. In a few seconds, condensation formed inside the tube and Mara released a breath she didn't realize she had been holding. The placement was successful.

Hooking up the suction device, she waited a few minutes. It didn't take long before the bluish tinge to his lips and fingernails began to pinken, and his skin was less clammy. "Are you feeling any better?" Mara stroked her hand down the side of Kiril's face.

"Maybe. A little, yeah."

"His color is coming back." Mikkarn held the tube firmly while Mara made a few sutures to hold it securely.

"And that, ladies and gentlemen, is the low tech

way to fix a pneumothorax." Mara smiled, supremely pleased with herself.

It wasn't long after that the guards brought their fallen comrade into the room beside Kiril's.

"He's still unconscious, Heirek?" Mikkarn glanced at the guard as he cleaned up the mess he and Mara had made with their equipment.

"He's in and out," Heirek said. "She hit him pretty hard, sir."

"He should take the next available tube," Mara said. "Kiril should be okay for as long as it takes. I can't do much for a head injury." She looked to the other two guards. "I'm sorry I hit him. Kiril needed help and he was going too slowly and in the wrong direction."

Heirek smiled. "No apology necessary, Doctor. You were right."

Mara smiled at Mikkarn as Kiril reached for her hand.

"Thank you for saving my life, Mara." Kiril squeezed gently. "Now, if you two would leave me alone for a few moments, I'd like to rest." Kiril winked at Mara. *I think Mikkarn needs to hold you.* Kiril's voice inside her head startled her and she jumped.

"Quit that!"

Kiril grinned. "But it's so much fun."

Giggling, Mara took Mikkarn's hand. "Let's go. Let the big, bad bodyguard have his beauty rest."

Without a word, Mikkarn let her lead him to a private room where she took him in her arms. He held her tightly for several minutes before she realized he was crying.

Without saying another word, Mara took Mikkarn's face in her hands and gently pressed her lips to his. She wanted to lose herself in the pleasure of his mouth moving tentatively against hers, but she reached for Kiril almost blindly. She needed to feel the bond the three shared.

When their kiss grew in intensity, she heard Kiril whisper, *I feel complete...*

Strangely enough, she did, too.

* * *

Since Kiril's near miss two days before, Mara had struggled to come to terms with her relationship with the two men. Once she was assured Kiril was out of danger and Mikkarn no longer needed emotional support, she went back home and locked herself in to think.

What was she supposed to do? What did she *want* to do? All this time, she had tried to avoid the two men in anything other than the most necessary aspect of her professional life. Now she wanted, *needed*, more.

That's it. Mara was tired of letting her wants and needs take second place. She was taking what she wanted.

* * *

The poolside door was open. Were they expecting her? Mara had trouble reading anything from either of them, but she suspected they were deep in their own pleasure. Entering the house, Mara paused just inside the door.

We were wondering when you'd finally show up. Mikkarn's voice was full of love and laughter.

Come upstairs. Kiril's deeper, seductive voice beckoned her. *There's something you'll want to see.*

Mara mounted the stairs quickly, following the sounds of masculine moans. Anticipation coursed through her and her nipples and cunt tingled. Finding a door at the end of the hallway slightly ajar, she slowly pushed it open. The very large bed dominated the room. The men upon it captured Mara's attention like nothing else.

Mikkarn lounged naked on his back. Kiril knelt above him, his big body also gloriously naked.

"Have a seat, Mara." Kiril's rumbling voice elicited a warm gush of moisture from her pussy and she whimpered as she sat in the oversized chair across the room. "Watch," he whispered.

Mara did watch, fascinated, as Kiril's thick erection disappeared into Mikkarn's mouth. Kiril's head fell back and the veins stood out on his neck. Both men groaned their pleasure. Kiril's shallow strokes became deeper, and faster. Mara couldn't resist the urge to cup her swollen breast.

"That's it. Turn yourself on," Kiril ground out through clenched teeth. "Your turn is coming."

Straddling Mikkarn's face, Kiril lowered himself to rest his weight with hands flat against the mattress, his face inches from Mikkarn's groin. Without breaking eye contact with Mara, Kiril lowered his mouth and enveloped Mikkarn's long, hard cock.

Kiril hummed as he sucked. That sound, punctuated by the occasional groan from both Mikkarn and Mara, filled the room, along with the scent of clean sweat, musky male, and a delicately sweet feminine smell. Not unpleasant at all.

While they pleasured each other, and her, if from a distance -- she knew this was more for her benefit than their own -- Mara took the opportunity to examine each man for the first time up close. Approaching them silently, she looked her fill.

Mikkarn's lean body was firmly muscled. The fine hair covering most of his body was as blond as the hair on his head. Even the coarse nest covering his sex was a pale, golden blond.

Kiril was very heavily muscled. Mara noted

several scars on his big body and knew he had experienced many battles, some of them probably on Earth. Rolling off Mikkarn, Kiril stood at the edge of the bed, positioning himself between the other man's legs. Mikkarn moved to the edge, spreading his thighs and bending his knees. Mara saw clearly the more recent scar on Kiril left by Tamche, and shuddered in remembrance.

"Do not think of such unpleasantness," Mikkarn said. "You saved him and Tamche cannot hurt him, or you, ever again. I seriously doubt she will ever get out of prison given the circumstances."

"You read my mind so easily." Mara spoke softly, mesmerized by the sight before her as Kiril squeezed a generous amount of lubricant into the palm of his hand and stroked himself until his cock gleamed with the thick gel.

Mikkarn hissed as the head of Kiril's cock slid into his ass. "You can do the same with us. You just have to reach for it."

Kiril pumped into Mikkarn with slow, steady, ever-lengthening strokes. Mara did as Mikkarn instructed and reached for his mind. The pleasure was incredible, from the fullness pressing into his ass, the pressure building in his cock and balls, and from knowing Mara enjoyed what she saw. She also felt a lingering darkness in his soul, something she knew would take time to heal.

Resting a hand on Kiril's arm, she halted his movements. "There is sadness within you. Your soul is as dark as Kiril's appearance. Why do you blame yourself when others die?"

Mikkarn blinked. "I do not blame myself."

"Liar," Kiril and Mara said in unison.

Mikkarn chuckled. "Okay, so maybe I just think

that with all the technology we have at our disposal, no one should ever die of anything other than old age."

"Well." Mara crawled up on the bed and stretched her body out next to Mikkarn's. "By learning what I tried to teach you, you've made a step in the right direction. But let me tell you something." She took his face in her hands, gently. "You have god-like power with healing, but you are not God. No matter what you do, no matter what you know, people will always die. It's all part of the circle of life."

Kiril gave a shallow thrust and Mikkarn cried out in surprise and pleasure. "Perhaps there are other things you can teach us, Mara. But right now, there are more important things I'm concerned about. Like just how many ways the three of us can fuck before we pass out from exhaustion."

Mara lowered her mouth to Mikkarn's and slipped her tongue inside, tasting, teasing. *This* was what she had been missing all her life and never even realized it. She had truly come home.

Losing herself in the passion of both men, she opened her mind to their cravings. Each wanted the other, each wanted her. Breaking her kiss, Mara stood and disrobed. It was past time they did this for real instead of in the strange dream world she visited every night.

"Stretch out on top of Mikkarn with your back against his chest." Mara never hesitated. She trusted both men implicitly. Carefully, she straddled Mikkarn's hips and let of her head rest on his shoulder, her legs on the outside of Mikkarn's. Mikkarn cupped her breasts as Kiril, firmly imbedded within Mikkarn, grasped her legs and lifted, hooking her knees over his shoulders, grasping her ass in his hands. Her shoulders supported the rest of her weight where they lay on

Mikkarn's chest and his knees helped to support her when he rested his feet on Kiril's rock-hard stomach. With a wicked grin, Kiril dove straight for her pussy.

Mara gave a sharp yelp and arched her back. Her ankles hooked together behind Kiril's neck, and she levered herself against his mouth, seeking the friction she needed.

Mikkarn's arms roamed her body, stroking, plucking her impossibly hard nipples, caressing her hips and ass as she sought her pleasure. "That's it, sweet. Fuck his mouth."

Mara was drowning in a sexual haze. Her climax, when it hit her, seized her muscles and took her breath. As she neared the peak, she screamed. She released every pleasure she had ever held back in that one gloriously hedonistic orgasm. Her breath coming in little gasps, her body drenched in sweat, she still wasn't satisfied. She wanted what she had denied herself for two long, torturous years. She wanted these men to fuck her senseless.

* * *

As the glory of Mara's climax faded, Kiril gently unwrapped her legs from around his neck. With Mikkarn holding her hips, Kiril once more spread her legs to rest outside Mikkarn's, exposing her to them both. Carefully, Kiril guided Mikkarn's cock inside her pulsing pussy. Mikkarn, his knees still bent, repositioned himself so that his feet were supported by the bed and gave an experimental pump, pushing his cock even deeper into her. Mikkarn's pleasure magnified his own and Kiril clenched his jaw to keep from taking his own pleasure. Not now. Not yet.

"She's so fucking *tight*!" Mikkarn gasped as he gave another experimental thrust, carefully, always mindful of Kiril's cock still deeply embedded within his ass.

"As are you," Kiril rumbled as he held Mara's knees against his chest, and started the steady, gentle rhythm once again. His motion drove Mikkarn's cock into Mara as he pulled her legs to him with each thrust of his body. He effectively fucked them both. Once he sensed they were all comfortable with the new, complicated position, he started to thrust faster, more forcefully. Before long, their rhythm was a driving force, longing to plunge them over the edge of sanity.

Mikkarn grunted, Kiril growled, and Mara whimpered. As one, they came in a glorious fountain of bliss, the pleasure so intense Kiril actually saw stars. Maybe even a couple of comets and planets as well. No one spoke words of undying love -- they didn't have to. All they had to do was reach for the others' thoughts and feelings and it was there. And they did love each other. Passionately.

When their spasms had ceased, when their bodies had no more to give, Kiril withdrew and cleansed himself. When Mara rolled to her side, sliding off Mikkarn's softening cock, Kiril washed her and Mikkarn as well. Climbing back into bed on shaky legs, he snuggled close to Mara, who was sandwiched once again between them.

For the first time in his life, everything made sense. He would never be without Mikkarn, he wouldn't have to worry about Mara leaving. They were mates. The love they felt for one another was incredible, and Kiril knew it would never fade. Sighing, completely happy and knowing his mates were as well, Kiril closed his eyes and slept.

Sleeping With the Enemy (Forbidden 3)
Post-Apocalyptic Sci-Fi Action Romance
Marteeka Karland

More bloodshed during the Gothe'maran-Earth War is the last thing Sergeant Taber Mahoney wanted to see. Hopefully, this one last battle will end it. Searching the dead to find the wounded, what he witnesses is enough to push him over the edge into madness.

Attacked by her mate -- an event all too familiar to her -- Akahana accepts her fate and sends a silent prayer that he will not find her in a future life. Prepared to die, she doesn't expect the dark warrior who brings death to give her life.

Even though she is freed from a mate who would smother her soul in fear and pain, can Akahana truly escape him? Will he haunt her mind and heart from the grave and never give her the peace she so desperately craves?

It takes more than technology to heal a fractured life, and even the love of one extraordinary man may not be enough. Besides, Akahana's mate may yet reach out from his grave, giving his final protest at this forbidden union.

Chapter One

Closing her eyes, Akahana tried to block out images she never thought she'd ever see. Her mate, a huge Gothe'maran male in full body armor captured a human child of not more than three. When she peeked carefully, she found the child looking directly at her, screaming in terror as Gamin's meaty hand closed around the girl's throat.

She couldn't have stopped the shrill "*No!*" that escaped her throat even if she'd wanted. In that instant, she knew she'd sealed her fate. Gamin tossed the child aside and stalked toward her.

She'd always heard that when one faced impending death, the souls of the Gothe'maran people who had gone before embraced the soul about to enter their ranks. Instead, Akahana saw only the souls of Earth killed by her people -- the Gothe'maran. The souls of Earth had been good people. Caring people. People who only wanted to exist in freedom, in their own cultures.

The last image to float in her mind was the face of the little girl.

Then Gamin was on her.

He backhanded her across the cheek with his closed fist and immediately followed it with a smashing blow to her jaw in one smooth motion. Blood poured from her mouth, but she didn't have time to spit it out before he hit her again. Ribs crunched, both her forearms snapped when she tried to block his crippling blows. He kicked her in the stomach, causing her to retch and gasp for breath that was becoming harder and harder to drag into her lungs.

When she fell onto her back, her eyes beginning to swell shut, Gamin grasped the neck of her tunic and ripped it with one sharp jerk. With a series of like movements, it wasn't long before he had her completely stripped of clothing.

She was unable to resist when he forced her legs apart and wedged his body between them. He was always aroused by violence and had taken her many times in this same manner. It was one of the privileges of being high in Military Command. He made enough money to purchase his own unregulated healing tube. No one monitored how often it was used or the type of injuries it was used to heal, and with no evidence, no one would believe that the mate of any Gothe'maran male was abused so, especially that of a decorated soldier.

Gamin freed his cock from the armor and his clothing in a series of quick, sure gestures. Scooping blood and spittle from Akahana's mouth and chin, he moistened his erect member and forced his way inside her. Akahana knew better than to protest or cry out, so she merely turned her head to the side.

Catching the image of her lifeless body in Gamin's mind, lying as she was now, Akahana knew he meant to kill her this time. She didn't mind, really. Although she loved Gothe'mar, Earth was a beautiful place filled with beautiful people, and the thought of spending her soul's eternity here wasn't unappealing. Besides, her life was a living death. She'd gladly leave this life and hope her soul's mate never found her again.

* * *

Sergeant Taber Mahoney of the United World Army of Earth surveyed the bodies on the field of what he hoped would be the last battle of the World Gothe'maran War. Despite all efforts, the blood had flowed for nearly ten years. Bodies, both human and

Gothe'maran, lay scattered like fall leaves over the landscape. Most everyone was dead, but those who weren't were transported to the Earthside Medical Command. He had personally checked each body carefully for any signs of life and used a handheld scanner to record each individual and to locate unrecorded body masses.

Only three left. Two adults and one child.

An image flashed through his mind -- a determined, fair-haired woman standing in his office haunted by the memory of a dead husband and child. He hoped Ms. Garrett had found peace.

With cautious steps, Taber made his way to the only other people alive in this wasteland, careful to keep to the shadows. In the fading twilight, it wasn't hard. The human child was huddled under a small bush, crying but not making a sound. The adult woman was Gothe'maran and very near death. At first Taber thought the Gothe'maran man over her was grieving or perhaps trying to help her, but he soon discovered the truth.

Aiming his scanner at the pair, he was horrified by what he saw. It was rape. Rape to the point of death for the woman, she was beaten so badly. Her whole body was covered with bruises and she had many broken bones. The scanner detected massive internal bleeding, including a slow but deadly bleed inside her head that guaranteed she would not live long if left untreated. The Gothe'maran was an officer by his uniform -- an officer for the rogue faction unless Taber missed his guess. The man's hips moved in rapid thrusts as he fucked the helpless woman. She didn't move, didn't make a sound. From her brain patterns, she was fully conscious and knew exactly what was happening.

Fury shot through him. His prized control and ability to use stealth as a weapon vanished, and he ran, screaming a battle cry, straight at the other man. His gun hung holstered at his side. He had no intention of using it. This kill, he wanted with his bare hands.

The Gothe'maran officer's head snapped up and he pulled himself upright, away from the woman beneath him. He wasn't able to un-holster his own gun before Taber was on him.

Taber dove into the air and caught the large man in the midsection, propelling him backwards and onto his back, effectively knocking the wind out of him. Before the woman's assailant could get to his feet -- or even to a sitting position -- Taber straddled him and hit him repeatedly across his face. Blood flew in all directions, splattering across Taber's face and covering his fist and arm and uniform.

Over and over Taber hit the other man. He kept hitting him until his hand would no longer close into a fist. Then he used the other hand. The man's face was a mass of bloody meat and smashed bone. Still it wasn't enough. When both Taber's hands were basically useless as fists, he took the man by the neck and banged his head against the ground.

He couldn't stop! It was as if he were looking at himself through a mirror. The rational part of his mind was horrified. What he was doing went against everything he'd ever believed in.

And he didn't give a fuck.

Then he felt a light touch on his shoulder.

"You can stop now." The voice was soft, feminine, and a bit muffled. "I think he's dead."

It was all it took to bring him back to himself. He dropped the man he'd just beaten to death in a pool of dark, congealing blood and sat back to one side of the body. He took a deep breath before looking over his shoulder. It was the woman the Gothie had been raping and beating.

Her face was swelling, and she looked worse than when he'd first seen her. Hair so fair it was almost white was caked in blood. Her eyes were so swollen, he wasn't sure if she could still see. How she was conscious at all was a mystery.

They stared at each other for a few moments before her strength left her and she slumped to the ground. Taber lunged for her and caught her head and shoulders as she fell over. He was afraid to touch her. Afraid he'd add to her pain, but it didn't matter. She'd finally passed out, his shirt firmly twisted in her hands.

* * *

Akahana was wrapped in warmth. Light and warmth. She floated somewhere between life and death, both beckoning to her equally. She was about to make her choice when another presence filled her mind.

The masculine presence was filled with anger and worry. He kept returning to the scene on Earth, Gamin in his grasp. Dying. His only goal had been to kill the man torturing the woman. His woman. Something deep inside him had claimed her as his own.

At first, Akahana shrank deep within herself, refusing to go to the huge man who had been her savior. She wanted no man ever again. But his anguished thoughts were filled with nothing but how his actions would affect her. Would she recover from her injuries? Was she comfortable in the tube? Was she as aware of him as he was of her?

Would she hate him?

Every time his thoughts drifted in that direction,

pain sliced through his heart, and a fresh wave of confusion swamped him. He didn't know what was happening.

Akahana did.

This man, Taber, was her soul's mate.

She didn't want to think about it. But despite her mind screaming for her to run from him, her heart recognized the goodness in him and reached out. She wanted a mate -- she just wanted one who wouldn't cause her pain.

With a tentative brush to Taber's mind, Akahana made contact as a mate. Her mind gently probed his, hoping he would realize what she was doing. He was startled at first, confused. He didn't know what to do. So Akahana introduced herself.

"I am Akahana Di'Var. You saved my life."

"How can you talk to me?"

Had she been awake and in her own body, she would have sighed. "It is complicated. I only wanted you to be at peace with what you did."

"You can forgive me for killing a man with my bare hands?"

"He would have killed me. I saw it in his mind."

"So you can read minds, then." It wasn't a question.

"No. Not as you perceive it, anyway. Every Gothe'maran can touch the mind of his or her soul's mate. It seems we have found each other against all odds."

"You were right." His voice sounded weary. "I guess it is complicated."

Akahana would have laughed if she'd felt like it, but she just couldn't summon the energy. "I'm tired."

"Rest then. I'll be here, watching over you."

"You don't have to."

"I know." There was a mental caress to her cheek as he tentatively reached for the unfamiliar and touched her mind. "Rest well, Dearheart. I'll be here when you wake."

The light surrounding her faded, replaced by a night sky filled with a myriad of stars, but no moon. She had a few moments to appreciate the beauty of it before her mind slowly sank back into unconsciousness. Back into a healing sleep.

* * *

Taber had never been so exhausted. His head pounded. He had been trying for hours to get back into Akahana's mind without success. He had an almost physical need to touch her mind again, to know she was alive and well. True, he could check the readout on the healing tube, but it wasn't the same. He could see her through the portal -- clear during the "day" cycle -- but only her outline was visible during the "night."

He hated not being able to see her at will.

He hated not being able to hold her, to comfort her.

He wanted this woman, but he wanted to protect her, make her happy. Shield her from all the bad things in the universe. He wanted more as well and cursed his body for betraying the lovely woman in that damned tube. She needed caring and love, not some horny soldier lusting after her lovely body.

She was the one he'd been waiting for his entire life. He never thought he'd find her. Now that he had found her, he would not let her go. No matter the personal cost. He would do whatever it took to win her heart.

It wasn't something he was used to feeling, and it was a very uncomfortable emotion.

Taber leaned back in the chair provided by the staff at Earthside Medical Command and took a deep, calming breath. The flowers he'd set on the table beside the healing tube earlier provided a cheerful color and pleasing smell in an otherwise stale, sterile environment. Closing his eyes, he went to sleep, imagining Akahana slept beside him, cuddled against him in his protective embrace.

* * *

Akahana's warm womanly body stretched languidly against his. She smiled up at him and caressed his jaw line.

His cock twitched at the simple touch, and the baser man inside him roared at him to roll her over and simply sink into her. Oh, God, how he wanted to do just that! Instead, he smiled back at her and lay there, pulling her closer against him, hugging her affectionately. He savored the feel of her skin, the smell of her hair.

For this woman, he could wait as long as it took.

"Why do you hold back?"

"Because you don't need a lover to devour you."

"You want to take me hard, fast, and violently. Yet you don't."

"Yes. The things I want to do with your body are probably illegal in most parts of the galaxy, but the only thing that stops me from fucking you every way I want is that I don't want to hurt you. I never want to hurt you in any way."

"Taber, this is your dream. You can give me as much pleasure or pain as you want, and it won't be physical."

"Dream." He mused over what she'd said. Damn! This was strange!

"Look at my body, Taber. Even after the healing

process is over, I will be marred. I am as you wish me to be now -- whole and beautiful."

"You are now as I see you. I have very little imagination."

She smiled. "You will understand. Later."

Taber brushed back her thick dark hair, tucking it behind her ear. "I will not add to your pain."

Akahana didn't say anything as she trailed her fingers down his torso to tangle in the hair at his groin. Taber inhaled sharply as her fingers made contact with his cock. He thought he'd lose his mind.

Her touch was tentative, yet firm. She obviously knew how to handle a man to create maximum pleasure. Moving over his body, she kissed and licked his chest -- his nipples and the valley separating his pectoral muscles. She nipped and sucked the taut flesh, blurring the line between pleasure and pain, all the while steadily gripping and pumping his cock.

"Akahana, you don't have to --"

"I want to. I can do things in the dream world I don't know if I'll ever be able to do in the real world." Down and farther still she went, following the line of his abdomen, over each ridge, kissing each muscle, making his cock jump in anticipation. When she kissed the flesh just above the tip of his now very fully erect cock, he couldn't repress the groan of anticipation and excitement.

With a swift move that took his breath, Akahana licked the length of his shaft from tip to balls. It took every ounce of self-control Taber possessed for him not to come all over himself. When she took one testicle in her mouth and rolled her tongue around the flesh surrounding it, occasionally giving the organ a squeeze with her mouth, Taber knew there was no way he could keep from coming.

Grabbing her head with both hands, he urged her to take his shaft in her mouth. She did. Eagerly. The head of his dick hit the back of her throat three times before every muscle in his body clenched, and he shouted her name. Spasm after spasm took his body, pumping his seed into her mouth, and he felt her swallow several times before his orgasm passed...

And he woke, still in the chair, with very damp underwear.

Chapter Two

Akahana awoke in a soft bed with covers tucked around her torso, the shared dream still fresh in her mind. Her arms were free, so she felt cocooned instead of trapped, and the familiar tingle her body always had after being healed was prominent in her muscles and bones. Judging from the sensitivity to pressure on her heels, she had been lying on her back in a healing tube for a very long time. When she turned her head to the side and opened her eyes, her first sight was a modest vase of colorful flowers on the table at her bedside.

"You're awake."

Akahana sat straight up in bed, startled by the sound of a very deep, familiar, masculine voice. Taber sat in a chair next to her bed. He was dark skin contrasted sharply with the whites of his eyes, his head gleaming in the moonlight pouring in from the window. She caught a hint of the tattoo covering his scalp.

He raised his hands in a non-threatening manner. "I didn't mean to startle you, Dearheart." His voice was so calm and reassuring she almost forgot what had happened to her. All she wanted to think about was the dream. "How long?" Her voice was gravelly, rough. She must have been in the tube for a very long while this time.

He shook his head. "How long... what?"

"In the tube," she managed to say. "How long in the tube?"

"Nearly three weeks. The doctors say it was far longer than it should have taken."

"Yes." She wasn't entirely sure she prevented the sadness and pain from entering that one single word. Perhaps having scientists know of this particular fact would work in her favor when her part in her husband's murder was investigated.

She tried to clear her throat, but she was parched. Her throat felt like it was stuck closed. Without being asked, her visitor stood and went to her bedside table. He took a small pitcher, poured liquid into a glass and handed it to her.

"Drink. It's water. I imagine you'll need several glasses before you feel normal." He guided her hands to her face, urging her to drink. "Just sip it slowly."

It tasted like sweet heaven. Perhaps it was as close to heaven as she'd ever get in any life. She didn't know what her past lives had brought, but this one had been nothing short of a living hell. One she didn't care to repeat.

"I need a Gothe'maran officer," she said.

"You need to rest."

"You don't understand. I've committed a crime and I must turn myself in. It's our way."

"What about the bastard who was beating and raping you? Do you think he would have turned himself in? I very much doubt it is the way of all your people to be that honest."

"Do you mock me?" She didn't want to be ungrateful. Perhaps she was simply trying to block out the fact that this man was the man she'd pulled off her dead husband's body.

"Not at all, Dearheart. I'm merely angry that you would be so willing to confess a crime when others would not. Now, what crime have you committed?"

"I didn't stop you from killing my mate."

From his indrawn breath, she knew she'd caught him off guard. He didn't know Gamin was her husband.

"Perhaps we should start from the beginning. I

think there are a few pertinent facts I'm missing."

"No." The sadness in her surprised her. Gamin had done nothing but beat her most of her life, yet she still grieved for him. It didn't make sense. "I need only to confess my deed and take whatever punishment is necessary."

He rose without a word and exited her room. When he returned, it was with not one Gothe'maran officer, but two. And a woman. She didn't recognize the woman, but the two officers were known to everyone.

Mikkarn was in charge of Earth's branch of Medical Command for this term, and Kiril was General Khan's right hand. At least, he had been when she'd last left Gothe'mar, before the wars.

"How are you feeling?" The woman's voice was very gentle, and she smiled easily at Akahana. She sat on the bed and took Akahana's wrist in her hand while she looked at the timepiece on her own wrist.

"I'm well."

"There is something you wished to say?"

"Kiril." The woman never looked up from her watch. "It can wait until I've examined her."

Akahana cringed and turned away. Such would have earned her a severe reprimand, even in public. Given the stature of Sub-General Kiril, he would probably actually strike her. After all, as Gamin had told her often enough, when in the presence of inferior officers, no one would question him, or go against his word.

No one said anything. The woman continued to touch her gently for several minutes before using her fingertips to turn Akahana's face toward them all again.

"My name is Mara. Taber says the man who did

this to you was your mate. He also says he is responsible for your attacker's death. Is this true?"

Akahana looked from one blank face to another. The two humans showed as little emotion as the two Gothe'marans. No disgust, no anger, nothing. They were simply waiting for her answer.

"Yes, but I think he was doing what he thought was right. I should have told him Gamin was my mate but I waited until it was too late. I don't think I even actually told him until I woke a few minutes ago." Her brow knitted in concentration as she tried in vain to remember. "There are things --" She had to look away then, embarrassed. "I just can't remember."

Kiril spoke next. "Taber also says you feel that by not trying to stop the incident, you have committed a crime. Is this also true?"

Confused, Akahana blinked several times. "Of course. It is my responsibility to defend my mate if at all possible." Tears formed in her eyes, and she brushed them aside angrily. "I was able to help. I simply didn't."

Mara stood and expelled an angry breath. "That's just one more thing about the great Gothe'maran society you two need to change."

Akahana was totally confused. What was she talking about?

Mikkarn crossed his arms over his lean torso. "Gamin Di'Var was a respected officer. I find it difficult to believe there isn't more to the story than meets the eye. I seriously doubt he would intentionally hurt a member of his family, especially his mate."

At the mention of "family," Akahana remembered the little girl. "The child!" Her exclamation drew everyone's attention back to her. "Did you find the girl child Gamin was..." she trailed off, unable to finish her sentence, suddenly ashamed.

Mara moved back to the bed and sat once again, taking Akahana's hand and bringing it to her lips tenderly. "Yes. She's fine. General Khan and his wife took her in, and she's doing wonderfully."

Akahana blanched. "General Khan." The very name sent chills down her spine. Gamin had worked closely with the general in the past. If he was involved, her death might well be as bad as her life. "Gamin served with him. The general will not be pleased to hear of my role in Gamin's death."

"We will have to see. Khan is nothing if not fair."

Taber stood then. "Perhaps there is more to the incident, but what I saw was not an honorable warrior."

"I still find it hard to believe." Kiril shook his head.

Taber took a threatening step toward Kiril, but Mara defused the situation with a snort. "Men are such pains in the ass sometimes, don't you think?" Akahana didn't know how to respond. In her reality, she would never have made such a remark. "What's your name, dear?"

"Akahana."

"Well, Akahana, let's worry about all that later. Right now, I'd like to put you into a healing tube for a well patient scan." She smiled. "Do you mind?"

"I --"

"You will release Senior First Lieutenant Gamin Di'Var's mate immediately!" The booming, angry voice coming from the doorway across the room belonged to her mate's first underofficer and closest friend, Davin Bakah. Akahana almost blanched, but managed to keep her expression neutral. This man wouldn't hesitate to kill her. In fact, he'd probably consider it

Gamin's last wish if he found out she could have stopped his death.

Mara faced the huge warrior and looked like she would have advanced on him if Kiril had not held her back. "Wanna make me?"

"Mara," Mikkarn hissed as he moved in front of the pair and addressed Davin. "Welcome to Earthside Medical Command. Is there something we can help you with?"

"I will take the woman back to Gothe'mar where Gamin has made arrangements for her care."

"She has experienced severe trauma and is not well enough for travel. I regret she will have to remain in our care a while longer." While Mikkarn was talking, the others were moving around Akahana. Especially Taber. The way the man clenched and unclenched his fists screamed violence, and the image of Taber beating the life from Gamin flashed through her mind. She whimpered.

"I must insist." Davin's gaze fixed on Akahana, and her insides froze. What had Gamin done? "She has been through the healing tube. She is ready to leave."

"I'm afraid it isn't that simple." Mara shouldered her way to Mikkarn's side. "It took three weeks in the tube to get her to this condition, and she still has a lot of healing to do. I'm not sure why, but she is rejecting the grafts and tissue regeneration. She'll have to stay until we can figure out why."

"It is not your concern, human." Davin's face contorted to an evil, hate-filled sneer. Akahana thought he would surely strike the small woman, but when the three warriors moved forward, Akahana began to realize that perhaps she needed to ask some questions. Mara was obviously protected zealously by her mates. But why would Taber rush to her rescue?

"She is the concern of Medical Command." Mikkarn's softly spoken voice held a wealth of menace. No one went against Medical Command. Only the highest officials in Military Command would even *question* an order given by one in Medical.

"And as such," Kiril spoke, clenching and unclenching his fists, "she is the concern of Military Command. I know you don't want to go against both infrastructures."

At first, Akahana thought Davin would argue the point and try to take her anyway. She could see the hatred in his eyes, which was something for a Gothe'maran. They were taught from childhood to suppress emotions -- especially the boys. Surprisingly, he backed down.

"Then I must insist on taking charge of her. You will do nothing without my permission, and she will go nowhere I am not allowed to follow."

"She is not property," Taber said softly. "Least of all yours."

"She is the mate of my commanding officer and best friend. It is my responsibility and *duty* to see to her safety now that he is gone." To the casual observer, Davin's face was probably an impeccable mask of non-emotion once again, but she saw the underlying menace. Davin would kill this human if he got the chance.

"Kiril." Akahana's head snapped toward the door and the new voice.

General Khan Mak'un!

"Khan." Kiril moved to the general, managing to stay between Mara and Davin. "It is good to see you, my friend." Kiril turned to the blonde woman at Khan's side. "I trust you are well, Anna?"

The greeting was clear: Kiril was establishing his

dominance over Davin by using his relationship with the general. It would be hard for Davin to protest anything Kiril decided.

"I am. It's good to see you again, Kiril." Anna's smile was warm and genuine. This was a woman Akahana would like to have known. In another life.

Khan took Kiril's offered hand, his face revealing nothing of what he was thinking. "We need to talk, General."

Khan raised an eyebrow, but allowed Kiril to lead him outside the room. Taber grasped Mikkarn's arm and mumbled something to him before turning back to Akahana. "I'll be right back. Dr. Mikkarn will take care of you."

"You can't fight Davin." She knew she was in trouble with Davin when she locked gazes with him. The subtle changes in the look in his eyes reminded her so much of Gamin, she wanted to vomit. Davin was definitely going to kill her. It was just a matter of when.

He caressed her cheek with a finger. "Yes, I can, Dearheart." And he followed Kiril and Khan out of the room.

* * *

Kiril looked back at Taber when he shut the door behind the three of them. "I didn't think I'd need to issue an invitation."

"She's terrified of that man in there," Taber said without preamble. "You can't let him take her."

Both the other men looked at each other, a wealth of meaning in that glance. "She told you this?" Khan prompted.

"I felt it. I can pick things up from her when her emotions are high."

Kiril shifted his feet. "Do you know what that

means, Taber?"

"She says it means I'm her mate." There was no reason to keep something like this from these two men. It could only help him if everything he'd learned about the Gothe'maran people was correct. "You should also know that she has no intention to take another mate. I get the impression that Gamin, the mate I killed, was very abusive to her."

"Abusive… how?" Khan waved a hand, indicating he wanted more information.

"Well." Taber looked the man in the eye. "He beat her almost to death before I got there. And I don't think that was the first time. I'm not a doctor, like Mikkarn, but I know a human body can become accustomed to things done to it repeatedly. A person who has seizures repeatedly and is treated with Valium or Ativan will eventually become tolerant to it. You can give that person a dose that would probably kill a person who has never had the drug, and it won't faze them in the least." He shifted his gaze to Kiril. "Now, I don't know how your healing tubes work, but something Mara said stuck with me."

Kiril nodded his head. "The grafts and regeneration aren't working properly on her. Makes sense." He scratched his chin. "But she'd have to have been healed *hundreds* of times…" Kiril trailed off and paled as the implication settled on him.

"You see my point." Taber crossed his arms over his chest. "Look." His focus shifted from Kiril to Khan. "She may not want me as a mate, but under your laws, it's still my responsibility to see to her safety. I can't do that if you let Davin stay near her."

"Relax, my friend." Khan laid a hand on Taber's shoulder. "Anna remembers you and would probably have my head if I went against you in this." He smiled.

"Besides, I can see no claim Davin could possibly have. Even if Gamin set up some kind of provision for her, your claim as mate will take precedence. You may be called upon to prove your claim, though. Are you prepared for that?"

"Prove my claim?"

"The Chamber of Souls. You would have to prove your claim as mate if Davin challenges you."

"Well, I guess that means I'm not prepared, because I have no idea what you're talking about." When Khan would have explained, Taber raised a hand. "Don't worry. I'll learn and be ready if it happens."

"In the meantime --" Kiril took a breath, "-- I'll deny Davin's request to stay with Akahana, saying she needs her rest and is to be disturbed by no one. That should give you time to learn what you must, Taber." He turned to Khan. "You'll back me up?"

"Always," Khan said without hesitation.

Taber wanted to rush back to Akahana -- she was very frightened. But he knew from years of hard battle that the last thing he needed to do was show his hand to this Gothe'maran warrior. If Davin smelled blood in the water, he'd move in for the kill. Instead, he let the other two men lead the way, and he took a spot leaning on the doorframe with his arms crossed over his chest.

"You're not taking her until I know without a doubt why she can't be healed." Mara was nothing if not human. No Gothe'maran -- man or woman -- could possibly be that stubborn. Taber almost smiled. Almost. Expressing amusement could be fatal at this point. Davin looked angry enough to kill, and for a Gothie, that meant the situation was likely ten times worse than it looked.

"I will take her back to Homeworld, where she

belongs, and where I may care for her as her mate wished. You cannot stop me. *Human.*"

"That *is* my mate, Davin." Kiril placed his hands on his hips and opened his stance, obviously ready to battle for his mate if necessary. "Take care how you use the word 'human.'"

Davin's jaw clenched, as did his hands. Taber had no doubt that if not for the presence of the two leaders from Military Command, he would have physically removed Akahana from her hospital bed. "I will require all necessities for my stay with the female. I will not leave her while she is here." He looked straight at Taber. "I do not want the human male to dirty her with his touch."

Kiril took a step forward, but it was Khan who spoke up.

"Two things, Davin." Khan stepped slowly toward the other Gothe'maran. Taber was surprised by the vehemence in his voice. He considered himself a fearless warrior, but he would have thought twice about facing Khan in battle at this particular point in time. "First, you will leave Earthside Medical Command immediately and not return until I personally contact you with *permission.*" Standing almost a head taller than the other man, Khan looked down at him and bared his teeth. "Second, you will learn to respect these people both in public and private. You are, currently, leader of a sizable number of warriors. Don't make me relieve you of your command."

Taber didn't dare breathe. He readied himself mentally to protect Akahana at a moment's notice, but he wasn't in the best position to get to her. Still, the tension in the air was too thick to risk igniting it by moving. Mikkarn stood between Davin and Mara with

Kiril moving beside him. Mara and Anna were between Akahana and everyone else while Khan stood nose to nose with Davin.

Gothe'maran and human alike, banding together to help a soul in need.

When this war had started, Taber was certain he'd never witness anything like this event. Now, he trusted everyone involved to help him protect a woman who might just change his life forever.

Taber was certain Davin would protest, but after a few moments spent eyeing the warriors lining the room, looking as if they were hoping he'd try something stupid, he straightened and brought the knuckles of his right hand to his forehead. "As you command, General." He spun on the ball of his foot and left the room without a backward glance.

"Yeah, I'm real sure he won't be back." Mara crossed her arms underneath her breasts. "We need to move her to a high security area, Mikkarn."

"I know." Mikkarn looked at Taber. "You'll need to stay with her, night and day."

"That's not a problem." Taber looked at Khan. "If you have time, can you find someone who can explain this Chamber of Souls thing to me?"

"I'll take that job." Anna smiled as she wrapped her arms around her husband's waist. "You'll need firsthand information." She gave Khan a sidelong look. "Which is more than someone gave me once upon a time."

"I thought we'd talked about you showing me respect in public." Though Kahn tried to look stern, Taber could see the obvious affection the very large man had for Anna. He hoped he and Akahana might look at each other like that one day.

"Yeah, well. I never was a very quick learner."

Akahana, who had been silent through most of the conversation, shook her head. "Is it always like this with all of you?"

Mara grinned. "No. It's usually worse." When Akahana opened her mouth to speak, Mara sat on the bed beside her and pressed a gentle finger to her lips. "We need to talk, my dear. I have just as many questions for you as you have for me, but you need rest. You're still not over the worst of your injuries, and I have a feeling you have a long road ahead of you. You're going to need your strength."

Taber's heart swelled with pride when Akahana's mind turned to him, along with her gaze, as if seeking his opinion. "Mara's right. But don't worry. I'm not leaving your side. I'll keep you safe."

"Safe," she said, her voice trailing off. "I'm not even sure what that means anymore."

"Let me put it this way." Taber knelt beside her bed and took her small, delicate hands in his own large, callused ones. "Once this is all over, if there is any way I can prevent it, you'll never spend another minute in a healing tube again. From a new injury, at least. Those days are over."

"We'll see." She managed a small smile. "Gamin will try his best to keep me, even from his grave. Davin won't give up as easily as you think."

"I know, Dearheart." Taber gave her his most charming smile. "But we'll all be ready for him."

Chapter Three

Akahana wasn't really sure what to think. After moving to a more secure medical suite where everyone left her to rest, it hit her that the women she'd met lived a life she had never dreamed existed. Her mother had submitted to her husband, as Akahana had submitted herself to her own husband. She was only now beginning to figure out how sheltered she'd been. It was just one more reason she found it hard to honor Gamin's memory.

She also wasn't sure she wanted to put herself in that position again. She didn't want any man to have a say in her life. And as nice as Taber was to her, that included him. But that didn't mean she couldn't enjoy her time with him.

As she fingered the delicate white petals of yet another vase of flowers, she couldn't forget their shared dream. She'd never before enjoyed sucking cock, but she had picked that out of Taber's mind and she couldn't seem to help herself. Oh, she'd tried to blame it on Taber -- he'd wanted her to perform that act, he was in control of the dream, so she had.

But deep down, she knew she'd wanted to. She had enjoyed it! His cock was magnificent! Even in the distorted images sometimes present in a shared dream, Taber gave her an impressive image of himself. His cock was as dark as the rest of him, with a thick, purple mushroom head. It had glistened with her saliva as she'd taken him into her mouth.

Thinking on it now, her hand wandered to her own cunt. Deftly, she manipulated her clit, dipping her finger to her pussy. She was surprised at how wet she found herself. Her stomach clenched as she stroked herself again. Oh, that felt *good*.

After a brief pause, she stroked herself again, this time dipping two fingers inside her pussy. She sighed and arched her back, relishing the pleasure she'd been denied for far too long. Even on the occasions she managed to block Gamin from her private thoughts, she had never truly enjoyed herself for fear her block wasn't strong enough. The one time he'd caught her…

No. She wouldn't think about that. It was over. He couldn't hurt her anymore.

And she wouldn't let anyone put her in a position where she'd ever be hurt again. She was learning about the choices she had in the "real world," and she liked what she'd found out.

I would never hurt you, Dearheart. The drowsy male voice was deep, seductive, sexy. *Your pleasure is the only thing that concerns me.*

Get out of my head! Her blocks were set. He shouldn't have been able to penetrate them, especially given his novice skills.

I can't. She could feel his confusion. He honestly didn't know why he could pick up her thoughts and feelings. *If I could, I would, because it is what you want.*

You expect me to believe that? You'd simply leave me alone because I wanted you to?

Yes. I have the greatest respect for your wishes. I always will.

I don't intend for you to always *be in my life, therefore I don't care what you respect.*

The second the thought entered her mind, she regretted it, but she wouldn't take it back. If hurting his feelings drove him away, so much the better. It would make things easier in the long run.

You won't even give me a chance to prove myself?

There's nothing to prove. I don't need any man in my life to be happy. I've had a soul's mate and found it wasn't as wonderful as everyone says. I'll pass this time.

She could almost hear him sigh in resignation. *As you wish.*

And his presence was gone. She suspected he'd become fully awake and lost the thread instead of severing it himself. Blocking him was going to be difficult, but she'd manage.

* * *

Taber couldn't sleep. Every time he did, he managed to find Akahana. And not only in his dreams. He knew without question he was seeing into her mind, and it disturbed him. Not because he could do it -- that part was actually pretty cool. It upset him because she didn't want him there, and he didn't know how to accommodate her. It was the only way he could think of to earn her trust, and the only thing he couldn't do for her.

She was the loveliest woman he'd ever seen. With her slender, delicate body, caramel-colored skin and white blonde hair, she looked like every Earth man's dream of a California girl. A fine dusting of silky white hair graced her darker skin, giving her a "glow" that was ethereal in its beauty. White eyebrows arched elegantly above her green, almond-shaped eyes.

Christ! The more he thought about her, the more he wanted her! It was useless to deny himself, because he simply was unable to pull his mind from her. The only thing that kept him from fully indulging in the most erotic fantasy of his life was his fear that his thoughts would bleed over to Akahana. He didn't know enough about his mind link with her to block his thoughts, as she seemed to be able to do.

There were times since she'd told him to leave her alone two days ago he was almost sure she was dead. It was only when his anxiety got so high he was on the verge of barging in on her physically that she would let her guard down. He wasn't sure if she was taking pity on him, or simply afraid he'd breach her privacy.

He sighed. He needed advice.

A chime at the door drew his attention away from his troubled thoughts. Scrubbing a hand over his face, he stood. Damn, he was tired. "Enter," he said. As the entry panel slid open, he was pleasantly surprised.

"Anna. Come in. Please." He stood aside and gestured inside.

"It is good to see you again, Sergeant." The smile she flashed at him warmed his heart. This woman's wounds had healed.

"You look happy. I'm glad."

"Things turned out quite differently than I expected."

"So it would seem." He offered her a seat on the sofa, and he took one in a nearby chair. "I assume you're here to tell me about the Chamber of Souls?"

"Yes. I thought you could use some enlightenment."

"Actually, that can wait." He debated all of two seconds before taking his problem to Anna. "I need some advice."

"Advice about what?"

"About this soul's mate business. Akahana acknowledges she and I are supposed to be together, but she refuses to let me get close to her." He stood and paced a few steps before turning back to Anna. "I don't know what to do."

"You do what you've been doing," she said without hesitation. "You be there for her, you see to her needs. She probably won't want you to do big things, but sometimes the little things are the ones that make the difference."

"You want me to court her." He made it a statement. No use looking too much like a dumbass.

"Exactly." She crossed her legs and sat back comfortably. "You can't make someone love you -- or even like you -- even if you are soul's mates. Sometimes, you just have to do it the hard way. The old fashioned way."

"Hell!" He plopped back down into the chair. "Running around inside someone else's head is hard. I was born and raised in Georgia. Courting, I can do. But how do I stay out of her head? She doesn't want me there, and every time I go to sleep, I either end up in her dream or pull her into mine."

"She knows you can't control that." Anna sounded more confident than he felt. "She may fuss at you for being there, but she knows. She's Gothe'maran. This is a part of everyday life for mates. Sometimes I can't stay out of Khan's dreams either. Especially if we're apart for any length of time."

"So, by forcing me to keep my distance, the problem is only getting bigger."

"Yes. Not just the need to touch mentally, but physically, as well."

"Are you sure she realizes that?" If their earlier conversation was any indication, he wasn't so sure.

"She does. At least, she'll remember. If you're right about the abuse you suspect she's suffered, she could have become adept at blocking Gamin, but your brain works differently. Don't give her a reason to really want to block you, and she'll never learn."

"Sound advice. Thanks, Anna."

"I'm just returning the favor." She smiled. "Though, as I remember it, you tried to do me a favor by keeping me out of the fighting."

He snorted. "That was sound advice, also. Had things been as bad as we thought they had been, you'd be dead now."

"That's beside the point. I got what I wanted anyway." She waved her hand in a dismissive gesture. "So, are you ready to hear about the Chamber now?"

"No." He needed to think. "Soon, but not now."

Anna stood, and Taber followed. "I imagine you have a lot on your mind. Let me know when you're ready."

"I will." He reached for her hand, and her grip was warm and firm. She had changed, but steel still ran in her veins. "Thank you, Anna. Please thank your husband for me as well. Having him on my side will give me the time I need to find out what actually happened to Akahana."

"Hum." She narrowed her eyes. "Finding the truth may be more difficult than you think. Personally, I suspect Gamin was part of a rogue cell hidden within Military Command. It's a theory Khan has been working on for some time, and this is the first information he's had to confirm his suspicions."

"Then my best bet is to get the information from Akahana."

"Yes. But you'll still need a witness." Anna sighed. "Even if Davin doesn't challenge your claim as mate to Akahana, you might still need the Chamber of Souls. When you're as focused on your mate as you must be when within the Chamber, there is nothing you can hide from the Souls of the Ancients."

Taber rolled his eyes and took Anna's arm, guiding her to the door. "I don't mean to be rude, but I really can't process this right now."

Anna laughed and rose onto her tiptoes to kiss his cheek. "Just respect her and you'll be fine. It's all about respect."

"Oh. I almost forgot. How's the little girl doing? And I heard your son wasn't killed at the Pilot after all -- how's he?"

Her soft smile turned absolutely brilliant. "They're wonderful. It's hard to believe Alex is ten, and little Doriena has recovered wonderfully. Alex will hardly let her out of his sight."

"It really is good to see you so happy, Anna. I thought about you often since I sent you off to war."

"Thank you, Sergeant. Goodnight," she said, and shut the door as she left.

Taber stretched and scratched his chest as only a man can do. It was time for sleep. If he met Akahana in a dream, so be it. He was dead tired.

* * *

Akahana knew Taber slept. She knew he dreamed of her. He reached out for her subconsciously, caressed her body sweetly, gently. She sighed and lay back on her bed. Did she dare to meet him in his dream? Did she dare submit to his touch?

Tucking her legs beneath the covers and pulling the plush blanket to her chin, she closed her eyes and snuggled into the warmth of her bed.

Yes. She'd take that dare.

* * *

"If you don't want me invading your dreams, you really should do me the same courtesy." Taber wasn't the least bit upset. Amused would be a better word to describe how he felt. Akahana couldn't help but grin.

He stood naked in front of a massive window overlooking an Earth city from high above the ground. Light from a full moon and thousands of lights from nearby buildings softly illuminated his nude form. He was an impressive male specimen. In every way.

The man was huge. Massive musculature set off rugged features, giving him a fearsome appearance. But for all that, for all the violence tightly leashed within him, he was probably the gentlest man she'd ever met. She knew this not because of any vast amount of time she'd spent with him, but because she could get inside his head and know him as well -- or better than -- he knew himself.

"I believe there is a saying on Earth. Something about becoming a part of what you cannot successfully defeat."

Taber laughed a full-bellied laugh full of all the humor and joviality she suspected was a vital part of his personality. "I think you mean 'If you can't beat 'em, join 'em.'"

"Was that not what I just said?" Akahana tried not to smile, but she giggled anyway. She reached out a hand to him. "I want to enjoy our time together, Taber. However long that turns out to be."

He took her hand without hesitation, pulling it to his smooth, heavily muscled chest. "Does that mean you're giving me a chance to prove we can be good for each other?"

"No." She answered as honestly as she could. "It means that I want to experience the pleasure denied me all my adult life. This is not about you being my mate. This is about me taking advantage of what the Universe has decided shall be my fate."

"Do you honestly look at this as nothing more than fate? Can you not see the potential for happiness like what Khan and Anna have found? Like what Mikkarn, Kiril, and Mara have found? Having a mate doesn't have to mean endless suffering."

"It doesn't mean I have to simply accept what is and hand my life over to someone else because he is my mate, either."

"I don't want control of your life, Akahana," he answered. "I have problems enough managing my own life. All I want is someone to come home to each night. Someone to hold me when I've had a bad day. Someone to love me because she wants to, not because she has to." He pulled her gently into his embrace and kissed her forehead. "I want someone to explore our mutual sexual fantasies with and I want to satisfy her in every way I possibly can."

"I want to talk about this later." She wasn't at all comfortable with what he was telling her. It was dangerously close to what she wanted herself but never dared to hope she'd ever find. "Right now, I want to get to the sexual fantasies part."

His rumbling chuckle vibrated deep within his chest and tickled her insides, leaving her excited and needy. Funny how that happened. One little expression of mirth combined with an enticingly naked man holding her closely, and her knees became weak and her cunt spasmed. She had never felt this way with Gamin, or any man before him. It was confusing.

Shaking her head slightly, she blamed it on the dream. Nothing was as it seemed when one dreamed. When she awakened, she'd feel differently.

At least, that's what she tried to convince herself. This man was special. And he'd crawled under her skin before she'd realized it.

She reached for his cock with her free hand and gave him a gentle squeeze. He sucked in a breath, and she could see the pulse at his neck accelerate as his arms closed around her and his mouth descended on hers.

She tried to devour him but he held her back, gently pulling away when she got too hungry. A couple of seconds was all it took for her to settle, and he started kissing her again. Slowly. Languidly. As if he had all the time in the world.

When he broke their kiss yet again it was because she hurried him by nipping his bottom lip and plunging her tongue deeply into his mouth. She realized the scenery had changed.

The city skyline had been replaced by a sky full of twinkling stars and a giant, full moon. She lay on her back on a bed of soft, sweet-smelling flowers with Taber resting beside her, his naked upper body covering hers. He lowered his head again, this time to her neck and the swell of one breast. That was when she realized she was also naked.

When he took a nipple into his mouth, she almost screamed. As it was, the tiniest of whimpers escaped her throat. His grunt of approval spurred her on, and she moaned again when he nipped the other nipple gently, then found her pussy and circled her clit with his fingertip.

He let his hands roamed her body, coaxing sighs and the occasional squeal from her even though she tried her best to hold back. The last thing this man needed was to know how he affected her. Even in a dream.

"I've never wanted a woman this much before. All I can think about is burying myself as deeply as I can inside your wet little cunt." He raised his head and stopped everything he was doing. "But I absolutely will not make love to you until you see it as just that. Making love. I'm not interested in meaningless sex. Not because fucking you senseless doesn't appeal to me, but because I don't want my heart broken any more than you want someone else in control of your life and body."

She blinked, then shoved him away from her and sat up. "I'm not interested in 'making love.' Love has nothing to do with sex. All I want from you is physical satisfaction. It's all I'm capable of."

He sat up slowly, and though a sexy grin spread across his face, she still felt the hurt inside him. "I think you're a highly passionate woman, Akahana. I think that you crave the love of another even more than most people because you've only known pain and heartache." His clothes appeared as if they'd been there all along -- dark pants with a white shirt that hugged him like a second skin. "When you're ready to love me like the mate you claim I am, I'll be here. However long it takes."

And he faded into the mists.

But she still felt his bruised feelings as if they were her own.

* * *

The dream slowly faded... and she woke in her bed. The covers had bunched around her as she'd thrashed about under Taber's masterful touch. She was surprised to feel a lump in her throat and tears spilling from her eyes. Rubbing a finger under one eye, she stared at the damp pad in amazement. Why did Taber feel so strongly about this? Why couldn't he be content with a little fun before moving on? She'd go back to Gothe'mar, he'd stay on Earth. She'd keep her newfound independence, and he wouldn't have to worry about adding another person to his life. She'd always been told that Earth men hated any disruption in their lives.

Then again, maybe that was just something Gamin had told her to ensure she never tried to leave their dwelling on Earth.

This was all so confusing. Everything in her life

she'd ever taken for truth had been turned upside down since she woke from healing. It was enough to plunge her into the depression she'd fought against all her life.

Wiping tears from her eyes, she got out of bed, went to the bathroom, and splashed cold water on her face. Patting herself dry with a towel, she looked at her reflection in the mirror. Her white hair had lost the luster it had once had, and there were dark circles under her eyes as well as a hint of a bruise on her left cheek. Gamin had changed her life in ways that would never truly heal.

Did she owe it to herself to let Taber prove his promises? Was he the only chance she had at a happy life?

She didn't have a chance to ponder it further, because as she stood there, a very large, solid male figure appeared behind her.

Davin!

She whirled around toward the door, but he grabbed her upper arm and pulled her to him, covering her mouth with one large hand. Fear churned inside her, leaving a bitter taste in her mouth, and she thought she might vomit. Desperate to escape, she lashed out at Davin, kicking and clawing at his shins and face.

She knew better.

When he wrapped both his hands around her throat and squeezed -- both preventing her from crying out and effectively stopping her assault -- she remembered that fighting was useless. This man, like her deceased mate, didn't care if he hurt her. He didn't care if he *killed* her. He'd come here to take her back to Gothe'mar. Dead or alive.

"Gamin promised you to me in the event he died

on this Universe-bedamned world. I get to fuck you until I'm tired of you, then I get to kill you any way I see fit." His face was inches from hers. In her collapsing sight, he was all she could see. Little dots began to invade her vision, and her lungs burned with the need for air. "I rather think I'd like to be soaked in your blood as I fuck you... as you die."

She couldn't fight against his greater strength if she couldn't breathe. She couldn't breathe unless he chose to let her. Gripping his wrists weakly, she quit struggling. Still he held on.

His eyes glistened with battle lust, and she realized he might not take her back to Gothe'mar to end her life after all. Eyes glazed in ecstasy, his pulse rate quickening -- his addiction for blood was overriding his common sense.

Two things passed through Akahana's mind before she passed out. The first was to wonder how Davin had been able to transport into a secure area of Medical Command. The second was an instinctive cry for help...

To Taber.

Chapter Four

Taber sat straight up in his bed. Sweat poured from his body. His heart raced and his chest felt like someone was squeezing it with a vise. At first he thought he was having a heart attack, but then he felt Akahana.

She was hurt, and in extreme danger.

Throwing the covers back, he took only enough time to pull on a pair of pants. Grabbing his gun and communicator, he signaled Mikkarn and Kiril and Khan on the run. "Something's happening to Akahana," he snapped.

"Impossible," Kiril responded. "That's the most secure section of Earthside Medical Command and, quite possibly, the whole planet."

"If it's impossible, then someone here has done something, and you have a traitor in your midst. Akahana is near death."

"I'm on the way." Khan was all business. He didn't question, he simply acted. It was a mark of a good commander. He had nothing to gain by asking for more information at this point, and the life of an innocent to lose if he delayed. Not for the first time, Taber was impressed with the man's ability to cut through the bullshit and dig out the important information.

Taber reached Akahana's room at the same time Mikkarn did. "Should we transport inside?" Taber asked. "Catch anyone inside by surprise?"

"If we do that, we'll have no way of knowing what we're actually getting into until we're right in the middle of it. Kiril will be here in two minutes. Our best bet will be to enter here and deal with whatever is inside until he and Khan arrive."

Mikkarn punched in his access code to Akahana's door and crouched as he covered Taber. Moving quickly inside the darkened room to the cover of an extended wall, Taber carefully peeked around it. He saw Akahana and Davin outlined in the light of the bathroom.

Akahana's body was limp, held up only by Davin's grip around her neck. Taber could no longer feel her presence. Blind fury overwhelmed him. Instead of rushing the man, he simply took aim and pulled the trigger.

Davin moved just as Taber fired, and the shot went wide. Tile from the bathroom wall exploded around Davin's head and shoulders. He drew his own weapon and fired in Taber's direction. Taber fired again, this time catching Davin in the upper thigh. The exploding tip of the bullet blew his leg apart, and Davin crumpled to the ground.

That didn't stop the Gothe'maran warrior, though. He fired several more times before pointing his destabilizer at Akahana's head. Before he could pull the trigger, Khan's voice bellowed over the noise. "You will stop, Davin!"

It was enough to make the man hesitate. Taber would have fired again, but Khan's hand on his shoulder stopped him.

Then Davin was gone. Transported back to wherever he had come from.

Taber ran to Akahana's side and would have picked her up, but Mikkarn stayed him and began examining her. Taber whirled on Khan. "You wanna tell me why you stopped me from blowing his brains all over the wall?"

Khan's outward appearance was calm and emotionless. God only knew what the man was truly feeling. "Because Davin obviously has his own agenda. I need to know what it is with regard to Akahana *and* the rogue faction."

"I thought you guys said you had all of them in custody?"

"Considering the fact that Davin was able to transport directly into a secure facility within Medical Command, I'd say there are more out there sympathetic to... something."

Mikkarn ran a handheld scanner over Akahana and shook his head. "She's got major damage to her trachea and hypoxia to her brain. She's lucky I thought to implant an anti-transport chip under her skin. Only a transporter with the proper code can move her." He looked to Kiril, who had moved in beside Taber. "She's alive. Barely. But without a healing tube, she'll die." His gaze shifted to Taber. "The problem is, I can't be sure the tube will work on her again. I can't guarantee she'll ever wake up, Taber."

"What do I have to lose?" Taber suspected he sounded as bleak as he felt.

"Nothing. Akahana's dead if we do nothing."

"Then do what you can." He watched as Mikkarn barked a set of instructions into his communicator, and he and Akahana disappeared. Taber looked at Khan again. "I'll take care of Davin."

"You can't do it alone, Taber." Kiril gripped his shoulder firmly.

"I have to. I'll find him. And when I do, he'll wish I'd killed him here."

"Taber." Khan blocked his way when he would have left. "There's another way."

"I don't *need* another way." Taber tried to shove the larger man out of the way, but Khan stood his ground. "All I need is to get my hands on the bastard, and I'll strangle the life out of him, just like he did my woman!"

"That's right." Khan grabbed him by the shoulders and shook him. "*Your woman!* Publicly claim her as your mate, and Davin will challenge. He won't be able to resist."

"How the *fuck* is that going to help?"

"Didn't Anna explain the Chamber of Souls to you?"

"No." Taber hesitated, uncertain. "She was too busy explaining the whole soul's mate thing, and I was too eager for a good night's sleep without worrying about invading Akahana's dreams. She was going to explain later."

"It is quite important that you know this, Taber."

"So I gathered. Tell me."

Kiril chuckled. "You're just like my Mara. If all humans are so demanding, I hope the Universe doesn't see fit to give me another human mate."

Taber would have growled, if he'd thought it would help. "Just spit it out."

"The Chamber of Souls is a place where the souls of our people wait to be reborn. It is said that each soul there remembers every past life he or she has lived, and in the Chamber is the only place where mates continually find each other. But they cannot express their love physically," Kiril explained.

"What do you mean, 'continually find each other'?"

Khan leaned against the windowsill overlooking a crystal lake with mountains surrounded by an aurora that reached halfway down their elevation. The atmospheric phenomenon appeared lower to the ground than previously possible -- a result of the atomic blast and the resulting radiation cloud as it spread across the country at the beginning of the war. When it was visible, being indoors was preferable. "Think about it," he said. "What are the odds that you and Akahana would find each other, halfway across the galaxy?"

"I see your point. One could go several lives without ever finding his mate." Taber took a breath. "So you're born, you die, and your soul ends up in this Chamber place where your 'soul's mate' will meet you when she dies."

"Yes. You don't find your mate in every life. And as we've recently learned with Mikkarn, Kiril, and Mara, a soul can have more than one mate. In their case, they are all three mates to each other. Knowing that, I have no trouble believing that Akahana could have more than one mate."

"Wait a minute, I'm *definitely* not any kind of mate to that Gamin character. I refuse to believe that, almost as much as I refuse to believe that he could have been her true mate. There has to be a glitch in the process somewhere because how could any higher power, or whatever determines a soul's mate, stick someone as gentle in nature as Akahana with someone as viciously mean as Gamin?" Taber paced restlessly about the room. "A person couldn't be that mean in only one lifetime. His soul would have to be rotten to the core."

Khan raised a hand to hush Taber. "You don't know that," he admonished. "None of us do. Perhaps it is something you can find out in the Chamber of Souls."

"Then take me there."

Khan shook his head. "You'd have to go into the Chamber, and that simply isn't possible at the moment."

"Well, why the hell not?"

"Because Akahana has to go in with you, and --" Khan paused before standing straight from his lazy stance and advancing on Taber. "And you have to make love to her in the Chamber."

Taber backed up a step -- not because he felt threatened by Khan, but in shock. "Never!" He pointed a finger at Khan. "I'll never subject her to that."

"You may not have much choice, my friend. It may be the only way to get Davin off your back. We can fight him -- even kill him -- but there will be others. I've been doing a little investigating, and unless I miss my guess, Gamin had a host of friends who are exactly the way he was." He turned his back and placed his hands on the windowsill. "First we must protect your Akahana, then there are more women we must find and protect. And they do not have other mates."

"Damn you all to hell," Taber muttered. "All I want is to make Akahana comfortable and let her heal."

"I know, my friend." Khan sounded troubled, and Taber was surprised at how much he'd grown to like him in such a short time. This man was nothing like the Khan the Merciless Earth had been told about. "It's just that this may be the only way to *truly* keep her safe."

"Okay. Start at the beginning." Taber desperately needed to understand what he was up against. "Why would I have to make love to Akahana in order to get inside the Chamber?"

Khan turned back to Taber. "Normally, one only enters the Chamber of Souls if he is challenging the validity of a mate claim, or if he is being challenged. Then both mates must enter, along with the challenger. The souls awaiting rebirth will wait for the couple to join, and if they are mates, they use the ensuing sexual energy. It is possible for mates to enter the Chamber to ask something of the ancient souls there, but it isn't something to enter into lightly." Khan leaned back against the sill, one hand bracing him, the other gesturing as he explained. "When a living being enters the Chamber, the souls draw energy from them. That energy can be either the person's life force, or the energy created when two mates join sexually. The only exception is during a challenge. If the couple engaging in sex are not true soul's mates, the challenger's life energy is not used, but rather the life energy of the falsely mated couple." Khan held up a hand when Taber would have questioned him. "Don't ask me why, it is simply part of life and religion as we know it. We do not question the ways of the souls, because they have given us advice and kept the peace for longer than recorded Gothe'maran history. Personally, I've always suspected that they can't stand for a couple to claim to be mates when they aren't because many of them have not been able to physically touch their mates for many lifetimes."

"It's not that I need to know why, so much that it is you've lost me. There is a difference in the 'energy' produced between mates and two people who just really like each other?"

"Oh, yes. But that's not all."

"Somehow I knew you were going to say that." Taber sighed and sat in a chair near Akahana's bed.

"Just because there is a mated coupling giving the souls energy doesn't mean any bystander inside the Chamber is safe. The stronger the sexual energy between mates, the more energy the souls want. It's like a drug. So anyone inside the Chamber is going to get sucked dry of energy if they stay too long without joining to a mate."

"God! This is so bizarre! Can you hear how bizarre you sound right now?" Taber scrubbed his face with his hand and rested his arms on his knees. "So where does Davin fit in all of this?"

"He'll challenge you if you make your status as mate to Akahana known publicly. He'll see it as a slight to Gothe'maran honor to have a human claiming his best friend's mate."

"So we get him into this Chamber of Souls, Akahana and I 'join,' and he gets zapped?"

"It might only age him, but I have a feeling that the link you and Akahana share is almost as old as the one Anna and I share. If that's the case, it will probably destroy Davin. And if that happens, no one in Gothe'mar or any other world will be able to question your right to be together. No matter how strongly they object."

"What makes you say that? Why wouldn't someone else just challenge us and bring their mate into the chamber with them?"

"Because it goes against the principles every Gothe'maran has lived in harmony with all his life." Khan paused a moment before continuing, as if unsure he should say anything further. "Before I found Anna, no one on Gothe'mar -- myself and my family included -- believed it was possible for one to find his soul's mate on another world, in another race of people. It was always assumed that a person's soul stayed within the boundaries of our home, and the souls never imparted knowledge to the contrary to the High Priest, the only one who can receive information from the souls without directly entering the Chamber. Now we know that not only is it possible to find a mate off world, it is possible to have more than one mate.

Mikkarn, Kiril, and Mara forged that path as they are all three mates to each other."

"It sounds like your whole society is being turned on its ear. How are people taking this?"

"Actually, for the most part, well. It is only the factions like the one Gamin and Davin represent that seem to have problems with it. I am not entirely sure what to do about them. If I seek them out and try to destroy them, I'm no better than they are. But I will not have my wife or children put in danger because of a closed-minded fool."

"Well, it sounds like you've got a lot to think about as future king of Gothe'mar."

"Yes. And you see why it is important for you and Akahana to enter the Chamber and prove you are truly mates."

Taber nodded. "The more evidence you have supporting the fact that true mates can be found outside the Gothe'maran race, the easier it will be to combat the ones who are against your own union."

"Partly, but it's not just me and my family I'm worried about."

Taber smiled. "I know, Khan. You're worried about every non-mated person on Gothe'mar. With space travel to and from Earth bringing humans to Gothe'mar and Gothe'marans to Earth, someone else is bound to find a mate."

"You're a wise man."

"Yeah, well. Tell me that after I convince Akahana to do this." He stood. "Assuming she heals."

"She will."

"I sure hope you're right."

"With Mikkarn and Mara as her personal physicians, she will be able to do nothing else. Neither of them would stand for it." Khan chuckled, and Taber couldn't help but smile.

"I see your point."

"Let's go to the Healing Room and see how she fares."

"Absolutely."

Taber reached out with his mind and found Akahana's essence. She was alive, but hurt very badly. Perhaps this was a good sign. Just in case, he did his best to enfold her in his love for her.

Please don't leave me, Dearheart.

Silence was his only response, but he knew she'd heard him. He'd just have to wait and see what happened. It was in the hands of the Universe now.

Chapter Five

Akahana sat straight up.

And hit her head on the healing tube lid before it had fully lifted.

"Where's Taber?" She might have been deeply asleep in healing, but his thoughts and feelings bled over into her mind. She knew everything. And they needed to talk.

"Careful, dear." Mara punched a few buttons on the control panel next to the tube before helping Akahana to her feet. Handing her a robe, she answered, "He'll be here soon. I sent him away a few hours ago to get some sleep. I called him as soon as I realized you were waking up. How do you feel?"

"My throat hurts." And her voice was gravelly, but she supposed that was a very small price to pay to be alive.

"It should pass in a day or two."

"Mara, Taber thinks he can defeat Davin by taking us into the Chamber of Souls."

"Mikkarn and Kiril said as much."

"You don't understand --"

Taber hurried into the room at that moment. "Akahana! Thank God!" He swept her up in a bear hug before setting her down and holding her at arm's length, looking her over. He gently gripped her chin and tilted her head back and from side to side, examining her neck.

"I'm fine, Taber. Really."

"Mikkarn and Mara weren't sure you'd ever regain consciousness."

"Obviously, I'm more resilient than they thought. Listen to me, Taber. You can't put yourself in the position of having Davin challenge you as my mate."

"What? How did you know?"

"You've thought of nothing else. It was impossible to shut out, especially when I had no control over my own mind because of the drugs from the tube."

Taber looked at her a moment. "Will you excuse us, Mara?"

"Sure, Taber. I'll go analyze the last set of test results and be back in a few minutes."

He waited until Mara left the room and the door was closed firmly behind her. "Okay. Khan has explained why I have to do this. Tell me why I shouldn't."

She wasted no time. Give it to him hard, with no buffer, and maybe she could convince him. "If you give him *any* excuse to be near you, he'll kill you. No matter the cost to himself."

"I've thought of that. Khan says it would go against everything your people believe."

"It does. But Gamin and Davin and the others don't operate like other Gothe'marans. They do what they feel is justified given the circumstances. In this case, kill the human at any cost. Believe me, if they thought they could get at Mara or Anna, they would. That isn't feasible. Make no mistake, even if it means his own death, Davin will kill you if he gets close enough."

"It is a valid concern, one I've wondered about." He pulled her to him again, this time enfolding her in his arms and holding her to his chest. "Khan and I have discussed this many times, and I have racked my brain to come up with something different. I have to admit, I'm stumped."

"We can't do it, Taber. We *can't*. I'm not really

sure I want to have you as my mate, but I know without a doubt I don't want Davin to kill you."

"And I don't want him to kill you either, Akahana. He almost did, you know."

"Yes. I know. I've felt the feeling many times."

Taber winced and her heart gave a painful lurch. Damn. She hadn't meant for that to sound as harsh as it came out.

"Look, Taber. I can take care of myself. I'll leave Earth, and Davin will never find me."

"You don't think so?"

Akahana could tell by the stubborn set of his mind she probably had no hope of winning this conversation, but at least she'd have her say. "No, I don't. In fact, I'll bet that if you don't publicly claim me as mate, Davin will leave us both alone."

Taber looked down at her and narrowed his eyes. "You don't really believe that." Then he became perfectly still.

Oh, man. She was in serious danger of him latching on to her and never letting go. Funny, the prospect wasn't as bad as she'd thought it was going to be. And all they'd done was share a few dreams together.

"You're trying to get him to chase you, so he'll leave me alone." His expression was shocked disbelief for a second or two before a slow smile spread across his face. "You love me, don't you?"

Akahana would have laughed if the situation had been different. "I didn't say that!" She had to regain control of the situation. If she'd ever had it. "I just don't want anyone hurt because of me."

"Dearheart, his people will come after me, anyway. We've got to stop this before it gets out of hand."

She pulled away from him and walked toward a nearby sink to splash some water on her face. "It's already out of hand. It's been out of hand for years. It's just now getting the attention of people in high places."

"How many women do these bastards have? We need to help as many of them as we can before we do anything else."

Akahana blinked several times. "I -- I don't know. I never saw other women. Not since I was mated to Gamin, anyway. I got the impression they were not mated because they frequently…" She trailed off, unable to finish because she was ashamed to admit what had happened.

"Did he let them touch you to punish you or because they wanted to?"

She blinked away tears that tried to leak from her eyes and turned her back to him. "A little of both, I think. Sometimes I never could figure out what I'd done to warrant punishment. He always said it was punishment, though."

"I'm beginning to see our cultures are alike in ways I wish they weren't," Taber muttered. "I'll leave it up to you, then. If you don't want to enter this Chamber thing, I won't ask you again. It's only for your safety I'd even ask in the first place."

"What about your safety? If I don't go into the Chamber, Davin and his people will hunt you down and kill you." She shivered at the thought of that. She didn't want to care. *Shouldn't* care. Taber was nothing to her, only in her life a short time and then gone. Could she live with that?

Her chest was tight and her breathing rapid. Her pulse pounded in her ears, and tears finally overflowed and spilled onto her cheeks.

"Relax, Dearheart. Breathe slowly and deeply."

Taber enfolded her in his strong arms and rested his chin on her head. "I'm with you," he whispered. "I'll always be with you."

"I don't want this, Taber." She sobbed quietly, not even bothering to wipe her tears. "I just want to live my life my way. I don't want to have to answer to anyone."

"No one said you had to, Akahana." He turned her to face him. "I don't want to control you. I just want to love you, and for you to love me in return. The rest is up to you. Do what you want with your life. I'll never stand in your way." He closed his eyes and took a breath. "I just want you to allow me to be a part of it."

"I'm so confused, Taber." She lifted a tentative hand to touch his face, to trace the line of his jaw and cheekbones. "Gamin's death freed me from his prison, and now I live in one of my own making. I'm afraid of losing my freedom, and I can feel the only happiness that will ever matter to me slipping away. If that happens, the whole point of freedom is lost. I don't know what to do."

"Listen to your heart, Akahana. This is an instance where your heart will not lead you wrong."

"It did with Gamin."

Taber sighed. "Did you feel this pull toward him that I know you feel toward me?"

"No. He frightened me from the moment I met him. I didn't have a sexual attraction toward him. I *never* had a sexual attraction toward him."

"What about his mind? Could you enter it at will like you seem to be able to do with me?"

"Not at first and never very easily." She closed her eyes and inhaled. By the Universe! He smelled good! "I never wanted to. I was too busy trying to keep him out of my mind to try to get into his. He was usually the one who initiated contact."

"Is there any possibility Gamin could have been telepathic? Could he have communicated with people other than you?"

Akahana started to answer in the negative. Who had ever heard of such a thing? Then she stopped.

"What is it?" Taber gently tilted her face to look at him. "What are you remembering?"

She shook her head, the thread of thought gone. "Nothing. That question triggered a memory, but it's gone now. I think it must have been one of the times I was nearly unconscious. I can't remember any more." She couldn't *think* when he stroked her back so tenderly. And *why* did he have to smell so good? It was a blend of clean, male sweat and soap. She looked up at him, losing herself in him against her better judgment.

"Don't try right now." Taber kissed her forehead. "You still need rest, and I don't want to be the cause of your rest being disturbed."

"Taber." She closed her eyes and inhaled deeply. "I never felt like this with Gamin. All I can think about right now is seeing if you taste as good as you smell."

Taber inhaled sharply, and his hold on her tightened slightly. She could feel the lust stirring inside him combined with something else. *Hope. Love. Need.* All combined to create an intoxicating elixir her mind could become addicted to. This was something she'd never felt from Gamin. His lust had surely swamped her many times, but he'd never loved her. He'd never *needed* her.

It had all been about control. This was *nothing* like her experience with Gamin. This, she could grow to like. "I want to kiss you, Taber."

He croaked a short laugh. "Like I'm going to object."

"But all I want to do is kiss you. Nothing else."

"At this point, Dearheart, I'll take whatever you want to give me."

"Then kiss me, too."

"Oh, God." Taber groaned the expletive as his lips descended to hers. She wanted to utter her own, but all she could do was whimper. His lips touched hers tentatively, then more firmly but still with exquisite gentleness. At first only their lips slid against each other, but Akahana instinctively darted her tongue out and into Taber's mouth.

The need and lust coming from Taber fueled her own desires, and in that instant she knew Gamin could not have been her mate. At least, not as she had always been taught to believe. She had never felt this building and feeding of her own emotions off the thoughts and feelings of another.

It felt like lightning sparked between them. She felt like she'd been punched in the chest, but at the same time, she couldn't get enough. Her insides heated, yet chills raised the fine hair on her body and puckered her nipples to stabbing peaks. She ached to have Taber take one of those nipples between the lips that were so expertly playing across her own.

She clung to him, tangled her fingers in his shirt before trailing one hand up his neck to the back of his head. The skin there was slick and slightly damp with sweat, and she found she rather liked the feel of it on her fingertips.

He held her closely, yet never doing anything more than kissing her, just as she'd requested. His body was hard next to hers, and she felt his cock harden and press tightly against her abdomen.

Everything combined to leave her breathless and wanting. Her breasts felt heavy and tender, her pussy tingly and damp. For the first time she could ever remember, she not only wanted sex, she needed it. Craved it. There was no fear or doubt. There was only this overwhelming sense of belonging.

Akahana wrapped both arms around Taber's neck and shifted her body as close to him as she could get, even hooking a leg around his hip to better align him to her.

Taber's hands dropped to her hips, and he gripped her flesh there, but still did no more than kiss her. But somehow it was exactly what she needed.

She was just about to suggest they explore each other a little more when the door opened behind them and someone cleared her throat. Mara had returned.

Embarrassed, Akahana set her leg down and tried to pull away, but Taber held her hip with one hand and wrapped his other arm around her back. He chuckled as he kissed the top of her head. "It's okay. Relax, Dearheart."

"I'm glad to see you finally accepting Taber, Akahana," Mara said. When Akahana peeked over Taber's shoulder, the other woman smiled warmly at her. "I think his connection to you saved your life. Your brain waves were decidedly more active, and you seemed to have a stronger will to live than before."

"We were just..." She trailed off, not knowing how to explain her current situation to Mara, but the other woman waved her off.

"I know exactly what you were 'just' and as your doctor, I strongly approve. I think you should 'just' more often."

For the first time in many, many years, Akahana giggled. Joy bubbled up inside her, and she buried her face in Taber's shoulder and laughed until tears streamed down her face. Life was suddenly worth living, and she'd be damned if she'd give into Gamin's will even after his death. Not anymore.

This was her life.

And she was taking it back.

* * *

Taber couldn't believe this was happening. Akahana insisted he stay with her that night, and now he lay naked in her bed waiting for her to join him. He wasn't sure he'd been this nervous when he was a virgin. He wanted tonight to be perfect, special. God! He wanted her so fucking *badly*! How could it be possible to need someone so badly?

And it wasn't just her body he wanted. Oh, he wanted to bury his cock in her cunt or ass or mouth -- wherever he could get to first -- but it was more than that. He wanted her heart as well. Not to control her, but because he'd earned her love and trust. He had to know she would always be with him.

When she emerged from the bathroom, she was wrapped in a bathrobe. The abundance of terrycloth should have been anything but sexy, but Taber couldn't stop wondering what was underneath.

It wasn't long before he found out.

She smiled shyly at him as she untied the belt and let the heavy robe slide from her arms and pool at her feet. She was the most exquisite woman Taber had ever seen. Her skin, a creamy caramel, made her white hair stand out erotically. Her eyebrows arched delicately over green, almond shaped eyes, and her pubic hair -- neatly trimmed -- framed her sex in the most tantalizing way. Her breasts were perfectly proportioned to her body, rounded and high, with dark pink nipples puckered tightly in her desire.

She took a step forward. "I'd be lying if I said I wasn't nervous about this, Taber."

"I know you're nervous." He smiled and reached a hand to her. "But I also know you're just as excited as I am, and that you've let go of your doubts about me." She reached for him, and he gently guided her onto the bed, her hair framing her face as it fanned out on the pillow. "I promise --" he propped himself up on one elbow to look down at her, "-- not to make you regret that decision."

"You won't, Taber." Akahana reached for him as she spoke and directed his lips to hers. "It's simply not in you."

Her lips were silky and moist as they met his. He groaned and covered her upper body with his own, kissing and licking at her lips. Her tongue played over his, and her sighs and whimpers with every stroke into her mouth were glorious music.

He skimmed the side of her breast with one hand, tracing her generous curves and savoring every inch of her sweet body. Her hand slid up his arm and around his neck, and she pulled him closer. Arching her back, she purred her enjoyment.

Taber cupped one breast in his hand, testing its weight and brushing a nipple with his thumb. He watched, fascinated, as the sensitive flesh puckered even tighter with his touch.

Unable to resist a moment longer, he dipped his head to her chest and sucked the nipple into his mouth. Her little squeal, along with the need pouring from her mind, encouraged him as nothing else could. She was definitely enjoying herself.

* * *

There was no pain. There was no fear.

Only pleasure existed in her world, a pleasure he

was a part of.

Akahana wasn't sure exactly what she expected at this moment, but the extraordinary amount of pleasure and satisfaction she was experiencing never entered her mind. It was just shy of obsessive, her need. Sure, she could deny herself -- walk away and never look back -- but why do that when everything he wanted centered around her pleasure? She could find no reason not to enjoy herself.

Besides, touching his skin was a pleasure unto itself. His arms were heavily muscled, and they alternately flexed and relaxed as they wrapped lovingly around her. Never in her life had she felt so important, so cherished.

She pulled at his hip, encouraging him to cover her more fully. When he moved over her, she slid her legs around him, settling him between her thighs. His already full erection brushed enticingly against her clit, rubbing, stimulating.

He rocked back and forth, simulating the act of sex, rubbing her clit with every stroke. She hooked her heels around the backs of his legs, resting her feet on his calves. She arched her back and tilted her pelvis, seeking his cock. As wonderful as she felt, she knew there was more.

She wanted more.

Their sighs and groans were the only sounds they made -- no speech was necessary. Their bodies spoke for them, and their minds twined, mixing their wants and needs until it was impossible to separate her thoughts from his.

With one thrust of his hips, and one tilt of her pelvis, Taber slid inside Akahana and both their worlds ignited. Akahana saw stars on the edge of her vision as her first orgasm overtook her and knew that

Taber felt much the same, but he held himself back. She got light-headed for a few moments as waves of glorious pleasure coursed through her, until only a gentle tingling in her pussy remained.

"By the Universe." Nothing she'd ever experienced even came close to this. Taber's body was tense above her with the need for release, and the lust reflected in his eyes took her breath. "What is this?"

Taber's laugh was tense. "You tell me. I don't know anything about this soul's mate thing."

"Apparently neither do I."

"Later." Sweat shone on Taber's face and head. "I want more."

Akahana laughed as she slid her arms around Taber's hips and grabbed his buttocks, pulling him to her. "Me, too. Love me, Taber. Show me how much you want my body."

"Not just your body, Dearheart." He bent his head to kiss the tip of her nose. "I want all of you. You are the strongest woman I've ever met, and I want to know that woman better."

"I'm not that strong." She wrapped her legs firmly around his waist, resting her heels on his ass. "You're that gentle. You're a very special man, Taber. Even if you weren't my mate, I'd be glad to have known you." She thrust her pelvis at him, causing him to groan. "Now, fuck me before I decide I don't want you for my mate."

Her teasing smile turned into a gasp as he thrust into her. "Well, I can't have that, now can I?"

Taber shifted his position, coming up onto his knees. Prying her ankles apart, he placed her feet on his shoulders. She immediately hooked her feet around his neck and used the leverage to thrust herself at him again. Taber wrapped his hands around her thighs to find his own leverage, and it wasn't long before they had their rhythm perfect.

Taber slammed into her, but no harder than she slammed herself into him. Akahana was as much the aggressor as he was, and she had trouble believing this was actually *her* acting this way. And it felt so damned *good*! Nothing in her experience could have prepared her for this. She felt so out of control, and knew that Taber had no more control over his feelings than she did. Somehow, knowing that made all the difference.

"Christ!" Taber ground out between clenched teeth. "I can't hold out much longer, Akahana. Come with me! Now!"

All she could do was hold on. His grip on her legs should have been bruising, but it fit the moment. As if he sensed her near discomfort, his grip eased and she felt him trying to hold back. Sweat slid down his skin because of his efforts, both at holding himself in check, and from the physical exertion. She could see his jaw working as he ground his teeth together.

"Don't hold back, my love. As your mate, my body is yours to take."

"No!" She could feel him try to hold off his impending orgasm, but he couldn't. "I will not use your body for my pleasure only."

"My pleasure is ensured, Taber. Come inside me. *That* would give me more pleasure than you can possibly imagine." And she meant it with all her heart.

For the briefest of moments, she wasn't sure Taber would take her at her word. But a brief moment was all it was. Once he was sure she meant what she said, he didn't try to rein in his passion. Adjusting his grip on her thighs, Taber threw his head back as he pounded into her pussy and roared his release. Arching his back in an effort to get inside her just a little deeper, he emptied himself into her grasping, pulsing cunt. Akahana's own release followed seconds after Taber's, and she gasped his name breathlessly as her body seized from her orgasm.

When it was done, when they both lay in each other's arms sated and very satisfied, Akahana turned to Taber and laid a gentle hand on his cheek. "I want to enter the Chamber with you, Taber. If our love can stop this nightmare I've been living, and your friends can keep you safe from Davin during this, I'd be a fool not to take that opportunity."

"You're still looking out for me."

"Always. I know you can handle yourself." She pushed him over and lay with her upper body covering his. "But I can't imagine losing you." She smiled at him as she drew lazy circles on his chest with a finger. "It's funny. I always promised myself if I was ever able to get away from Gamin, I'd never again let a man have any influence over me." She dipped her head to kiss the line of his jaw. "Now, I only feel fortunate to have finally found my true mate."

If he thought anything about the comment, he didn't say anything. Which was probably a good thing. Akahana wasn't sure she could explain. But she had no doubt in her mind that Gamin was not her true soul's mate. How he had managed to be able to get inside her head and project his thoughts to her, she couldn't even begin to imagine, but somehow he had. What she could communicate with Taber went deeper than simple thought. It was feelings, understanding of those feelings, and a blessed union that her soul rejoiced in.

She crawled over Taber's body, straddling his hips. His jaw clenched as he stared at her breasts. His hands rested lightly on her hips.

"You are such a giving lover, Taber. You can't

imagine how big a difference that makes to me." She reached between her legs to guide his semi-erect cock inside her pussy. "I never imagined pleasure such as this existed."

"You're worth anything I've given you and more, Dearheart. And any man who would say otherwise is either a damned fool, or the biggest liar in the universe."

She moved slowly, rotating her hips in little circles, enjoying the slowness and deliberateness of her play. Taber didn't hurry her, or encourage her to move faster. He simply rubbed her legs in feather light touches from hip to knee. Akahana used her link with him to gauge his reactions, and when she sensed he was close to coming, she sped up her motions slightly.

It wasn't long before her own orgasm started building. As Taber neared his release, Akahana pushed hers back so she could come with him, take the fall together. She opened herself up to him completely. He could feel her pleasure and her growing love for him.

When he gripped her hips harder and thrust against her firmly twice, her body tensed with her own release. She shouted once and collapsed onto Taber's chest, wrapping her arms around him as best she could. It was only a moment before she fell asleep.

Sated, satisfied...

And happy.

Chapter Six

On the trip to Gothe'mar, Taber felt the nervousness he always associated with a coming battle. He paced the small cabin he and Akahana shared and finally left her to jog around the deck when the pent-up energy became too much. She had been a constant presence in his mind. Though she didn't say anything, sensing he needed quiet, her presence, both physical and mental, comforted him as much as anything could.

When they reached the spaceport orbiting the planet, Taber was a bundle of energy. The thought of the two-hour ride planetside in one of those ridiculously small shuttles was intolerable.

"Can't we use a transporter?" He sounded whiny. He was *not* whiny.

"I'm sorry, my friend." Taber could tell Khan was trying valiantly not to laugh at him. "Space around Gothe'mar is too crowded to risk it. You could end up in a different location altogether, or with another man's legs."

"Or as a woman." Mikkarn's attempt at a joke was *not* amusing, and Taber gave him a scathing look. It didn't faze the other man in the least.

"If I didn't need you on the planet, I'd have to kill you just for the tension release."

Mikkarn shrugged. "Mara might have something to say about that."

Kiril snorted. "Yeah, like 'don't look at me, you deserved it.'"

Taber barked a laugh before he could stop himself. These three men, and their women, had come to mean a great deal to him. They had proven themselves invaluable in protecting Akahana, and in making things easier for him to handle in a culture and society he was unfamiliar with. He felt like he needed to say something, but he didn't know what words to use.

Khan simply grasped his shoulder and looked at him as if he were a commanding officer sending a soldier into battle. "All will be well. See to your mate. The priest and I will deal with Davin." His softly spoken words gave Taber encouragement. Taking care of Akahana was his job, his part in the mission. Others would take care of the rest. As when he was in the field, he had to place his trust in the ability of other soldiers, and he could not think of a better soldier than Kahn the Merciless. It made the wait getting to the planet tolerable.

Akahana remained silent, and, though for the most part her mind was closed to him, she was never far from his side. Always close enough to touch if he wished. He could feel her fear of what was to come, but it was him she was worried about.

When they disembarked, Kahn led them toward the Temple Beyond -- a great housing complex where the Chamber of Souls was located. Taber reached to his left, and he took Akahana's hand without looking in her direction. Her grip was cool and firm. He knew there would be no emotion showing in her face, no hint of what she was really feeling.

She was Gothe'maran. Part of a warrior race. The ideal companion in battle.

As he looked at her then, she looked back. *No fear, my love. Only desire. And love.*

Her words were a mere shadow in his mind, and he wasn't sure he'd actually heard them, but she was right. If Khan was right, and there was no reason to believe he was wrong, there could be no room for fear or doubt.

"Davin should already be inside the temple," Khan said softly. "Should he challenge, as is expected, the arrangement is for an invisi-cell to confine him while inside the Chamber. The priest will set the timer as you enter so you and Akahana will have a chance to get deep inside the Chamber. Davin will only have a few seconds before the cell activates and stops him immediately. He will only be able to go a few steps before that happens. That should give you time to prepare."

"Prepare." Taber grunted. "How *does* one prepare for this?"

Khan smiled. "You don't. Just do what the souls tell you. They will not harm you if you are true mates. It is Davin who should be worried."

The structure was the most imposing Taber had ever seen. Great pillars dominated the entrance, and there was a reverence about the place Taber had never before witnessed. This place was at the heart of this people's most sacred beliefs. The imposing superstructure looked like it was encased in gold and diamonds as the sun's light reflected from it, creating elegant shadows and sparkling reflections on the pool in front of it. Above all, there was an air of anticipation. If Taber didn't know better, he'd swear the temple itself expected him.

Inside, a thin, aging priest dressed from head to toe in shimmering gold robes met them in front of an ornate silver door that should have been gaudy. Instead it was the most beautiful piece of craftsmanship Taber had ever seen. It opened to reveal an immense Chamber surrounded by windows and shrouded in mists.

Khan frowned. "The Chamber within has always been dark. Has something changed?"

"The souls are showing their disgust for the human bastard." Davin's voice dripped contempt as he turned to address Akahana. "Gamin had plans for you. As his mate, it is your *duty* to honor him in death as he wished."

"Gamin was not my mate, Davin. I'm not sure how he managed to get inside my head, but having found my true soul's mate, and feeling what a true mate's link is like, it is simply not possible that the links could be that different."

"You *lie*!" Davin all but exploded, and Taber stepped between the warrior and Akahana. "Gamin cared for you, instructed you how the wife of a Gothe'maran warrior should be, and gave you a life of luxury, and you dare repay his kindness with lies against him?"

"I only tell you the truth as I perceive it. Taber is my mate. There is no question."

"But there is." Davin sneered. "I challenge your Claim of Mates, and further, I challenge your claim that Gamin was not your mate." He turned to the priest. "Once she is proven to be dishonorable, I demand you turn her care over to me so that she can live as her mate intended and set forth in a private Document of Command."

"Gamin put in his *will* how he wanted Akahana cared for?" Taber was so shocked at Gamin's attempt to control Akahana -- even from the grave -- that he spoke before he could stop himself.

The priest frowned at him before he turned to Khan, clearly not knowing what to do. When the other man didn't offer any guidance, the priest faced Akahana.

"What is your wish, Ma'am?"

"Her wishes are not the issue!" Davin was clearly

about to lose control of his anger. Taber wasn't at all sure this was going to work without a fight. Looking at Khan, Mikkarn, and Kiril, he could tell they had drawn the same conclusion. "She is to return to her home, here on Gothe'mar. It was the wish of her mate!"

"She is a free person, my son," the priest said reasonably. "She can make her life choices regardless of what her mate wants or wanted."

"It's okay." Akahana's softly spoken words cut through the tension easily. "If he's right, and I'm lying about Taber or Gamin, then I'll go wherever he wishes." She looked at Davin, squarely in the eye, crossing her arms under her breasts. "But if I'm right, and he manages to leave the Chamber of Souls alive, he and the rest of Gamin's men must leave me, Taber, and our children alone as long as our souls exist."

Davin smiled viciously. "You will have no children."

She uncrossed her arms and took a swift, sure step forward, her head held high, a look of determination on her face. "Then we have something in common."

Taber felt a swelling of pride. When he'd found this woman, there was no way she would have stood her ground with Davin. The impression he'd gotten from her then had been that of a whipped dog. She had resigned herself to a life of no choices and constant pain.

Now she was taking back control of her life.

The priest stepped to Davin and readied a small device that would set the invisi-cell once he was inside the Chamber. Davin frowned at the priest. "I must protest again. This is an unnecessary waste of time and a slight to my honor."

"Not from what I've seen. General Khan has

insisted on this security measure and I agree with him. There will be no violence in this temple I can prevent." Davin merely grunted and allowed the device to be set.

"The two of you should disrobe and enter the Chamber of Souls while I finish this. Once it is set, Davin will have thirty seconds before the timer activates, and he will not be able to move beyond a two-foot diameter until it's powered down."

Taber and Akahana did as requested and stepped to the Chamber entrance. Before they entered, Taber looked at Akahana. She was beautiful. Confident, just shy of stubborn in her stance. When she looked at him, his breath caught. He had been worried about being too keyed up to "perform," but it didn't look like that was going to be a problem, either. One glance from her, and he was randy as a goat.

Together, the couple stepped inside.

The mist was like a murky, amber fog. Taber could feel the mist clinging to his skin and the air was damp when he inhaled. After a second or two, his skin started to tingle, and he grasped Akahana's hand more firmly.

"It's starting," she whispered.

They both turned toward the Chamber door. Davin made it four steps inside before the invisi-cell activated. The rolling autobot generating the cell shadowed Davin's movements from a foot away. Once the cell was activated, his movement around the room was severely limited. With his presence inside the Chamber, the power struggle began.

The tingling on Taber's skin soon became an itching-burning sensation, and he realized he'd better get to "joining" with Akahana as soon as possible. But Akahana had frozen where she was, listening to something only she could hear.

Then they were alone. The mists closed in on them, blocking out everything around them until all they could see was each other.

"What's happening? What do you hear?" Taber's battle senses were screaming at him.

"They're trying to protect us." Her whisper was a mere breath, as if any sudden noise might break whatever spell was being woven.

"Protect us from what?" Taber backed them across the room in what he thought was the direction of the entrance. When his back hit something solid, he used his hands to feel on either side of him until he found the cool silver of the door.

"Get us *away* from the door, Taber," she whispered. "Davin was just inside the entrance."

"We need to get out of here."

"Not with Davin so close. *Now get us away from the door!*" Even as she whispered, she sounded -- and felt -- almost frantic. A moment later, all hell broke loose.

A flash of white-hot light knocked Taber to the floor, followed by a deafening explosion. Somehow, he managed to wrap his arm around Akahana and pull her underneath him, but he knew she'd taken as much of the blast as he had. His skin burned -- was still burning -- and he crawled away from the heat source with Akahana beneath him, forcing her along with his body between her and the immediate danger.

A second explosion rocked the temple, then a third and a fourth.

"We've got to get out of here!" Taber shouted to be heard over the roaring, the wind from the blast blistering his bare skin. Damn everyone for making both of them go in unprotected!

"We can't." Akahana had turned to her back and

wrapped her arms around his neck. "It's in the hands of our ancestors now."

"You've *got* to be kidding." Placing his life in the hands of fellow soldiers as he did his part in the mission was one thing -- to cower in the corner while they bailed his ass out of trouble was something else.

"There's nothing else we can do. I don't know how, but Davin managed to circumvent not only the security of the priesthood, but that of the souls in the Temple, as well."

"Khan said the souls within this place feed off of sexual energy," Taber said, "that they normally demand sexual energy from mates or take it from any life force that enters."

"Yes. That's correct," Akahana confirmed.

"So why haven't they sucked all our energy away?"

At one end of the Chamber, where smaller explosions still rocked the temple, an eerie green light started to grow and burn, and the waves of tremendous heat coming out of the light warped the wall behind it.

"Move deeper into the Chamber, Akahana!" Taber stood and dragged Akahana to her feet, running into the mist as hard as he could.

Help us!

The voices speaking as one in Taber's head broke his concentration, and he almost tripped as he ran.

We cannot deflect the energy…

The voices faded in his mind, and the mist lessened slightly. An almost overwhelming sadness filled Taber, and he instinctively reached out mentally to Akahana. The sadness was not hers, but she felt it, as well. Absorbing the emotion rather than fighting against it, she seemed to better understand its cause.

"What is it? What do I need to do?" Taber knew Akahana had the answers, but his link to her was too new for him to pick it out of her mind. In his indecision, she became the aggressor, the leader. She pulled him deeper into the Chamber, and he followed her willingly, eagerly. He knew his life couldn't be in any better hands.

When she stopped, she pulled him to her, pressing her body against his. A jolt of lust surged through him as his adrenaline found an outlet, but he gave it no more than a passing thought.

"We're probably going to die, Taber." Well, she didn't believe in pulling any punches. "Whatever Davin used to set off those explosions was designed to produce Pedderon radiation."

"What does that mean?"

"Simply being in possession of elements used in the production of such radiation is the only crime which *requires* death."

"Sounds extreme."

"Because it is the only thing a living being can do to destroy a soul. That is the only purpose of Pedderon radiation." As she explained, Akahana wrapped the fingers of one hand around Taber's semi-erect cock and squeezed gently. "Our only hope is to feed as much energy as we can to the souls within this Chamber to sustain them until the priests outside can rid themselves of the blaze."

Taber's cock jumped at her attention, rapidly hardening as she stroked him with firm, aggressive touches. "Sexual energy." His murmur was lost as he buried his face in her neck. "This is insane."

"Open your mind, Taber." Akahana's mouth was millimeters from his ear, her breath warm and enticing. Shivers slid down his body from his ear straight to his dick, and it was only a matter of seconds before he had the best hard-on in the history of the world. "Our lust feeds their lust and vice versa. Let them lead us, because they know what they need to overcome such a catastrophe."

His mind was beginning to cloud with his own lust, but he managed to process what she said. And that was hard when she took his earlobe between her lips and sucked, none too gently. He could feel what she was talking about. Not only her sexual need combined with his own, but the needs of the whole collective of souls, as well. They reached out for Akahana and him, a few of them expressing love for their mates in a void filled with endless sexual frustration.

Taber's arms tightened around Akahana against his will. He needed to pull her lush body more firmly against his. Her hand, trapped between them, gripped his cock, and he growled his appreciation. When she stuck her tongue in his ear, he was ready for a more active participation.

With a roar, Taber pushed Akahana away from him and gripped her waist. Lifting her in the air, he dove for her pussy with his face. She must have caught the image in his mind, because she gripped his wrists and swung her legs over his shoulders. Within a couple of steps, he had her braced against the wall of the Chamber, and he went to work.

Darting his tongue to her pussy, he licked her folds apart and found her clit. Turning his head from side to side, he wedged his head between her legs, allowing for a firmer hold on her cunt.

Her sighs turned to whimpers, then to groans and finally screams when his tongue parted her folds again and found her drenched opening. Akahana ground her pelvis into his face, bringing his mouth into impossibly tighter contact. Breathing was difficult, but at this point, Taber really didn't care.

Her smell was intoxicating, her screams of pleasure more fulfilling than he had ever thought possible. Loving a woman had never given him such pleasure or satisfaction. She was all that mattered in his world.

And the souls came to life. *Now you understand the meaning of soul's mate, my brother and sister.*

Power surged around them as they loved. In one gust of wind with the force of a thousand hurricanes, the green glow was forced back and contained. In the sudden quiet within the Chamber, Taber heard the distinct hum of an autobot being activated. One glance to his left, and he saw Davin within the invisi-cell, pounding his fists against the barrier.

Knowing the danger was contained, Taber didn't worry about Davin another second. In one swift move, he lifted Akahana once again and lowered her down his body until his cock was positioned at her slick entrance.

"I don't know the words, but I'm telling you now. I'm claiming you as my mate in the eyes of your people."

"Those are the only words you need." Her smile was nothing short of satisfied. Given her protests before, Taber was a little surprised.

"You don't mind then?"

"No." She caressed his cheek as she wiggled closer to him, impaling herself on the head of his cock. "They're right. I know now what it truly means to have a soul's mate. How Gamin managed to deceive me, I don't know. But he was never my mate."

Taber thrust upward, the rest of his cock filling

her. She was so *tight!* He wanted to thrust inside her so wildly that they both went up in flames as quickly as possible, but making this last seemed more important.

She pushed herself upright, her back and shoulders fully against the slick glasslike substance of the wall. Gripping him with her legs, she used her hands to push her breasts together and squeeze. That about did it for Taber. Coming had never seemed more important to him than it did at that moment. Against his will, she pushed his pace and quickened their tempo.

Sweat began to form on both their bodies and Akahana slid easily up and down the wall as Taber fucked her. Although the only voices he heard seemed to be coming either from Akahana or the voices inside his head, he felt as if people surrounded them.

Watching them.

Mimicking their actions.

The emotion was almost overwhelming. All around him, there were souls who wanted desperately to make love to each other, but had no physical bodies. He could feel the satisfaction they gained from being allowed to share in this moment.

Dipping his head to Akahana's chest, Taber sucked a nipple into his mouth as she kneaded her breasts and offered them to him for his pleasure. She gasped and pulled him to her with one hand. "By the Universe! Taber, I need to come."

He grunted and released her breast with a pop. Gripping her hips more firmly, he thrust in earnest. Their rhythm increased, as did the force with which Taber fucked Akahana. She gripped his shoulders and looked into his eyes, the lust in her matching his own.

"That's it, Taber. Fuck me harder. Make me come." She snarled at him, her face almost savage in its intensity. Sweat made her skin shine, and tiny droplets clung to the tips of her eyelashes, scattering with each of his upward thrusts. Her hair clung to her face and shoulders, and her cheeks were red with heat and passion.

Finally, when he sensed she wanted control, he shifted the slightest bit closer to her. She braced her hands on his shoulders as she shifted higher up on his hips, riding him at her own pace.

She bounced and ground her pussy onto his cock so he penetrated her as deeply as possible. She let out a bloodcurdling scream as Taber felt her cunt spasm around his cock and gave himself over to her passion. His own yell of satisfaction came mere moments later when he emptied himself into her. His juices, combined with her own, overflowed and trickled down his balls to either drip to the floor or down his leg, mixing with the sweat from both their bodies.

The energy surrounding them was like nothing Taber had ever felt. The mist and fog had long since disappeared, and the center of the Chamber radiated with a glowing amber light, almost white in its intensity.

Taber knew he'd been injured in the initial blast, but any pain he felt was rapidly fading as the light from the Chamber bathed their naked bodies in a cool, cleansing breeze.

Akahana's breathing was as rapid as his own. Her eyes were closed, but a smile lingered on her lips. When she opened her eyes, all he saw was her love shining back at him. Neither said anything as the light around them faded to a soft amber glow.

It wasn't long before the Chamber door burst open and Khan, Mikkarn, and Kiril entered, the priest close after them yelling, "Don't enter the Chamber while you have no mate at your side!"

"What the fuck happened?" Kiril swept the area with his eyes before moving toward them. "There were horrible explosions, and it felt like the whole place was coming down."

"Davin set off some kind of device containing a banned radiation," Taber said. "I thought we were goners."

"By the Universe," the priest murmured from across the room. The invisi-cell was intact, but nothing remained of Davin. The priest, however, wasn't looking at the cell. He was looking toward the center of the Chamber at the amber light.

The image of Gamin, sad and regretful, faced them.

You are allowed to enter this Chamber because the Others have allowed it for one purpose. I am being expelled from them, never to be born again.

Taber glanced at Akahana. She stood tall and proud as she faced the image of the one who had caused her so much pain and had almost taken away any chance she had of happiness.

Akahana, I deceived you and all our people when I claimed you as mate. I am one of only a handful of true telepaths among our people, and I used this power so I might gain status by claiming a mate.

She interrupted him at this point. "But why me? Why did it have to be me?"

Gamin looked at his feet. *Because I'm not a particularly strong telepath, and for some reason, lifetime after lifetime, I seek you out. We are not mates, but you always want a mate so badly you are receptive to my thought patterns. This is why I am being expelled. I don't have the morals to keep my gift, and since it cannot be passed to another, nor taken from me, it has been decided that you should never have to live a life like the one I held you in this time ever again.*

"Which brings me to my other question." The confidence this woman held warmed Taber's heart. "Why did you treat me like this? What was it inside you that made you hold me prisoner and torture me every single day of my life?"

Because you were everything good and decent that I could never be. I thought if I hurt you badly enough, you'd become as evil as I had. But you didn't. You never let yourself hate the way I did. I doubt it is in you to hate someone that much. He paused a moment. *I won't ask for your forgiveness because I don't deserve it. Just know that you're loved by this man whose heart you've claimed, and that he is your true soul's mate.*

Surprisingly, she smiled and looked at Taber. "I already knew that." Turning back to Gamin, she said, "May the Universe grant you the peace the Chamber of Souls in the Temple Beyond could not."

Closing his eyes, Gamin's image flickered, then vanished.

You have learned your lessons well, brother and sister, the voice that was many voices praised them. *We thank you for sharing your passion with us. Go in peace and love.*

"We must go now." The priest was already urging them toward the door.

Once outside, Akahana wrapped her arms around Taber's chest and snuggled against him. "I love you, Taber. Take me home."

"Gladly, Dearheart. Does it matter to you if we live here or on Earth?"

"You will always have a place among us, Taber." Khan extended an arm toward him, which Taber gladly took.

Kissing the top of Akahana's head, he looked to

her. "Your life here has been nothing but grief. If the memories are too much, we can get a fresh start on Earth."

"As long as you're with me, no memory can haunt my days or nights. If you want a life here among our new friends, I have no objections."

"Then, I'd love to leave Earth for a while. All the blood I've spilt there is something I'd like to forget."

"You'd be a good representative for Gothe'mar to Earth, if you want to leave behind military life. If not, I have a place for you in Military Command," Khan offered.

"No military life for me, thanks. I've had my fill. Representing Gothe'mar sounds like a challenge I'd love to undertake."

"Well then." Mikkarn stepped forward with a stack of clothes and a wicked smirk on his face. "You might better serve your cause if you were dressed."

Taber looked at Akahana, who was giggling into his chest. "I don't know. Being naked in the arms of a beautiful woman has its advantages."

"So does walking out into public dressed," the priest urged.

Akahana kissed the center of his chest and turned to Mikkarn, taking their clothes. "Come on," she said, "let's get dressed and go show the Universe how happy two enemies can be together when all that matters is their love."

New Beginnings (Forbidden 4)
Post-Apocalyptic Sci-Fi Action Romance
Marteeka Karland

Alex and Doriena Mak'un have been raised together, but they are most definitely not brother and sister. They have always been attached to each other, but when Doriena is hurt during war games at Military Academy, something unexpected happens.

While Doriena heals physically, she is pulled mentally into arguments between Alex and his best friend, Bakac. Both men recognize it immediately for what it is -- she is soul's mate to both of them. But Alex is torn between what he wants and what he perceives as right.

While Alex is intent on pushing Doriena away with his intense sexual appetite, Bakac tries to hang on to her with both hands... with his intense sexual appetite. All the while, a protective father rages, and a mother secretly hopes all three can overcome a Forbidden union and find the happiness each so desperately seeks in a New Beginning.

Chapter One

Alex was late. He knew it, but he didn't care. Thrusting mindlessly into the cunt of his latest lover, he tried to ignore his growing impatience to get home. He knew once he returned, he'd be obligated to take Doriena to meet Bakac. The man might be his best friend, but he'd be damned if he'd let him anywhere *near* his little sister.

Tisheena moaned beneath him and he forced his thoughts back to her. She was really beautiful. Classically Gothe'maran. Her skin was a rich, creamy mocha and her hair dark as night. But she was too thin for his tastes. He generally preferred fleshier women, but Tisheena was lusty enough, and she didn't expect a commitment.

And she had a very tight cunt. That helped make up for the lack of cushion.

She raked her nails down his back and settled her hands on his ass, clenching and squeezing and urging him to fuck her harder. He obliged eagerly.

"By the Universe, Alex!" He loved how her voice became thickly accented and husky when she was turned on. "Fuck me! I want to come on your thick cock."

Who was he to disappoint her?

Moving up onto his knees so he could get better leverage, Alex pulled Tisheena's legs over his shoulders and gripped her thighs. Then he began a furious pounding. Over and over he thrust into her, pulling her back against him with each forward surge. The staccato rhythm they pounded out echoed in the vast bedchamber, as did Tisheena's screams of delight and pleasure.

Realizing she was too close to hold back much

longer, Alex redoubled his efforts. He rammed into her so hard, he scooted them across the bed, and Tisheena had to brace herself with her hands above her head on the wall behind them. With two last thrusts, Alex shouted his orgasm just as Tisheena's muscles clenched around him and she exploded in her own pleasure.

Breathing hard, he rolled over. Nice. Very nice.

"You're always such an enthusiastic lover, Alex." Tisheena smiled as she patted down her hair. Alex managed not to snort at that. Not matter how wild their fucking, she never had a hair out of place. That she enjoyed their sex play, Alex had no doubt, but he knew if she ever found the right someone, Tisheena would be a handful.

He wasn't the right someone.

And neither was she.

"I have to go." Alex didn't particularly like leaving right after sex, but this time he didn't really have a choice. He was in enough trouble as it was.

Tisheena stretched, thrusting her breasts up at him. "So soon? I'd hoped you'd stay tonight."

He smiled at her and gave her one last tongue-filled kiss. "I'd like to, but I can't. My sister's home from a month at the Academy and I promised her I'd be home tonight."

"She's not really your sister." Tisheena pouted. "She's not part of your family at all."

"No, but I owe her the same respect I'd give a full blooded sibling, and I give it willingly."

His stepfather and mother had taken Doriena in after the Earth Gothe'maran War when they couldn't find her parents. Alex was only ten when she came to live with them, so she was raised as his sister.

Tisheena shrugged. "I suppose. But you can't blame a girl for wanting a warm man in her bed, can you?"

Chuckling as he dressed, Alex said, "I seriously doubt your bed will remain empty for long."

She grinned. "True, but I always have such a good time with you. You're always welcome here, Alex. Come by whenever you like."

"You're an elegant Gothe'maran lady, Tisheena. I'm glad to know you."

"Oh, please!" She waved a hand in dismissal. "We enjoy each other, Alex. Not only the sex, but each other's company as well. Believe me, I'm not a lady. I'm a royal bitch and everyone knows it. I simply tolerate you better than most."

"Take care of yourself."

"I always do, my dear." Standing up from the bed, she pressed her naked body against him and kissed him, reaching down to squeeze his cock through his pants. It swelled under her touch. "If you need to relieve that later, you know where to find me."

Wishing he actually did want to stay a while longer, he said, "Keep the bed warm. I may take you up on the offer." Alex winked at her as he left. He wished he actually felt that lighthearted. Dreading the moment he walked through the door and had to look his sister in the eyes, Alex started home.

He just wasn't sure he was dreading it because he knew he'd broken a promise, or because he was afraid this time Doriena might just see right through him. He was afraid she might figure out the reason he didn't want her around Bakac was for his own protection and not hers.

* * *

"Is that a destabilizer wand in your pocket, or are you just happy to see me?" Doriena Mak'un cocked an eyebrow as she addressed her stepbrother. The man had just said "good night" to his latest distraction, and the evidence of his failure to relieve himself properly was prominent.

"You're a pain, Doriena," Alex growled. "Mind your own business."

"This *is* my business. You were supposed to be home *three hours* ago! Now you've ruined everything!"

"Don't exaggerate," Alex snapped. "You should have had Dad take you to the tournament."

"Yeah. Like Dad is going to take me to meet Bakac Kemka. You know he only agreed to let me go because he's your best friend." Doriena was angrier than she could ever remember being. Angry and hurt. "The deal was I could go to the Spars as Bakac's partner *only* if you went with me. Instead, I'm sitting home, and Bakac is fighting with someone else helping."

"So?" Alex shrugged and shouldered past her to the kitchen. "The Spars are too violent for you anyway."

"They are not! They're just *games*, Alex. But being there with the reigning champion would have given me extra status in the Academy!"

"It would have labeled you as Bakac's woman."

"How is that a bad thing? I'd like to be with Bakac." Doriena couldn't help but smile. "He's the best looking guy I've ever seen."

Alex rounded on her and gripped her shoulders hard. "You don't have a clue what that means, Doriena," he growled. "You're not ready for that kind of relationship."

"How would you know?" She spat the question with as much contempt as she could muster. "You're never here. You don't spend any time with me. How could you possibly know what I'm ready for?"

"I know Bakac. I know the Gothe'maran people. Believe me --" He shoved her away from him and crossed his arms over his chest as he leaned against the wall. "-- being a human female makes you definitely not ready. Hell, *I'm* barely able to deal with their sexual appetites."

Doriena just looked at him. She'd heard about Bakac's taste in sex play, and she wasn't sure Alex was wrong in his assessment of the situation. She tried to be strong, tried not to let him see how truly hurt she was that he'd broken his promise to her.

Truth was, she was just as attracted to Alex as she was to Bakac. His dark blond hair fell below his collar, but was always neatly groomed. Sometimes he wore a goatee that emphasized the differences between him and most Gothe'maran men. There were very few blonds among their people. Mikkarn was the only one Doriena could think of. Every now and then, there would be a man or woman with snow-white hair, but few blonds. He was definitely as formidable as any male of the Gothe'maran race. He was muscular in an athletic way. He didn't carry as much bulk as many Gothe'marans, but his finely toned muscles were sexy as hell.

He had always looked beautiful to her, but the fact that he was her brother always made her feel guilty. Well, stepbrother, anyway.

Right now, it didn't matter. He wasn't acting like a brother, he was acting like a *man*. All stupid and superior acting when he was just silly. She wanted to pout, but the truth was, she was just plain hurt.

"Go away," she whispered. "Go away, and don't speak to me again."

Alex rolled his eyes. "When you're older, you'll thank me for this."

She whirled on him. "You're not my father! I'm old enough to know what I'm ready for and what I'm not. I'm nineteen!" When he straightened and would have interrupted her, she shoved him back against the wall. "I was old enough to enter the Warrior's Academy for Military Command -- I'm certainly old enough to know about the more carnal side of the Gothe'maran male."

He simply stared at her a moment. She wasn't certain -- she wasn't nearly as worldly as she would have him believe -- but she could have sworn she saw a hunger in his eyes the likes of which she had never witnessed before. It didn't take a genius to figure out the meaning of *that* look.

It excited her beyond belief.

Before she could be sure, it was gone and the heat turned to icy resolve.

"You're a child compared to me and Bakac," he said softly. "Stick to boys your own age, or you might find out just how much you don't know." With that, he headed up the stairs.

When she heard the door close, Doriena slumped against the wall. She felt like crying, but that wasn't the way she dealt with things. Tears only proved she was weak. A member of Military Command *never* showed weakness. If she wanted to be the first female officer in Military Command, she couldn't afford to show even the slightest hint of weakness.

Straightening, her back ramrod straight now, she calmly walked out the door. If Alex wouldn't take her where she wanted to go, she'd go herself. She'd have to face her father's wrath later, but damn it, this was her life. She wanted to live it.

* * *

When Alex heard Doriena leave the house he

immediately moved to the window. She was heading toward the transport pod. He'd just bet she was going to find Bakac herself.

Damned girl!

She had no idea what she was getting herself into. Bakac was nice enough, but not for his little sister. It was the nature of the Gothe'maran to be intensely sexual -- they were a warrior race in a culture embracing peace. All that pent up emotion had to go somewhere. He'd had his share of Gothe'maran women, and if the sexual appetites of the men were anything near what he'd experienced with women like Tisheena then there was no way Doriena could handle it.

Unless she wasn't as innocent as he thought.

She was a beautiful young woman. Not painfully thin, like most Gothe'maran women, but her limbs were sleek and layered with fine muscle. If she stayed at the Academy, she'd undoubtedly develop quite a physique in a few years. Usually she kept her flame red hair secured tightly at the base of her skull, but on the rare occasions he'd seen it down, it flowed like an orange flame down her back to brush the top of her ass, emphasizing the fact that he wanted to bare the tempting bottom and spank it until it was as red as her hair. It was enough to make him avoid her for weeks. How could he possibly face her with the biggest hard-on in the Universe?

He immediately squashed that thought. She was his little sister, for crying out loud! He had protected her from men like Bakac all her life. He knew better than anyone how men looked at her. Because from time to time, he caught himself looking at her the same way -- with a sexual, predatory hunger.

God! This fascination with her was getting way

out of hand.

Okay, so he'd kept any and every man he could away from her. His baby sister was *not* going to be exposed to the more violent nature of his stepfather's people.

Which brought up another problem. She was doing very well at the Academy. If things kept going like they were, she would graduate with honors in a couple of years and take her place among the other officers in Military Command.

Correction. She'd take her place among the other *male* Gothe'maran officers in Military Command.

He knew it was what she wanted, knew she wanted to follow in their father's footsteps. He also knew she wasn't anywhere near ready for the responsibilities that went with that job. Oh, Doriena was responsible. He just didn't think she could make the shitty calls. The ones that she knew going in would result in the death of a comrade. He had no doubt she could cut the work. She was hardworking, physically and mentally strong, highly intelligent -- everything an officer needed to be. But she was too damned young! And too tenderhearted.

Definitely too young and tenderhearted to seek out Bakac.

Decision made, Alex headed back to the ground floor and the door.

"Alex." His mother's voice. "What's going on? You were supposed to be here hours ago. Are you just getting home?"

"Mother." Alex pinched the bridge of his nose. How was he supposed to explain to his mother that he'd been out fucking around -- literally -- so he wouldn't have to take his sister to meet his best friend? "Yes. I just got home, but I'm leaving again."

"Where's your sister?"

Alex took a breath. "She left."

"It wouldn't have anything to do with her missing the Spars, would it?"

"Maybe."

Alex's mother, Anna Mak'un, wife of General Kahn Mak'un, approached him, a dangerous look on her face. It was something Alex had rarely seen.

"Do you have any idea where she went?" Her voice was deceptively calm. Alex knew his mother well enough to know she was working herself into a good "mad," but he'd be damned if he knew how to defuse her. Mainly because he knew he deserved it.

"I suspect she may have gone to seek out Bakac on her own."

He expected the explosion in that moment, but that deadly calm stayed firmly intact. It was almost worse than if she'd lashed out at him. He hated for his mother to be mad at him.

"Do you feel anything you said or did directly influenced her decision to leave this house knowing she was going against the wishes of her father and I?"

There it was. If he told the truth, he was in trouble. He didn't even want to think about what would happen if he lied. Because she *always* knew when he lied.

Oh, well. Better to get it over with.

"I think it was a combination of both."

His mother was a phenomenal woman, which was probably one of the reasons his father adored her so much. Even almost thirty years after they'd met, the affection the two of them had for each other was more than obvious to everyone who encountered them. In fact, the tender looks and caresses were commonplace and expected when the couple were in the same room.

She was also a terrifying woman to have angry with you. He'd been on the receiving end of her wrath more than once, and it was never pleasant.

She simply looked at him a few moments, the silence stretching on and on. He desperately needed to break the tension, but didn't dare speak. Just when he thought he couldn't take another second of the blistering silence, she turned and walked away. As he watched her go, his father emerged from his study and immediately enfolded his wife in his arms.

"Are you going after her?" It didn't surprise Alex that his father knew the topic of conversation. He and his mother could easily communicate with each other telepathically thanks to years of practice with their connection as soul's mates.

"Would it do any good?"

Kahn didn't bat an eye. "Probably not, if she was angry enough to leave in the first place." There was a brief pause. "You realize she's not coming back."

Alex's stomach gave an awful lurch.

"What do you mean?" He had to ask, but deep down inside, he knew what his father meant.

"She's been planning on leaving for months now. Moving to Academy housing. In your... umph!" His mother punched Kahn in the ribs, even as she clung to him. "In *our* --" he glanced down at Anna, "-- zealousness to protect her, I fear we've pushed her away from us."

"She wouldn't dare." Even as he said it, he knew how false that statement was. Doriena would most certainly dare. "Can't you stop her -- forbid it or something?"

"If I thought it would help, I would."

"I think the two of you have done enough." Anna sniffed. "I should have intervened a long time ago."

"Maybe if you had, she wouldn't feel like she had to leave home to enjoy freedoms every other Gothe'maran female has here." Kahn sighed, nuzzling his wife's head in a gesture Alex had seen a thousand times when something worried his mother.

Without warning, Anna pushed away from Kahn and moved from the two of them a few steps. "Men," she muttered under her breath. "You don't have a clue what you're talking about." When Alex opened his mouth to say something, she cut him off. "As usual."

"Anna." Kahn's voice should have sounded reprimanding -- would have with anyone other than his wife -- but the effect was ruined by the wince as Anna turned her sharp, intelligent, angry eyes on him.

"Oh, come on! Listen to what you're saying," she spat. "You really think Gothe'maran females enjoy as much freedom as men?"

"Now, Anna." Kahn's tone suggested he would try to reason with Anna, but Alex knew his mother all too well. When she was in this kind of lather, it was best to let her have her say. He'd also seen his father try to reason with her almost every time she got this angry, and he always failed. He would have thought Kahn would have learned better.

"Don't take that patronizing tone with me, Kahn Mak'un! You know very well what I'm talking about. If men and women were equal here, my Doriena wouldn't be the only woman in the Academy. You're ruler here. Do something!"

Alex's father sighed. "Anna, you know this is a male dominated society. Men have always been the warriors protecting Gothe'mar in Military Command. It's going to be hard to change over a thousand years of thinking."

"Which --" Alex cringed when his mother turned her angry, piercing gaze on him, "-- is why I wanted her to stay here instead of at the Academy." She poked him in the chest. "Get her back here."

"I don't think it's up to me, Mom. She's got to do what's best for her."

"So?" Anna shrugged. "Make her *want* to come back home."

He blew out an exasperated breath. "And just how in the Universe am I supposed to do that?"

Kahn placed a hand on Anna's shoulder. "You'll have to figure that one out on your own, son."

Alex ran a hand through his hair. Yeah. Right. A surge of anger went through him as he thought all of this could have been avoided if he'd only come home like he'd promised Doriena he would. That feeling intensified every passing second, and when he reached his suite, he punched the wall just to relieve a little tension.

It might have helped if he wasn't so worried about Doriena. He had a bad feeling something was very wrong.

Chapter Two

Leaving home was the hardest thing Doriena had ever done. A little more than a week after she'd left the relative peace and tranquility of the royal estates, explosions flashed and boomed all around her. Men shouted orders and fired all manner of exotic weapons at an enemy none of them could see.

Doriena should have been at least a little bit scared, or excited, or… something.

What she was, was pissed as hell.

None of it was real.

This was a Gothe'maran military academy. Gothe'marans never did anything halfway. Until she joined the Academy. This was the first exercise where live ammunition wasn't used. Ever.

At first she thought it was because she was a woman. Her mother had alluded to that assumption several times, but in recent months, she had discovered it was because she was the daughter of General Kahn Mak'un. One simply did not put the general's daughter in harm's way. For *any* reason.

Which was why she knew she'd never go far in Military Command.

Which was why she was doing this to begin with. She'd always hated being told "no."

The night sky lit up like day with brilliant flashes of light. Noise bombarded her, and all she wanted to do was look around her and laugh hysterically, but she couldn't. If she was ever going to prove to her teammates she wasn't a fragile porcelain doll, she had to do it better and faster than everyone else.

The exercise today was an obstacle course. She had to climb fences, through razor wire -- blunted, of course -- and swim pools without getting her gun wet.

She had to fight "enemy soldiers" hand to hand and hit moving targets with flash grenades and blunt laser flashes from her destabilizer gun.

And she just *knew* there was no way she would fail. The Academy couldn't afford to let the daughter of its favorite general flunk out.

"Doriena! Move your ass!" Bakac yelled as he boosted another soldier over the wall in front of her. He was senior instructor for this exercise, and it was apparent he was also her personal bodyguard. Much as she really wanted him guarding her body, this wasn't exactly what she had in mind.

Ignoring him, Doriena looked around her. There were a few men shouting orders, a few struggling with the wall, the stronger ones shoving the weaker ones out of the way and using them as stepping-stones when necessary… it was literally every man for himself. Well, if she couldn't fail, she'd help out a few of her classmates.

One very large warrior pulled a man off the wall when the smaller man impeded his progress not two feet from her. If not for Bakac's presence, and who she was to begin with, she had no doubt she would have been the one pulled off that damned wall.

"Soldier!" Her voice carried more authority than she thought possible. "You will stop your advancement and help your brother!" When he only looked at her, smirked, and continued upward, Doriena ran to the wall and jumped as high as she could. Without a second thought, she grabbed the man's ankles and hung on for dear life.

"What the *fuck* are you doing?" The warrior yelled down at her as he tried to shake her loose. Once she got a solid grip on one ankle, she braced her feet on the wall and threw all her strength into pulling the man from the wall. With a mighty battle cry, Doriena gave one more tremendous yank. The man's grip let go and both of them fell to the ground.

Which was the one part of this she hadn't thought out. The man was probably twice her size and weight, and he landed on her chest from about eight feet up. The breath left her body in a *whoosh*, and she felt the sharp snapping of many ribs. She couldn't breathe.

"That should teach you, you little bitch," the man hissed. "Just because you're the general's daughter doesn't mean you can tell the rest of us what to do. You are *not* my commanding officer, lady." Standing, he spat on her before leaving her to scale the wall.

Every breath was a struggle. She tasted blood and knew she had probably punctured a lung. But there was no way in hell she was going to let that big thug get away with what he'd just done.

Once again, she jumped for the warrior, who was already almost as high as he was before she pulled him off the wall. This time, however, she climbed up his body and put herself on above him. Her body *screamed* in pain, but she climbed every inch. Once she was above him -- him swearing at her and threatening her bodily harm all the while -- she stomped his hands as hard as she could. Her boots were thick with sole and tread, so she knew every blow had to be misery for him. Still, he held on for several minutes before he finally let go and fell to the ground a second time.

Doriena lowered herself before jumping. Landing on her feet with a thud, she crumpled to the ground. The warrior was getting to his feet, but it looked as if his hands were useless.

That didn't mean he was helpless, though.

He came at her with murder in his eyes. Doriena

struggled to her feet, but didn't make it before he kicked at her. Falling back to the ground and rolling quickly, she managed to avoid his kick, just as she'd been taught. When he roared his frustration and came at her again, she rolled to one side before he would have reached her. Using his own weight against him, she stuck out a foot and shoved hard as he passed her, and he stumbled a few steps before finally falling.

He would have gotten up a third time, but Bakac placed a booted foot on the man's head, shoving it back into the ground. "I could kill you for what you did, soldier." He had to raise his voice to be heard above the noise, but Doriena was certain only the soldier and she heard Bakac's words. "Not only did you attack a member of the Mak'un family, but you pulled another soldier off that wall to save your own ass. Cowards are not welcome in Military Command."

"It's just war games!" the soldier panted, rolling over when Bakac removed his foot. "No one was in any real danger, and he was slowing me down. I was working on a record time."

Bakac moved so quickly, Doriena almost didn't see him. He dropped down to one knee and backhanded the soldier so hard Doriena heard his cheekbone crack. "This exercise simulates a real battle, you *bakkara*! Had you been in a real battle, you would have condemned that man to death. Which means your life would have been forfeit."

Doriena winced. Bakac never swore at his troops. He told her it was demeaning and served no purpose other than to show disrespect and earn him a healthy dose of resentment. For Bakac to have called this man the Earth equivalent of a son of a bitch meant he was very angry indeed. And that this man was probably looking at his last day at the Academy.

"But it isn't a real battle," the downed soldier managed to get out as he spat blood from his split lip. "They're not even using real munitions." He glared at Doriena. "Because of *her*, none of us will get any battle experience before we actually get in the field as part of Military Command."

Again, Bakac backhanded the man. His already broken cheek sunk into his face even more. Bakac looked at him as if to say, "Go ahead. Say something else stupid." Wisely, the soldier kept quiet, probably more from pain than common sense.

Bakac turned to Doriena. "Let's get you to Medical."

"I have to finish the exercise." Even to her own ears, she sounded too weak to continue. But she knew that not finishing even one exercise, no matter the reason, would knock her out of the Academy completely. The Gothe'maran didn't give second chances under any circumstances.

"You can't. You're not physically able."

"I *will* finish this, Bakac." She tried to make her voice firm, but she wasn't altogether certain she succeeded.

"You can try." Bakac nodded as he spoke. "And when you finally collapse, I'll take you to Medical and you'll *still* not complete this course. I'd be willing to bet you have ten minutes at best before you're unconscious from blood loss or lack of oxygen." When she opened her mouth to speak, he added, "And that's with you sitting still. If you try to continue on, you'll go down even faster. Either way, I'll be taking you to Medical and I think you'd prefer to enter under your own power. Yes?"

"I really hate you sometimes, Bakac."

He smiled. "No, you don't. You just hate to lose."

"But this isn't just losing. This is my entire career."

"Listen to me, Doriena." Bakac knelt and brushed one fiery red curl from her forehead. "I have no doubt in my mind -- have never doubted -- that you would make one of the finest officers in Military Command since your father retired from active service to concentrate on governing Gothe'mar. But this isn't you. You have too gentle a soul to expose yourself to this kind of violence."

Doriena was starting to feel the effects of her injuries, but she needed to finish this conversation. "I -- " she began and had to stop for breath. "I am as --" Another breath. "-- tough as you and Alex put -- put together."

"Undoubtedly," Bakac said without hesitation. "I'd not be so foolish as to question that. I just think that your soul would be better suited for peace instead of war."

Something in the way Bakac looked at her gave her pause. There was something she was missing, but she couldn't quite figure it out. "I think I need to get to that healing tube, Bakac."

"Yes. I think you do."

She expected he would have helped her to her feet, or worse, tried to carry her off the faux battlefield, but he simply stood there. He offered a hand when she needed one, but let go of her as soon as she was steady. He let her walk until her legs simply wouldn't hold her any more. Then he simply scooped her up and ran as hard as he could to Medical Command.

She passed out long before he made it.

* * *

"If she dies, I'm going to kill you."
"It's not like I made her go after a warrior almost

three times her size. I got there as quickly as I could."

"You should have anticipated!"

"Could you have?"

Blessed silence.

"It doesn't matter. I gave you one set of instructions. One simple task and instead of keeping her out of harm's way, you almost let her get killed."

There they go again.

Doriena had been listening to Alex and Bakac go at it for nearly an hour. What she couldn't figure out was how she was doing it. She was in the healing tube. Had been for several hours if what the two men were saying wasn't exaggerated. She should have been oblivious to the outside world, but here she was, privy to the conversation of two insufferably stubborn and infuriating men.

Alex blamed Bakac, Bakac refused to accept blame, when in reality both men felt guilty as hell. They just didn't want to admit it to the other.

Drugs. It must be the drugs. She was bound to have been given drugs of some kind when she was placed in the tube.

Fine. If she was hallucinating, she'd damn well play along.

If the two of you don't shut the fuck up and give me a little peace and quiet, I'm going to kick both your asses when I get out of here.

Again, silence.

Did you hear something, Alex?

Err... no. I absolutely did not hear anything. Especially not Doriena.

I thought not.

Maybe it's your guilty conscience playing tricks on you.

And there they went again.

She was definitely going to kill them both. Once she figured out what the *hell* was going on.

* * *

Bakac sat at Doriena's side. He had been there since they had removed her from the healing tube a little more than one day ago. He glanced to his left to find Alex with his head propped on his hand, his elbow resting on Doriena's bed. Neither of them had spoken since they first took her out of the tube, and it was likely they wouldn't.

Neither of them knew what to say.

Doriena had clearly spoken to both of them while in the healing sleep of the tube, and they didn't really know what to make of it. Several times, Bakac had thought to ask his father's brother, Kiril, what that meant, but he had always backed down.

Mainly because he already knew the answer. The problem was what it meant for Alex and him.

He loved Alex like a brother, but he didn't think he could actually have a sexual relationship with the man.

Sorry. Not his style.

Getting up, Bakac paced the room several times before stopping at the window. The view was breathtaking, even for a native of Gothe'mar. Nothing could compare to an average day at the Northling Valley, the northernmost city of Gothe'mar.

Winter kept the city in mostly darkness, but summer yielded the most beautiful auroras in the known galaxy. Stunning light displays arced the length of the horizon in a myriad of exotic colors.

And all he wanted to think about was how Doriena would look by the Crystal Lake in this same light. He wanted to see the lights reflected in her hair and to hear her cries of joy as he made love to her all evening.

He'd tried too hard to keep his interest in Doriena to himself. She was his best friend's sister for crying out loud! He also knew how Alex felt about him pursuing a relationship with Doriena.

Hands off!

"What are we going to do?"

Bakac looked over his shoulder at Alex. He should have known the other man would have been smart enough to figure out what was going on between the three of them.

"I'm not sleeping with you."

Alex snorted. "That's okay. I'm not sleeping with you either." Alex looked at him for a long minute. "And I don't want you sleeping with my sister."

"She's not really your sister, you know."

"Yeah, I know. But I still have to protect her. Quite frankly, I don't want her doing with *either* of us what we do with other women. It's a little unsettling."

Bakac snorted. "It's a *lot* unsettling. You think I don't feel this overwhelming need to protect her too? Why in the Universe do you think I agreed to act as bodyguard to her during the more vigorous exercises? Not because I like *you* that much."

There was silence between them for a moment. Alex opened his mouth to speak, but Dr. Mara Jenson entered the room. "Good evening, gentlemen." She was always so bright and cheery. Almost too much so for Bakac's taste. He cringed.

Mara stopped and looked at Bakac. "Something wrong?" Just like that, her demeanor changed. She still smiled, but Bakac could sense the warrior stretching her arms for battle.

Damn! No wonder Kiril loved her. She was a woman with a warrior's heart.

Just like his Doriena.

"Nothing, Doctor." He cleared his throat to keep from smiling. "I was just thinking how I couldn't stand your bubbly personality. I think I prefer the warrior woman."

Mara blinked a few times, as if trying to decide whether to be insulted or not. Then she chuckled. "Well, you *are* Kiril's nephew. I suppose that is to be expected."

Alex stood to embrace the older woman. "It's good to see you again, Mara." When he let her go, he turned back to Doriena. "Will she be okay?"

"Oh, of course." Mara waved off his concern. "She's perfectly fine. She just needed a little more rest than normal." She frowned slightly. "She didn't rest well in the healing tube. Her body tried to, but it was like something kept waking her up."

Bakac looked at Alex and the other man met his gaze squarely.

Mara looked from one of them to the other. "What?"

"Nothing," Alex mumbled and paced to the other side of the room from Bakac.

"Well." Mara continued to look at Alex. "She should be waking up shortly. I've contacted Kahn and Anna. They will be here soon."

Alex groaned. "Damn."

"Hey, I gave you guys two days' reprieve. It's time to take your medicine now."

Bakac had to smother a grin. Oh, he knew he was probably in a world of trouble as well, but he doubted he was in as much trouble as Alex.

Chapter Three

Doriena floated in a sea of endless, puffy clouds in an excited aurora. The colors swirled around her and changed like images in a multifaceted mirror. A soft warm breeze caressed her nude body, and she stretched much like her cat might.

Soothing images floated through the clouds, and she knew there was a doctor somewhere -- probably her mother's best friend, Dr. Mara Jenson -- trying her damnedest to make her comfortable and relax her troubled mind. Healing tubes were great, but Mara had pointed out on many occasions the best medicine is sometimes restful sleep.

Well, this was certainly soothing.

At least it was until her imagination kicked in.

Coming toward her in the distance were two very large, very nude males. They were both formidable in appearance, but nothing about them scared her in the least. She had no doubt who they were.

Her stepbrother and Bakac were two men she had always thought unattainable. There was nothing she could ever recall to lead her to believe either of them was interested in her as more than a sister or friend. In fact, although she had pursued Bakac recently, she knew in no uncertain terms he considered her off limits in a physical way because of Alex.

But, oh, she had fantasized!

Like now.

Both walks might have been cocky, both grins sexy, but each man was very different in both appearance and demeanor. Alex swaggered, blatantly arrogant. Bakac was more sensual, contained power that needed no arrogance to showcase himself. Both men had bodies that would do any god on any world proud and were enough to cause her to cream instantly. Had she not been bonelessly relaxed already, she would have surely melted into a puddle of sensual goo.

Neither said a word, but both reached for her. She lay on her back, suspended in the air between them, Alex at her head, Bakac at her feet. Alex's hands kneaded her shoulders and down the length of her arms gently but firmly. Bakac did the same with her feet and legs and before long, muscles still sore from her ordeal began to loosen and relax.

They worked her limbs for what seemed like hours. She didn't want them to stop, so they didn't.

Still, neither said a word.

After a time, something changed in the nature of their touches. Neither of them massaged anything other than her limbs, but the feel of their hands became almost erotic. Alex rubbed and kneaded the underside of her arm while Bakac massaged her feet and ankles, and the two of them were flipping sexual switches she didn't know she had.

Her cunt clenched once when Bakac stimulated a particularly sensitive part of her foot and she couldn't help the gasp that escaped her lips. When he smiled, she gasped again.

It was the most seductive smile she had ever seen, and in that instant everything changed.

Subtle touches were now sexual torment.

Alex bent to lick the well of her collarbone as Bakac grinned once more before sucking her big toe into his mouth. It took all her strength of will not to jump. As it was, she cried out at the unexpected sensation and arched her neck to guide Alex more firmly against her flesh.

Two mouths feasted on her in two different ways, each with an erotic quality all its own. Alex apparently preferred a more straightforward approach, whereas Bakac favored teasing and tormenting. Each had devastating consequences on her nervous system.

Leaving her foot for a short time, Bakac gave her that heart-stopping grin before making a swipe from her heel to her big toe. She tried to watch, fascinated, as he sucked each toe on each foot, but Alex turned her head to him and took her mouth in a gentle kiss.

Well, gentle and plundering at the same time.

There was not a spot in her mouth within reach of his tongue that he did not explore. She surrendered willingly, eagerly. All she wanted was these two men.

Always.

Forever.

Alex kissed her so completely, so totally satisfying her every curiosity about what his lips would feel like on hers, she almost missed Bakac's advance up her leg. He nibbled and licked and sucked his way to her knee and started working on the inside of one leg. Just when she pulled herself away from Alex to watch Bakac's progress, he stopped and started all over again with her other leg.

Doriena lay back with a groan and Alex smiled down at her. He trailed kisses up her neck, across her jaw line to her mouth, up her cheeks to her temples, and finally settling on her left ear. He licked around the shell, dipping his tongue ever so slightly inside and pulling back to blow gently. The cool sensation sent chills over her body and she whimpered a little and stiffened with the unbearable pleasure these two men so expertly created with their mouths.

Damn!

Bakac made his way back up her other thigh, and

she again looked down at him, expecting him to dip his head and finally put her burning clit out of its misery. Instead, he stopped and snared her gaze. He looked so fierce that Doriena should have been afraid of him.

But she wasn't. She had known Bakac most of her life. She trusted him the same way she trusted Alex. If the two of them wanted to take her down the road to dark, carnal pleasures, she'd follow them willingly. Never looking back.

"Be careful what you wish for, little warrior," Bakac's voice whispered inside her head. "Our passions are darker than an innocent such as you could ever imagine."

No sooner had Bakac stopped speaking than Alex bit her neck, sharply, before laving the small hurt with his tongue. Doriena cried out before she could stop herself…

* * *

Doriena awoke to find both men staring at her from opposite sides of the room with identical looks of lust in their eyes. Unfortunately, her mother and father were there also.

"Doriena!" Her mother was at her side in an instant, checking her pulse, pushing her back into the bed when she tried to rise. "Are you all right? You screamed in your sleep."

"I -- I'm fine, Mother," she managed to stammer. She felt guilty as hell, like she'd been caught doing something naughty. Which she had, except no one knew.

She managed to convince herself of that until she looked at Alex and Bakac again. They knew *exactly* what she had been dreaming. She was sure of it.

And she knew what that meant, too.

Worse, they were right. She wasn't ready for this. "Mom." She reached for her mother, who enfolded her in her arms and held her tightly.

"I'm so glad you're okay. Thank God Bakac was with you."

"It would have been okay if he hadn't been." She pulled away from her mother then, feeling defensive now. "My status chip would have alerted Medical of my need for assistance."

"It shouldn't have happened at all." Bakac stared at her a moment before turning to Kahn. "Your daughter pulled an apprentice warrior from the wall. Her injuries occurred because he fell on top of her."

Her father looked at her sharply, his eyes piercing. He was in "General" mode now. Over the course of her life, she had seen this switch many times, though she had never been the cause of such a look before. "You pulled another warrior from the wall during a battle?"

Honesty was always the best approach with her father. He always gave an opportunity for one to explain one's actions, so she kept her answer short and focused.

"Yes. I did."

"And you had a reason for doing this, yes?"

"I did."

"Then explain yourself, apprentice."

"Kahn." Her mother placed a hand on Kahn's shoulder, but he brushed her off, not looking at her. Her mother seemed miffed, but didn't press whatever issue she had.

"He was pulling the slower warriors from the wall to better his own time. Apparently, with the threat of real weapons fire removed from the battle, several warriors are using the advantage to set record completions. I shouldn't have let my anger cloud my judgment, but this particular warrior has put others in danger more than once."

Kahn looked to Bakac. "Is this true?"

"Yes, sir." Bakac didn't hesitate in the slightest. "It was well known, sir."

"Then why was this not stopped by someone other than an apprentice warrior?" Kahn's words exploded throughout the room. Doriena had never seen her father actually angry. Gothe'marans were experts at hiding any emotion, especially during battle. Her father might show love and affection as a father and husband, but as a member of Military Command, he never showed emotion.

Until today.

"I will deal with this at the Academy." He looked directly at Bakac. "Then I will hear why you didn't tell me about this personally."

"Father." Alex spoke for the first time. His voice sounded husky, like he desperately needed a drink of water. He cleared his throat. "Bakac had another duty that interfered with everything else. I have no doubt that, if he'd had the time, he would have told you what was going on."

Kahn's eyes narrowed as he turned to Alex. "And that duty?"

"He was shadowing Doriena night and day. The only time he had a break was when she was at home, which ended when she left to stay at the Academy. Thanks to me, he's had no time for anything other than keeping an eye on Doriena."

Alex looked as if he was preparing to say more, but one look from Kahn and his mouth snapped shut. Her brother wasn't one to back down from anyone, but he had too much respect for their father to argue with him in front of others.

She sucked in a breath.

She actually *felt* his frustration at not being able to defend himself and Bakac. She felt the love and respect he had for both their parents. And his lust for her was simmering there in the background. He was hoping no one noticed the damned raging hard-on he had at the moment, and he was hoping like *hell* he didn't have to fuck Bakac. Literally.

She couldn't help herself. The giggle broke free before she could stop it. Everyone looked at her, but her eyes locked with Alex's and she had to swallow another giggle.

"I am *not* changing my mind about that!" Alex's outburst was enough to draw attention away from her, and she looked at Bakac. He was not amused. In fact, he looked very uncomfortable indeed. Apparently, he felt the same way Alex did.

Anna looked at the three of them in turn. Doriena felt a sinking feeling in her stomach. If anyone could put this together, it was her mother. She just hoped Anna could keep that little bit of information to herself.

Kahn's head whipped around to his wife and the disbelieving look on his face answered *that* question. "Absolutely not!"

"I'm not sure you have a say in this, dear." The faintest smile graced Anna's lips. Doriena was more than a little relieved to know there was at least a chance that her mother was on their side.

"I most certainly *do* have a say. She's my daughter!" He slashed his hand through the air in a quick angry motion. "*I forbid it!*"

"She's a grown woman, Kahn."

Kahn pinned both Alex and Bakac with a deadly

glare, which was something considering both men were on opposite sides of the room. Turning from one to the other, he said, "Don't get me wrong, I love you both. Bakac, you've been like a son to me, and Alex is not only my son, but my heir. I accepted him as my own when I took his mother as my mate." He turned back to Alex. "But if either of you make her cry -- even once -- and I find out about it, I swear by the Holy Universe, I'll kill you both!"

Doriena had never seen her father look so fierce. Apparently, this was why he'd gotten the name "Kahn the Merciless."

"Father," she said softly, "do you really think I could have found a man anywhere who would have my well-being so firmly in his mind? You've raised Alex and I as siblings. For all intents and purposes, he is my brother." She glanced at him out of the corner of her eye. "He may make me crazy sometimes, but he's always been there for me. And Bakac has apparently been willing to put his career on the line to protect me when I was supposed to be working on my own. Could *you* have found anyone who would do that?"

"I don't want to talk about this." Kahn held up his hand. "You're my daughter. You don't need anyone but me." He glared at the two men. "Especially two who have lived in your shadow most of their lives and still seek their own pleasures. They will only bring you heartbreak."

The stabbing in her heart surprised her. Her father's words hurt. It took her a moment to figure it out, but the pain wasn't her own. It was Alex's.

When she looked at him, his face was blank, but he focused on nothing. He just looked straight ahead somewhere above Kahn's head. Like a soldier being dressed down by his superior.

"Dad!" She never called him that unless she wanted his undivided attention. "How can you possibly say that?"

"Because it's true." He scrubbed a hand over his face. "Doriena, you have no idea what passes as sexual entertainment for these two." He waved a hand at the two men, momentarily taking his eyes off his daughter. "Don't bother trying to deny it -- I'm head of Military Command and ruler on this world. I know your tastes, whether I want to or not." Turning back to Doriena, he continued, "Trust me when I say you're not ready for this."

"I know," she said softly, "but I've never backed away from anything my whole life and I'm not about to shrink away from my soul's mates simply because I'm not as worldly as they are." When Kahn would have spoken again, she interrupted. "Would you have given up Mother if she had stretched your limits sexually?"

Anna cleared her throat and coughed once, softly. "Don't answer that or I'll kick your ass right here, Kahn."

The great Kahn the Merciless actually blushed.

And he conceded defeat as gracefully as he could.

"Well, if you need me to kill either one of them, don't hesitate to ask." He gave the men another menacing look, then said, "Damn it, Doriena. You're not supposed to grow up."

She watched her father leave, followed by her mother who smiled and winked at her. "Don't worry, dear. He's just afraid to lose you." Then Anna looked at her son. "He's really very proud of you, Alex. You've grown into a fine man. But fathers and daughters have a different relationship. You'll understand someday."

After Anna left, Doriena looked at Alex and Bakac. No one spoke for a few moments.

"Well," she said after she cleared her throat, "I'll be leaving soon, I'm sure. Perhaps we should all go someplace private and discuss this later?"

Alex said nothing, but Bakac straightened from his place leaning against a wall. "I think that would be wise. We'll meet you at my mountain estate tonight."

"Meet me?" She had expected they would all go together.

"Yes. I want you to have the means to leave if you wish."

Doriena swallowed. What the hell could they possibly do to make her want to leave? She tried to reach out to them, but couldn't sense anything. Everything she had ever been taught about soul's mates suggested that their connection had to grow and develop over time, but not being able to pick feelings, emotions, or even thoughts out at will was damn inconvenient.

"Father's right, Doriena." Alex spoke, never looking at her, but at Bakac, as if he simply couldn't meet her eyes. "We have advanced tastes. Bakac is wise to suggest you have a way out if you can't handle it."

"You're making me nervous." She tried to laugh it off, but her words were true. For all her bravado, could she really handle not one, but both men?

Not bloody likely.

"Good." Alex rose from his seat beside her bed and headed for the door, not saying another word.

Bakac followed, leaving Doriena to contemplate their future.

Chapter Four

"Are you sure this is the right thing to do, Alex?" Bakac always deferred to Alex in matters of Doriena, but this was different. And not what Bakac would call conducive to winning the heart of their souls' mate.

"Do you want to spend the rest of your life repressing your needs? She has to know what we want, the same as we need to know what she wants." Alex gripped the carrying case that contained the week's end entertainment. To Bakac, he didn't look certain at all.

"And if those wants don't coincide?"

"Then it's best we find out now."

"Will it change your desire to claim her as your mate?"

"Not my desire, Bakac, but I won't trap her in a relationship she can't stand, the same as I won't trap myself."

"Well, I'm telling you now, Alex, if she doesn't like my darker nature, I'll repress myself to the other side of the Universe and back before I'll give her up. Just because she's not ready for this stuff now doesn't mean she won't be if introduced properly. Sometimes you just have to be patient."

Alex didn't say anything, but Bakac got the distinct impression he was trying to scare off Doriena. Well, the things in that carrying case would probably do it. He'd just have to make sure they progressed carefully.

For this little adventure, he'd have to stay in tighter control of himself than ever before in his life.

So much for showing Doriena his true nature.

* * *

Doriena had been to Bakac's mountain estate only once. It was nestled high up in the Mandorian Mountains overlooking Northling. The view was breathtaking. Great trees spired majestically around the front and sides of the estate, and a mountain lake was situated in the back. Bakac always told her the lake was cool in the heat of the summer, while heat from an underground fissure warmed the water in the winter, creating a natural hot spring. Secretly, she had always wanted to swim naked in that lake. Perhaps she'd get her chance.

Instead of taking a transport pod to the estate entrance, she opted for a chartered drive. It took several hours, and she needed that time to prepare herself.

If that was possible.

She knew Alex wanted to shock and frighten her, and she wasn't sure it wouldn't work. Taking a deep breath, she concentrated on her training at Military Command. If there was ever a time when she needed to repress her emotions, it was now.

* * *

What the *fuck* was keeping Doriena? Alex paced back and forth between the bedroom and the window of the great hall that overlooked the estate's entrance. He'd been waiting for over three hours and was beginning to think he really *had* scared her off.

Then he saw the small conveyance making its way up the side of the mountain, and he knew what she had done.

He blew out a breath of air. If he'd given her a specific time to be here, he'd punish her first thing. But he hadn't.

More importantly, he hated that he cared. He didn't want to get his hopes up because what he had told Bakac was absolutely correct. He would refuse to take her as his mate if she couldn't accept his sexual appetites. Bakac could do as he wished, but he would not live his life in sexual repression.

Damn it.

Funny how he felt the need to remind himself of that.

Once he knew she was on her way, would in fact be there very soon, he went back upstairs to Bakac's gym which they had converted into a "play room" for the week's end. With Instamovers, it had only taken them half an hour and the effect was... disturbing.

All the windows had been covered. All the equipment had either been removed or refitted to use as a device of restraint. Toys of every imaginable use were placed around the room.

And the thought of tying Doriena down made his blood *boil*! He got an instant hard-on every time he imagined her creamy, freckle-dusted flesh stretched out and helpless before him. His to do with as he pleased.

The plan had been for him to await Doriena and Bakac here. He had already dressed the part -- they both had. Black leather pants with a flap at the crotch for easy extraction of his cock, black armbands that emphasized his muscles, and a calm exterior he didn't feel on the inside.

He'd never been this nervous about being with a woman in his life. Perhaps he wasn't as jaded as his father thought.

* * *

Bakac had dressed similarly to Alex, minus the arm bands and flap over his crotch. He wore instead a loose gray shirt hanging open to about mid chest. He had seen Doriena enter the property, too, and took his place in the great hall to welcome her, and to gauge her nervousness. Alex might be set on scaring her away from them, but he intended to hang on to her with both hands.

And arms, and legs, and feet, if necessary.

If she left Alex, he still had her as a sister. Bakac had nothing.

The door chimed, bringing him out of his depressing line of thought. Slowly, deliberately, he made his way to let Doriena in the house. When he opened the door, he felt like he had been punched in the gut.

She was stunning.

Her leanly muscled body was encased in a form-fitting outfit the same color as her hair. And there really wasn't much of it. Although it was long sleeved and long legged, it was designed with so many gaping holes, it looked like it might have been ripped to shreds instead of intentionally created that way.

Or like it would be easy to rip off that delectable body.

She was muscled, and very lean, but she had womanly curves in the right places. Her hips were gently rounded, and her breasts even more generous than he could have possibly imagined. How she'd managed to keep those hidden all this time, he had no idea. Her muscled abdomen was exposed from just below her breasts to dangerously low below her navel, strong arms and legs bare in several places from shoulder to wrist and hip to ankle. And that magnificent cleavage! Large, rounded, high breasts there just waiting for him to grab each of them in his hands and bury his face between them.

For a moment, he just stood there, unable to form a coherent sentence. Doriena shuffled her feet and looked away from him when he said nothing. Still, he couldn't even invite her inside. Never before had he been this awestruck over a woman.

Finally, she took a deep breath. "I guess this wasn't quite what the two of you had in mind."

"No!" He was practically yelling at her. "Sorry." He ran his hands through his hair, then grabbed her arm and yanked her inside.

Once the door was closed behind them, he pulled her into his body and held her there. She came to about mid chest on him, so he bent down and picked her up. "Wrap those long, strong legs around me, Doriena." His voice was husky in his need, and he didn't give her time to comply before he took her mouth with his.

At first she was tentative, unsure of herself, but a few moments later and she was kissing him as hungrily as he kissed her. Her legs tightened around him, her pelvis thrust against his belly, trying to get the needed friction in the needed places.

She surprised him by snaking her tongue inside his mouth to duel with his. It was all he could do not to simply rip that ridiculously skimpy outfit off her luscious curves and fuck her right there.

But they had plans, and he'd just bet she was a lot stronger than either of them -- or Doriena herself -- gave her credit for.

* * *

Doriena's head spun. Bakac's kisses were intoxicating. His big hands on her ass kneaded her flesh, pulling her cheeks apart, and she could just imagine how *that* would come in handy.

When she moaned and managed to bring her pussy into contact with his leather clad cock, which was now hard as stone underneath his pants, he spun her around and slammed her back up against the door.

With an animalistic growl, he fisted his hand in her hair, yanking her head back to look at her.

He ground himself into her, and she slid up and down the door, helpless in the wake of his lust. Not that she cared. She used her legs to draw him into her and braced herself against the wall as best she could. His face was as fierce as the most aggressive warrior caught in a blood lust, and it was clear he was oblivious to anything else around them. He had only one goal in mind.

It was fine with her. The only thing she wanted at this moment was to explode into the orgasm that hovered just out of her reach.

"No!" Bakac growled as he sped up his movements. "Do not come! Not until I say you can!"

Doriena was shocked, but also suddenly desperate. She wanted to follow his instructions, though she had never been one to let another control her life. There was something naughty about his order -- and make no mistake, it was an order. Not only did she want to follow his order, she needed to. It was slightly unsettling.

He pushed harder and harder, pushing her closer and closer, but she fought. She wanted to come so badly, she could feel it, but she didn't dare. His features grew more and more strained, and she knew he was fighting it himself. Finally, with one more thrust he shouted and snarled. Doriena was almost sure he hadn't come. He was still holding her, but she sensed he was more turned on than ever.

"Bakac! What in the Universe are you doing?" Alex's face was just as fierce, something she had never seen in her brother. "Bring her upstairs."

Bakac was breathing hard and the lust gleaming in his eyes was so intense, it was scary. He just looked at her a moment before resting his forehead against hers. "I'm sorry." His whisper was so low, she almost didn't hear it. "I didn't mean for this to start out this way."

She smiled. "Like I didn't enjoy myself."

"*Now*, Bakac!"

Bakac snorted. "Looks like the master has spoken."

Doriena would have laughed if she hadn't been so weak in the knees. If she was in for more experiences like this one, she was definitely in over her head.

But she couldn't have been happier about it.

* * *

Alex felt the lust building in Doriena. It was the first time he'd actually experienced her emotions, and he was shocked and more than a little angry for her to be experiencing such intensity with Bakac. They were supposed to be doing this together, damn it!

What if this little scheme backfired? What if he succeeded in pushing her away, but she clung to Bakac? Could he live knowing his soul's mate was with someone else? His plan was to push her away sexually, but to keep her affections as a sister, but if Bakac didn't have the same goal, he might very well lose them both.

He had to think.

His thoughts were interrupted when Bakac and Doriena entered the room. Bakac had her cradled protectively against him, and the look in the other man's eyes said Alex had best not push her too far.

He had been right. Bakac meant to keep Doriena, no matter the cost.

Doriena struggled out of Bakac's arms -- the big man didn't seem to want to let her go -- and stood before him. She didn't say anything, but she didn't have to. Her outfit spoke for her.

The woman had come to fuck.

"I see the two of you started without me."

"It couldn't be helped." Bakac stepped forward, slightly in front of Doriena. Alex knew the protective gesture warmed her heart. He also knew Doriena wasn't afraid of him. He wasn't nearly as hardhearted as he tried to make her believe, and after nineteen years of living with a man, Doriena knew him.

Alex looked from one to the other. "Well, we've only got the weekend." He pinned Doriena with his sharp gaze. "If you're still willing, that is."

"I'm ready for anything you have in mind." She stepped toward him and smiled as she placed a hand on his face. "You can't frighten me off, Alex."

His emotions were in complete turmoil. What if she was just what he needed? What if she not only tolerated what he was about to put her through, but enjoyed it? What if she not only enjoyed it…

But craved it.

Just thinking about that possibility got him hard.

It also scared the hell out of him.

It was difficult for him to think of her as a sex object. All his life, he had tried his best to protect this girl. Now she stood before him ready to submit to his most carnal desires and he wasn't sure *he* could go through with this.

Either she was becoming very adept at picking up his emotions, or he was giving away too much himself because she moved into his arms and hugged him fiercely. "Alex," she whispered, "I'm not your sister." She pushed away and looked at him. "When the war between Earth and Gothe'mar ended, Father told both peoples in order for us to coexist there had to be a new beginning. We all had to reinvent how we thought about each other. It's taken almost twenty years, but trade now thrives between our peoples."

"What's your point, Doriena?"

"My point..." She took his hands and placed them on her breasts. He swallowed reflexively. "It's time for a new beginning for the three of us. The two of you can't think of me as your little sister --" she looked over her shoulder at Bakac, " -- or your best friend's little sister. You have to start thinking of me as your souls' mate. If you don't, the past will be our only barrier."

Bakac snorted. "Well, that and the general."

"It's not that easy, Doriena." Alex might have stubbornly clung to their past relationship, but he also clung to her breasts -- a sure indication he was letting himself get used to the idea she was his soul's mate. His thumbs absently brushed the pebble-hard nipples he found beneath the flimsy material covering them.

"Oh really?" She raised an eyebrow. "Even if I were to rip this silly outfit off and impale myself on that hard cock?" Her hand closed over the steel-hard member beneath his pants. It wasn't long before her exploring fingers figured out how to loosen the flap, and she wrapped her hand around his thick cock, stroking the length of him.

He swallowed.

"Well, Alex," Bakac said as he moved behind Doriena, gripped her hips and pushed his pelvis into her bottom, "make up your mind. Doriena is a passionate woman, one that I want for my own. She is my soul's mate and I'm keeping her." He bent his head to Doriena's neck and looked Alex in the face as he nibbled her skin. "You're not going to scare her off, because I'm not letting you be the ass you'd planned to be. If you don't want her, then leave. But I intend to introduce her to a wonderful world of dark pleasures with or without your help."

"Goddamn you both!" Alex grabbed Doriena's waist with one hand, and pulled one leg around his hip with the other. No sooner had the words left his lips than he claimed Doriena's mouth with his.

* * *

Doriena welcomed him. He still had reservations, but she knew she could help him overcome them. This week's end was supposed to be to teach her a lesson, but she was hoping she could teach the two of them a thing or two.

Not the least of which was she was perfect for both of them. Always, deep in her soul, she had known she belonged with both of them. She had just never put it all together and given herself the mental "okay" to seek a physical relationship with two men.

She was sandwiched between the two sexiest men on the planet. They were vastly more experienced than she was, and they were going to drive her insane with sexual pleasure for three nights and two days.

Starting now.

Chapter Five

Doriena's flesh was a heady mix of salty sweetness. Bakac glanced around the room, giddily, trying to decide where to start, when he spied an odd looking contraption. It took his mind a while to figure it out, especially since his thought processes were slowly but surely turning to mush in the sexual haze surrounding him, but it was definitely worth the wait. Where the hell had Alex come up with *that*?

It would do nicely.

Alex looked like he might start ripping clothes off any second now. He kissed Doriena like this was truly their only weekend together, his growls and snarls as loud as Doriena's heavy breathing and whimpers. He totally dominated her, his bigger body almost enveloping her in his need to get closer, to get inside her.

Bakac grinned and shook his head. Alex was really getting into this.

"Alex." His voice sounded too husky. He could never remember being this excited about tying a woman up. When Alex looked at him, annoyance flashing in his eyes, Bakac jerked his head in the direction of the apparatus in question.

* * *

When Alex saw where Bakac wanted to go, he picked Doriena up, urging her legs around his hips, and carried her to an apparatus guaranteed to push her limits and, in turn, maximize her pleasure, a modified weight bench he had adjusted especially for this occasion. He ground his cock into her as he sat her down, letting her know without words what he wanted from her. Well, part of what he wanted. Truth be known, he wanted everything from her. He was just afraid to let her know. She deserved much better than either himself or Bakac.

She deserved someone like their father.

But damn him, he couldn't deny himself this one week's end. She was determined to go through with this, and he was just human enough to let her.

He laid her on the slightly inclined surface and, before securing her hands, buried his face between her legs and inhaled. By the Universe, he had to have her. Now. Yesterday.

Gripping two of the ragged holes in her outfit at the thighs, he ripped the scant material from her body. The fiery pelt at her sex beckoned him like nothing ever had. He wanted to devour her, to dip his head once again and not come up until he had drained every ounce of passion from her body. She whimpered but he couldn't take his eyes off her pussy.

"Eat me, Alex," Doriena cried. When she threaded her fingers in his hair, it was enough to snap him out of the sexual haze. Yes, he wanted to fuck the shit out of her, but not yet.

Not yet.

"Her hands." He managed to raise his head and growl an order at Bakac, who was leaning against the wall with his arms crossed over his massive chest. The smirk on his face was the final dash of ice water to bring him back to reality. He stood. "The wrist restraints are on the wall. Fasten her in."

Doriena's chest heaved and the grin on her face was positively giddy. She was enjoying the hell out of this. That wasn't supposed to happen. Was it?

Alex watched in fascination as Doriena stretched her arms for Bakac. Her body lay before him, perfect in every way. Muscles bunched and flexed as she made herself comfortable, her eyes never leaving Alex's. She didn't hesitate when Bakac spread her legs, secured straps just above her knees and tied her. Doriena lay there, spread out for both men. Ready to be fucked.

And she smiled.

Damn.

She might have been tied, but Doriena looked anything but helpless. It would be impossible for such a powerful body to look helpless. She wasn't bulky, like a man, but sleek and powerful. Like a cat, or the pet *tarae* their mother had. He wanted to see all that power unleashed in one explosive orgasm.

As he stood there, looking down at Doriena, he had the sudden urge to chuckle, which didn't at all fit his mood. He shook his head slightly and reached for the feeling, to see where it came from, but the feeling was gone before he could grasp it.

"Are you going to fuck me, or stand there?" Even bound and spread out at his mercy, she still had a smart mouth on her. He thought briefly about gagging her, but that wouldn't be in her best interests.

"Before we begin…" Alex went to a nearby storage unit to retrieve something for Doriena, "…we need to establish a couple of things." He turned around, and Doriena's eyes widened when she saw what he held. A little, brown, very worn out teddy bear. "We need to establish a safe word."

"Buggly Bear? You kept him all this time?" Finally! He'd succeeded in focusing her on a memory from a long time ago. If anything would bring her to her senses, this surely would. He hoped this would remind her exactly what he was capable of. He ignored her question as if it meant nothing to him. As if she was just like the woman she'd seen him with several years ago.

"If we begin something you are uncomfortable with, you need only say 'Buggly Bear,' and we'll stop. It's your safe word."

He could feel a flash of hurt from her, then confusion, but neither emotion stayed with him long. He simply couldn't tell how she felt beyond the brief encounters when her emotions were high.

"Are you sure you want to continue?" Alex kept his voice as calm and neutral as he could, yet somewhere deep inside him was confusion and anger at her reaction. Again, just as briefly as the emotion came, it was gone.

"Why?" Her voice was small and she didn't look nearly as confident as she had a few moments ago. "Why are you doing this?"

"Because you have to know the kinds of things I want. Did you think that just because a few years had passed, I'd have changed? If you can't give me what I want, I suggest you save us both the pain and aggravation and tell me now."

"You're a bastard, Alex." Her voice was a bit shaky, and he suspected she was near tears, but she held back. Her fists were clenched, and the muscles in her arms and abdomen stood out in stark relief under the delicately freckled cream of her skin. "If you don't want me, say so. I'm sure Bakac will be happy to keep me for himself."

Bakac! He had been so intent on scaring Doriena into admitting she wasn't ready for this, he had been oblivious to the other man's presence. Turning to face him now, Alex had never seen the man look so furious.

"I saw her memory, Alex. You deliberately made her remember something that terrified her. Besides that, I never knew you were such a sick *bakkara*."

Alex couldn't disagree with him. Even though

the woman at the time had asked -- begged -- for what he did to her, the memory was disturbing. She had been very into pain and had asked to be flogged, had asked to bleed under his lashes. He had complied, but it wasn't something he had ever done again or had ever wanted to do. Bondage and spankings were one thing. Hard core BDSM was something else.

The problem was, Doriena had accidentally walked in on the worst of it at the tender age of thirteen. Even before she had seen the mess he'd made, she had an anxious look on her face. She had been clutching the bear Alex himself had clutched as a child. When she saw what he was doing, she had backed away, a look of horror on her face. She had dropped the bear and run out of the room. Unfortunately, she had also run away from him, both literally and figuratively. He hadn't seen her for weeks after that and when he finally cornered her one evening in her own bedroom, she hadn't spoken to him nor did she accept Buggly Bear from him. It was almost a year before she did speak to him, and their relationship had never been the same. They had managed to establish an uneasy peace after that, but neither had spoken of that incident in the six years since it had happened.

"It wasn't me, Bakac. You've been in situations where women wanted something you didn't."

"I'm not talking about what you did back then. I'm talking about you dredging up a memory like that for her. You're just trying to make yourself feel better. Forcing her to make the decision about whether or not you get to fuck her. It's an act of a coward!" Bakac shoved Alex from his place standing between Doriena's legs. "I never thought of you as a coward, Alex. Besides, she's made her decision or she wouldn't be here, and you're a damned fool for making her doubt her decision."

The other man dismissed Alex then. His attention focused totally on Doriena. She looked at him with need, a need for him to take her demons away.

Bakac petted her tense thighs, and gradually, her breathing settled and her face relaxed. She no longer looked upset but he'd be damned if he knew what she actually felt.

"Don't worry, my lovely," Bakac soothed. "I can still take you on a journey into forbidden passion." He dipped his head to Doriena's cunt and made one long swipe. She tensed again, but this time in anticipation.

Alex watched, fascinated. He knew he had no right to stay, but he couldn't make himself leave. The growing sexual desire within Doriena called to him as nothing else could. She was his soul's mate. He couldn't leave her. Not now.

Not ever.

* * *

Doriena was hurt and confused by Alex's strong desire to be rid of her. She couldn't believe he had made her relive that incident on this day of all days. This was supposed to be a special time. Yes, she knew from the beginning he would try to push her away, but she had never guessed he'd wanted it that much. Perhaps he truly didn't want her.

Bakac's soothing touches, however, were a balm to her bruised feelings. He looked at her like she was the only woman in the world, like he found her beautiful and always would. When he licked her pussy with one hot, wet stroke of his tongue, she resolved to put Alex out of her mind. If he didn't want to share his life with her, so be it.

But the more Bakac worked her, the more she saw how her wetness coated his mouth and chin when he stopped to look at her with a heated gaze, the more she wanted to include Alex. Perhaps it was her link with him as her soul's mate. It just didn't seem right.

She turned her head slightly and looked at Alex. At first, he was intent on Bakac and what he was doing to her pussy, but it wasn't long before she caught Alex's attention. She licked her lips.

"Are you sure you don't want to help, Alex? Are you so intent on scaring me away that you won't be here to help me through this?"

"You have Bakac," he said dryly, looking to the other man, who was again feasting on her cunt. "Why would you need me?"

"Because you're my rock, Alex. Even when things became strained between us, you were still there for me, and I still looked up to you. I needed you, even if it was just to pick a fight with you. I needed to know you'd always be there. I still need it."

She felt him hesitate, then reach for her with everything in his being. He took a step, two, then knelt and fused his mouth to hers.

"'Bout damned time." Bakac lifted his head long enough to mutter the words before settling into her cunt in earnest.

Had she not been bombarded with not only her own lust filled emotions, but the lust filled emotions of the two men, Doriena would have laughed out loud. As it was, she tried to reach out to Alex, only to be reminded abruptly that she was restrained effectively. She knew she couldn't move, but she pulled with her arms all the same.

"Alex," she panted when he left her mouth to suck and nibble at her jaw and neck, "get me out of this so I can touch you." She glanced between her legs. "Both of you."

Alex ignored her and continued to torment her flesh. When he reached the opening at her cleavage, he simply tucked his fingers under the material and ripped. Her nipples, now exposed to his gaze and the cool air, hardened in response. She wasn't sure which had the greater power over her.

When he sucked one nipple into his mouth, she cried out as she arched her back, thrusting her chest into him. Bakac still sucked and lapped her clit and pussy, and the sensations were almost overwhelming. Two men whom she loved beyond reason pleasured her beyond reason.

Love.

Yes, she'd always loved Alex, but Bakac was another matter entirely. He seemed to take their attraction in stride, but despite her attraction for him, she had never thought of her feelings as love. Was it possible to love him as deeply as she loved Alex?

When Bakac stood and straddled the bench, aiming his cock at her pussy, she knew the question would have to wait for later. She was about to lose her mind.

A vein stood out at Bakac's temple, a testament to his own passion. His face was flushed, and sweat made his body glisten. She was awestruck at the sheer power of this man's body. She had always known he was strong, but the man was absolutely massive. He made her feel tiny in comparison, fragile. His skin was a dark golden hue, like warm caramel. Muscles bunched and rippled under his skin with each movement, and his powerful thighs settled against her bound ones.

His cock was long and wide, nestled in dark curls, and she watched in fascination as it came closer and closer to her cunt.

"Watch as he enters you, Doriena." Alex had moved from her breasts and now knelt by her head, speaking softly into her ear. "I'm sure this will be the first of many times tonight, but always remember this first time. This is the time he claims you."

She did watch, hypnotized. He stretched her and it burned erotically. Oddly, the slight pain enhanced the pleasure the two had been building. Slowly, with agonizingly careful strokes, Bakac worked himself inside her until his balls rested on her ass.

He paused, and Doriena took a deep breath of anticipation.

Alex turned her face toward him and delved into her mouth fiercely with his tongue at the same time Bakac started to stroke. It was as if the two men were connected somehow. The more aggressively Alex kissed her, the harder Bakac pounded her cunt, each thrust jarring her body so that she wondered how she was able to continue kissing Alex.

With a growl, Alex stood and thrust his own cock at her mouth. She opened eagerly, taking the plump head into her mouth and running her tongue around the silky skin. Again, she tried to reach for him -- a move of instinct to grasp his cock in her hand as she sucked him -- but, again, her movement was cut short. She would have let out a frustrated screech if her mouth hadn't been full.

Bakac's deep grunts mingled with Alex's as both men fucked her from opposite ends. Nothing in her existence could have prepared her for the pure sensation flowing through her. She could feel the pleasure and excitement building in each man, and it fed her own lust to unbelievable levels.

Bakac rammed into her with one powerful surge after another, his hips meeting her flesh with sharp slaps of skin on skin. Alex's thrusts, at first shallow, became increasingly deep, and she almost gagged a time or two before he backed off, but knowing he was so out of control thrilled her beyond belief.

All three of them were panting hard. Doriena's breasts bounced with each thrust of both men. She pulled fiercely at the bonds at her wrists, trying to brace herself as best she could. Almost overwhelmed by the combined need, she reached blindly for her own release, but with the tilt of her pelvis, Bakac's position perpendicular to her outstretched body didn't allow enough friction on her clit.

Which, no doubt, was what the two of them planned. Neither of them did anything without a plan.

"That's it, my beauty." Alex's voice was hoarse, gravelly. "Suck my cock like you want it." His fist in her hair tightened, and she knew he was going to come. She braced herself for the hot jet of his seed, but at the last moment he pulled out and the sticky, milky-white fluid spurted over her breasts and neck. Two more thrusts and a shout through clenched teeth, and Bakac pulled out of her needy cunt and shot his own load over her belly.

Both men were breathing hard. *Goddamn!* She needed to come worse than she needed to breathe. She was trembling all over, her muscles ached from being clenched so tightly, but she'd be damned if she could relax.

"Please don't tell me you're going to leave me like this." She hated sounding like she was begging, but well, that was exactly what she was doing.

"For the moment." Bakac grinned. "But don't worry. I promise that before this evening is over, you'll be more satisfied than any woman has a right to be."

"I still don't see why you guys got to come and I

didn't," she grumbled.

"Frustration is good for the orgasm," Alex chuckled.

"Now I know why you tied me up. You were afraid I'd kill you."

Bakac knelt and gave her a searing, open-mouthed kiss. "Trust me, *A'Tal*, my angel. I won't leave you dissatisfied for long."

She *did* trust him. She trusted him on the battlefield, and in the bedroom, err, playroom. He wouldn't let her down. She had always known that about him, but he was proving it to her in everything he did. It was because of him Alex was trying to come around to her way of thinking. It was because of him she was even alive to enjoy this exquisite frustration.

It was Alex she was worried about. He was trying, but even now, she could feel him trying to distance himself from her. She refused to let him.

"What's next?"

Bakac laughed out loud. "Impatient wench. I like that."

"Hell yes, I'm impatient! I want Alex's cock buried in my cunt. I want more of your lovely cock. By the Universe, I want to *come*, damn it!"

"Hmmm." Bakac was trying to sound playful, but she felt the underlying worry inside him. They had to keep Alex focused. "I think that can be arranged. At least, we might be able to let you come. What do you think, Alex?"

The other man stood there, where he had spent himself, still staring at Doriena's come-covered breasts. Glancing up at Bakac, he brought himself out of whatever thoughts haunted him and looked around the room. "Yeah," Alex breathed, "I have an idea."

Both men worked to free Doriena, and she

massaged her wrists as soon as she was free. Her thighs ached from being spread open so long, and she had bruises around her wrists where she had pulled against her bonds, but she didn't really care.

Alex headed across the room, and she reached for Bakac when he knelt to pick her up. Normally she would have refused such treatment, but she wasn't sure her legs would hold her at the moment. Besides, he had already carried her once. It wouldn't hurt to let him do it again.

When he stopped beside something that looked like a huge swing hanging from the ceiling, Doriena just looked at him. "You've got to be joking."

"I never joke." Bakac set her on her feet and turned her away from him.

"Yes, you do. What are you doing?" He had pulled her arms behind her back and was tying them there. He was careful to wrap her wrists in a soft, padded material before binding them.

"You didn't think we were going to leave you loose, did you?"

"I just don't see why you have to keep me tied up. I want to touch you guys, too."

Bakac spun her back around to face him. "Later. Right now, it's time for you to surrender control of your body to us."

"Somehow, I knew you were going to say that."

Bakac lifted her by the waist and set her in the swing. Her ass slid snugly into the meshy material. Once again, Bakac spread her legs. This time, he snapped her ankles into cuffs attached to two of the chains holding the swing suspended.

She was exposed. Totally at their mercy. She loved it! It was an extremely vulnerable position. And it got her hot just waiting to see what they would do next.

Alex returned with something wrapped with a towel, his cock already beginning to harden. He devoured her with his eyes. The more helpless she was, the better he liked it. Doriena could see it in his beautiful face.

"Nice job, Bakac."

"Just fuck her, Alex. I want to see her come apart. Then --" he gripped his own cock and stroked, almost absentmindedly, " -- I want to fuck her again."

Alex walked around the swing, trailing a finger over Doriena's skin as he went. He stopped beside her and knelt until his face was mere inches from hers.

"Do you want to continue?"

"Without question." Her voice was husky with need. If her lust had died down during Bakac's preparation, it was back with a vengeance. "Please, Alex. Don't fight what's meant to be. I love you. I always have. I always will."

An expression came across Alex's face Doriena hadn't seen in a very long time. He used to look at her like that, when she was a kid. Only now, along with an unconditional, tender love, there was a lust so hot she was afraid she'd go up in flames on the spot. He didn't say another word -- he simply situated himself on a stool that put him between her legs.

* * *

Alex had been going about everything with mindless lust. He didn't want to think about it. He didn't want to think that he might not be good enough for her. He still wasn't sure he could ever be what she deserved, but knowing she loved him made it a little easier. Perhaps that was why she had two soul's mates. Perhaps where one of them was lacking, the other would be strong.

As he sat and reached for an adjustable butt plug and a tube of lubricant, he caught a whiff of the musky smell from her cunt. Unable to resist, he dipped his head between her spread legs and took a slow lick from cunt to clit. *Goddamn, that's good!* He sucked each lip into his mouth briefly, then her clit. Then he simply buried his face in her pussy, his nose occasionally brushing her clit.

Doriena squirmed and arched her back, using the straps where her feet were propped as support. When he inserted a finger, then two, inside her, she threw her head back and screamed. She moved her pelvis as much as her bonds allowed, and Alex found himself wondering what she'd be like unbound and free to do as she wished. Would she pull his head into her cunt more firmly? Would she pull his hair, urging him above her and inside her moist heat? Would she scratch and claw his back like a *tarae* in a mating frenzy?

All of the above, most likely.

When he noticed Bakac above Doriena's head, kneading her breasts and murmuring softly to her, he remembered he had something he needed to do. As always, there was a method to his every movement. Alex immediately ceased his drinking from her pussy and found the butt plug and the lube. Greasing the wedge-shaped instrument liberally, he set it aside and coated two of his fingers.

Carefully, slowly, he rimmed her anus. She cried out in surprise and sat up as much as she could to watch his movements.

"Do you want to watch, *A'Tal*?" Bakac licked the shell of her ear as he made eye contact with Alex.

She nodded, and Alex had the distinct feeling it was all she was capable of at the moment. While he continued to rim her ass, Bakac went to a nearby console and retrieved the mini viewer and camera. After testing the viewer and placing the camera at an angle that provided the best advantage, he placed the glasses-like viewer on Doriena's face and adjusted the camera one last time. The tiny projection gave her a bird's eye view of what Alex was doing to her.

"Do you like to watch, Doriena?" Alex asked as he stretched her ass with his two fingers, working her open with slow gentleness. He wanted to simply plunge himself into her and be done with it, but hurting her like that wasn't something he could even conceive of.

Again, she nodded as she lay back fully within the swing. Bakac went back to her breasts, sucking and licking each peak, under each globe, before pushing them together and taking both nipples into his mouth. Besides the extra stimulation from Bakac, Alex made a show of examining the butt plug to make sure it was lubed well. Her breaths came in shallow, rapid gasps, and Alex smiled wolfishly at her as he placed the wedge-shaped object at the entrance to her ass.

"Take a deep breath," Alex said. "I want you to push against me gently and it will slip inside you easier. Once it's inside, we can adjust it."

* * *

"Okay." Doriena bore down slightly when she felt the tip of it push into her. As it eased past her opening, there was a small amount of pain, but more than anything, she was more excited than she'd ever been in her life. She could see the image in Alex's head of the three of them in an erotic embrace and knew this was a necessary step toward achieving that goal. Her ass was virgin. He was simply ensuring she could accept them.

Alex wasn't as ruthless as he'd have her believe. She doubted he would have done any different had she been any woman. She was beginning to understand that the women he'd been with over the years, even the woman he'd lashed bloody, knew exactly what they were getting into. Some of them probably even begged for it.

With the combination of Bakac at her tits and Alex pushing the butt plug up her ass, she knew she was definitely close to begging.

It took a couple of stops and starts, but he finally got the plug in with a minimal amount of pain. She felt full, stretched, but not uncomfortably so.

"By the Universe," she managed to breathe out. "Alex, I need to come. Please."

He made one final adjustment to the plug and stood. She could see the rectangular base flat against her cheeks in the mini viewer, and she watched it move when she contracted her muscles. *By the Universe, that was hot*! Bakac stopped his assault on her breasts and moved to Alex's side and looked down at her.

"Tied." Bakac looked at her like she was the sexiest woman he'd ever seen. "Covered in come, with a butt plug up her ass to ready her for my dick. I've never seen anything like it, Alex. Her lovely face is sweaty and flushed, her muscles stark in her tension…" He trailed off.

"Yeah, sexual frustration is becoming on her."

"You're right, Alex." Bakac knelt and swiped her clit once with his tongue. "Guess she'll have to wait for that orgasm."

Doriena was certain they heard her frustrated scream halfway down the mountain.

Chapter Six

Alex needed to think. He had stepped away to relieve himself and had taken the opportunity to sort out his emotions. Something was really strange. He wasn't sure, but he thought he was getting two sets of emotions. The reason he thought that was he was getting both frustration and fascination. Now, logically, both those emotions could be coming from Doriena, but up until now, he'd only been able to read her strongest emotions.

No matter what, he was *not* going to fuck Bakac. Absolutely not. No.

There. Now that was settled he felt better.

Except, watching Bakac teasing Doriena to a fevered pitch was driving him *wild*. Yes, he felt Doriena's excitement, but he also felt something else. He felt Bakac's appreciation of the softness of her skin, the slightly salty taste of her sex, the feel of her hardened nipple on his tongue.

He shook his head. This wasn't good at all. Maybe Bakac wasn't feeling the same duality of emotions. Maybe even if he was, he wouldn't say anything. Maybe…

He was *not* going to fuck Bakac!

Pushing everything else aside, Alex approached the couple again.

"If you don't let me come soon, Bakac, I swear by the Holy Universe I'll kill you when you let me out."

Bakac chuckled. "Who says I'll let you out? I like you like this."

"Bakac!" Her screech was filled with so much frustration, it was all Alex could do not to yank Bakac away from Doriena and show him exactly what it felt like to be bound and played with. He shook his head.

That was Doriena's fantasy. One she intended to follow through on unless he missed his guess.

"Don't worry, A'Tal, I'll let you come. But if you're so hot you're screaming, it will be so much better."

"I seriously doubt an angel would find herself in this position, Bakac." Doriena panted her reply, referring to the pet name Bakac had taken to calling her. A'Tal. My angel. "You probably shouldn't call me that."

"But you are an angel, Doriena. If you've fallen from grace, it's entirely our fault." He paused before picking up a slim, golden dildo and putting a thick coating of the lubricant over the shiny surface. "But I'm not sorry for it." And he carefully inserted the tip into her cunt.

Doriena screamed and pushed against the straps at her feet in order to tilt her pelvis upwards. Sweat made her skin glisten, and the thatch of fiery curls was damp with sweat and the remains of semen from their earlier romp. The butt plug was still firmly in place and now, with the addition of the dildo, she had to feel full to bursting. Still, he caught frustration and fascination.

And lust.

He was pretty sure that was coming from both Bakac and Doriena as well as himself.

He knelt down beside Doriena's head. "Are you still watching what Bakac's doing to that lovely pussy? Do you still like watching?"

"Please, Alex. I'll do whatever you guys want, but please let me come."

"Soon, baby. Just a little longer."

"I can't hold out much longer. I think I'm going to go crazy."

Alex chuckled. "You're stronger than that. If not, you would have never made it to Military Academy in the first place."

She snapped her head toward him. "I got kicked out of the Academy! And I assure you, I'm very capable of losing it if you guys don't let me come soon. When I do snap, I'm going to ravage both of you. Hell, I may force you to ravage each other."

Alex jerked his head toward Bakac. The other man stopped his torment of her pussy and clit enough to stare back.

"Doriena." Bakac never took his eyes from Alex. "I am *not* going to fuck Alex." That was all he said. He went back to sucking Doriena's clit, his eyes closed and a look of bliss on his face. He was, however, more subdued. Alex sincerely hoped Bakac didn't feel his own almost overwhelming fascination at the thought of having sex with Bakac. Alex, however, did feel a sense of curiosity coming from Bakac before it was firmly snuffed out.

Alex just wasn't sure if that curiosity was Bakac's, or his own.

Either way, this was wrong. Their first time together should be as comfortable as possible. He and Bakac exchanged looks, and he caught the image of the upstairs bath from Bakac.

* * *

She was going to kill both of them. All it would take was about eight seconds on her clit and she'd come, but Bakac always stopped just short of her orgasm. The *bakkara* was doing it on purpose, too.

The most frustrating part of all of it was not being able to move. Alex intended this to scare her off, but what he was doing was ensuring she stayed, if only to show him what this felt like.

Finally, Bakac removed the dildo and stood. Alex moved between her legs, and she thought it was all going to start over again, but instead, he removed the plug from her ass and set it aside.

Without a word, both men untied her, and she stood on wobbly legs. She looked from one of them to the other.

"You two have one last chance." She wasn't sure how she managed to force the words out and stand at the same time, but she did. She was so unsteady on her feet it took all her concentration just to keep standing.

Bakac picked up the discarded dildo, scooped her up and headed out of the room and to the second floor of the residence. "I know. You want to come. Didn't anyone ever tell you a submissive is supposed to wait until her master tells her to come?"

"No one ever said I was submissive, you ape." She laughed and punched his chest. By the Universe, he was a huge man. She always felt tiny and delicate next to Bakac. She felt feminine.

"You are the most beautiful woman I've ever seen, *A'tal*. It's time Alex and I showed you exactly how lovely you are. The Universe knows you deserve better than either of us can give you, but perhaps we can give you what you need together."

Bakac entered a bath chamber and set her in the shallow pool. All around her was a tropical paradise. It reminded her of pictures she had seen of Earth. Plants surrounded the pool, and flowers perfumed the air delicately. Bakac washed her body. He didn't say anything, he just rubbed her body down with a lightly fragranced soap.

It felt like heaven. It wasn't enough to get rid of the sexual frenzy they had built, but it took the edge off. Curiously, it was a tad disappointing.

When he'd finished, he scooped her up, dried her off with a soft, fluffy towel. Alex was waiting on them with the bed turned down when Bakac carried her into the bedchamber.

"So, Alex." She stretched her sore muscles as she lay back on the bed. "Have you decided to keep me, after all?"

"I've decided you're too stubborn to scare off. I guess that means I don't have any other choice but to keep you."

Bakac slid between her legs and kissed her lower belly.

Alex lay beside her, tracing lazy circles on her nipples with a finger. "You said this was a new beginning."

She couldn't believe Alex was trying to make conversation. Bakac forsook her belly for her clit, once again winding her so tight she thought she'd break. As if that wasn't enough, he slipped that stupid dildo back inside her pussy for a few more strokes. "That's exactly what this is. We prepared you my way. Now, we make love to you Bakac's way."

She couldn't help herself. She giggled. "I'm sorry, Alex, but anytime there's a dildo involved, I seriously doubt you could call it making love."

Both men laughed at that, but they continued to stroke her body. Alex moved to kiss her with all the tenderness and passion Doriena had known was inside him, and Bakac used all his considerable skill of mouth and hands to bring her to the brink of orgasm again and again.

When she thought she'd die from all that tightly coiled sexual frustration, Bakac removed the dildo and kissed his way up her body. Alex rolled to his back, taking Doriena with him, her back to his chest. Bakac stroked her pussy one last time before looking at Alex and gently guiding Alex's cock inside her anus.

She hissed at the increased size, but the pain was minimal and served to heighten her already hypersensitive senses.

"Is it too much?" Alex moved gently within her, and she found herself moving with him without even realizing it.

"No. It's perfect." Her gasp came just as Bakac made one last swipe with his tongue on her clit. She didn't miss the fact that it was dangerously close to Alex's cock.

Bakac got to his knees between her legs. Alex held her knees apart with his own legs, and Bakac squeezed easily between them both and guided himself into Doriena's cunt.

It took a few seconds for everyone to become comfortable, but when Doriena began to gingerly pump her hips at them, both men started to move. There was no rhythm to their movement -- in fact they seemed to deliberately move at a random pace. It felt to Doriena like each man was desperately trying to ignore the other. She almost chuckled.

Almost.

Whatever was going on between them was definitely good for her body. She was so stuffed she felt like she was going to burst, but in a very good way. Her orgasm, when it finally came, was going to be so explosive, she was very afraid she would never be able to go back to the way things had been.

And she didn't intend to.

These men were hers. They just didn't know it yet.

Chapter Seven

Bakac thought the Universe was going to open up and swallow him whole. There was no way this much pleasure wasn't a sin against all the Universe held holy. Thrusting into Doriena's tight, hot cunt was indescribable.

Feeling Alex separated by a few layers of skin and tissue just a few inches away in Doriena's anal canal, sliding against him, was just as sinfully erotic. Bakac tried to ignore the other man and concentrate on Doriena -- she was what this was all about. Her pleasure. But the faster they moved, the more friction they created, he found himself trying to move so Alex was pleasured by his movement as much as Doriena was.

Her feet were propped on Alex's bent knees, and she whimpered with each thrust. Bakac had just managed to convince himself she didn't know what he was feeling when she opened her eyes and looked him straight in the face. For several moments she held his gaze then a slow, wicked smile spread across her face.

Slowly, deliberately, she turned her head and found Alex's mouth. She kissed him as the two men pumped into her faster and faster. Alex grabbed her breasts and squeezed like they were his only lifelines in a great sea of pleasure. His groan and Doriena's whimper were music to Bakac's ears, and he knew in that moment he would give anything in the Universe to hear those sounds every day for the rest of his existence.

Lust swirled like a living thing around the three of them. Doriena could no longer move, so ragged were the movements of the men. Sweat scattered from Bakac in a fine mist to settle on Alex and Doriena. The droplets blanketed the two people he loved most in the Universe.

New beginnings.

He'd grab this one with both hands.

* * *

Alex felt the change in Bakac. He knew the man was trying to ignore the physical attraction neither of them was able to suppress. Hell, he was trying his damnedest to ignore it as well. But that damned Doriena picked up on it. Alex suspected she had been trying so hard to convince the two of them she belonged right where she was, she didn't catch it at first. Once she relaxed, Alex imagined his and Bakac's pull toward each other was as obvious as their pull toward her.

Doriena now knew the pull of soul's mates went three ways, and she was apparently more than willing to push all of them together in every way possible.

She gripped his wrists as he kneaded her breasts with his hands in rough, jerky movements and turned her head to kiss him passionately. Her tongue slipped inside him deeply and for the first time in a very long time, he felt like the scared, inexperienced virgin. Ironic, since he had equated this vixen between him and his best friend to that very thing.

By the Universe, the woman could kiss! His heart raced, his body broke out in a fine sweat, and he thrust like mad into her ass. He grunted with each up stroke -- he couldn't help it! *She knew he had a budding attraction for Bakac*. And she was encouraging it.

Still, he wasn't prepared when, still gripping his wrists, she reached out for Bakac. Before Alex knew it, two sets of hands molded Bakac's arms and shoulders, and one set was his own. With one last groan, he pulled Bakac down as he raised his own head. The two men met in a torrid kiss that set Alex's blood on fire.

"That's it, Alex," Doriena encouraged. "Kiss him like you've wanted to since we started this weekend. He's wanted this as much as you have. Give it to him."

The moans, whimpers and screams of all three of them filled the mountain estate's main house. They moved at an almost impossible speed given the awkward positioning, but they simply couldn't stop the inevitable explosion building among them.

With Doriena between them, with their lips locked in a passionate kiss, both Alex and Bakac exploded inside the woman they both loved with all their hearts. Spasm after spasm pulsed come deep inside her body. Bakac reached between them and strummed Doriena's clit with a finger, setting off her own orgasm. Alex gritted his teeth as her ass squeezed his sensitized cock. Bakac shouted as the last of his pleasure rippled away, and he rolled them all to their sides to collapse in a heap of exhausted flesh.

* * *

They explored each other all week's end long. Doriena experimented with sex in every possible fashion with her men, and they experimented with each other. It was a week's end Doriena could only have dreamed about before.

Once it was over, however, there was reality to face.

Kahn.

This wouldn't be pretty.

The three of them went back to Kahn and Anna's home expecting an explosion.

They weren't disappointed.

"Where the hell have the three of you been?" Kahn's roar made Doriena's ears ring. He looked angrier than she could ever remember seeing him.

"Kahn," Anna said gently, a sharp contrast to Kahn's hostility, "we discussed this. It's not something you have any control over."

"I do have control over it!" His bellow wasn't quite what it had been before, but was still way too loud for Doriena's comfort. "Besides, she was supposed to report back to the Academy two days ago!"

Doriena's heart skipped a beat. "What?" She wasn't sure she had actually voiced the question out loud until Kahn continued.

"I had to bully almost every member of the Ruling Council to get you back in, and you didn't even bother to show!"

"But, Father." Doriena couldn't believe he'd done this. "Why would you do something like that? I failed to complete an exercise. It's automatic expulsion, no matter the circumstances."

"Don't you think I know that?" Khan paced the room like a caged animal. All the while, Anna stood with her arms crossed under her breasts. Doriena suspected her mother was letting her father rid himself of some leashed energy. If he had been looking for her all week's end, he was probably more than a little relieved, and angry, and all kinds of emotions she couldn't even begin to name.

"Does she still have the opportunity to reenter the Academy?" Alex said quietly. "Can she still go back?"

Doriena looked at him sharply. Did he want rid of her already?

Alex turned to her. "No, Doriena. Don't ever think I want rid of you ever again. I've learned my lesson on that subject." His eyes were intense. Whatever her answer, it was very important to him.

She glanced at Bakac, who was standing much like her mother. Not moving. Not saying a word.

"Yes." Kahn broke the silent communication with his presence. "She can, and she is."

"That's enough, Kahn." Anna finally crossed to her mate and pushed him back a few steps into a nearby chair. Leaning over him, her hands on his shoulders, she said, "When Doriena first applied, you did everything you could to get them not to accept her. You were so afraid of losing your precious baby girl that you tried to trample her dreams of following in your footsteps. You gave in on that one, but only because you saw how brokenhearted she was when her application met with a solid block. Unanimous denial."

Doriena bit back the hurt gasp barely in time. In an instant, a hand was on each shoulder offering support. Bakac and Alex would always be there for her. She knew that beyond any doubt.

"Are you telling me now that you'd rather see her in Military Command, an organization that can send her into battle and mortal danger at the whim of the Ruling Council, just to avoid having to see her mated?"

It was Alex who stiffened this time. After all this time, he still wasn't good enough for his father.

"That's enough." Doriena approached Kahn, a fierce need to protect and defend both men in her heart. Especially Alex. He was the one being hurt by their father's fears. "If there are two men in this Universe who could ever make me happy, it's these two." She stepped into her mother's place in front of her father and took his face in her hands. "Daddy, I love both of them. I can't be happy without them. Could you be happy without Mother?"

Kahn looked away, clearly not wanting to admit she was right. "You told me once the only thing in this Universe you ever wanted to do was make sure Mother, Alex and me were as happy as we could be. I know that means you have to ensure our protection, but it also means giving us the means to follow our hearts."

Her father looked at her then. She actually saw tears in his eyes before he blinked them away. "You're supposed to be my baby girl."

Doriena smiled. "I'll always be your baby girl, Father. Besides, if I mated with someone not in the family, you'd intimidate them too easily. I don't want a wimp for a mate."

Finally, Kahn smiled. Not only that, he actually chuckled. "Well, at least you've got good taste."

"Of course she does, dear," Anna sniffed. "She takes after her mother."

Kahn really did laugh then. "No denying that." He looked at the two men standing there, trying to be as unobtrusive as possible. "My mate tells me, quite regularly, I've been an ass to the two of you. I'm truly sorry."

Alex grinned. "It could have been worse. Believe me, I wanted to kick my own ass when I realized what was going on."

"What are you going to do about the Academy, Doriena?" Bakac asked softly. "Are you going to return?"

She looked at her mates, and her mother and father. "No." All four let out a collective breath, and Doriena giggled. "I won't lie, it is very tempting, but I think I'd rather spend my time planetside. Perhaps I could teach at the Academy one day."

"You were top in your class at everything,

especially hand to hand combat." Kahn scratched his chin. "It is very possible that could be arranged."

"It would certainly be a step in the right direction," Anna voiced. "Gothe'mar needs strong women in influential positions, and I can't think of a better place."

"I have time." Doriena embraced her mother, all the while looking at the three most important men in her life. "After all, even new beginnings with the best of intentions take time."

Chocolate Kisses (Forbidden 5)
Post-Apocalyptic Sci-Fi Action Romance
Marteeka Karland

When Tianna completes a family tradition by welcoming a new neighbor with her famous Chocolate Brownie Sheet Cake, she doesn't expect the oversexed, oversized Gothe'maran man to be so... well... oversexed. And oversized.

A short story in the *Forbidden* universe.

Chocolate Kisses

Knock, knock, knock. The sound reverberated as Tianna rapped politely on the door. It was customary for one to greet a new neighbor, but Tianna had misgivings about it this time. Her mother would roll over in her grave if she knew her youngest daughter hadn't made a new neighbor welcome with the Darnell family's Chocolate Brownie Sheet Cake. It was a tradition in her family that hadn't been broken in over one hundred years. The only thing that gave Tianna the courage to walk up to the new tri-level mansion across the street was the thought of being the first to screw it up. She'd already put it off for three weeks. Damned house was completely out of place in this little country neighborhood anyway. She doubted anyone else had approached him either.

She'd seen the man who owned the house, Rikardi Lyyons, and had confirmed he was indeed the owner with the movers. He terrified her. OK, so terrified was a harsh word, but any man who rode a big black hog in a leather suit, black helmet, and looked good doing it was *not* a man she wanted to get anywhere near. Add to that he was the new ambassador to Earth from Daysom in the Gothe'mar Empire, and he spelled trouble. She was a good girl. Good girls didn't associate with men like that.

Except that she'd become obsessed with him. She watched for him to come home. She couldn't get any work done for it. When he got home, she made every excuse she could to go to her mailbox, or check her rose bushes, or pick up doggie dung from the front of her yard. *Anything* to get close enough to his house to see him. See what he was doing. It was freaking creepy! And she had never been so compelled to do anything in her entire life.

He'd also become the star of every erotic fantasy she had. When she pleasured herself, it was Rikardi's face she saw when she closed her eyes, his hands on her body as she stimulated herself, getting ready for sex. Instead of one of the many dildos in her collection, it was always Rikardi's cock she imagined inside her, bringing her to orgasm.

She shivered and shook herself.

Ding dong, ding dong. When no one answered her knock, she rang the bell, stubbornly refusing to leave until he answered and took her cake. She'd meticulously cut it into perfectly symmetrical squares and placed it carefully on a serving platter and she'd be damned if she'd let all this hard work go to waste. Besides, maybe if she had one close encounter she'd see he wasn't really "all that" and get back to her life.

She knew he was there. She'd watched him pull in the drive on that sexy as sin motorcycle, his sexy as sin ass clad in all that leather. So where the hell *was* he?

Tianna blinked. She couldn't believe she'd just mentioned his ass, even to herself. She'd just decided maybe this wasn't such a good idea when the door was flung open. The man who stood in front of her wasn't a man she'd ever seen before, but he had the same hugely muscled build as Rikardi.

He wasn't wearing a shirt. Normally, that wouldn't have been a problem. She'd seen lots of men without their shirts before. But she was so sexually energized this was just one more thing to cloud her judgment. He had the best-looking chest and abdomen she'd ever seen, even in magazines and movies. Lightly hair dusted, muscled, tanned… what's not to like? Powerful shoulders and arms completed the look, and Tianna had to grip her plate of chocolate cake to keep from dropping it.

Wait a second. Had she thought his arms completed him? Those sinful leather pants were just as good, the way they clung to his ass...

Tianna swallowed. How was it possible for two men in the same house to be this good-looking?

The man looked her up and down then asked, "How much do you weigh?"

Tianna blinked. "I'm sorry?"

"How much do you weigh?" He repeated his question, but with a touch of annoyance. Like a man who was used to having his orders obeyed without the slightest bit of hesitation.

She felt compelled to tell him. She couldn't have stopped herself from telling him what he wanted to know if her life had depended on it.

"A-about a hundred and ninety-seven pounds." She felt her face heat. Why she hadn't simply refused to tell him was beyond her, and saying she was so close to two hundred pounds mortified her. It was one thing for one of the sexiest men in the world to see she was a large woman, quite another for her to place a number on her weight.

"Good." He looked supremely satisfied. Tianna was certain she looked as confused as she felt.

He grabbed her free hand and practically dragged her inside. Tianna almost dropped the plate as he led her through his house to a huge sunroom on the west side. She could see her own house from there, particularly her bedroom.

"I came to welcome Mr. Lyyons to the neighborhood --" Her well-rehearsed speech started in a squeak that she couldn't correct. He didn't look like he was paying much attention to her, anyway. When she finally noticed what he was preoccupied with, she dropped the plate with a little squeal.

"Miss Darnell. Tianna." Rikardi sat on a plush, very large couch. What startled her enough to drop her plate of prized Brownie Sheet Cake was the fact that he sat there totally naked. When Tianna didn't answer him, he simply smiled and continued speaking. "I wondered when you'd finally come to me, though I didn't expect Damion to be the one to bring you."

Was it common practice for the man to converse with complete strangers while in the nude? "You -- you're *naked*!" It wasn't just that, though. Rikardi was frigging huge. Apparently, distance distorted size considerably. All of him was bulky, solid, ripped muscle. His legs sprawled out in front of him as he lounged. His skin was dark and hairless, except for the nest of jet-black curls around his cock. And his cock, even at rest, looked positively frightening in its size. Yeah, Tianna's lower torso was clenching and dancing for joy, but her mind was dumbfounded, and she was sure her eyes almost bugged out of her head.

Damion frowned and looked at Rikardi. "I thought you said she was of high intelligence."

Rikardi chuckled. "Oh, she is. She's one of the most intelligent women I've encountered on this world, but she's a tad shy."

"She's not an innocent, is she?" Damion said that as though the mere thought left a bad taste in his mouth.

"She's not a virgin, but she's not very experienced. Her tastes are borderline exotic for this culture," Rikardi replied, then grinned and added, "at least, not with anyone other than herself and her toys." Tianna didn't think it was possible for her face to get any redder. She could feel the heat rising from her in waves. She didn't know if it was possible to die from embarrassment, but she was damned close to finding out.

Damion raised an eyebrow. "How do you know her tastes, Rikardi? I thought you said you hadn't touched her yet. Have you been in her mind?"

Rikardi's grin turned positively cocky and he puffed out his chest a little. "Oh, yes. Several times. It's hard to stay out when she's constantly bringing me into her fantasies." Yes. She might just die of embarrassment... if she were lucky. "I'm looking forward to seeing if your methods of self-pleasure have prepared you for me." Rikardi stood now. Yep. The man was fricking *huge*. He towered over her and was several inches taller than Damion -- who was also fricking huge. Even being a "big girl," she felt small compared to them. Had she been a "normal-sized" woman, she'd probably have run screaming. But, as Rikardi had so cheekily pointed out, her tastes were exotic. She liked big men -- in every sense of the word -- and Rikardi sported the biggest cock she'd ever seen, and it was rapidly growing as he looked her up and down. And what did he mean by "prepared you for me"? Her heart thudded so hard in her chest she was sure her shirt moved with each beat.

He turned that dark smile on her, his perfectly straight, white teeth flashing her a wolfish grin. "I want to see you as I've long imagined. I want to see that exquisite body naked. Strip."

His voice was melodious, almost hypnotic. Without thinking, she almost reached for her jeans button before she realized exactly what she was doing.

"I most certainly will *not!*" Tianna had to shake her head to clear it of the spell he wove around her. It had been a really long time since a man had told her to strip. Well, at least a sober man. Now, she remembered how much she loved the feeling of being sexy, and this man looked at her like she was a piece of that delicious Brownie Sheet Cake he wanted to eat. "I don't know you." She turned to Damion. "Either of you. I'm not just hopping into bed with you because you say so."

Rikardi shrugged. "You don't have to 'hop' anywhere. I'm more than happy to carry you." That was the only warning she got before he scooped her up as if she weighed no more than a child and left the room with her.

At first, Tianna was so surprised all she could do was shriek and wrap her arms around his neck. Then, she thought to protest, but his skin felt so good. Smelled so good. She wanted to see if it tasted so good.

Rikardi took her up the stairs two at a time and she truly thought she'd died and gone to heaven. This was a perfect man for her.

"Remember that, sweet. I am *the* perfect man for you. No one else."

"Not now, Rikardi," Damion growled from a couple of steps behind them. "You need to complete the first stage of the claiming first. She needs to know you can satisfy her every need before she knows the rest of it."

Tianna groaned. It was going to be complicated. It was always complicated. They were weirdo aliens with a taste for kink who wanted to get laid. Rikardi had been playing the Peeping Tom inside her head, learning what she liked, and this was their chance to get the BBW and not have to commit to a second session. They'd give her some line of malarkey to make her think they were insane or something, and it would look like she was the one who didn't want to continue the "relationship."

She should put a stop to this now. Right now.

Oh, God. Maybe after Rikardi quit that nibbling and sucking at her neck. Her skin prickled and burned slightly where his lips made contact with her neck. It felt damned good. She decided maybe she'd wait before stomping out of the house and back to her own home.

They'd made it to the top of the stairs at some point and entered a huge bedroom done in rich, masculine colors. The carpet was a deep crimson and the drapes were a lush hunter green trimmed in gold. Three huge windows allowed warm, golden sunlight into the room, giving the effect of spotlights being directed in strategic places. One of them being the plush-looking king-sized bed, dressed in the same beautiful green as the drapes, sitting proudly on a dais three steps off the floor.

Tianna was mesmerized as the bed got closer and closer with every step Rikardi took. Then he was climbing the steps and she was set gently atop the silk comforter in the middle of the bed, only to be followed by both men. They sandwiched her between them, invading her personal space quite deliberately. Rikardi faced her and hooked one of her legs around his hip while Damion snuggled close behind her, pulling her bottom to rest against his pulsing groin.

"Will you freely give of yourself so that I may prove myself worthy to be your consort?"

Rikardi's words sounded formal, and Tianna knew this would be a really good time to scramble to her feet and run like the wind, but instead she simply breathed out, "Yes," and the fun began.

Rikardi's mouth captured hers in a firm but gentle kiss. He wedged his thigh between hers and pulled her leg higher so that he contacted her sex through her jeans. Her breath caught and she clamped down on his thigh, holding him to her. Lord, it felt good to be touched like this!

His hands shaped her thigh and hip over and over, gripping, squeezing, and gently rubbing until she longed for him to do that to her bare flesh. Hesitantly, she laid her hand just above his hip and gingerly stroked. When he grunted his approval, she began a tentative but eager exploration of whatever skin she could reach.

His mouth sucked carefully yet insistently at her lips until she opened with a sigh and his tongue dove in. It was quite obviously a determination not to leave until he was good and ready. Her head rested on his other arm, and he curled it round her head possessively and fisted her long, auburn hair, positioning her just where he wanted her.

She was so caught up in Rikardi's masterful touch, she almost forgot about Damion until she felt his hand graze her hip. Automatically, she reached back to touch him. When she found bare, warm flesh, she jumped a little. Both men chuckled -- Damion in her ear with a warm breath, Rikardi into her mouth. She sighed when Rikardi plunged his tongue in deeper.

I think you're overdressed for the occasion, little Tianna. Rikardi's voice was but a whisper in her mind. His lips molded hers insistently but tenderly, and she jumped a little when she registered he hadn't actually spoken.

This really should have creeped her out, but all she really cared about was getting as naked as possible as fast as possible. She wanted her flesh mashed between theirs. Now. *Yesterday.*

She started to disengage herself when she realized she *was* naked between them. "Wha --"

"Shh," Damion said. "Later. Just enjoy."

What the hell? You only live once. Tianna sighed and surrendered to whatever they wanted. She might go back to being little Miss Prim and Proper when it was all over, but for now, she'd enjoy everything they had to give.

It was like a silent signal went out to each man. Rikardi rolled to his back, taking her with him, and she sprawled on top of him, her breasts mashed wonderfully against his chest. She tried to push away, to take at least some of her weight from him, but he held her fast, both arms snugly around her waist and back.

"You're not going anywhere. You gave me permission to prove I could pleasure you, and that's exactly what I'm going to do." Rikardi's look was fierce, proud. This was a man with something to prove.

"I'm too heavy for this," she protested. "I'll hurt you."

"Look at me, Tianna," he said, obviously annoyed. "I'm six feet eleven. Over three hundred pounds. If you were one of those waify, skinny women this world and Gothe'mar both seem to adore, I'd seriously hurt you during love play. You're absolutely perfect for me." His lips found hers again, and he kissed her more thoroughly than she could ever remember being kissed in her thirty-five years. She kissed him back just as eagerly. She felt like she'd been starving, only to be set before a banquet table and told to eat her fill. She wanted to taste everything.

When she felt the soft, unmistakable sensation of a tongue probing her cunt -- which had to be drenched by now -- she squealed inside Rikardi's mouth and arched her back.

So responsive, Rikardi. She already loves your touch.

I told you she was a rare prize. I chose with great care, my captain.

Again, the words were those of the men pleasuring her in the most wicked of ways, but their voices were inside her head.

Later. She'd deal with it later. Right now, she wanted this experience. Needed it. Craved it.

Two fingers entered her. She knew it was two because they scissored inside her, brushing against the walls of her sex. Damion spread her gently, no doubt readying her for Rikardi's massive cock. At the thought, she groaned. Very soon now, that cock would be inside her. Two fingers soon became three, then four as Damion stretched her. Occasionally, his tongue lapped at her pussy and his teeth nipped at her ass cheek, creating as much pleasure as Rikardi's masterful kiss.

And, oh, could the man kiss! She felt every stroke of his tongue shooting lightning straight to her clit. She'd never been kissed so thoroughly in her life. It was as if he couldn't get enough of her. Like all he wanted to do in the world was taste her, tease her, tempt her to do things she'd only dreamed about. Part of her forbidden fantasies included a man who would fill her completely and stretch not only her body, but her mind as well.

He definitely filled her mind and senses, and she was certain that magnificent cock would fill her body. The only phallus she'd ever had in her pussy that matched his was a toy she'd bought out of curiosity. The thing measured in at twelve inches long, and she was barely able to close her hand around it. At first, she'd thought she'd never be able to get it inside her, but after using a few other toys of various sizes and working her way up to her enormous new toy, she'd managed it, and found she loved the burn as it stretched her. The thing had rapidly grown to be her favorite plaything for long nights spent alone. She was able to take all of it now with shorter periods of stretching herself. It was still almost unbearably tight, but when she was in the mood, it was the most erotic thing she'd ever experienced. Rikardi wasn't quite that big, but he was damned close.

She was still kissing Rikardi when Damion's fingers slid out of her, and she felt the blunt tip of Rikardi's cock at her entrance. Bracing herself, she stiffened her body, and Rikardi broke his contact with her lips.

"Don't be afraid." Rikardi's whisper washed over her like warm water, relaxing and soothing her. "Damion wouldn't have brought you here if you couldn't handle me."

"I'm not scared." She smiled as she spoke. "I'm experienced enough to know that thing ain't going to slide in easily in one stroke." She leaned in to kiss him firmly on the mouth. "Maybe *you* should relax."

The chuckle behind her sent chills racing over her body. "She's got you there, Rik."

The big man growled beneath her. "Just put a condom on my dick and help me get inside her. You're not here to make fun of me." He didn't sound irritated and some of the strain left his face.

He didn't really have to say anything. Tianna already felt his cock pushing slowly into her. He stretched and burned her, but she loved every blessed second of it. She needed this, needed him.

"Why *is* he here, if you don't mind me asking." It was stimulating beyond belief to have both men focused on her, but she wasn't sure about actually having sex with both of them.

"I'm here --" Damion said as he moved back into her line of sight, "-- as a witness that you consented willingly, and to help if necessary. Rik isn't a small man. Sometimes, more... stimulation is needed. Of course, if he does his job and proves himself, it won't be necessary anyway." His grin was infectious, but only until Rikardi pushed deeper inside her.

She pushed back against Rikardi, sinking down on his big cock. When the burn became too much, she rose slightly and carefully impaled herself again. It took several such attempts before she finally had him fully inside her, and she closed her eyes, savoring the moment.

When she opened her eyes, Rikardi was looking at her intently, his face strained and tense. She couldn't help the satisfied smirk she knew graced her features. Rikardi gripped her hips and clenched his jaw, the muscles in his face flexing and relaxing as he gritted his teeth together. Tianna was deliciously full. She loved this feeling, and she intended to savor it as long as she could.

Without comment, they began to move as one, he rocking forward gently as she sat down. He slid his hands around her to grip her ass, and Tianna was in heaven. Every cell in her body seemed sensitized. Everything was magnified. The sounds of their combined breathing and moaning, the taste of him still on her tongue where he'd kissed her, the touch of his skin against hers, all of it seemed to drive her toward the biggest climax of her life. She was stretched and full, complete as she'd never been before. It was as if every carnal experience in her life, everything she'd ever desired and craved had been compressed into this one man.

Gradually, she picked up the tempo, wanting

everything he had to give. She wrapped her arms around him, burying her face in his neck. She took a deep breath and filled her nostrils with his masculine scent. She didn't want this to ever end.

Her clit grazed his pubis with every stroke, setting her lower body on fire with the need for a climax. She held off, biting her cheek in an attempt to mute the sensations coursing through her.

It didn't work.

She threw her head back, and with a shout of utter satisfaction, she came. Pulse after wonderful pulse flowed through her. Her pussy clenched and milked Rikardi. Never had she felt the presence of a man inside her so acutely. The sheer size of him left little room for the spasms of her inner muscles. The resulting sensation drove her climax even harder, and she couldn't help the screams that now erupted from her.

Rikardi had a death grip on her ass, and the moment her orgasm started to fade, he let go of a roar of his own. The sound was almost deafening and utterly satisfying to Tianna. He dug his fingertips into her plump cheeks and gave one final plunge into her and she felt the pulsations of his cock as it expanded with each spurt of his semen into the condom. Sweat drenched them both, and Tianna felt like she'd run a marathon. Her lungs hurt as she struggled to get her breathing under control.

"Wow," she breathed.

"Yeah." Rikardi sounded as breathless as she was. "Me, too."

Damion chuckled from his place on the bed. Tianna jumped, startled. She'd totally forgotten he was there. "I'm no expert, but I'd say you proved your point, Rik."

Rikardi looked almost vulnerable, as if her judgment might somehow shape him as a man. "Did I?" he asked, one hand moving to caress her face. "Did I prove I could pleasure you as no other? Am I worthy to be your consort?"

Tianna blinked. He'd said this before. "I'm not sure I understand what you mean."

"He means," Damion said, now dressed and looking amused, "he wants to be your boyfriend."

Tianna looked at Rikardi, who might have been blushing, though it was hard to tell with his skin color. This was insane! *She* was the one who was supposed to be nervous and embarrassed.

"Look at you." She extended a hand to indicate his rock-hard, bulky physique. "You're every woman's dream. You could have any woman you want. Why would you want someone like me? I'm fat, I've been on my own for a long time, so I'm pretty bitchy, and I'm not exactly what one would call a prize catch."

"You're perfect for me. There's enough of you to take me on for a hard ride, and I don't feel like a freak standing next to you. We complement each other. Not to mention you're the most beautiful woman I've ever seen. Give me a chance to get to know you. You get to know me. I promise you won't be disappointed."

She thought for a moment. "Before I answer that, tell me what's with the thing where my clothes vanished and the speaking in my head thing."

"They are but two of many talents of our people. Some of those talents are even more exotic." He winked at her and kissed her nose.

"Will there be lots of sex involved in this 'getting to know me' thing?"

He gave her a slow smile. "Absolutely."

"Then count me in."

Marteeka Karland

International bestselling author Marteeka Karland leads a double life as an action romance writer by evening and a semi-domesticated housewife by day. Known for her down-and-dirty MC, out of this world Post Apocalyptic Sci-Fi, and Dark Fantasy action romances, Marteeka takes pleasure in spinning tales of tenacious, protective heroes and spirited heroines. She staunchly advocates that every character deserves a blissful ending.

Marteeka finds joy in baking, and gardening with her husband. Make sure to visit her website to stay updated with her most recent projects. Don't forget to register for her newsletter which will pepper you with a potpourri of Teeka's beloved recipes, book suggestions, autograph events, and a plethora of interesting tidbits.

Marteeka at Changeling: changelingpress.com/marteeka-karland-a-39

Want more? Check out Wanda Violet O. -- Teeka's BDSM Erotica side at changelingpress.com/wanda-violet-o-a-226

Changeling Press LLC

Contemporary Action Adventure, Sci-Fi, Steampunk, Dark Fantasy, Urban Fantasy, Paranormal, and BDSM Romance available in e-book, audio, and print format at ChangelingPress.com – MC Romance, Werewolves, Vampires, Dragons, Shapeshifters and Horror -- Tales from the edge of your imagination.

Where can I get Changeling Press Books?

Changeling Press e-books are available at ChangelingPress.com, Amazon, Apple Books, Barnes & Noble, Kobo, Smashwords, and other online retailers, including Everand Subscription and Kobo Subscription Services. Print books are available at Amazon, Barnes and Noble, and by ISBN special order through your local bookstores.

Changeling Press LLC

ChangelingPress.com